# LINDBLAD LIBERATION

Joseph McRae Palmer

LINDBLAD LIBERATION
Copyright © 2024 Joseph McRae Palmer
www.josephmcraepalmer.com

This book is a work of fiction. The characters, incidents, and dialog are drawn from the author's imagination and are not to be construed as real. Any resemblance to actual events or persons, living or dead, is fictionalized or coincidental.

No part of this book may be reproduced in any form or by any electronic or mechanical means, including storage and retrieval systems, without written permission from the author, except for the use of brief quotations in a book review.
ISBN (paperback) 978-1-961782-23-5

Cover design: Donna Cunningham@BeauxArts.design

## *Prologue*

Alright, folks, buckle up. You're about to dive into the second installment of my story. And let me tell you, things are going to get strange. We're talking Syderealium and marac Soul Ravager strange. Now, if you're a history buff, you probably think you know all there is about Soul Ravagers from the UHC-Kergan Wars. But the Syderealium? That's a whole different beast. The UHC government has gone to great lengths to keep that under wraps, because true power—like the kind found in the Syderealium—is terrifying. Horrifying, even.

So, what you're about to read hasn't been screened by UHC censors or sanitized for your reading pleasure. Nope. This is the raw, unfiltered truth. Why am I doing this, you ask? Well, maybe I'm reckless—or just too stubborn for my own good. But I trust you'll figure it out. Besides, at this point, I'm too old to care about getting tossed in jail for spilling these secrets. At my age, I've got more gray hair than common sense, and honestly, prison doesn't sound all that bad. Three square meals, a bed, and no one asking me to save the universe? Sign me up.

Now, if you've been with me from the start, you'll

already know Destiny Austin and Clemen Busto, my dear comrades. Destiny's got a sharper shot than my ex-mother-in-law's tongue, and Clemen, well, he's the gruff yet lovable voice of reason in our little band of misfits. You also remember Her Highness, Zeta—back when she was just plain old Zeta, not yet sitting on the Nova Throne like it's her personal recliner. If you thought she met her maker when *Thunder* crashed, you're dead wrong.

You'll soon find out how she returned. It's a tale as twisted as a politician's promise, and you'll want to stick around for it. You've flown with us on *Thunder*, witnessed its birth as we took to the black yonder during the early years of the UHC War of Liberation. You've been with us through battles, retreats, and victories. So, let's continue this journey together. Keep your eyes peeled and your mind open— you're about to see where no UHC history book dares to go.

# 1

My protomatter-encased foot sank into the scorching sand, each grain pressing against the sole with a tactile precision only carbon nanobots could convey. The quarter-inch-thick protective layer shielded me from the desert's harshness. Still, every pebble, every granule of silica rubbed against my foot like a subtle reminder of the unforgiving terrain of Western Arizona's wilderness.

I pushed off with my rear foot, the muscles in my leg straining as I trudged toward the faint trail Gunny Clemen Busto was breaking ahead. His camouflaged suit shimmered like a mirage, blending into the heated air, barely visible ten paces in front of me. Meanwhile, I was moving with all the grace of a drunken moose, each step feeling like it was powered by stubbornness alone. The sun beat down relentlessly from the southern sky, turning our suits into stifling ovens despite their reflective coating—because clearly, the Dominion military thought slowly roasting was the key to stealth. I was pretty sure I'd be fully cooked by the time we got where we were going.

My throat felt like sandpaper, dry and raw with each attempted swallow, but I resisted the urge to drink. Busto had warned us: conserve water. We had no idea where, or when, the next drop would come in this desolate wasteland.

A sharp curse broke the silence behind me. I glanced over my shoulder to see Destiny Austin hopping on one foot, her face twisted in frustration as she inspected her raised boot.

"That's the second one!" she yelled, her voice echoing in the still air.

I stopped, turning back to her. "What now?"

"A thorn! They can't get through the suit, but I can feel every damn prick. It's driving me crazy."

"Turn down the sensitivity on your suit's feet," I advised, though her muttering suggested she wasn't keen on taking suggestions at the moment. Still, she jabbed commands into her wrist panel, her scowl deepening.

Ahead, Busto's voice barked across the sands. "Keep up, you two!" He was already a good sixty feet ahead, his silhouette a ghost in the shimmering heat waves.

I raised a hand to signal we'd heard, and we resumed our slow march, each step sinking into the loose, treacherous sand that swallowed our feet like quicksand. Nearly three hours of this—this endless desert—stretching out toward the horizon as we headed east toward Elkin, Arizona. Busto's pace wasn't the problem; it was the stops, the constant halts where he made us kneel and scan the empty, barren landscape. The most excitement I'd seen so far was a lazy snake curled and sleeping in the shadow of a jagged rock.

When Destiny finished adjusting her suit, we resumed our trudge, kicking through patches of brittle, yellowed weeds and passing stunted trees that looked more like twisted bones than anything alive. I didn't recognize the species, and I wasn't about to ask—each one looked like it had given up on life in this godforsaken place a long time ago. Honestly, I couldn't blame them. If I could've rooted myself into the ground and waited this heat out, I might've considered it.

We caught up to Busto, who stood staring at the horizon. "There's a road up ahead," he said, pointing at a faint depression in the ground.

At first, I thought it was another dry arroyo, but the tire tracks—faint and worn—gave it away. They rose briefly on a bank of dirt, the first fleeting sign of civilization we'd seen since we left *Thunder*'s crash site behind.

The road itself was rough, unpaved, a scar through the desert. Pickup trucks or SUVs might brave it, but the fine, powder-like sand that filled its dips and ruts would make it a challenge for any conventional ground vehicle.

"We'll follow it," Busto declared, the command settling over us like a welcome reprieve from the endless ocean of sand. "It should lead us close to Elkin."

Relief flooded me as I moved toward the harder-packed ground. Each step in the sand had felt like wading through water, dragging my legs against the shifting surface. The sweat pooled under my suit, trickling down my back. The suit's cooling system wasn't terrible, but it wasn't enough. I wanted the arid air to penetrate and let my sweat evaporate and soothe my skin with its cool breath.

Above us, a falcon circled, riding a thermal like a king surveying its empty kingdom. I envied its freedom. Hours ago, *Thunder* had been our wings, cutting through the atmosphere with ease. Now, our beautiful ship was shattered, broken by a crash I'd barely managed to control after our battle with the Kergan frigate.

We'd lost Zeta too. The igna had been our chief engineer, my Heliacal consort, our military adviser, and our friend. Now she was gone, vanished when her capsule had ruptured in the fight with the frigate. No body, no remains —just the empty shell of her capsule, which we buried. A hollow ceremony for a hollow death.

# 2

Endless dunes of sun-bleached sand and scrub stretched in every direction, the barren landscape broken only by jagged rocks and brittle, dried weeds that cracked in the relentless heat. Even in winter, the Arizona desert felt like a furnace, the late afternoon sun baking everything under its unforgiving gaze.

Each step I took down the dirt road kicked up clouds of dust, the weight of the day pressing down on me.

Busto marched ahead, silent and focused, his broad figure casting a long shadow across the ground.

Sweat trickled down my forehead, stinging my eye, but my protomatter suit's faceplate sealed me off from any attempt to wipe it away. I shook my head in frustration, but the bead of sweat clung stubbornly, blurring my vision.

"Wish I was back on *Thunder*," Destiny muttered from behind me, her voice dry and laced with sarcasm. "At least the A/C worked."

She adjusted her grip on the flechette gun she carried with both hands, casting me a wry look through her visor.

Even fully armored, her wit was a constant, undiminished by the miles of burning sand or the fact that we were stranded, hundreds of miles from Wolf Jaw.

"Not anymore," I replied, the words heavy with the memory of the crash. *Thunder* was nothing more than a mangled wreck now, scattered across the desert like the carcass of some ancient beast.

We'd been lucky—if the chromatic battery had shorted out on impact, we'd have been vaporized in an instant, mere flashes of plasma in the vast, empty desert. Maybe we should've ejected. Maybe we should've bailed when the Raider became unflyable. But we didn't. It was my decision. I flew us down, hoping for a miracle.

I shifted my torso harness, feeling the straps dig into my shoulders, the weight of our gear growing heavier with every step.

The road ahead curved sharply around a massive boulder perched atop a low rise, its weathered surface casting a long shadow over the path.

A flicker of yellow caught my eye—a butterfly, fragile and bright, its wings flashing against the backdrop of endless sand. It struggled against the wind that blew in from the northwest, each beat of its wings a desperate fight for survival in the desolation.

Busto reached the boulder ahead of me. I watched him pause, lift his gun to his shoulder, then step slowly around the block of dark gray basalt.

After observing for a few seconds, instead of advancing, he stepped back behind the rock with his back to it and looked at us. He signaled with his hands for us to drop to the ground.

I immediately lowered myself to my belly on the sandy road surface. I hadn't seen anything, but I trusted Busto.

"Gunny, what is it?" I asked over our tactical radio link.

"There's a pair of hostiles about a hundred yards up the road," Busto said. "Two maracs. They appear to be holding up a small group of humans."

"How many humans?"

"Four or five. I didn't get a good count, but there are adults and children."

"I'm coming closer to take a look."

"Okay, just keep out of sight."

I crawled forward and heard Destiny doing the same behind me.

I kept the bulk of the boulder between me and the rest of the road ahead.

The road's hard surface bit my knees uncomfortably, and the dust made my active camo waver.

I reached Busto, and he pointed over his right shoulder, indicating where I should look.

Staying on my belly, I slithered up to look around the boulder.

The road appeared ahead. A group of figures were gathered.

I brought my gun up to my shoulder and looked through its magnifying optics.

Four humans sat in the sand at the side of the road: a man, woman, and two older children.

Looming above them floated two maracs in battered armor.

One of the twelve-armed aliens held a short flechette gun aimed at the man and appeared to be talking to him, though I couldn't hear anything from this distance.

The second marac was digging through the bags of a pack animal of some kind. Maybe a donkey or mule. I was no good at identifying types of domesticated animals.

Discarded items were strewn on the ground around the marac as the octopus-looking alien pulled out objects from the saddle bags, momentarily studied them, then tossed them.

The children clung to the woman, hiding their faces in her blue blouse.

The man's arms appeared to be tied behind his back. His face was flushed, eyes large, and he seemed to be pleading with the first marac.

"Looks like a hold-up to me," I said.

"Yeah, that's what I thought, too," Busto said with a tired shadow in his gaze.

Destiny crawled up next to me and looked at the scene through her gun optics. "Those don't look like Kergan soldiers, to me," she said.

I noticed a pair of what looked like dirt bikes parked on the side of the road about fifty yards beyond the maracs. Their configuration was odd, and I knew that they were what the maracs were riding around on, not the humans.

"This looks like a highway robbery, I think," I said.

"It makes for a good distraction," Destiny said. "We just cut through this bend, and we can avoid them."

Busto shook his head vehemently. "No way. We need to help them."

Destiny hung her head. "We don't *need* to. This is the perfect setup. We can slip past those maracs without them ever knowing we were here."

"If you're too scared, then go right ahead," Busto said. "I suppose I can catch up with you later."

I slid back into cover behind the boulder, rose to my knees, and held my hands out. "Hold on, guys. We're not splitting up."

Those maracs may not have been Kergan soldiers, but

they were armed and looked dangerous. Maybe they were part of some kind of paramilitary group or counterinsurgency unit. But to me, it didn't matter. They had accosted fellow humans, were holding them captive, and were digging through their belongings, looking for something. It was clear to me that the small group of humans—most likely a family—were the prey, and the maracs were the predators. It made my blood boil.

Memories of my dead mother and father came to me. I had been part of a family in the distant past, when I was a small child. Mom and Dad loved me and protected me. Then they died and left me. I knew they had no choice in the matter. When you died, that was it. But I was convinced that if they'd still been alive, they would want me to help this family.

"I want us to rescue them," I said.

"Kory, maybe they're only robbing them and will soon let them go," Destiny said. "But, if we go in there with guns blazing, we could get them killed."

"There're only two maracs," Busto said. "We have the element of surprise on our side if we move quickly. They're not expecting to encounter humans armed like we are out in this desert."

"I agree," I said. "And, besides, that family probably knows this area. If we rescue them, then maybe they can help us."

Destiny sighed. "Okay, okay, you've made your point. I just didn't expect us to become some kind of knights errant, is all."

"What's the plan gonna be?" I asked Busto.

As a former Marine raider, he was our expert on ground tactical warfare. I always deferred to him in these sorts of situations.

"We need to flank them," he said. "From this location, the family and the animal are in the line of fire." He gestured in a direction north of the road. "See that rise up there?"

Destiny and I nodded.

"I'm going to take Destiny with me up to the top of that. We'll have clear shots from there. Kory, you stay here and keep an eye on the situation. You can also provide fire support in case the situation goes bad."

"Okay," I said. "Let's do it, and quick, before something else happens."

Destiny and Busto took off in a loping run, trusting that their active camo and the distraction of the humans would keep the maracs from noticing them.

I lay belly down in the dust, studying the maracs through my gun optics.

The second marac found something interesting in the bags of the pack animal and examined it. A small box, which it had opened and was rifling through it.

The first marac held its gun up, aimed at the torso of the man.

The man began yelling. Over the gusty wind, I could hear him pleading for his life.

"If you're gonna do something," I said over our comms, "you better do it quick."

"*Roger, we're almost there,*" Busto replied.

I aimed my gun at the head of the marac who was threatening the man. I had a very narrow, clear shot, but it was chancy. If I took it, I risked hitting one of the children, who lay just beyond the marac's floating body. The alien could squeeze off a shot at any moment. Should I do it?

Then, the marac seemed to relax and lowered the muzzle of its gun.

"*We're in position,*" Busto said over the comms. "*On my*

*count of three, engage."*

*"Roger,"* Destiny said.

*"One...two..."*

I aimed at the first marac, preparing to fire in case Destiny and Busto's shots missed. Not that I had much confidence in my own shot—I just hoped I could drop the marac before it went on a murdering rampage, or at the very least, not hit one of my own team by accident. Because knowing my luck, if it came down to me, I'd probably just scare it into a worse mood.

*"...three!"* Busto cried.

Both of the maracs leaped in the air, and a fraction of a second later, I heard the cracks of Destiny and Busto's guns echoing across the desert.

The two maracs slumped in their armor. The first dropped its weapon, and the second the box it had been digging through.

The family of humans froze in place for a few seconds. Then the two adults flung themselves to the ground, the woman pulling the two children underneath her.

As soon as I was sure the maracs were eliminated, I jumped to my feet and sprinted toward the scene.

Running on the hard road in my protomatter suit—which augmented my strength and speed—I completed the dash in under ten seconds.

At the end of the run, I jumped up and smashed my body into the first marac, who still floated in the air, shoving him away from the family.

I grabbed the second alien and also pushed it away.

Both of the maracs had been shot through their globular heads. Gaping exit wounds spilled out gore and purple blood onto the ground.

One of the maracs was still twitching.

I pulled out my laser pistol and shot it again in the head. At that short range, it vaporized about half of it.

Busto and Destiny came running out of the desert and joined me, holding their flechette guns ready.

"We're clear, two down," I said.

"Destiny," Busto said, "go up the road about a hundred yards and check for threats."

"Roger." She started jogging up the road.

I turned toward the family, who lay face down in the dirt. The children were crying.

"It's okay," I said. "You're safe now."

I moved to the man and grabbed his arm. His hands were tied behind him.

"Hold still, I'm gonna cut you free." I shouldered my gun, pulled out my combat knife, and sliced through the bands.

The man turned over and grasped his wrists, massaging them. He squinted against the bright sun. "Just take it! Just don't hurt us! Please!" He scrambled over to the woman and placed himself between her and the children and myself.

I realized I still had my blade held in front of me in a threatening way.

I put it back in its sheath, disengaged my active camo, and held my hands out in a hopefully peaceful gesture. "Sir, calm down, you're no longer in danger! We're here to help."

Busto was walking around our perimeter and checking for any other threats. He was ignoring the human civilians so far, leaving me the job of making contact.

The man's eyes darted between me and Busto, his chest heaving. "Who... who are you people?"

I opened my helmet faceplate, letting him see my face. "My name's Kory Drake. We're not here to hurt you. Those maracs were robbing you, right?"

He nodded slowly, still shielding his family. "Yes...they ambushed us on the road. Said they'd kill the children if we didn't cooperate."

"Well, they're dead now," I said, gesturing to the alien corpses. "You're safe."

The woman sat up, pulling the children close. "Jonathan," she said, her voice shaky, "I think they really are here to help."

Jonathan relaxed slightly, lowering his arms. "Thank you," he said. "I'm Jonathan Marsden. This is my wife Martha and our children."

I nodded, trying to appear as non-threatening as possible. "Nice to meet you, Jonathan. Are you all okay? Did they hurt anyone?"

Jonathan shook his head. "No, we're alright. Just shaken up." He glanced at the marac corpses. "I can't believe you took them out so easily. Where did you come from?"

"It's a long story," I said, not wanting to get into the details of our crashed ship. "We're...travelers. Got separated from our group."

Martha stood slowly, dusting off her clothes. The two children, a boy and a girl, clung to her legs. "You saved our lives," she said softly. "How can we ever repay you?"

Before I could respond, Destiny jogged back. "All clear up ahead," she reported. "No sign of any other Kergans."

I nodded at Destiny, then turned back to the Marsdens. "We're just glad we could help. But if you really want to repay us, we could use some information about the area. Maybe a safe place to rest for the night."

Jonathan's face brightened. "Of course! Our farm isn't far from here. You're welcome to stay with us as long as you need."

I exchanged glances with Busto and Destiny. We needed

to be careful, but shelter and local intel could be invaluable.

"That's very kind of you," I said. "We'd appreciate that."

Martha bent down to comfort the children, who were still wide-eyed and trembling. "It's okay, little ones. These nice people saved us from the monsters."

The girl, no more than six or seven, peeked out from behind her mother's skirt. "Are you soldiers?" she asked in a small voice.

I knelt down to her level, softening my expression. "Something like that. We're here to help people."

She nodded solemnly, her eyes wide. The boy, a few years older, stepped forward. "That was awesome! You totally blasted those aliens!"

"Graham!" Martha scolded, but I could see a hint of a smile on Jonathan's face.

I stood, scanning the area. "We should move. More maracs might come looking for their friends."

Jonathan nodded. "Our farm's about five miles east. We can make it before dark if we hurry."

"Let's get your stuff packed up," I said, moving to help gather their scattered belongings.

# 3

The road to Elkin cut through the desert like a scar, a path of cracked asphalt surrendering to the encroaching sands. Ahead, the Marsden family's silhouettes danced in the heat haze, their ragged clothes clinging to their forms, offering scant protection against the relentless sun. I trailed with my crew, our rear-guard position a silent promise of safety.

Our protomatter suits hummed quietly around us, a symphony of nanobots and diamond matrices that shielded our skin from the scorch of the day. My suit's heads-up display painted ghostly arcs of tactical data across my vision, but even it couldn't predict the fury brewing on the horizon.

A gust hit us first, a harbinger that smelled of dust and desolation. Then, with a howl that drowned out all conversation, the sandstorm descended. Particles pelted us, fine as needles, each grain a microscopic blade etching into the world. I squinted through the maelstrom, the wind's wail echoing the chaos churning within me.

"Zeta..." Her name was a whisper lost to the gale, my

thoughts swirling as violently as the sands that obscured the sun. Guilt gnawed at me, a relentless vermin with teeth of regret. Pilot error. My error. If not for my reckless pursuit, if not for my need to chase down that damned frigate, she would be here, her presence a calming balm rather than this biting storm.

I could almost hear her archaic cadence now, offering wisdom or perhaps chastising me gently for my folly. But there was only silence where her voice should have been, a void as vast as the desert itself.

"Keep moving!" I shouted over the roar, my voice carried away as quickly as it left my lips. We pressed on, figures blurred in a world smudged by wind and earth. Alone. That solitary word echoed in my mind, its weight heavy as the responsibility now resting squarely on my shoulders.

We had lost Zeta, our beacon in this post-apocalyptic chaos, and I couldn't shake the feeling that it was all my doing. I should have known better, and I should have flown smarter. The past clawed at me, but the storm pushed us relentlessly forward toward Elkin, toward an uncertain future carved from the dust.

The sand bit at my faceplate, and I squinted against the relentless storm. A gust whipped past, carrying Destiny's voice with it.

"Wouldn't it be ironic if we got lost in this? Like finding a needle in a—"

"Shut it, Austin!" Busto's retort was almost as sharp as the granules pelting our protomatter suits.

"Come on, Gunny, lighten up. It's not like the sand can eat us," she shot back, her tone laced with irritation.

"Both of you, cut it out." My words sliced through the tension, or at least I hoped they did. We needed focus, not infighting.

"Destiny," she turned to me, her face hidden behind her faceplate, "how far to Wolf Jaw?"

"Five hundred miles, give or take," she estimated, her eyes scanning the horizon as if she could see our destination through the storm.

"Damn." That was too far without backup. "We're blind and deaf out here—no contact with the Dominion, no Zeta."

"Do they even know about *Thunder*? About Zeta?" Her brow furrowed behind her faceplate.

"Unlikely," I said, the wind snatching my words away. "We need to get back in touch. And find a new advisor."

"Great. No pressure, huh?" Busto chimed in, sarcasm heavy in his gritty voice.

"None at all," I replied, matching his tone. The weight on my shoulders grew heavier with every step towards Elkin.

Sand whipped across the lonely road, biting at our suits like a swarm of tiny, relentless insects. In their tattered clothing, the Marsden family certainly were feeling it much worse. But they trudged ahead, while behind them we followed, a beleaguered convoy wrestling with more than just the elements.

"We can't just sit around in this dust bowl," Destiny argued, sweeping her hand through the air as if to clear the stubborn grains. "Wolf Jaw is where we need to be."

"Lost the ship, lost Zeta," Busto countered, his voice gruff against the howling wind. "Why flee when the Kergan are here, waiting to be fought?"

"Because running headfirst into a fight without a plan is what gets people killed, genius." Destiny's words were sharp enough to slice through the storm.

"Enough!" I barked. My patience was wearing thin; sand was not the only irritant in this blasted wasteland. "We gave our word to Zeta, remember? To the base? Or did that slip your mind along with any common sense?"

Busto's scowl deepened beneath his bushy eyebrows, but he knew a losing battle when he saw one. He let out a resigned sigh, his shoulders slumping momentarily before squaring them again. "Fine. We head to Wolf Jaw. But first, we need wheels. Elkin might have someone crazy enough to drive through this mess."

"Or desperate enough," I muttered, turning the idea over in my mind. Gold coins and chips clinked softly in my pocket—a sound that suddenly seemed a lot like opportunity knocking.

"Let's move, then," I said, gesturing forward with a nod. "No use wasting daylight, even if we can't see much of it."

"Double time," Busto commanded, his voice rising above the whine of the wind that picked up fine grains of sand, peppering our faces. The Marsdens were a good distance ahead, and we needed to close the gap. My boots pounded the cracked earth as I surged forward.

"Jon!" I called out as I finally caught up, brushing dust off my faceplate. "We're aiming for California. Know anyone in Elkin who's got a ride?"

Jon turned, his face shadowed beneath the wide brim of his hat, "Vehicles? Not many running ones left. Fuel's scarce as honest politicians these days." He gestured towards the town with a sweep of his arm. "Try the Tumbleweed Tavern. If there's anybody willing or able, that's where you'll find 'em."

"Shortages?" I asked, the word leaving my lips like a bullet.

Martha's face creased with concern as she joined in. "Ain't just fuel, Kory. Ban'ach and those Nebula Nomads— the bandits—have taken most of it. And people too...lots of folks gone missing."

My gaze flicked between them. "Abducted? For what?"

"Nobody knows," Jon said, his tone heavy, burdened by unspoken fears. "Could've been us today if those robbers had their way."

I nodded, filing away every scrap of information. Every fact was ammunition, and I was going to need plenty.

"Thanks," I said, already turning back to signal the crew. "We best head to this tavern, then."

"Be careful," Martha warned, her voice carrying the weight of genuine concern.

"Always am," I lied with a tight smile, feeling anything but.

The sand whipped around us like a living thing, hungry and relentless. I pushed through it, thoughts racing as fast as the storm. Abductions. Not random, not with the Kergans' reach casting shadows across Earth. I could almost see the marac overlords pulling strings, their alien eyes gleaming with dark purpose. Selling humans? Eating them? Or worse—turning them into something unrecognizable, tools of conquest?

"Jon," Busto's voice cut through the howl of the wind, "these Nomads, they ever spill blood?"

"First days, yeah," Jon shouted back over the storm, his words laced with a chill. "They killed those who stood up to them. Now we play nice, give 'em what they want. No choice."

I chewed on that, my jaw tight. Elkin was backed into a corner, no different than any outpost under siege. But Wolf Jaw, at least, didn't have its own citizens hunted like wildlife.

An investigation. Yes. That had to be the next move. Find out why, find out where. Those lost souls deserved that much. Who was this Ban'ach? Why were the Nebula Nomads picking on this small town?

"Let's keep moving," I ordered. "The sooner we get to this tavern, the better."

The town of Elkin slowly emerged out of the dust storm, like the shallow sea floor revealing itself as a skiff approached the shore. The outlines of buildings, blurred by the blowing dust, promised shelter and rest.

Dust devils danced mockingly across the main street of Elkin, nearly a ghost town haunted by its own slow decay. The paved road was a cracked artery leading to a heart that barely beat. Gravel crunched under our boots, the graded side roads fanning out like weathered scars on the earth's skin. Buildings, once proud, now slouched; their windows stared blankly, the paint flaking away like dried scales. No rhythm of life here—cars sat abandoned, relics of better times.

"Desolate," I muttered, eyes squinting against the sand-laden gusts.

"Surviving," Busto corrected with a grunt as we trudged forward, protomatter suits shielding us from the worst of the storm.

A growling chorus broke through the wind's howl—a pack of ribs and fur, more skeleton than canine. The dogs approached, driven mad by hunger, desperation in their bloodshot eyes. Instinctively, I stepped forward, hand on my sidearm, my voice a commanding bark. "Back off!"

"Get!" Busto echoed my command, his presence an unspoken threat.

The dogs hesitated, then scattered, tails tucked, leaving us in peace. The encounter, brief as it was, a harsh reminder of nature's unforgiving rule: adapt or perish.

We turned onto a gravel road, following the Marsdens'

lead. Each step kicked up dust, marking our passage in ephemeral clouds that were quickly swallowed by the relentless tempest. Half a mile felt like an eternity, but eventually, a ranch house emerged from the bleak landscape, a solitary haven amidst the chaos.

"Home sweet home," Jon announced, gesturing toward the single-story structure. A barn, a shed, and a fenced yard with a cow, two horses, and a mule completed the picture of rustic life clinging stubbornly to tradition.

"Appreciate the hospitality," I said, glancing at Martha, who smiled back warmly. We'd drop our gear, catch a moment's rest, then on to the next task.

"Let's unload quick," I instructed the crew, "then we hit the Tumbleweed Tavern. Need wheels to Wolf Jaw.

"Hopefully, we're not overstaying our welcome," I added, though the sentiment was met with gracious nods from our hosts.

"Two days, tops," I assured them, though in my gut, I knew timelines had a way of unraveling fast.

"We don't have much space in our house," Jon said. "But you can stay in the hayloft of our barn." He seemed embarrassed by his suggestion, so he held out his hand and quickly added, "It's not as bad as it sounds. I'm certain you'll be much more comfortable there and have better privacy."

I nodded. "Thanks, Jon, it will be fine. We appreciate your hospitality."

# 4

The Tumbleweed Tavern greeted us with a chorus of clinking glasses and low murmurings. The place was an old Western movie come to life, complete with a balding man in a white apron tending the bar like he'd been doing it since the frontier days.

Four customers occupied stools, hunched over their drinks, while another half dozen sat at tables scattered around the room, most busy with plates of steaming food.

The air was rich with the smell of cooking meat and beer, layered on top of dry wood and dust.

It was all so familiar yet alien at the same time, as if I'd stepped through a portal into one of those ancient films my dad used to watch. Cowboy hats perched on tabletops, worn boots clumped against the wooden floorboards every time someone moved. It was a cliché wrapped in nostalgia.

I made my way to the bar, conscious of the laser pistol hanging from my holster.

The clothes Martha lent me were snug, straining against my muscles, reminding me that these weren't mine.

Protomatter suits would have stuck out worse than a sore thumb here, but I couldn't help feeling like a pretender in this garb—everything about it rubbed wrong.

Busto, though, looked almost comical; smaller than me, his borrowed clothes hung off him like a kid playing dress-up in his father's wardrobe.

*Feels like I'm in a costume,* I thought, glancing around. But the weight of the pistol was real enough. We were here for something important. We had a job to do. And part of me relished that.

"Evening. What'll it be?" the bartender asked, wiping his hands on a rag.

"Name's Kory," I said, meeting his gaze. "And these are my friends."

"Sheldon Stafford," he replied, nodding. "Owner of this here Tumbleweed Tavern. Got beef stew tonight, comes with bread."

"Do you take gold?" I asked, fishing out one of the chips we had with us as part of our survival gear from when we escaped from the wreck of *Thunder*.

"Depends on what you got," Stafford said, eyes narrowing slightly as he inspected the chip of yellow gleaming gold.

I held it up, letting the dim lamplight catch the glint.

"That's good for ten meals, twenty drinks," he declared after a moment, satisfied. "Want me to start a tab?"

"Yeah, do that. We'll take three stews and beers to start."

"Coming right up," Stafford said, tucking the chip into his apron pocket as he turned away.

I settled onto a barstool, scanning the room again.

My attention snagged on a man in the back corner. He was alone, gray hair like steel wool under the low light. A badge pinned to his vest marked him as some kind of lawman. Rugged. Intent on his papers and notes, spoon paused mid-air, his focus split between the meal and the task at hand.

A couple of stools over, a young woman nursed her beer, eyes darting toward me now and then. Each time our gazes met, color rose on her cheeks, and she'd quickly turn away, engaging the older man beside her in hushed conversation.

*Interesting crowd*, I thought, taking it all in.

Stafford emerged from the kitchen, balancing a tray that sent the scent of rich beef stew wafting through the room.

The aroma hit like a freight train—savory and warm, mingling with the earthy smell of fresh bread. My stomach growled in response, reminding me of how long it had been since our last decent meal.

"Here we go," Stafford said, setting down bowls with steaming heaps of stew in front of Destiny, Busto, and me.

The broth shimmered under the dim light, chunks of tender beef swimming amidst potatoes and carrots.

The bread, golden and crusty, begged to be torn apart.

"Smells damn good," Busto grunted appreciatively, leaning forward to inhale deeply. His eyes closed briefly, as if committing the scent to memory.

"Better pace yourself, Gunny," Destiny quipped, poking at her own bowl with amusement. "With your tiny stomach and all, we wouldn't want you to explode. Kory's might survive, though. It's already stretched to capacity."

"Ha!" Stafford chuckled, his laughter rolling like distant thunder. "You folks ain't from around here, are ya?"

"California," I replied, careful to steer the conversation away from anything too revealing. "Just visiting. Looking for a way back."

"Ah, California," Stafford mused, wiping his hands on

his apron. "Heard it's a tough place these days. You need transport?"

"That's right," I said, keeping my tone casual but direct. "Know anyone who could help with that?"

"There are few with working vehicles left," he admitted, shaking his head. "Fuel's scarce. But see that fella over there?" He nodded toward the man with the badge. "Marshal Batts. Might be able to lend a hand."

"Thanks," I said, filing the information away.

I glanced over at Batts again, watching as he scribbled notes with the air of someone who had seen more than most. Just what we needed—a lawman with connections.

"Enjoy your meal," Stafford offered with a grin before moving off to tend to other customers.

I turned back to my stew, the weight of our mission pressing down once more. We needed to get home. Fast. The Brooks family would be worried about us, and the town of Wolf Jaw was depending on us for some of their supplies of food and fuel.

I shoveled the last spoonful of stew into my mouth, savoring the rich, savory warmth that flooded my senses. Tender chunks of beef and perfectly cooked vegetables melded together in a way that reminded me of the home-cooked meals Dora Best used to make back in Wolf Jaw. But this? This might actually be better. The bread—crusty on the outside, soft and warm within—accompanied the meal perfectly, though I wished for a bit of butter to elevate it further.

"That was incredible," Destiny sighed, pushing her empty bowl away.

Busto nodded in agreement, already downing the last of his beer.

"Best I've had in years," I said, meaning every word.

Elkin's ranches must supply the best beef if Stafford could whip up something like this.

"Drinks done?" I asked, glancing at the others.

"Yeah," Busto replied, wiping his mouth with the back of his hand. Destiny gave a nod as she took the final sip from her mug.

"Alright, let's move." I stood, feeling the weight of the gold chips in my pocket—a reminder of our task at hand. If we were to buy a ride home, the yellow stuff would likely speak loudest.

We crossed the tavern floor, weaving between tables, until we reached Marshal Batts' corner.

I cleared my throat slightly, drawing his attention away from the papers he was immersed in.

"Excuse us, Marshal Batts," I began, keeping my tone respectful but firm.

"Strangers in town," Batts noted, his eyes sharp beneath the brim of his hat. "Been watching you."

"Is there a problem?" I asked, meeting his gaze head-on.

"Not yet," he replied, his voice carrying the weight of authority. "And I'd like to keep it that way."

I chose to sidestep the implied warning. "We're looking for transport back to California," I explained, cutting straight to the point. "Heard you might help."

"Destination?" he asked, folding his arms across his chest.

"Wolf Jaw," I answered. "We can pay—in gold."

Batts leaned back in his chair, considering.

His eyes flicked over us, assessing.

I stayed silent, waiting, the room buzzing around us.

Batts sat there, arms crossed, eyes distant—thinking. The silence between us stretched like a taut wire.

Finally, he nodded to himself, as if settling some internal

debate.

"I *could* help you," he said slowly, his voice gruff but measured. "But what you're asking...it's a lot for this town."

"Gold's not enough?" I asked, keeping my expression neutral. We needed this transport more than anything.

"Fuel's scarce," Batts replied, shaking his head. "Only used for official business around here."

"Official business?" I repeated, raising an eyebrow.

"That's right." Batts leaned forward, his gaze sharp and unwavering. "I've got a problem. A big one. And maybe you can help."

"Go on," I encouraged, though impatience was gnawing at me.

"Got a gang terrorizing Elkin," he began, his tone growing serious. "Nebula Nomads. Mostly marac fighters, but they've got humans in their ranks, too. Been stealing from our folks, abducted over a hundred people these last six months."

"That's rough," I acknowledged.

"There are four Army scouts here, who're willing to fight back," Batts continued. "But we don't have enough numbers. You look like fighters"—his eyes darted to the laser pistols strapped to our sides—"and with your help, we could take 'em down."

"Free transport in return?" I asked, cutting to the core of the deal.

"Exactly," Batts confirmed. "Help us with this, and I'll make sure you get to California."

I considered his proposal, weighing our need against the risk. His offer was tempting but perilous, too. We were strangers in Elkin, yet embroiled in its troubles, whether we liked it or not.

I weighed Batts's proposal, mind racing. Shouldn't the

citizens handle their own problems? But then again, these Nebula Nomads were only here because of the Kergans. I'd sworn to fight those invaders wherever they reared their ugly heads. Maybe this was part of that promise.

"Alright," I said, glancing at Busto and Destiny. Busto gave a curt nod, his eyes steady with resolve. Destiny rolled her eyes, shrugged—a gesture of reluctant agreement. "We might be able to help. But we need more details."

"Fair enough," Batts replied, a hint of relief in his voice.

He folded his papers with methodical precision, tucking them into his vest pocket. His hat found its place on his head with a practiced motion, shadowing his sharp features.

"Got another engagement," he said, rising from his chair. His cowboy boots thudded against the wooden floor, each step measured, deliberate. "But I'm expecting the Army Scout Team to show up here any minute. You wait around, you can talk to them."

"Will do," I nodded, extending my hand.

Batts grasped it firmly, a handshake that spoke volumes. No frills, no unnecessary words—just an understanding.

"Good luck," he offered simply, turning away.

We watched as he walked toward the door, his authoritative presence lingering in the air even after he'd exited the tavern.

We took our seats at Batts's vacant table, the wooden chairs creaking under our weight.

The tavern buzzed with the low hum of conversation and clinking glasses.

I leaned back, trying to ease the tension that had coiled in my muscles.

"Look at these folks," Destiny said, her voice dripping with amusement. She gestured subtly to the patrons around us, all decked out in cowboy hats and boots. "It's like we walked into a Wild West reenactment."

"Yeah," I chuckled. "We're the only ones without spurs."

"Hey, Busto," she continued, a mischievous glint in her eyes. "You being a Mexican, better watch yourself. They might toss you out for historical accuracy."

Busto blushed, a rare sight. He shot Destiny a glare that could cut steel. "Keep it up, Destiny," he replied, his voice gravelly but laced with humor. "I'll make sure they throw you out first. After all, they didn't have sharpshooting sassy ladies back then."

Destiny snorted, feigning offense, but there was warmth beneath their verbal sparring—a camaraderie forged through battles and close calls.

Suddenly, the tavern door slammed open.

The room fell silent.

Three maracs floated in, their tentacles undulating like liquid shadows.

Behind them, two human males stumbled forward, eyes glazed and movements erratic.

Each of them bristled with weapons—pistols strapped across their bodies, long guns slung over their shoulders.

"Look at these yokels," one of the humans sneered, his words slurred and dripping with contempt. He swayed slightly, steadying himself against a nearby table. "Staring like they've never seen a real man before."

The tension in the room spiked.

Conversations died mid-sentence.

Eyes flickered nervously between the newcomers and each other.

I felt the air grow heavy, charged with an unspoken threat.

My hand instinctively hovered near the laser pistol at

my hip, senses on high alert.

    Something dangerous was about to happen.

# 5

The shorter, drunker human leered at the pretty young girl, now sitting alone at the bar. "Hey baby, why don't you come sit on my lap?" She shrank back in fear, eyes wide.

I tensed, my hand inching toward my holster. But I held back. For now.

The maracs drifted through the tavern, cold eyes scanning the room as if searching for someone.

The biggest one floated at the front, a flechette gun fondled by one of his many tentacles.

His gaze brushed over me, studying me for a long moment.

I met his stare unflinchingly until he finally looked away.

That's when I saw the drunk stumble toward our table, his bloodshot eyes fixed on Destiny. "Well, ain't you a pretty little thing," he slurred, reaching out to stroke her face with grimy fingers.

Destiny slapped his hand away. "Touch me again, and you'll pull back a stump."

The man's face flushed crimson. "Bitch! You'll pay for that!" He raised his meaty hand to strike her.

Time seemed to slow.

I launched myself out of my chair, raw protective fury pulsing through my veins.

In one fluid motion, I slammed my fist into the drunk's face with a sickening crunch.

He crumpled to the floor, blood gushing from his shattered nose as he wailed for help.

"Not again!" Busto cursed, dropping down beside the table for cover.

Destiny dove behind the table too, her hand flying to her hip.

But I was already moving.

Adrenaline surging, I grabbed the groaning heap of a man and hoisted him over my head with a roar.

The bastard was heavy, but I was bigger, and rage made me even stronger.

With a grunt, I hurled him across the room.

He smashed into the floor, leaving a smear of blood the color of rust.

Breathing hard, I glared at his moaning form, fists still clenched.

Damn. I hadn't meant to go that far. But seeing him about to hit Destiny, my street sister, my closest thing to a family, I'd just...snapped.

Now, we were neck-deep in a mess.

The drunk's pals were on their feet, hands darting toward weapons.

I'd been so focused on protecting Destiny I hadn't thought about them. Stupid, reckless.

And heavily armed, too, bristling with serious firepower. These assholes were definitely Nebula Nomads, the bandit scum who'd been terrorizing the town.

*Rats.* In my blind rage, I'd just painted a huge target on all our backs. Destiny and Busto were gonna kill me. If these bastards didn't do it first...

Heart pounding, I widened my stance, ready to fight like hell to defend my crew, my family. Even if it was my own damn fault. No way I was letting these pricks lay a finger on Destiny or Busto.

Not while I still had breath in my body.

I tensed, prepared for the carnage about to erupt. My mind raced to formulate a plan. We were outnumbered and outgunned. But we weren't going down without one helluva brawl...

Chaos erupted.

Customers dove for cover, some bolting past the maracs in a desperate bid for the exit.

I glimpsed Stafford, the bartender, ducking behind the bar. Smart man.

The biggest marac, a hulking purple monstrosity, floated forward. It snarled something in its alien tongue, leveling a flechette gun at my chest with a suckered tentacle.

"Get fried, calamari," I spat back.

Wrong thing to say.

The marac's beady eyes flashed with rage.

It took aim, barrel rising to my head.

I heard the whine of it charging to fire.

Time crystallized.

I moved on pure instinct, hundreds of hours of Busto's relentless combat drills kicking in.

In one fluid motion, I drew my laser pistol from its holster, thumbed off the safety, and snapped it up.

The marac's finger tentacle tightened on the trigger.

I was faster.

A searing lance of blue-white light cracked from my pistol's muzzle, straight and true. It punched through the center of the alien's bulbous skull.

The thing's head burst like a rotten melon. Gobbets of steaming purple flesh splattered the walls.

The stench of charred meat permeated the air.

A smoking, fist-sized hole gaped in the wall behind it.

For a stunned heartbeat, the marac swayed. Then, it collapsed to the floor with the heavy finality of a fresh corpse.

But there was no time to process, no chance to feel the weight of the kill. The two remaining maracs were raising their own weapons, multiple arms moving in eerie unison.

Stafford popped up from behind the bar, clutching a sawed-off shotgun. "Drop 'em now, you squiddly scum!" he bellowed. "I'll paint the walls with ya!"

The thunderous cocking of his gun punctuated the threat. He swung the scattergun back and forth, trying to cover both aliens at once.

"You're gonna be an oil slick when the boss gets done with you!" one of the bandits yelled at me, voice quivering with rage and fear. "Ban'ach will cut out your spine for this!"

The invocation of their leader's name sent a chill down my own spine. Ban'ach. Jon Marsden had told us about the leader of the Nebula Nomads.

"Pick up your buddy and get lost!" Stafford roared, jabbing his shotgun at the dead marac. "While you still got heads to think with!"

The drunk who'd started this whole mess blubbered nearby, cradling his battered face. "He zapped Bl'rko!" he wailed in a pitiful keen. "Poor Bl'rko! He never hurt nobody!"

I almost snorted at that. I'm sure "Bl'rko" had hurt

plenty. But gallows humor died in my throat as the gravity of the situation sank in fully.

The drunk humans and marac picked up the body of their comrade and fled through the door.

My pulse throbbed in my skull, adrenaline still electric in my veins. The copper tang of blood mingled with the ozone stink of expended laser fire.

I met Destiny's wide eyes across the room and saw my own grim realization mirrored there.

Busto glowered at me, tight-lipped.

Dammit. In mere minutes, everything had changed. By killing that marac, I'd just signed our death warrants. Painted bullseyes on the backs of everyone I cared about.

The Nomads would be out for blood now. Our blood. This was no two-bit beef, solved with fists and forgotten by morning.

This was war. And I'd just fired the first shot.

With a trembling hand, I holstered my pistol, its weight suddenly heavy on my hip. The reality of what I'd done crashed over me like a tidal wave. Self-doubt gnawed at my gut.

Had I made the right call? Pulled the trigger too quickly? Maybe there could've been another way...

No. I shook off the second-guessing. That piece of garbage had been getting ready to ventilate me. It was him or me. I'd done what I had to do.

Stafford stowed his shotgun back under the bar, muttering curses. He caught my eye and gave a solemn nod. An acknowledgment. Gratitude and sympathy in one gesture.

"Well, that went to hell fast," Destiny remarked, her tone dry but her eyes still wide and wary. "Guess we can cross 'quiet drink' off the agenda."

Busto slid me a hard look. "You know this ain't over, Kory. Killing a Nomad...their boss won't let that slide. You just brought a world of trouble down on us."

I clenched my jaw, a muscle ticking. Busto only voiced the dread already coiling in my own mind.

We'd been marked now. The vicious chieftain of the Nomads, Ban'ach, would be howling for retribution. And something told me she wasn't the "eye for an eye" type.

She'd want a mountain of eyes to pay for this insult. Starting with mine.

My fingers curled into fists. Let her try. We'd handle whatever she threw our way. Together. Like always.

I'd spilled first blood to protect my family. To protect Destiny. And I'd do it again in a heartbeat.

No matter the cost.

Stafford ambled over, concern etched into the lines of his weathered face. "You okay there, son?"

I managed a tight nod. "Yeah. Thanks for the backup."

He waved a dismissive hand. "Those Nebula Nomad bastards had it coming. Been terrorizing my tavern and this whole damn town for months now."

Busto leaned forward, his dark eyes intense. "How many of them are there, Stafford? In the gang?"

The barkeep scratched his stubbled chin, considering. "Hard to say exactly. They come and go. But if I had to guess...maybe thirty or so."

Destiny let out a low whistle. "Thirty bandits? Ouch, Kory, you sure know how to pick a fight."

A chuckle rumbled in my chest, the tension easing just a bit.

Busto cracked a smile, shaking his head. Even Stafford huffed a quiet laugh. For a moment, the gravity lifted, replaced by a camaraderie forged in the heat of battle.

Stafford cleared his throat. "Can I get you folks anything? On the house, of course. Least I can do."

"Just some water would be great, thanks." My throat felt like sandpaper, the adrenaline still buzzing through my veins.

As Stafford turned to go, I added, "We're actually waiting on the Army Scout Team. Need to talk to them about a proposal from Marshal Batts."

The barkeep paused, nodding. "Good people, those scouts. They usually come in around this time for dinner, catch up with the locals. I'll send 'em your way when they arrive."

True to his word, he returned shortly with a pitcher of blessedly cold water and three clean glasses. Setting them down, Stafford clapped me on the shoulder.

"Thank you again. For everything." Sincerity rang in his voice. "You ever need anything, you just say the word."

With that, he retreated back behind the bar, leaving us to our thoughts and the uneasy calm that settled over the tavern.

I poured the water, the simple act grounding me. Busto and Destiny each took a glass, sipping slowly.

We sat in silence for a long moment, the weight of what had just transpired hanging heavy in the air.

Five minutes crawled by, each second ratcheting up the tension coiling in my gut. The adrenaline ebbed, leaving behind a bone-deep weariness and a throbbing ache in my knuckles where they'd connected with the bastard's jaw.

I flexed my fingers, savoring the pain. A reminder that I was alive. That we all were, despite the odds.

The tavern door creaked open, and I tensed, hand flying to my holster. But instead of more marac thugs, in walked four humans clad in weathered military fatigues, an assortment of well-used pistols on their hips.

Two men, two women, moving with the coiled grace of those who'd seen combat. The easy camaraderie between them spoke of a team forged in fire.

The Army Scout Team. It had to be.

Smiles and greetings erupted from the locals as the soldiers entered, a hero's welcome. They returned the salutations with easy charm, clearly at home among the townsfolk.

One of the women, a wiry blonde with a scar bisecting her eyebrow, caught sight of the scorch marks and the blown-out wall. She barked out a laugh.

"Damn, Stafford, looks like we missed one hell of a party!"

Stafford grinned back, relief plain on his face. "Nothing I couldn't handle. Had some help from my new friends here."

All eyes turned to us, curiosity and appraisal mingling in their gazes. I met their stares evenly, chin lifted, shoulders back.

# 6

The soldiers strolled over to our table.

"Staff Sergeant Ivor Rowbottom," one of the men announced, his voice cutting through the tavern's murmur like a knife. He had a tall, athletic build—sharp features etched with discipline, scars whispering stories of old battles.

"Private First Class Moriko Appleton," came next. She was focused and intense, eyes like laser beams scanning every inch of the room. Her lean frame spoke of agility and purpose, her words measured and deliberate.

"Corporal Balbino Vila," the second man chimed in. He carried himself with an easy kind of confidence, like someone who always knew where the exits were. His presence was steady and grounded.

"Sergeant Cindy Montana." A nod punctuated her introduction. There was something about her—a certain calmness that belied the chaos of war. She moved with quiet assurance.

"Destiny Austin," I reciprocated, nodding toward

Destiny, her eyes narrowing ever so slightly in appraisal. "And that's Clemen Busto, former Marine Gunnery Sergeant." Busto gave a nod, curt and respectful, the scars on his face catching the dim light.

"Pleasure," Rowbottom said, offering his hand. We exchanged firm shakes and polite nods—soldiers and insurgents, meeting over tables sticky with spilled beer.

"Grab a chair," I said, gesturing to the empty seats around the table. They did, pulling chairs to join us. The wood scraped against the floor, a sound like fingernails on a chalkboard.

While they settled in, I sized them up. Rowbottom radiated authority, every move calculated, like he was playing chess while the rest of us played checkers. On the other hand, Vila had a watchful gaze, probably the kind of guy who'd notice a pin drop amidst artillery fire.

Appleton, she was different. Her eyes darted around the tavern, missing nothing. There was a fierceness in her, a readiness that couldn't be ignored. And then Montana—her kindness shone through like a beacon in the gloom.

As they sat, a sense of calmness began to form—a shared understanding among those just looking for a quiet place to chat. Maybe this would work out after all.

"Marshal Batts wants us to help take down the Nebula Nomads," I said, breaking the ice. "He thinks with your scouts and a citizen posse, we might just have a shot."

Rowbottom glanced at the marac bloodstain smeared across the tavern floor, remnants of our earlier scuffle. A smirk tugged at his lips. "Looks like you've already started cleaning up the neighborhood."

"Yeah, Kory's been redecorating," Destiny quipped, her voice dripping with mock admiration. "I think he missed his calling as an interior designer."

I felt the heat rise in my cheeks, laughter bubbling up despite myself. "Alright, alright," I chuckled, waving off the jabs. "So, Rowbottom, tell me about your team."

"Well," Rowbottom began, leaning forward, elbows on the table's sticky surface. "We were part of the 11th Armored Cavalry Regiment—scouts sent to Arizona to deal with the Kergan Invasion."

"The 11th ACR?" Busto echoed.

"Yeah," Rowbottom nodded. "Our M3 Bradley was tasked with recon near Elkin, behind enemy lines. Things got hairy real fast. Kergans ambushed us—caught us off guard."

"Lost our driver," Vila added quietly, his voice low but steady.

"Most of us made it out alive, though," Rowbottom continued, a somber edge to his tone. "I'm the team commander. Vila here is the gunner—best shot I've ever seen. Appleton's our dismount observer, keeps us informed, and Montana's the medic. She patched us up and kept us moving when things went south."

"You must be a tight unit, if you're all still together," I observed, a hint of envy bleeding into my voice. My crew had been through hell together, but we'd always been a ragtag bunch—held together by common goals rather than military discipline.

"Had to be," Rowbottom said, meeting my gaze with those sharp, authoritative eyes. "It's the only way you survive out there."

"Yeah," I agreed, feeling the weight of his words. It's what we needed if we were going to make it through this and return to Wolf Jaw.

"Sounds like you're exactly the kind of allies we need," I admitted, glancing around the table. That sense of shared purpose I'd felt earlier? It burned brighter now, like a beacon cutting through the fog of war.

"Tell me, Rowbottom," Busto leaned in, his gravelly voice cutting through the ambient noise of the tavern. "What happened out there when you lost the Bradley?"

Rowbottom's eyes flickered with an intensity that seemed to darken the room. "It was a routine recon, or so we thought." He paused, drawing everyone into his tale. "We were moving through a narrow pass near Elkin, keeping an eye on Kergan movements. All was quiet—too quiet."

"That's when they hit us," Vila interjected, his voice low and simmering with frustration. "An ambush. Hidden beneath scrub and rock, Kergans swarmed like hornets from a nest."

"Driver didn't stand a chance," Rowbottom continued, his tone somber. "Took a direct hit to the front armor. Armor-piercing round. We were sitting ducks."

"How'd you get out?" I asked, curiosity piqued.

"Appleton spotted a weak point," Rowbottom said, nodding towards the young observer who sat silently beside him. "She saw a break in the enemy line, just wide enough for us to make a run for it."

"Montana patched us up as we moved," Vila added, admiration shading his words. "We fought our way through, all the while dodging fire, until we were clear."

"Made it here by the skin of our teeth," Rowbottom finished, eyes meeting mine with a mixture of pride and grim determination.

"Impressive," I said, the weight of their survival pressing upon me. Each scar told a story—a testament to their tenacity.

"Where were you during the war, Busto?" Rowbottom asked, shifting the spotlight.

Busto hesitated, a rare flash of vulnerability crossing his face. "Missed it," he admitted, almost sheepishly. "Was on reserve status, waiting for the call-up. Never came."

"Former Marine Raider, though," I chipped in, glancing at Busto. His modesty needed no embellishment, but the truth deserved recognition. "Now he's one of us—part of the crew, fighting back however we can."

"You're insurgents?" Rowbottom's eyebrows arched in surprise.

"Yeah," Busto confirmed, his tone firm. "Different kind of battle now."

"Interesting," Vila mused, leaning forward, curiosity etched across his rugged face. "What's your story, then?"

"Well," I began, leaning back slightly in my chair and catching Rowbottom's eye, "we were serving under a military adviser from the Collective Dominion. They gave us an alien warship with which to fight the Kergan."

"Alien warship?" Appleton's eyebrows shot up, eyes wide as saucers.

"Yeah," I grinned, though it was tinged with bitterness. "Didn't end well, though. We lost her in battle against an armored Kergan frigate. The thing was a beast. Cut through us like butter."

"Zeta," Destiny chimed in, her voice softer now, almost reverential. "Our military adviser. She's missing, probably dead."

"Sorry to hear that," Rowbottom offered, his voice sincere.

"Thanks," I nodded, trying to shake off the weight of memory. "We're making our way back to California now. To our base." A pause, then a hopeful glance at Rowbottom. "Think you could give us a ride?"

Rowbottom chuckled, a deep rumble that seemed to

shake the dust from the rafters. "Ride? In Elkin? Bicycles, if you're lucky. Most have been stolen by the Nomads."

"Figures," I muttered, more to myself than anyone else. My mind drifted as Rowbottom continued talking, his words fading into the background for a moment.

I found myself studying the scout team again. Half a year since the US military supposedly surrendered, yet here they were—cohesive, disciplined, still operating like soldiers. It was impressive, really. They hadn't lost their edge or camaraderie, much like my own crew. Both teams behind enemy lines, still fighting what felt like a losing battle.

Maybe, just maybe, Rowbottom could be a valuable ally. I had to admit, there was a certain comfort in knowing we weren't alone out here. Even if my ego didn't want to admit it. As if reading my thoughts, Destiny nudged me, bringing me back to the present.

"What's the plan, Kory?" she asked, her voice cutting through my internal musings.

"Plan?" I quipped, flashing a grin. "We find some bikes—or maybe roller skates. Then we take on the world."

She rolled her eyes and jabbed me with her elbow.

I nodded and leaned forward. "Alright," I said, bringing the conversation back on track. "Our crew's aiming for California, to get back to our base. But Batts—" I nodded toward the tavern door, imagining Marshal Batts' stern presence just outside. "He's offered us a deal. Free transportation if we help Elkin with its little bandit problem."

"Sounds like Batts," Rowbottom replied, his voice gruff but intrigued.

"Yeah," I continued. "And we heard your team's already itching to take on the bandits."

Rowbottom exchanged glances with his team, nods passing between them like silent communication. "We've been ready," he confirmed, eyes scanning our laser pistols on the table. They gleamed under the dim tavern lights, deceptively small yet deadly.

"Impressive sidearms you've got," Rowbottom acknowledged, "but it'll take more than that to handle the Nomads."

"Most of our firepower is stashed at the Marsdens'," I admitted, leaning back in my chair and crossing my arms. "Got some advanced rifles from the Collective Dominion—" I saw Montana's eyes flicker at the mention of the Marsdens. Recognition. "You know them?"

"Good people," Montana remarked simply, her words carrying weight.

"Right. Well, those rifles can punch through Kergan battle armor like it's paper. Plus, we've got protomatter armored suits and tactical comms."

"That's really good," Rowbottom nodded, a hint of admiration in his voice. "But we'll need to be smart about this. Break the bandits into smaller groups. Destroy them in detail."

"Divide and conquer," Busto chimed in, his gravelly voice cutting through the air. "Makes sense."

"Exactly," Rowbottom agreed, eyes gleaming with strategic intent. The plan was forming, solidifying, as we sat there in the Tumbleweed Tavern debating it. Two teams, one goal. And maybe, just maybe, a fighting chance.

"Abductions," Destiny said, breaking the silence with a voice like flint. Her eyes locked onto Montana, sharp and unyielding. "We've heard about them. What's going on?"

"Not much to say," Montana replied with a tight shrug, her words clipped and matter-of-fact. "Young adults vanish, no trace, no word from the Nomads. Like they've been swallowed whole."

A chill ran down my spine. Elkin was a ghost town in more ways than one. Montana's deep brown eyes met mine, filled with an unspoken urgency.

"Elkin's got dozens of orphans now," she continued, her voice softening just a fraction. "Parents gone, leaving kids behind. People like the Marsdens—" she paused, took a breath, "they're lucky. For now."

"Jon and Martha are ticking time bombs," I muttered, recalling the couple's faces etched with fear—their gratitude when we'd saved them from those bandits. "We had a run-in with two of those Nomads. Sent them packing permanently."

"Good work," Rowbottom nodded, approval coloring his tone.

Orphans. The word stuck in my throat like ash. Memories clawed at me, unwanted and raw. I could see it—the cold walls, the sterile floors of state-run orphanages that felt more like prisons. My fists clenched under the table. Kids shouldn't have to live like that. Not ever.

"Where are they?" I asked, forcing the words past the lump in my throat. "The orphans. Where do they go?"

Montana's gaze softened, just a flicker. "Urbana Fontana's place. She's a widow who turned her home into an orphanage for them."

"Mrs. Fontana," I repeated, mentally noting the name. I'd find time. Visit her. See those kids. Offer something—hope, help, anything.

"Yeah," Montana confirmed, nodding slightly. "She's doing what she can."

"Then it's settled," I said, my voice firm, final. We'd handle the Nomads. But first, there were other debts to pay.

Other promises to keep.

"Right," Rowbottom echoed, understanding threading through his voice.

"Let's make it happen," I vowed, feeling the fire ignite within.

"Agreed," came the consensus.

The Tumbleweed Tavern buzzed around us, but at that moment, all I saw was the road ahead.

"Alright," I said, leaning in over the table. "Let's take down these Nomads."

Rowbottom nodded. His eyes were steady, calculating. "We can make it work. I'll talk to Marshal Batts. Get back to you with the plan."

"Sounds good," I replied, extending my hand. His grip was firm, solid—a promise sealed.

"To the Nomads' end," Rowbottom declared, and our hands parted.

"To their end," I echoed.

"See you soon," Rowbottom said, nodding at me before turning away.

"Yeah." I watched them go, the buzz of conversation swallowing their retreating forms.

"Time to head back?" Busto asked, his voice cutting through the noise.

"Yeah. Let's move," I replied, standing up.

The Tumbleweed Tavern melted away behind us as we stepped out. The night air hit me—cool, crisp. Stars hung overhead like scattered diamonds.

"Back to the Marsdens'," I said, leading the way. Gravel crunched underfoot as we walked, shadows stretching long and thin beneath the moonlight.

# 7

I jolted awake, heart hammering against my ribs like a caged animal. The suffocating darkness of the Marsdens' hayloft pressed down on me, every shadow twisting into a potential threat.

The sweet scent of hay mixed with a faint, acrid odor that didn't belong.

Below us, the creaking of floorboards groaned louder than they should have in the stillness of the night. Footsteps —too many to count—shuffled stealthily beneath, accompanied by hushed whispers that prickled the hairs on the back of my neck.

I reached out blindly to my right, fingers brushing against Destiny's warm shoulder. She slept soundly, her breath steady and unaware.

To my left, Gunny Busto was a silent mound in his sleeping bag.

Panic tightened my chest. I leaned closer to Destiny, my lips barely an inch from her ear. "Destiny," I whispered, voice barely audible. No response. It was as if she were submerged in a dream too deep to rouse from.

A floorboard creaked loudly below, followed by a stifled curse.

My pulse quickened.

I shook Busto's shoulder firmly. "Gunny," I hissed, urgency sharpening my tone.

His eyes snapped open, instantly alert, years of military training pulling him from sleep to readiness in a heartbeat.

"Someone's below us," I mouthed, barely breathing the words. "It's not the Marsdens."

His gaze hardened. He nodded once, silently reaching for his own weapon.

I grasped my laser pistol, the metal cold against my clammy palm, and inched toward the edge of the loft.

Peering through the gaps in the wooden slats, I could make out shadows moving in the murk—figures slipping between the barn stalls like wraiths.

A sudden clatter echoed as something was knocked over.

The intruders froze.

My heart leaped into my throat.

In the faint sliver of moonlight slicing through a cracked window, I caught the glint of a weapon.

These weren't just thieves.

"On my mark," Busto whispered, his voice barely audible. "We engage."

I nodded, muscles coiled like a tightened spring.

But before we could act, a chilling sensation washed over me—a cold that seeped into my very bones. The shadows below began to coalesce, swirling upward like a serpent made of smoke.

A figure emerged at the top of the ladder without climbing it, as if the darkness itself had given birth to form.

Tall and indistinct, the silhouette loomed, four eyes gleaming with an otherworldly light.

I raised my pistol, aiming squarely at the intruder's center of mass.

"Stop!" I commanded, my voice firmer than I felt.

The figure tilted its head, a grotesque mimicry of curiosity.

Before the word was fully formed, agony exploded in my skull. It was a searing blaze, an inferno behind my eyes.

My body betrayed me, locking every muscle into place.

Panic surged as I tried to move, to shout, but nothing obeyed. I was trapped, my mind screaming against the confines of my own flesh.

Blindness swallowed me whole, and a bright afterimage burned across my vision.

I could feel something—someone—looming over me, examining me with a detached curiosity that made my skin crawl. Like an insect pinned beneath a magnifying glass, I was laid bare, exposed, and vulnerable. Not with my eyes did I see this, and yet I could perceive them somehow.

The shadow brushed against my mind, a cold caress that sent shivers racing down my spine.

I fought against it, desperate, every instinct urging me to protect my crew. But I could only listen to the silence, helpless and paralyzed.

My mind screamed, but my body stayed as still as the desert night.

I willed myself to move, to fight against whatever held me captive. It was like trying to pull free from quicksand—every tug felt like my spine was unraveling, being stretched beyond its limits.

*Move, dammit,* I urged myself silently, desperation clawing at the edges of my consciousness.

Every instinct told me that we were in danger, that something sinister lurked behind the whispers threading through the barn.

Gritting my teeth, I forced my focus inward, tugging again at the invisible chains binding me.

The sensation was excruciating, a searing line of fire tracing down my back. But I pushed through the pain, driven by the primal need to defend myself.

Then, with a suddenness that left me gasping, something inside me seemed to pop—a release, an opening—and the shadow loomed closer to my mind, though I remained blind, deaf, and dumb.

I sensed shining nodes. It wasn't light the shadow emitted, but energy—a pulsing, throbbing presence—nodes of power connected like grapes on a vine, larger ones interspersed with thousands of smaller nodes.

Millions of even tinier nodes filled the spaces between, a vast network I perceived not with sight but with my consciousness.

*What... is this?* I thought, awed and terrified. Somehow, impossibly, I could feel it all, this intricate web of energy strewn before me, attracting me.

*Hold together, Kory*, I reminded myself, steeling my resolve. Whatever this was, whatever it meant, it seemed hungry, and I knew one thing for certain: I couldn't let it win. Our lives depended on it.

A whisper coiled through my mind, soft yet strong. It wasn't sound, but something deeper.

"How interesting," the shadow murmured, almost curious.

My instinct was to cringe, but I couldn't move—anchored by an invisible force.

"Who's there?" My thought shot out to the nodes, jagged

and raw.

I felt a probing sensation like fingers rifling through the pages of my mind.

"How are you doing this?" the voice asked, laced with surprise.

I didn't know what it meant. My confusion must have been palpable because the presence seemed to chuckle at my ignorance.

"You don't even know." The shadow laughed again, mocking me. "*Flairsparked*," it mused, tasting the word as if sampling fine wine. "A flairsparked human, indeed. How... quaint."

I tried to speak, to demand answers, but no words came.

Silence stretched taut between us until I realized I had actually spoken—not with voice, but with thought.

"I don't understand," I formed with my mind, forcing it through whatever barrier separated us. "Who are you?"

Laughter followed—a low, cruel ripple that made my skin crawl.

This was no friendly spirit.

The laugh lingered, long enough for doubt and fear to creep in.

Were they ignoring me?

"I am Ban'ach," it finally said, humming with satisfaction.

It was the leader of the Nebula Nomads! Somehow, she was in my mind!

"Welcome to the Syderealium," she said.

That name was unknown to me but carried weight, each syllable heavy with menace.

I was no stranger to threats, but this one felt different—otherworldly.

"What's the Syderealium?" I pressed, defiance curling

my thoughts.

"I am not your teacher," Ban'ach replied, dripping with mockery. "*I* am your punishment." A pause. Then, a sigh. "A flairsparked being like you would typically interest one of our savantes, but you, Kory Drake, are simply too delectable to pass up."

The implication hit hard.

Flairsparked?

Delectable?

Ban'ach was no normal marac. That was clear.

Whatever she was doing, she saw me as prey, something to feed on. And flairsparked—whatever that meant—or not, I wasn't about to let her have the better of me. But how was I to fight inside this...Syderealium?

At that moment, I noticed that the vine of energy nodes representing Ban'ach was not the only energy network. I also perceived another vine of nodes closer to me, and somehow, I knew this was *me*.

Interconnected bubbles of vitality numbering in the millions. Most were tiny, but a few were larger.

They were all connected to each other through a network of threads.

Ban'ach's body—not her physical one, but this vine of energy nodes—seemed to be surveying mine.

I felt her probing through my nodes as if she were searching for something.

I felt violated, as if she were molesting my body.

"Stop!" I pleaded silently. "Please!"

She ignored me and continued.

After a while, she stopped at a particularly large pair of bright balls of light hanging near the center of my clustered body.

"Ah!" she cried out in pleased surprise. "What have we

here?"

She seemed to hold the nodes, even though I could see no hands. But I felt her fingers in my mind tugging at something.

"As an appetizer, these will do *quite* nicely. Don't worry, this will be over soon."

Something pulled at my mind, its force increasing gradually, the pain rising until a shard of glass seemed to be poking at my brain.

I screamed.

It felt like my very being was unraveling.

Then, when it seemed like I could no longer tolerate it anymore, when I was about to surrender to the void, the pain stopped.

Ban'ach still loomed over me, but now her body of nodes was holding something. It was one of *my* nodes!

She had detached it from my own vine.

She moved it closer to her body, nesting it amongst a particularly large cluster of her own nodes, and somehow, she attached it.

The thief had stolen something from me! What could it be?

Then, her attention focused on me again, and the pain began to build in the same way as before.

Needles pressed on my mind.

I flailed out at her clumsily, trying to block her.

"Ta ta ta, stop!" she yelled. "It won't do you any good."

The pain cut off, and I saw her again carrying one of my nodes and connecting it to her body.

I could feel something missing.

A gap in my mind.

A void in my...memories?

"What did you take!" I cried.

"You are quite the bruit," Ban'ach said in a conversational tone, casually, as if she hadn't just raped me. "Under a more...sedate setting, I would consider adding you to my stable. I've never seen a flairsparked with so much potential as you. But that just makes doing this that much easier. It's a good thing you aren't trained."

She focused on me again.

I tried to flee, willing my body of nodes to move, to put distance between Ban'ach and me. But though I could move, it seemed to be random.

Ban'ach chased after me.

But just as often as I successfully moved away, in the next moment, I would lose control and move closer. It was like Brownian motion.

Ban'ach giggled. "Look at you! You have no control at all."

She placed herself right in front of me, screaming. "Hold still!" I felt the weight of her body—this mental body—pressing me down and holding me in place.

Suddenly, in the distance, at the edge of my perception within this Syderealium, a third body of nodes appeared.

It shone brilliantly, flying in a straight line toward Ban'ach and me. It was just another vine of bunched-up nodes of vitality, but to me, it seemed familiar as if I'd met the being before.

The newcomer flew closer, never deviating from their path. "Begone!" they roared.

It was Zeta!

She was alive!

I don't know how I knew it was her at the time. I suppose it was because we had been friends, had bonded with one another, such that our minds were familiar.

Somehow, Zeta had found me within the vast

Syderealium. She had heard my cries of agony.

"Begone!" Zeta cried again, and an unseen force flung Ban'ach away from me.

"An igna specter!" Ban'ach screamed. "How?!" Then she fled.

Zeta stopped in front of me. "You are injured! Kory, you must go back!"

"Zeta! How are you here?" I said.

"Not now. Zeta shall explain later." Her body flew circles around me, studying my body. "But you must end this projection. You are untrained, and it is very dangerous for you to be here."

"I don't know how. And I don't want to leave you! How are you here?!"

"Go, now. Zeta shall return to you soon. It is her solemn promise. We shall speak of the Syderealium henceforth."

I felt her shove me into what felt like a whirlpool, falling into an emptiness.

My eyes opened, and I jerked up to a sitting position. Hands grasped me and shook my shoulders.

"He's awake!" Destiny yelled.

I felt her hugging me to her breast.

"They're gone!" Busto said from the top of the hayloft ladder.

"Kory! Talk to me!" Destiny hissed in my ear.

I tried to speak, but only a croak escaped my dry throat. I tried again. "Water," I finally managed.

She brought me my water flask, and I drank deeply.

I let out a moan and lay on my back, rubbing my eyes.

"Ban'ach," I said.

"How do you know?" Busto said from my side, his fingers pressing gently into my throat, checking my pulse.

"Didn't you see her?"

"No. There was movement by the ladder. Then nothing. But I checked my watch. We missed a couple of minutes somewhere. Whatever was here is gone now."

"Dest, and you?" I asked, turning my head to my sister.

"Same thing. Why? What did *you* see?"

I told Destiny and Busto about my strange experience in that place called the Syderealium and about meeting Ban'ach and Zeta there. I told them Ban'ach had stolen something from me. She had assaulted me.

"Weird," Destiny said. "It was some kind of psychic attack."

"No," I said. "I don't think that's the right word. And isn't it strange how I saw Zeta? I think my mind is playing tricks on me. I think I hallucinated something."

"I don't know, dude," Busto said. "*Something* happened. *Somebody* was here."

I could feel a new gap in my mind. But how do you identify something that's been stolen from your memory? It's not like there is an obvious hole that you can point to and say, "Oh, my memory of Brook Johnson, my childhood best friend, is missing." If you can't remember it, then how do you know it's missing?

I also felt physically weakened and depressed. Like the only thing I wanted to do was curl up inside my sleeping back and hide my head under a pillow and sleep for the next century.

Destiny lay down next to me and hugged me. She pressed her cheek to mine. "Kory, you're so cold. Are you okay?"

I just moaned in response, trying to hide my eyes from her.

"What's happening?" Busto said.

"I don't know," Destiny said. "This isn't like him."

She massaged my temples with her fingers. "Come on, Kory, don't do this. What happened?"

With my face hiding inside the crook of my elbow, I said, "I don't want to talk about it."

"What did Zeta say to you?"

I groaned and tried to shift away from her, but she just held on tighter, spooning me, wrapping one of her legs around mine. This was my sis. She didn't like to see me hurting.

"Come on, you lout! I'm not gonna let you shut me out like this. Tell me what Zeta said!"

"You won't believe me when I tell you," I said. "Trust me."

She patted me on the back. "Brother, I've got a wild imagination. I've had weirder Tuesdays. What's the worst thing that could happen? That you tell me of aliens? Laser pistols? Marines?"

"I heard that," Busto mumbled.

"Ghosts," I said. "Zeta is supposed to be dead."

"We don't even know that for certain," Busto said. "We don't know how the igna life-cycle works."

Busto made a good point.

There was obviously something going on here I didn't understand. So, I tried to remember what Zeta had said and repeated it back to them.

"She's coming back?" Destiny said, her head leaning over mine and trying to pry my elbow away from my face.

I finally relented, turned on my back, and looked at the barn roof. "That's what she said."

Why did I feel so drained? I did not have a depressive personality. On the contrary, Destiny accused me of being overly energetic. Even manic sometimes.

Whatever was causing it, it had to do with whatever

Ban'ach had stolen from me. It felt too physical. That's how I knew that what had happened hadn't been a hallucination. It had been real.

Busto eventually returned to his sleeping bag and, a few minutes later, was snoring lightly.

Destiny lay there next to me, hugging me. I knew she was worried about me, but I couldn't think of anything to say that would put her at ease. *I* was worried.

We lay there holding each other for a while, just like old times on the street when all we had was a single blanket to share.

Laying in the darkness, my mind wandered, probing at my memories, trying to find what was missing. How would I even know when I found it?

Abruptly a loud *crack* sounded in the room like a gunshot had gone off.

All three of us jumped to our feet with our pistols in hand.

Floating in the middle of the room was a familiar white octahedral capsule.

"Zeta?!" I yelled and stepped over to her.

I reached out and brushed my hand on her capsule. It felt hot and smooth and had soft white light glowing on the edges.

"Friend Kory!" Zeta's pleasant female voice said. "Destiny! Busto! Zeta has returned!"

# 8

My heart surged with relief at the sight of her—my friend, alive. I had feared the worst, and even after her miraculous intervention in the Syderealium, seeing her there in that place that was so alien, so incomprehensible, I hadn't truly believed she was truly there.

"About time you caught up with us, you laggard," Destiny said with a teasing smile, her voice cutting through the tension.

Zeta drifted deeper into the room, her movements smooth and deliberate, like she was a shadow untethered from the ground. Her gaze seemed to scan the walls, calculating, absorbing every detail. "This is not the base," she said, her voice calm and distant.

"Zeta, how did you find your way back?" I asked, the disbelief still buzzing in my veins.

That's when I realized I could once again feel my link to Zeta. Like a piece of twine tied to my heart whose tug indicated where she was and what she was feeling. At that moment, she felt content.

"We thought you were dead, princess," Busto said.

"Yeah, Gunny even had a funeral for your capsule," Destiny said. "It became probably the most honored piece of scrap metal on the planet."

"But Zeta did indeed perish," Zeta said.

I moved closer to her and sat on the floor. "How is that possible? How did I see you in the Syderealium?"

"All beings, both living and dead, have a presence in the Syderealium. Those who are living are generally confined to the material plane while those who are dead may travel more freely." She spun on her vertical axis. "Some few living beings can separate from the material plane. We call them flairsparked. Kory Drake is one such person, which is why wise Zeta selected him as her heliacal consort."

"That still doesn't explain how you're here now," I pressed, my pulse quickening.

"Zeta was recalled from the Syderealium by the Supreme Council and ordered to return to the material plane," she explained, her voice as steady as ever.

"Uh...so you're, like, undead?" Destiny said with a raised eyebrow, skepticism clear on her face. "Well, that's one way to get out of morning meetings!"

"No, silly Destiny, Zeta has been given a new igna body. Zeta has also ascended and been granted permission to access the Syderealium. That is how she could assist Kory in his encounter with the Soul Ravager."

"Ban'ach?" I asked, my breath catching slightly at the name.

"Indeed. You are a victim of Ban'ach's sydereal assault. Brave Zeta rescued you from great peril, Consort. You are an untrained flairsparked, and Zeta must train you."

"Zeta," I said, leaning forward and fixing her with a glare. "You need to explain what is going on. This isn't making sense."

Slowly, over the next several minutes, we got an explanation out of our alien friend. According to Zeta and the igna understanding of existence—what they call the Omniverse—it comprises an infinite number of dimensions. Some of those dimensions are organized into material subspaces, one of which is our known universe. Other material subspaces exist orthogonally to our own, and these represent different universes. They aren't parallel universes but rather *orthogonal* universes. There are an infinite number of orthogonal universes, though the set is smaller than the Omniverse, being a subset of it. However, the set of dimensions lying outside of any other material universe is called the Syderealium, and it is there that reside the consciousnesses of beings from the material universes.

Living beings are normally confined to portions of the Syderealium that intersect with one of the material universes. Their physical bodies hold them there. When they die, their sydereal bodies—called glyphshades, which are the portion of their consciousness that is free to travel through the Omniverse—detach from their physical bodies and become free to traverse the Omniverse.

"So, this glyphshade is like our soul?" Busto asked.

Zeta swayed side-to-side a few times. "That is a primitive description derived from your civilization's religious beliefs. Describing a sydereal body as a soul only works as an analogy, but in the sense that it is immortal, then yes, a glyphshade is like a soul. However, its organization as a distinct body is of finite duration. Glyphshades lacking a corresponding body in a material universe eventually disassociate into primeval sydereal energy, making it available to be formed once again into one or more protoconsciousnesses.

"Creatures lacking sentience tend to disassociate almost

immediately after the death of their bodies. But sentients, like you and Zeta, will persist for a time within the Syderealium. This is what happened to Zeta after her previous physical body perished. The greater Zeta's willpower, the longer she would have staved off disassociation. Many igna endure for millennia inside the Syderealium after physical death.

"The wisest of those igna who persist are chosen to serve on the Supreme Council of the Collective Dominion. This governing body called Zeta back to the material universe and granted her a new body so that Zeta may complete her mission with the humans."

"For what purpose?" I asked.

"Zeta was told very little," she said, "and most of what information she received she is not permitted to share with you."

I didn't like the idea of Zeta being here on some kind of secret mission directed by this Supreme Council. It made me feel manipulated. Why not just tell us the truth? But at the time, I was so happy just to see Zeta again that I didn't press her on the question.

"What's the longest that one of these...glyphshades has existed for?" Destiny asked. "Long enough to start charging rent?" she quipped.

"There are beings—powerful glyphshades—of whom nobody knows when they emerged or from where. There are rumors that some of them never even inhabited material bodies but have always existed freely within the Syderealium. They collect sydereal energy unto themselves and are dangerous."

"So, basically cosmic gods with a power complex? Great, just what we needed—immortal energy hoarders with no origin story!" Destiny smacked her palm on her forehead.

"Joking aside," I said, "I think Destiny makes a good point. These beings sound a lot like gods."

"Friend Kory," Zeta said, "again, you draw upon an analogy in an attempt to comprehend what is beyond your understanding. But if it helps you picture these beings, then by all means call them gods, for they are effectively immortal and so powerful and knowledgeable as to appear omnipotent and omniscient from the perspective of a living human."

"That's terrifying," Busto said. "They could just wipe us out?"

"Unlikely, brave Busto," Zeta said. "These sydereal... gods rarely take interest in the business of the material universes. They are more of a threat to those glyphshades who travel freely through the Syderealium. Like those whose bodies have died, or the flairsparked who find themselves in the Syderealium."

"Is that why you said it was dangerous?" I asked.

"Indeed, Consort, each time you project into the Syderealium, you risk drawing the attention of one of the god-like glyphshades. Either that or lesser beings who are nonetheless powerful, such as the Soul Ravagers."

"Who are they? You haven't yet explained."

"There is little Zeta is permitted to explain, but she will say the following: Soul Ravagers are an ancient order of the flairsparked marac who use the Syderealium to feed upon glyphshades as a means of manipulating their physical bodies and increasing their cognitive power. That is what Ban'ach was doing to you in the Syderealium: feeding on your sydereal body."

The heavy depressive weight still had not left me, despite my happiness at seeing Zeta. "Is that why I don't feel right? Ban'ach took something from me. I saw it and felt the pain."

"What did she take?" Zeta asked.

"I don't know yet. I just feel something missing, like a hole in my soul. I feel sadness and anxiety and a desire to give up and run away somewhere where nobody will find me."

"Regretfully, Ban'ach has stolen some of your energlyphs from your glyphshade and thereby decreased your willpower and increased her own."

"Can it be healed?" Destiny asked.

"No, for there is nothing remaining to repair. The gap can only be filled with something to replace it. But if what was taken is fundamental to Kory's mental makeup, it may be impossible to compensate for it fully."

An idea occurred to me, one that had been cooking in my mind ever since I saw Ban'ach flee. "What if I could steal my nodes back?"

"What does Kory mean by nodes?" Zeta asked.

"Um...that's what they looked like in the Syderealium. Balls of light connected to a network like a bunch of grapes. Some big, many tiny ones, and thousands in between. All grouped together."

"Ah, yes, interesting. Zeta believes you are describing an energlyph. Your brain has interpreted them as nodes in a network. How interesting. Zeta perceives them differently. No matter, what is important to understand is that an energlyph encapsulates a life experience that influences a sydereal body and even affects the physical body. Large energlyphs are like gravitational bodies that attract and influence smaller energlyphs."

"Ban'ach stole two of my largest energlyphs. It was excruciatingly painful. She attached them to her body.

They're part of her, now!"

"Zeta is not surprised, for that is what Soul Ravagers do, though Ban'ach appears to be a more discerning predator than most. Fortunate for you. Otherwise, you might be nothing but a catatonic body at this point. That monster could have wiped your mind."

"The point I was about to make was this: If she stole them from me, then I can steal them back," I said.

"Nay!" Zeta cried out suddenly. "Never shall you speak of such a thing again!" The ferocity of Zeta's response caught me completely off guard. I even raised a hand to ward her off, thinking she was about to attack me. "For that is what Soul Ravagers do! It is what the sydereal gods do! It is evil! You cannot fix an evil with another evil!"

Destiny stepped forward and interposed her body between Zeta and me. "Back off, you gas bag!" She held a hand up to Zeta. "What else is he gonna use? Spit out some carefully worded sarcasm? Sometimes, it takes a little evil to cancel out the deluxe, all-inclusive kind!"

"All I want to do is steal back what is rightfully mine!" I said, trying to reason with her.

"Nay, it cannot be done," Zeta said in a calmer voice. "Do not contemplate it. Whatever has been taken from you, you must live past it and be strong. Zeta knows you are a sufficiently potent flairsparked to do it. Zeta promises you that Kory can live beyond this without having to resort to the despicable practices of the Soul Ravagers."

I kept my own council. I knew that if I ever had Ban'ach within my power, I would find a way to get into the Syderealium and steal back what was mine. I still didn't know precisely what the marac gang boss had taken, but it was something fundamental to my being. But, for now, I would play along with Zeta because I needed her help. I needed this training she was talking about.

So, I lied.

"Zeta, I promise not to do it," I said, putting as much sincerity behind my voice as possible. "But please train me so this doesn't happen again. I want to know how to defend myself inside the Syderealium."

"Agreed, that was always Zeta's intent," the alien said.

Suddenly, Busto's hand shot up, his voice a sharp whisper. "Quiet! Someone's coming."

Zeta's soft glow vanished as she ducked behind a crate.

Busto, Destiny, and I crouched low, our pistols drawn, ears straining for the sound.

Footsteps. Light but hurried. Whoever it was, they weren't trying to hide.

The ladder to the loft rattled as the intruder climbed.

In the moonlight, the figure became clear—Jon Marsden.

Before any of us could speak, his panicked voice cut through the silence. "Have you seen my kids?!"

# 9

"Your son and daughter?" I lamely asked Jon.

"Yes, Hattie and Graham. Have you seen them?" Jon begged, holding his hands stiffly to his sides.

It was the middle of the night, not long after midnight. "They're not in their beds?"

"No! We've turned the house inside out looking for them!" Jon said while frantically pulling at his hair.

"I don't know where they are," Busto said. "Jon, slow your breathing down. Calmly tell me what happened." He rested a hand on the frightened father's shoulder.

Jon rubbed his hand through his scalp. "We heard a loud bang, like a gunshot, in the backyard."

That must have been when Zeta appeared. It had sounded like thunder.

"I got up," Jon continued, "and shined a flashlight in the kids' bedroom just to make sure they were okay. But their beds were empty! So, I woke Martha up, and we started searching the house, thinking they might have gone downstairs for water. But why would they both go? And why not go to the bathroom? And their shoes are still there. And their clothes."

"Can we look again?" Busto asked. "Maybe we'll notice something you didn't."

Jon threw his hands in the air and shrugged. "Of course! I don't know what else to do. Martha's beside herself with worry."

We descended the loft ladder and followed Jon back to the house. Zeta remained hidden behind. I didn't want the Marsdens to know about her yet.

Jon showed us the kids' bedroom. The beds were messy as if somebody had been sleeping in them not too long ago.

Busto approached them and felt around under the covers. "Still a little warm," he said. "They haven't been gone long."

"What's that?" Destiny said, pointing at the window facing toward the house's front.

I approached. A piece of folded paper sat on it. It looked out of place, so I picked it up and opened it. A messily scrawled message was written on the inside.

*Kory Drake, We have the two children. If their parents ever hope to gaze upon their faces again, you will surrender yourself to the Nebula Nomads. You have 24 hours. After that, the only thing left to return will be their screams on the wind. -Ban'ach.*

I sighed and handed the message to Jon. He read it, then cried out, pacing back and forth, agony written on his face, and pounding his fist on his thigh.

The sound of the front door opening and closing came to us upstairs, and a moment later, Martha came racing into the room. "There you are! I went up and down the street and—" She noticed Jon's expression and yelled. "Honey! What happened!" She held her hands to her face and started crying. "Where are my babies!"

I explained what was on the note. The husband and wife clung to each other.

Guilt twisted my insides. This wasn't the Marsdens' fault. They never would have become targets if they hadn't helped us by giving us shelter and food. I wasn't going to let those kids die because of me.

"This is between the bandits and me," I told the couple. "I'm sorry you got caught in the middle. I'm going to turn myself in tomorrow."

Destiny grabbed my arm in an iron grip. "The hell you are!"

"Ow!" I pried her hand off me. "What else am I supposed to do?"

Busto stepped between us and faced the Marsdens. "There's no guarantee the Nomads would honor the deal. I don't trust them. The best thing to do is recover Hattie and Graham."

"But how?" Jon said.

I thought about Zeta and her ability to find things. "We have ways of tracking these bandits. Can we have some of the kids' used clothing?" I asked Martha.

Her red eyes stared at me briefly before she realized I'd asked her a question. "Of course. Anything! I don't care, just as long as you find them!"

I looked around. Then, my eyes settled on the pillows on the two beds. I grabbed them and peeled off the pillowcases, keeping the latter and returning the pillows. We were going to use Zeta as a bloodhound.

"Gunny," I said, "go wake up the Army scouts and tell them we need their help."

"At this hour? Those army pukes aren't gonna be happy," Busto said with an obvious distaste for the task.

"Say whatever you need to, but we need them."

Gunny rolled his eyes, but the former marine finally gave in. "Fine, but waking up an Army ranger reject is like trying to get a cat to do pushups. Don't expect miracles."

I took a few minutes to talk to the Marsdens, explaining that we would do everything within our power to recover their kids. I don't think I was very successful at consoling them. I didn't have kids of my own, but I had to imagine that the feeling of being powerless and their failure to protect their offspring made them feel like terrible parents, which they weren't. Both of them seemed to be wonderful with their kids. It made me wish for...

For what...?

My mind grasped for something. The Marsden's reminded me of somebody important to me.

Yeah, my parents.

*My parents?*

Destiny and I were returning to the barn and edging across the backyard when this question occurred to me. I froze in midstep.

That hollowness I'd felt ever since my encounter with Ban'ach suddenly loomed like a sinkhole, threatening to swallow me.

I tried to summon the face of my mother but failed. I dug down deep for the comforting feeling of snuggling with her but found nothing. I cast my mind into the past for the rich, deep sound of my father's loving voice.

Silence.

I now knew what Ban'ach had stolen from me: the memory of my parents.

I collapsed to my hands and knees in the middle of the yard, dizzy, feeling like I was walking a tightrope across an abyss and had suddenly awoken and realized I had nothing to hold onto and no safety net below to catch me.

Destiny cried out something and ran to me. She squeezed my shoulders and spoke. Her words didn't register.

Ban'ach had stolen my parents from me. Yeah, it was only my memory of them. But that was all that remained of my dead mother and father. And she'd taken them. She spotted those two shining energlyphs in the Syderealium that represented my parents and their interconnection with the rest of my mind. The greedy thief had recognized how much strength those two jewels gave me and taken them for herself.

I imagined her sitting in a quiet room somewhere, treasuring the strength she'd stolen from me. It was *my* strength. Now, *she* thought she owned it. She thought she could benefit from my past, the life I'd lived, and the things I'd achieved through the strength of the memory of my dear parents.

A ball of starfire ignited inside me. I raised myself upright on my knees, looked up at the star-strewn sky, and roared with rage.

In response to my outburst, Destiny jumped back and held her hands to her chest.

I finally came to myself after I don't know how long. My throat stung from the roar I had screamed out into the night. Beads of sweat ran in torrents down my face and neck.

"Kory?" Destiny said in a whisper, tentatively reaching out to me. "What is it?"

In response to Destiny, I shook my head. I had no way to explain to her what I had discovered. I'd rarely talked to her about my parents because it was such a private memory. Now, I regretted it because even *she* couldn't remind me of what I'd forgotten. She couldn't restore the memories that had been stolen.

And they were more than memories. That's something I'd learned on my own about the Syderealium. The energlyphs—those nodes of energy—represented more than just memory. They were somehow the building blocks of my consciousness.

Energlyphs comprised the emotional meaning of all the knowledge packed into my head from my short but full life. Though I could no longer remember my parents, I could see the gap that had been ripped into my psyche by depriving me of them. My very motivation to survive in this god-awful world had been taken with them. It was suddenly like I no longer had anything to live for.

"Talk to me," Destiny commanded me with steel in her voice.

I waved her off and stumbled to my feet, every step toward the barn feeling heavier than the last. The shock of what I'd just realized pressed down on me.

But I couldn't let myself fall apart. Not yet. There were two kids out there, stolen away, their fates hanging by a thread, and Ban'ach—she'd tear into them just like she tore into me if we didn't get to them in time.

Was that what waited for them? Would they lose everything, too, piece by piece, until they were nothing but hollowed-out remnants?

Destiny followed me in silence, her face tight with worry, but she didn't dare speak. Maybe she sensed I was on the edge, that something inside me was fraying, coming undone.

I must've looked like a madman, and somehow, I was. Less than two hours ago, Ban'ach had ripped through my mind and violated the deepest parts of me. What did she expect me to be after that? Whole?

Ban'ach was as good as dead to me. I didn't know how yet, but I would take back what she stole—my memories of my parents—and then I would erase her from existence.

There was no room for mercy, no second thoughts. Someday, somewhere, somehow...it didn't matter. I would find a way to end her.

Until then, the hatred she left burning inside me would fuel every step. If I couldn't rely on the love for my parents I had once felt, I would let my rage push me forward, keeping me sharp. I would make Ban'ach regret not finishing me off, regret leaving me alive, and just sane enough to hunt her down.

# 10

About 30 minutes later, Busto returned with Ivor Rowbottom, the leader of the Army scout team, and Cindy Montana, their medic. Rowbottom wore a pair of gray sweats, and his face was still puffy from sleep. On the other hand, Montana looked like she'd been awake for hours and greeted us with a smile.

We met in the Marsdens' living room. Jon and Martha were both present, sitting on their sofa, looking scared.

"Before we get started," I said, "we have somebody for you all to meet." I opened the rear door and gestured for Zeta to enter.

The octahedral capsule of the igna floated into the room. The eyes of Jon, Martha, Rowbottom, and Montana locked onto her. Montana took a step backward, and Jon seemed to forget for a second that his kids were missing.

"This is Zeta of the Collective Dominion," I told them, pointing to my alien friend. "She is my crew's military adviser and just returned from a visit with her leaders."

"Well met, humans. This being is designated Z374,

though most call her Zeta."

Seeing uncertainty and anxiety in their faces, I said, "She is friendly to humans. Zeta has been of huge assistance to my crew in the last couple months. She's going to help us find the Marsdens' children."

Rowbottom continued staring at Zeta, then shook his head as if rearranging his thoughts. "Gunny Busto showed me the message from Ban'ach," Rowbottom said. "Kory, I hope you understand that if you choose not to turn yourself in and the 24 hours expire, then those kids..." He looked at the Marsdens and seemed to reconsider his words. "Well, we don't want to cross that line."

Destiny stepped forward. The petite black girl looked tiny, facing the tall, powerfully built Army staff sergeant, but that didn't deter her. "So your solution is to have him turn himself in? Uh uh. *Not* going to happen."

Busto held up a hand. "Rowbottom, we can't trust these bandits. You know that. Even if Kory turning himself in was a viable option—and I don't accept that—we have no reason to trust the Nomads to do what they say."

"I think it's a trap," Destiny said. "It's just a way for Ban'ach to get her hands on Kory and give herself even *more* power over us."

Rowbottom waved his hands. "Yeah, yeah, I understand. Don't get me wrong. I don't trust that creepy marac anymore than you do. Probably even less. I'm just saying that Kory holds those kids' lives in his hands."

"Sergeant Rowbottom, Zeta does not agree with your logic," Zeta said calmly. "The Nebula Nomads are the ones who chose to abduct the children and hold them hostage. Not Zeta's consort, Kory Drake. Furthermore, the bandits may still choose to torture the children"—Martha moaned and held her hands to her face—"or use them as bait to further weaken Kory's resolve. Face the fact that Ban'ach and her subordinates have chosen to use these children to shield themselves and seek vengeance on Kory by hurting his friends, the Marsdens."

"These are classic bully tactics," Busto said. "We've all seen something like this before. The bully identifies their target's greatest weakness and attacks that. Kory is their target, and his greatest weakness was the exposure of the Marsdens' children because they are his friends."

"Okay, I got it," Rowbottom said. "So, what do you plan to do about it? The children could be anywhere."

"You don't know where?" I asked.

"I have some ideas. Most likely, they're being held up at the Mineral Park Mine. That's where the bandits seem to shack up most of the time."

"Where's that?"

"It's a copper and silver mine about four miles southeast of town. An open-pit mine. It's been closed since the invasion, and the Nomads have taken up residence there."

I looked at the alien. "Zeta, if I give you belongings of the children that have their scent on them, can you use your nanobots to track them down?"

"It is possible," she said. "The trail is still fresh. But we must move quickly."

"Let's spend the next few hours searching for the kids. We can develop a rescue plan once we know where they're being held."

"But we've got less than 24 hours!" Jon said, rising to his feet. "We don't have time to conduct a search!"

"Jon," I said, "don't underestimate Zeta's abilities. The Nomads certainly don't know about her, and I'd like to keep it that way for as long as possible."

"Kory, what do you need from my team?" Rowbottom asked.

"Gunny, Destiny, and I will accompany Zeta in her search. It will probably take us to this mine. I'm assuming you can arm yourselves appropriately. Could you provide security for our line of retreat? In case we run into trouble?"

"Sure. But you do realize that we're gonna be on foot, right?"

"There's no working vehicles at all? Even for something like this?"

"No. Marshal Batts will only crank up his SUV for the most extreme emergency, and not even this qualifies."

I shook my head. I'd need to ask Zeta to manufacture some gasoline once we had some downtime. "Well, we should probably tell Batts what is going on, even if he can't provide immediate help. How can we stay in contact?"

"My team has a half dozen AN/PRC-152 tactical radios. It's got enough range to reach the mine. Why don't you take one of them?"

Zeta bobbed up and down. "Consort, Zeta can program your suit radios to interface with the scouts' AN/PRC-152."

"Truly?" I asked.

"Indeed. Sergeant Rowbottom need only tell Zeta what channel to use."

Zeta and Rowbottom chatted for a few seconds and came to an agreement on channels.

"Okay, everybody," I said to the group. "If nobody else has anything to say, then let's gear up and move out. Rowbottom, can you take care of informing Marshal Batts?"

"Sure," Rowbottom nodded.

"My crew won't wait for you, but I'd like you to be standing by in case we run into trouble."

"That's fine. I'll get them awake and move out within

the hour. We'll move south and set up a watch post at the Gracy Holding Pond." He showed me a hand-drawn map of where that was. It was a man-made pond about a mile west of the primary buildings at the Mineral Park Mine.

"Sounds good to me." I clapped my hands. "Gunny, Destiny, Zeta, let's move out."

I jogged down the gravel road heading south. My body was wrapped in my protomatter armor, carrying my laser pistol on my hip and a flechette gun cradled in my arms.

Busto ran ahead of me about 10 yards in front, and Destiny trailed.

Zeta flew at my side.

We were about 3 miles south of Elkin, a distance we had covered in just ten minutes with the help of our suits' augmentation. It was about 3 am on this early winter morning, so the sky was perfectly dark, other than a sliver of the waning moon to the south. The integrated vision enhancement built into our armor made the scene look like daylight.

"You still got the trail?" I asked Zeta.

"Aye, Consort. The bandits must have come by here with the children on foot. The trail of their pheromones is quite strong."

Before heading out, I gave Zeta the two pillowcases of Hattie and Graham, and she'd sampled them. From those, she'd easily picked up their scent at the front of the house.

"On foot," I said. "Poor kids. I can't believe they forced them to walk. But better for us." It made them easier to track.

We continued our ground-eating pace for another mile, then turned east onto a dirt road that led to the Mineral Park Mine.

Puffs of dust rose from each of my footsteps, smelling metallic and reminding me of the aftermath of crashing *Thunder* into the desert. Now that Zeta had returned to us, that memory no longer stung like it had.

As we headed east, I thought about the implications of Zeta reappearing. Though we were still stranded hundreds of miles from our base in Wolf Jaw, at least we had our igna military adviser once more. That meant we could rebuild *Thunder*, bigger and more powerful than ever since we'd now qualified for the corvette hull. I was anxious to return to the base and return to our duties. But I'd never be at peace doing them if we didn't first rescue these kids and take care of these bandits.

Busto slowed our pace as we approached the mine. I expected to run into some kind of bandit guards at any moment, so we took it slow, pausing frequently to observe the terrain ahead.

The trail Zeta followed was taking us up a road that led to a group of buildings and large sheds on the northern edge of the mine.

A 400 ft hill rested directly to the west of the buildings, along with a couple parking lots and holding ponds.

Busto left the road—and the scent trail—and directed us up the hill's flank.

We climbed a rocky ridge, reaching the summit, giving us an excellent view of the buildings.

"How about here?" Busto said.

"Zeta agrees with this location."

"Okay," I said. "Do your thing."

We rested on the ground, drinking water, while Zeta began to deploy her nanobots in a search pattern that could reach over a thousand-foot radius around us.

So far, we'd seen no sign of the bandits other than their

scent as we followed the children's trail.

"Contact, at our 11 o'clock," Busto said, pointing toward one of the buildings below.

I fixed my gaze on the location and used my suit to magnify.

A male human was walking outside. He was armed with a rifle of some kind and smoked a cigarette. He was probably on watch.

It was 4 am, and sunrise was still three hours away. With our active camouflage enabled, the guard had zero chance of detecting us where we were hiding.

While we waited for Zeta's search, I studied the layout of the mine. From our location at the summit of this hill, I could easily see all of it.

The mine was of open-pit design and quite large. It encompassed a diameter of about a mile, with several active pits being worked on and a half-dozen holding ponds.

Scattered through the terrain were clusters of buildings.

On the south side, there appeared to be some kind of plant or refinery being fed by long conveyor belts and an electrical substation. Perhaps it was a smelting plant.

I didn't know much about how mines worked, so most of what I saw was a mystery.

Around that time, we got a call from the Army scouts on our radios. They were en route to their watch post. It took them much longer to get moving than I'd hoped. They were at least an hour away if we needed help.

About thirty minutes after we arrived, Zeta suddenly said, "I found the children."

I jumped to my feet and approached her. "Where?"

An icon appeared in the tactical display of my HUD. It was the glowing outline of a large building to the southeast of our position, about 200 yards distant.

Inside the outline were two green dots.

Two red dots rested nearby, along with a third dot moving around inside the building.

"Zeta has highlighted the building on your tactical map along with markers indicating the children's location and nearby hostiles."

"Neat," Destiny said. "Now, if only you could point out the best spot for coffee after this."

"What are their surroundings like?" I asked Zeta.

"The children are being held in an office inside that building, which appears to be a large maintenance garage for servicing the mine's fleet of vehicles. Two armed maracs are guarding the children, with an armed human roaming around the garage."

"Did you see Ban'ach?" I asked, hoping to track down the thief who'd stolen my parents from me. Or at least my memory of them, though that was as good as killing them all over again.

"Nay, Consort, the Nomads boss is not in the nearby vicinity."

"Do the children look like they'll be there a while?"

"They are sleeping on a shared cot in the office. There are food and bathroom facilities nearby and seating for the guards. Zeta guesses that the Nomads plan to hold the children in that location for some time. At least the rest of the day."

"Okay." I turned to Busto and Destiny. "Let's head to the scouts' watch post and reconnect with them."

"Why don't we just walk in there and rescue the children right now?" Destiny said. "There are only three guards nearby, and I doubt they're expecting us so soon."

"I'm worried about a trap," I said. "Finding the children was too easy. I think Ban'ach *wants* us to find them and try to rescue them. I don't want to make the move without overwatch from the scouts."

"I agree," Busto said.

Destiny smirked. "Fine, but if this trap comes with dramatic speeches and evil laughter, I'm charging extra for patience."

I grinned. "Well, if we're lucky, maybe Ban'ach will monologue long enough for us to grab the kids and sneak out while she's still bragging."

Soon after, we picked ourselves up and moved westward to find Rowbottom and his team.

# 11

I studied the faces of the townspeople who had joined us, each reflecting a mixture of fear, determination, and the weight of what was to come.

The late afternoon sun cast long shadows over the group as we gathered in the fading light, the air thick with anticipation.

It had taken hours to hammer out the details of our plan, and organizing the players had proven more challenging than expected. Yet, here we were—eighteen men and women, and one igna—huddled in a hidden draw in the low mountains west of the Mineral Park Mine.

I'd chosen this location to avoid detection; the bandits could easily spot us if we took the roads.

All that stood between us and the mine was a rugged ridge to the east. We would have to climb it, cross the other side, and descend into enemy territory.

The thought of the children captive just beyond that slope gnawed at me. Time was running out, and so were our options.

Marshal Batts had received the news with unsettling indifference. I expected more—shock, urgency, anything—but the weight of so many months of kidnappings seemed to have hardened him.

Maybe he had grown numb to the losses, and I couldn't decide if that made him stronger or weaker. Still, he had agreed to rally a citizens' posse. Despite their inexperience, they had heart. But I wondered if heart alone would be enough.

Busto stood at the group's center, laying out our plan with military precision. His voice was calm, but the gravity of the situation was unmistakable.

I glanced at a rancher gripping a worn, bolt-action rifle as though it might slip through his fingers. His knuckles whitened, and with a clumsy shuffle, the weapon tumbled from his hands.

He scrambled to pick it up, red-faced, avoiding eye contact with the others.

His nervousness was contagious. Around him, the townspeople fidgeted, their faces pale, their eyes darting toward the mountains.

These weren't soldiers—they were farmers, ranchers, and shopkeepers. And we were asking them to face hardened marac criminals, killers who wouldn't hesitate to take more lives.

My stomach twisted with doubt.

Clad in his black protomatter armor, Busto looked more like a machine than a man—an imposing figure ready to lead us into battle.

Destiny and I would be at his side, forming the assault and extraction team.

The weight of my own protomatter suit felt heavier today, as though the responsibility of the mission pressed down on me from all sides. We were no longer just fighting for survival but for the lives of others.

The Army scouts stood nearby, silent and still as stone, their faces hardened from years of service. Dressed in combat fatigues and light body armor, they were the only ones who looked genuinely prepared for what was about to unfold.

Their M4 carbines gleamed under the dying sun, each one well-maintained, ready for action.

Vila and Appleton carried AT-4 rockets slung across their backs, their eyes scanning the horizon for any sign of movement.

The soldiers' experience showed not only in their equipment but in how they held themselves—unwavering, steady. They knew what was coming and weren't afraid to face it.

The scouts would initiate the diversionary attack to the north, striking a cluster of buildings near the mine. If all went as planned, the bandits would be drawn away from the garage where the children were held, allowing our smaller team to slip in undetected. But plans never go as expected, and I braced myself for the inevitable surprises.

Ten more humans, all from Elkin, including Marshal Batts himself, would cover our retreat. They'd establish a sniper post overlooking the mine, their hunting rifles trained on the area.

Batts had assured me they were crack shots, used to taking down prey from long distances. But hunting deer was a far cry from hunting marac bandits.

I studied their faces once more—Batts' cold resolve, the doubt simmering just below the surface in the others—and I wondered if they truly understood the danger.

The wind picked up, whistling through the dry brush

and kicking up dust around our boots. I squinted up at the ridge, knowing what lay beyond it, knowing the risk we were taking.

The thought of those children, terrified and alone, spurred me forward. There was no room for hesitation now. We had to move.

I knelt behind a jagged boulder, its rough surface biting into my palms, at the top of a low ridge west of the garage's parking lot.

My heart hammered in my chest as I glanced at Busto and Destiny, both crouched low, waiting for Busto's signal.

The air was thick with the tension of anticipation, and the oppressive silence made my skin prickle.

With her unnerving calm, Zeta had taken a position with the posse on a low hill to the north after infiltrating it without a sound.

So far, there wasn't even a hint that the bandits had noticed our approach, but the stillness made me uneasy.

*Too easy*, I thought.

"Bravo team, this is Alpha actual, are you go?" Busto's voice crackled quietly over the radio. Our team was Alpha, the Army scouts were Bravo, and the posse had taken the name Charlie team.

"*Alpha team, Bravo actual, we are go,*" came Rowbottom's steady response. Despite the controlled voice, I could sense the readiness behind it.

"Execute," Busto said, his voice clipped and sharp with purpose.

The radio clicked twice—affirmative.

"Here we go," Busto muttered, the gravity of the moment hanging in the air like a storm about to break.

Destiny grinned, though the tension was clear behind

her smile. "Well, if we're not back by dinner, I'm blaming Rowbottom's version of 'go.'"

No sooner had she spoken than a deafening crack rang out from the northeast, the sharp sound reverberating off the mountainsides.

My pulse quickened.

The scouts were making their move. An M4 chattered in short bursts, followed by the distant echo of answering fire —likely the bandits.

Then came a whistling noise, a sound that turned my stomach into knots, followed by a gut-punching boom that shook the ground beneath me.

A column of smoke rose into the sky, stark against the late afternoon glow.

"That was an AT-4," Busto said grimly, as though commenting on the weather.

He lifted his head just enough to peer over the boulder. For what felt like an eternity, he scanned the area, then ducked back down. "Two armed maracs just flew out of the garage toward the diversion," he said.

His voice was calm, but the urgency beneath it was unmistakable. He clicked the radio, "Bravo team, Alpha actual, be advised. Two maracs are moving on your southern flank."

Two clicks answered him. The tension in the air thickened.

"Let's move, you two," Busto ordered, his voice dropping to a dangerous tone.

I double-checked my active camo, ensuring the shimmer enveloped my body before gripping my flechette gun tightly. The barrel felt solid and reassuring.

Busto led the way, gun at his shoulder, and I followed Destiny close behind, the three of us moving as a single unit.

As we advanced, we swept our gazes across the terrain, scanning every shadow for hostiles.

The parking lot stretched out before us—wide open, nothing but fifty yards of exposed asphalt.

Every nerve in my body screamed at me to find cover, but we had no choice.

We ran across the lot, our boots slamming the pavement, breaths loud in my ears.

I braced for the crack of gunfire at any moment, my finger hovering near the trigger, but it never came.

I pressed my back to the cold, steel wall of the garage, my breath coming in sharp bursts.

Busto slid over to a set of double doors and quickly peered through a small rectangular window.

The sound of automatic gunfire and small detonations echoed from the north, relentless and frantic.

I knew the scouts were running low on ammo—they couldn't keep this up for long. We had to move, and fast.

The sharp crack of a hunting rifle rang out from the hilltop, its distinct echo setting my teeth on edge. Charlie team was getting a piece of the action now, too.

*"Bravo, this is Charlie,"* Batts' voice came over the radio. *"You've got hostiles trying to flank you on the north. We're engaging."*

More rifle shots followed, their harsh cracks cutting through the chaos.

I tuned out the noise, focusing on the task at hand.

We still didn't have the children. Everything else was background noise until we did.

"This is Alpha team, we are entering," Busto said into the comms, his voice steady despite the whirlwind around us.

Without hesitation, he kicked the door open and sprang

through, flechette gun at the ready.

Destiny and I followed, our weapons raised, eyes scanning every dark corner of the cavernous garage.

The place was enormous, and my heart sank at the thought of how long it would take to clear. But we didn't have time for that.

Zeta's tracking on our tactical screen showed the children's location—and the hostiles nearby.

We moved with purpose, the oppressive silence inside the garage only broken by the distant thrum of the ongoing battle.

I led the way to a back corner behind a mining truck so massive its tires dwarfed me, towering over my 6'4" frame.

The truck was propped up on jack stands, thick steel beams holding its enormous weight.

I pressed my back to the corner of the truck, then whipped around it, gun at the ready.

A shadow shifted.

My pulse spiked as I saw the shape of a marac, rifle raised toward me.

I squeezed the trigger, and three flechette darts flew from the barrel of my gun, screaming through the air at hypersonic speeds.

The marac jerked back, purple blood splattering the wall behind him, one dart piercing his head, killing him instantly.

More gunfire echoed inside the garage. Destiny's voice came through the comms, calm but sharp. *"One down."*

We regrouped, the three of us moving like a well-oiled machine.

More radio chatter crackled between Bravo and Charlie teams, but I barely registered it. Our focus was laser-sharp —the children.

We leapfrogged past another row of massive mining trucks, their enormous frames like hulking beasts in the shadows.

As we cleared the last truck, the door to the office came into view. It was unguarded, and that made my skin crawl.

"Clear!" Busto called, advancing toward the door.

I took the rear, scanning the shadows behind us.

A flicker of movement high above caught my eye. My blood ran cold.

From the truck bed, a marac rose, weapon gleaming in his hands.

I fired, my shots going wide but forcing the marac to duck.

"They're behind us!" I shouted, diving for cover behind a steel drum as Busto tossed a grenade toward the truck bed.

A brief moment of silence—then the grenade flew back across the floor and detonated. The maracs had batted it away like it was nothing.

The firefight intensified. More marac heads appeared above the truck bed, and then, horrifyingly, humans joined them, weapons raised.

We were outnumbered.

My heart pounded in my chest as I shouted, "Fall back! We're outnumbered!"

Weapons blazed from the dump truck as flechette rounds, laser beams, and bullets flew in every direction, tearing through the air with deafening speed.

I ducked behind one of the vehicles, heart hammering in my chest as I returned fire, but the maracs were entrenched —the truck bed served as a near-impenetrable fortress.

My flechette rounds barely scratched the surface of the steel sides.

Busto dropped to his knees and scrambled under the chassis of one of the mining trucks. He was pinned but safe for now, though he couldn't return fire without exposing himself.

I cursed under my breath.

They'd baited us, and I'd walked right into it. The bandits were entrenched, waiting for us, and I'd led my team right into the kill zone. My only relief was that the Nomads had botched their timing—they should have had us dead already, but their disorganized attack had saved us for the moment. Still, we were in serious trouble.

Suddenly, the office door burst open, and two more maracs floated out, laser pistols drawn.

Busto had a clear shot but didn't take it, likely afraid his rounds would hit the office behind them—and the children inside.

This was the trap I had feared all along. Zeta's nanobots hadn't detected the bandits in the dump truck. They had been hiding, waiting for us, and now they were closing in.

The maracs moved toward us like sharks circling wounded prey. If we didn't act fast, we were done.

One of the maracs came into my line of sight, and instinct took over.

I fired two darts into its torso, and it crumpled to the floor, dead before it hit the ground.

"Busto!" I yelled over the comms. "You've got to move! I'm going to drop a grenade into that truck bed, but I don't want it landing on you!"

"Roger that," he said, his voice taut with strain.

A burst of gunfire echoed, and then Busto came hobbling toward me, favoring his left leg.

When he reached me, I saw a stream of blood trickling from just above his ankle, the wound ugly and raw.

"Are you okay?" I asked, my voice tight.

Busto looked down at his leg with surprise. "Huh, so that's what's been hurting. Didn't even notice." He flashed me a weak grin. "Yeah, I'm good."

He straightened, his face going serious. "Where's Destiny?"

I shook my head. "I don't know."

I was just about to activate the grenade when I caught a flicker of movement at the back of the dump truck.

Suddenly, the entire truck bed lit up with blinding flashes of light, like a series of rapid-fire explosions.

Ten seconds later, Destiny vaulted over the side of the truck, landing with a thud on the concrete floor.

"Clear!" she shouted, her laser pistol glowing orange from the heat of prolonged firing.

Her chest rose and fell with deep breaths, but her expression was one of pure, hardened focus.

I stared at her in disbelief, my mouth hanging open.

My little street sister had just single-handedly wiped out the entire band of bandits hiding in that truck. I didn't know whether to cheer or collapse.

I moved toward her, awe giving way to relief.

Before I could speak, her pistol whipped up, aimed directly at me.

My stomach dropped, heart freezing in my chest.

And then she fired.

The beam seared the air above my left shoulder, missing me by inches.

Instinctively, I dropped to the floor, barely processing what had just happened.

"That was close!" Busto said, crouching beside me, looking past my shoulder.

I turned, and there behind me, sprawled on the ground,

was a human bandit with a smoldering hole burned clean through his forehead.

His pistol was still gripped in his hand, aimed right at me.

My entire body went cold. I hadn't even seen him. If Destiny hadn't acted when she did, I'd be dead.

I swallowed hard, the gravity of it sinking in.

I couldn't afford to slip up like that again. This wasn't the streets anymore. One mistake, one missed step, and you were gone.

Busto didn't hesitate. He bolted for the office door, and Destiny and I followed, guns ready and hearts pounding.

We burst into the office, bracing for hostages or a firefight, but the room was empty save for Hattie and Graham, huddled in a back corner, their hands and legs bound.

Relief washed over me, but I didn't lower my weapon. Not yet.

Destiny was at their side in a heartbeat, untying them with quick, practiced movements.

The children's eyes were wide with fear, their small bodies trembling, but they were alive—and that's all that mattered.

"How are you, kids?" Destiny asked, her voice soft but urgent as she worked on their bonds.

Hattie whimpered, her voice shaky. "I—I can't feel my legs."

Destiny rubbed her hands over the girl's legs, coaxing circulation back. "You'll be fine, sweetie. We just need to get you out of here."

The little girl nodded bravely, though her lip quivered.

On the other hand, Graham was quiet, his face set with a stubborn defiance that seemed far too old for a child.

Busto called over the radio, his voice steady. "This is Alpha team. We have the children in custody and are proceeding to extract them to rally point Zulu."

Charlie team's response came through almost immediately. "*Roger that. We've got you covered.*"

Destiny took Hattie's hand while I reached for Graham's, but the boy pulled his hand away, straightening with determination. "I'm okay," he said, his voice stronger than I expected.

I nodded, respect for the boy rising within me. "Alright, let's move."

We crossed the garage quickly, stepping over the bodies littering the floor. "Just ignore the bodies," Destiny whispered to the children as we passed the carnage.

Graham didn't flinch. "It's okay," he said quietly. "We've seen dead maracs before."

The weight of his words hit me like a punch to the gut. These kids had been through more than any child should.

We dashed for the exit, Busto leading the way through the door with Destiny and me close behind, keeping the children as protected as possible.

My heart pounded in my ears, waiting for the inevitable crack of gunfire, but thankfully, none came.

Five minutes later, we reached the rendezvous point, hearts still racing, and waited for the other teams to disengage and meet us.

The relief was palpable, but my muscles remained tense, knowing the battle wasn't truly over until we were all out of there.

## 12

We crouched in the shadows of the first rally point, the wind biting at our exposed skin, kicking up dust, and carrying the scent of burnt metal and smoke.

The mountains around us stood like silent sentinels, watching over the chaotic battlefield we'd left behind.

My eyes flicked between the children, Busto, and Destiny. Their faces were still flushed with adrenaline, though the terror in the children's eyes remained as stark as ever.

"We wait here," Busto muttered, adjusting his rifle, his face a grim mask of focus. He winced slightly as he shifted his leg, blood still trickling from the wound near his ankle, but he waved off any offer of help.

"*Alpha team, this is Charlie actual,*" Batts' voice crackled over the radio. "*We've disengaged and are on the move to your position.*"

"Roger that," Busto replied, his voice steady but strained. His eyes shifted toward the children. "We need to get them out before more bandits catch wind of the extraction."

I glanced around nervously, my senses on high alert. Every rustle of the wind, every creak of the rocks made my pulse spike. Ban'ach had set a trap once; I couldn't shake the feeling there might be more lying in wait.

Destiny knelt beside Hattie, who was leaning against the rocks, still rubbing her legs to get the blood flowing. "You're doing great, kid," she said softly. "We'll get you home soon." Her voice was gentle, but I could hear the urgency beneath the calm. She was on edge, too, though she was doing a better job hiding it than I was.

Graham stood quietly next to me, eyes narrowed as he scanned the horizon. For a kid who had been through hell, he was surprisingly calm. I caught a glimpse of determination in his eyes that reminded me too much of myself—young, hardened by life too early.

Minutes passed, each one stretching painfully longer than the last. My mind kept racing to worst-case scenarios. What if the scouts were pinned down? What if the maracs regrouped? What if Ban'ach was still watching, waiting for the right moment to strike again? My fingers gripped the flechette gun tighter, knuckles white with tension.

Finally, movement appeared on the horizon. I caught sight of the familiar silhouettes of Charlie team and the scouts as they descended the ridge, moving quickly but cautiously. Relief washed over me, but only for a moment. Vila from Bravo team towed a marac behind him, its twelve arms bound with a rope.

As they approached, Marshal Batts raised a hand in greeting, his expression hard but focused. "We encountered some resistance," he said, eyes scanning our group and lingering on the children, "but nothing we couldn't handle. And the scouts caught a prisoner."

Busto nodded. "Good. That'll be useful, I'm sure, but the priority right now is getting the kids out of here before anything else goes sideways."

"Agreed," Batts said curtly, his gaze drifting toward the darkening sky. "But we need to move fast. There's more of them out there, and I don't want to stick around for a second wave."

I felt the weight of those words press down on my shoulders. I could still feel Ban'ach's presence lingering, like a dark cloud hanging over us, waiting. She was out there, somewhere, watching. And she wouldn't stop until she had what she wanted.

Busto stood up, wincing as he put pressure on his injured leg. "All right, let's move. Charlie team, you take point and secure the path ahead. Bravo team, you bring up the rear. Alpha will stick with the children."

We fell into formation, the weight of the situation pressing down on us as we moved quickly but cautiously across the rough terrain.

The wind howled through the rocks, and the distant sound of burning buildings echoed faintly behind us.

Every step felt like we were being watched, hunted. I kept expecting to hear the crack of a rifle or the explosion of a laser aimed at our backs. My heart pounded in my chest as we weaved through the low hills, the rocks casting long, eerie shadows in the fading light.

"We're getting close," Batts whispered over the radio, his voice barely audible. "Just a few more minutes, and we'll be clear."

But those few minutes felt like an eternity.

Suddenly, the ground seemed to shake, a low rumble growing beneath our feet.

My eyes darted to the horizon, and my heart dropped.

A dark, hovering shape loomed over the distant hills—a Kergan shuttle, larger and more menacing than anything we'd seen during the initial engagement.

Busto cursed under his breath. "They're sending reinforcements."

"We need to move faster," I hissed, grabbing Graham's hand and pulling him along, though he barely needed the push.

The shuttle was too close for comfort, and we had precious little time before they'd be on us.

The radio crackled again, this time with a voice that sent chills down my spine. "*Kory Drake, you have something of mine.*" It was Ban'ach, her voice dripping with malice, the threat clear beneath her words. "*And I'm coming to collect.*" How had she gotten onto our encrypted radio channel?

My breath hitched. I looked at Busto and Destiny, both of whom had gone stone-faced, their eyes locked onto the shuttle descending in the distance.

"We need to split up," Busto said, his voice low but urgent. "We'll buy you time to get the kids out. You know what she's after."

My chest tightened. It was me. Ban'ach wanted me. But I couldn't abandon the team—or the children. "No," I said through gritted teeth. "We stick together. We face her head-on."

Destiny's hand came to rest on my shoulder, her expression softer than I'd seen it in a while. "Kory, we'll handle it. You have to get those kids out. You know you're the only one Ban'ach is really after. Don't give her what she wants."

I clenched my fists, torn between my desire to fight and the reality of the situation. Destiny was right. If I stayed, I'd be putting everyone—including the children—in more danger. Ban'ach wouldn't stop until she had me.

"Go," Busto said firmly, his eyes locking with mine. "We'll cover you."

I swallowed the lump in my throat, the weight of the decision bearing down on me.

With a quick nod, I grabbed Graham and Hattie's hands.

We bolted toward the second rally point, the cold wind biting at our faces as the sound of the Kergan shuttle grew louder behind us.

As we ran, I couldn't shake the feeling that this was only the beginning. Ban'ach wouldn't stop hunting me. Not until she had what she wanted. And I wasn't sure I could run forever.

The roar of the Kergan shuttle echoed across the sky, growing louder with each second.

My heart pounded in sync with the children's hurried footsteps as we dashed through the rocky terrain, trying to stay ahead of the incoming threat. But no matter how fast we ran, Ban'ach's presence loomed, her words still searing in my mind: I'm coming to collect.

Busto and Destiny stayed behind to slow her down. Leaving them behind felt wrong, but I couldn't let her get to the children. They had already been through too much.

Over the radio, Busto's voice crackled through. "*Charlie team, Bravo team, this is Alpha actual. We're throwing the net. Divert and disperse. Split 'em up!*"

I didn't know what Busto had planned, but whatever it was, I hoped it worked.

As we sprinted toward the safe extraction zone, the noise of the Kergan shuttle shifted—less ominous now, more distant.

I heard small explosions, like a series of controlled detonations. Busto and the others were laying down enough fire to make them think we were in more places than we were.

Good. The Kergans were distracted.

"Just keep running," I said to Graham and Hattie as we pressed forward.

We reached the second rally point—a hidden clearing surrounded by tall trees and rocky outcrops, safely concealed from the eyes of overhead pursuers.

Finally, the shuttle's roar faded into the distance.

My heart settled just a bit. We had done it. We'd thrown them off.

After half an hour of quiet, the rest of the teams regrouped, faces grim but determined.

Busto limped forward, his leg still bleeding but his face hard with purpose. "It worked. We lost them," he said, voice low and breathless.

Destiny emerged from behind a rock, helping one of the Charlie team members. "Took a bit of convincing, but they've bugged out," she said with a smirk. "They'll be chasing shadows for a while."

I let out a breath I hadn't realized I'd been holding.

We had made it. Now, all that was left was to get the kids back home.

"What about the prisoner?" I asked Batts.

"I'll take care of him. He's going into the town jail. You can talk to him later."

We agreed to that and then headed out for home.

The journey back to Elkin was quiet. The adrenaline had long since burned out, replaced by exhaustion.

Hattie clung to Destiny's hand, her eyes still wide with a mix of fear and relief.

Graham, ever stoic, walked beside me, his small hands

curled into fists, but his eyes focused ahead.

The sun was setting when we reached Jon and Martha Marsden's farmhouse, casting long shadows across the dry earth.

As we approached, the porch light flickered on, and the front door flew open. Jon Marsden rushed out, his eyes wide and frantic, followed closely by Martha, her face pale.

"Mom! Dad!" Graham cried, running ahead.

Hattie limped behind him, but her face brightened as she saw her parents.

Martha knelt and wrapped them both in her arms, tears streaming down her face. "Thank God...thank God," she whispered between sobs. Jon stood behind her, eyes wet but with a steady expression. He placed a hand on her shoulder, giving a silent nod of thanks.

I stood back, watching the reunion unfold.

Some of me felt relief, but it was muted by the knowledge of what had happened—and what still lingered in the shadows. Ban'ach wasn't gone. She had just been delayed. I would have to face her again, and soon, and I would find a way to recover the memories of Mom and Dad.

Jon stood up, approaching me with a firm handshake. "Kory, I don't know how to thank you," he said, his voice heavy with emotion.

"You don't have to," I replied, glancing at the children as they clung to their mother. "Just make sure they're safe. Things are only going to get more dangerous from here."

Jon nodded, his face set with grim understanding. "We'll be ready."

Martha wiped her tears and looked up, her voice shaky but strong. "Thank you. You brought them back to us. We'll never forget this."

I gave a tight nod, unable to find the words to respond.

Destiny, standing by my side, placed a hand on my arm. "You did good, Kory," she whispered, her usual sarcastic edge softened.

But as I stood there, watching the Marsdens hold their children close, I couldn't shake the feeling that this was just a small victory in a much larger, darker war. Ban'ach would come again; next time, I might not be so lucky.

I clenched my fists, feeling the weight of what lay ahead. I had bought us time—but time wasn't enough. Not with Ban'ach out there, waiting for her moment to strike again. But for now, the children were safe. And that would have to be enough.

For tonight.

# 13

We left the Marsdens' farmhouse just as dusk settled over the horizon, the orange glow of the setting sun sinking behind the distant hills. The silence between me, Zeta, Destiny, and Busto was heavy—unspoken but palpable. We had won this round, but Ban'ach wouldn't let us walk away so easily. Her presence lingered in my mind like a shadow that refused to dissipate.

As we walked through the dry, brittle backyard of the Marsdens' property, my thoughts spun. Each victory felt like a fleeting reprieve, pushing us closer to an inevitable confrontation. I wasn't ready. Not yet. But I didn't have a choice. Ban'ach had taken what was most precious to me, the memory of my parents and my feelings for them. It was like stealing my identity.

Destiny once told me, *Being a parent should be a life-long job, and doesn't go away when your kids become adults*. Both she and I had lived our teenage years without parents, so I knew she was referring to the way things *should* be in an ideal world. Though my parents had been dead for over fifteen years, I had continued leaning on them. That was until Ban'ach stole from me what little remained of them.

Destiny, ever perceptive, broke the silence first. "Kory, you good?"

I glanced at her, but the words caught in my throat. How could I explain this cold, constant sensation of being empty? I just nodded, focusing instead on the horizon.

Busto, limping but resolute, remained quiet. His mind seemed as preoccupied as mine, probably already planning our next steps. We all had our battles to face. For me, though, Ban'ach was more than just an enemy—she was a force that had stripped away my very soul.

When we reached the barn, the interior lay in eerie quiet. The lights flickered when we turned them on, and the occasional shadow seemed to move in the background. People knew war was on our doorstep. The Kergan Empire might have conquered Earth, but the fight wasn't over.

When we reached the loft, Zeta hovered in her capsule, as inscrutable as ever. Her presence, though alien and detached, seemed more focused tonight.

Zeta's energy pulsed faintly within the capsule. "Ban'ach will not cease her pursuit. She is relentless by nature, Kory Drake."

Busto grimaced, his voice low. "She's changed tactics. That shuttle wasn't part of the usual Nomad setup. She's escalating."

Zeta's hidden gaze seemed to shift to me. "Ban'ach's focus is clear. She seeks your glyphshade, Kory. You are flairsparked, and she desires what she has not yet claimed."

I clenched my fists, feeling the weight of her words. "She's not getting it," I muttered. "Not this time."

"Zeta reminds you," she said, her tone sharpening, "Ban'ach nearly succeeded once before. And next time, she will be better prepared."

Destiny folded her arms, casting a glance between Zeta and me. "So, what now? We just wait around, hoping Ban'ach doesn't pop up out of nowhere again?"

Zeta tilted her head slightly, her formal posture unmoved by Destiny's casual tone. "There is an alternative," she began. "Zeta recommends that you undergo training. You may be flairsparked, but your current abilities are insufficient to withstand Ban'ach's full power."

I frowned, frustration bubbling up. "I don't even know how, Zeta."

Her capsule hovered closer, her voice softening though it retained its distant authority. "Zeta has observed you. You are raw. There is untapped power within you—potential you have yet to unlock. If you are to stand against Ban'ach, you will need to learn to manage your sydereal strength. You must learn to command your presence within the Syderealium."

My mind spun. Could I really tap into something stronger? The thought of facing Ban'ach again, unprepared, made my stomach twist. I needed to be stronger, but a deep-rooted fear gnawed at me: what if no amount of training would ever be enough?

"We can begin immediately," Zeta continued. "There is little time to waste. Ban'ach will strike again soon, and you must be ready."

Destiny looked at me, her expression more serious than usual. "You sure about this, Kory? We've all seen what Ban'ach can do. We need you whole if we want to keep this fight going."

Her concern weighed on me, but I knew what had to be done. Ban'ach had stolen from me, and I was determined to regain my memories. And the gang boss seemed determined to get the rest of my glyphshade. She would come for everyone I cared about if she had to. "I don't have a choice, Destiny. You need to understand something."

I rubbed my chin, reluctant to talk about my parents. The loss of their memory was still so tender. "I know what Ban'ach stole from me. She stole my memory of my parents. I *must* have them back; otherwise, I lose who I am."

We stood in the loft, the faint hum of the wind thrumming the walls, the naked lightbulb overhead casting a sterile light across the floor. Zeta's capsule hovered, her true form hidden from our gaze. The energy in the room felt cold, distant—just like her.

"Kory," Zeta began, her voice even and detached. "Zeta understands your desire to reclaim what Ban'ach has taken. However, Zeta has already stated that she will not aid you in such an endeavor. It would be wrong—an act of theft and corruption."

I stared at her, my pulse quickening. "But they're my memories. She took them from me! I'm not stealing anything—I'm just taking back what's mine."

Zeta's capsule shifted slightly, her presence growing heavier. "What Ban'ach has taken is no longer yours as you once knew it. Your memories have been consumed, twisted into something else. To reclaim them would be to steal an energlyph, just as Ban'ach has done to you. Zeta will not condone this. Zeta cannot assist in such evil."

Destiny, leaning against the wall with a smirk, chimed in. "So, what? Are we supposed just to leave those memories in Ban'ach's slimy hands? That doesn't sound right."

Zeta fixed on Destiny, calm and unwavering. "It is not about what feels right, Destiny Austin. Energlyphs—once taken—become intertwined with the taker. To recover them is to corrupt the natural order further. Zeta cannot endorse such a violation, even in the name of justice."

I clenched my fists, the anger bubbling just beneath the surface. "So, what am I supposed to do? Just let her keep them? My parents—everything I have of them—is gone because of her. You're telling me I should just...give up?"

Zeta's floating form seemed to pulse as though responding to my frustration. "What Ban'ach has stolen cannot be restored to its original state. Your memories, your energlyphs, now serve her will. To seek them out, to attempt to take them back, would make you no different from Ban'ach herself. Zeta will not help you descend into that darkness."

Destiny's brow furrowed, her usual quips falling silent as she seemed to process Zeta's words. "Wait...so if Kory tries to get them back, he'd be... what? Like Ban'ach? How does that even work?"

Zeta's voice remained calm, though a hint of something —disapproval, perhaps—crept into her tone. "By seeking to reclaim your energlyphs through force, Kory Drake would become like those who steal in the Syderealium, feeding on the essence of others. He would become a Soul Ravager. This is not a path Zeta can allow you to walk."

I swallowed hard, the weight of her words hitting me. "But they're my parents. They're all I have left. If I don't get them back, then...what's left of me?"

Zeta's capsule hovered closer, her form still and unwavering. "What remains of you is who you are now, Kory. To cling to what has been stolen, to lose yourself in the pursuit of what was, is to forsake your future. Zeta believes you are capable of more than such folly."

I let out a shaky breath, feeling the knot of frustration tightening in my chest. "So what, then? I just let her win? Let her keep what she stole?"

Zeta paused, her energy pulsing faintly in the dim light. "There are battles yet to come. Ban'ach has not won. Zeta will help you train, to protect what remains of your glyphshade, but Zeta will not aid you in becoming a thief of energlyphs. Such actions can only lead to greater loss and unbalance the Syderealium."

Destiny shook her head, a dry laugh escaping her lips. "So, we're just gonna play defense? That's not exactly a winning strategy, Zeta."

Zeta's voice remained cold, as if Destiny's words had no impact. "The path forward is not one of vengeance, Destiny. It is one of preservation. Kory must learn to defend himself and those he cares about, not seek to reclaim what is already gone."

I wanted to argue, to push back, but deep down, I knew she was right. Ban'ach had taken my memories, but trying to steal them back wouldn't bring my parents back—not really. It would only pull me deeper into the very thing I hated most.

I nodded slowly, my chest still tight. "Fine. No stealing. But I still need to be ready. I need to be strong enough to protect what I have left."

Zeta's capsule pulsed gently as though acknowledging my decision. "Zeta will help you prepare. The path ahead will be difficult, but you will not face it alone."

Destiny gave me a sideways glance, her usual smirk back in place. "Well, I guess you're signing up for Syderealium boot camp. Let's hope Zeta's training comes with snacks."

Despite myself, I smiled faintly, the tension easing just a little. Ban'ach might have taken my memories, but I still had a fight left in me. And this time, I wouldn't be going in unprepared.

# 14

The air in the loft was heavy with silence as I sat cross-legged on the hay-covered floor, Zeta's capsule hovering beside me.

The faint hum of energy that always surrounded her seemed to pulse in time with my nervous heartbeat. I had agreed to this—to training that went beyond anything I'd imagined—but now that we were about to begin, a part of me questioned if I was ready.

Zeta's voice broke the stillness, calm and steady as ever. "Kory Drake, Zeta shall guide you through the process of entering the Syderealium. This is not a skill one simply acquires—it is a delicate balancing act of mind and willpower. Only those with true potential can master it."

I nodded, trying to settle the unease that gnawed at my insides. "What do I have to do?"

Zeta floated slightly closer, her capsule glowing faintly. "You must focus your mind entirely on a concept beyond the material world—something that transcends the limitations of human thought. Zeta has chosen a number for you to meditate upon: Champernowne's constant."

I frowned. "Champernowne's constant? What's that?"

Zeta's voice grew softer, almost reverent. "It is a transcendental number, a sequence that never repeats, never resolves into any pattern. By meditating upon it, you will train your mind to move beyond the finite, to understand the infinite in ways that free you from this material universe."

I took a deep breath, the name ringing strange in my ears. Champernowne's constant...a sequence of numbers stretching endlessly into chaos. It was fitting, I supposed. Zeta instructed me to close my eyes, and I did as she asked, trying to quiet my mind.

"Begin by visualizing the number," Zeta said. "One. Two. Three. Four. Five. Six. Seven. Eight. Nine. One. Zero. One. One. One. Two..." Her voice continued on the sequence. She taught me that the constant was zero point, followed by the counting digits concatenated together forever.

I followed her voice, each digit unfolding in my mind's eye, repeated over and over like a mantra.

The room around me faded away, the cold floor beneath me forgotten as the digits consumed my focus.

Champernowne's constant—an endless, nonsensical sequence with no pattern. How was I supposed to comprehend something like that? I could barely keep track of my own thoughts most days, and now I was expected to wrap my head around an infinite patternless sequence that made number theory look like child's play.

*Yeah, no pressure. Just meditate on pure chaos—what could possibly go wrong?*

And yet, time slipped from my awareness as the numbers stretched into infinity.

My breath slowed, and soon, the rhythmic chant of

numbers was all I could hear. There was no room for anything else—no thoughts, no fears, no memories—just the number.

Zeta's voice seemed to come from a distance. "Now, let go of the sequence and reach beyond it. Feel for the edge of the material plane."

It was like slipping into a void, a quiet nothingness where the universe's rules no longer applied. The constant wasn't a number anymore—it was a sensation, a pull like I was floating somewhere between reality and dream.

Suddenly, I felt a shift—a strange tug, as if my consciousness was being drawn toward something.

And then it happened: the room around me dissolved completely, and in its place was a vast, luminous landscape that stretched endlessly in all directions. This wasn't the world I knew. It was something else—something enormous and alive.

I remembered it. I was in the Syderealium once again.

I blinked, staring in awe at the shimmering expanse before me.

Colors I couldn't name swirled through the air like living things, and I felt as though I was standing at the heart of the universe itself, surrounded by the very essence of existence.

Zeta floated beside me, no longer a capsule but a bunched network of energlyphs.

The Syderealium seemed to magnify her presence.

Her voice, though still formal, held a note of surprise. "You have entered the Syderealium, Kory Drake. Zeta did not expect you to succeed so swiftly."

I turned to face her, still trying to process what I was seeing—what I was feeling. It was like nothing I had ever imagined. "I...I did it?"

Zeta hovered closer, her gaze fixed on me with what could only be described as approval. "Indeed. Zeta is...pleased with your progress. Your talent for traversing the Syderealium is rare, even among the flairsparked."

Her words brought a strange sense of accomplishment, but beneath that flicker of pride, there was a deep, gnawing unease. This place—the Syderealium—was incredible, even beautiful in its own bizarre way, but it was also terrifying. I could feel it in my bones. Ban'ach had been here too. She knew this realm far better than I ever could, like a predator that already knew every shadow, every hiding place.

And there were other dangers, far greater and darker than Ban'ach. The gods Zeta had mentioned—because, apparently, one soul-ravaging monster wasn't enough. Now, we had cosmic deities in the mix. I could barely navigate this place without mentally tripping over myself, and now I had to worry about bumping into immortal entities? Awesome. Nothing says "you're in over your head" like being a rookie psychic wandering through a god-infested plane of existence.

Still, I had taken the first step. I had entered the Syderealium, and with Zeta's help, I would learn to control it. I would learn to defend myself. And when the time came, I would face Ban'ach here—on her turf. I would surprise her, and despite my promise to Zeta, I would find a way to take back what was mine.

Zeta's normally detached manner had softened just a fraction as she studied me. "You have proven capable, Kory. There is much more to learn, but Zeta is confident you will become a formidable presence within the Syderealium."

Destiny's voice broke the solemn air, echoing faintly from the material plane. "So...did you guys manage to not break reality, or am I gonna have to mop up some existential goo when you're done?"

I smiled faintly, though the awe of the moment still held me in its grip. "We're good, Dest. For now."

But deep down, I knew this was only the beginning. I couldn't help but laugh inwardly at the absurdity of it all. Me—a psychic? Who would have ever thought? People like fortune tellers, astrologers, and spiritual mediums had always struck me as total kooks. Yet here I was, diving headfirst into something that felt like a bizarre blend of those worlds. Zeta, no doubt, would disagree with my comparison to pseudosciences, but that's exactly how it felt.

Zeta spent the next couple of hours guiding me through various sydereal exercises. She taught me how to control my sydereal body and, most importantly, how to protect my energlyphs from being stolen. She also showed me how to exit the Syderealium if I was ever forcefully projected into it again.

The act of entering the Syderealium was called sydereal projection, and it was achieved by meditating on a transcendental number of my choice. It is strange how something as abstract as numbers can act as a key to a dimension beyond reality. Maybe it felt simple for me, but Zeta hinted it wasn't easy for others.

During my training, I learned to protect myself from simulated attacks on my energlyphs. When I asked Zeta how she was attacking me, she refused to explain. "Your desire for revenge clouds your judgment," she said. "This knowledge would destroy you."

I was left to guess at her methods, which, honestly, felt like trying to solve a puzzle with half the pieces missing and the instructions in another language. You'd think watching her glyphshade in action would give me some clues, but it wasn't that straightforward. Turns out, my psychic detective skills are about as sharp as a spoon. Still, I managed to sense when I was under attack and throw up a mental shield to stop my energlyphs from being yanked away. It was often painful, sometimes excruciating, but hey, I've survived my own cooking—so how bad could it be?

"Very good, friend Kory," Zeta said, her tone impassive. "Zeta is confident that you now possess the necessary skills to defend yourself should Ban'ach confront you in the Syderealium again."

"That's it?" I asked, surprised. "We've only been at this for a couple of hours."

"The knowledge of the Syderealium is as vast as its dimensions. Zeta could never teach you all there is to know. What Zeta has taught you are the techniques to defend yourself from the types of attacks Ban'ach and other Soul Ravagers use."

I rubbed my temples, feeling the weight of it all. "Well, that's something, I guess. My head hurts."

We exited the Syderealium, and I could see the world again through my real eyes.

Destiny sat next to me. She looked like she'd been there the entire time, watching over me. It warmed my heart.

Destiny shot me a sideways glance, raising an eyebrow. "Well, look who's back from the psychic deep dive. I was starting to think I'd have to come in there and drag you out myself. You looked peaceful, though—kind of like someone drooling during a power nap." She grinned, giving my shoulder a light punch. "Glad to have you back in one piece."

# 15

My crew and I sat around the video monitor. I was watching the live image of a marac bandit resting in the Elkin police department's one and only police interrogation room. The marac had been stripped of all his belongings and clothing. He was naked because nobody had marac-compatible prison suits.

It was the morning after the rescue of the Marsden children. We were waiting for Marshal Batts and a deputy marshal to enter the room and begin the interrogation. The room didn't have one of those fancy one-way glass windows with the hidden room like you see in movies and TV shows. All we had was the output from a video camera hanging on the ceiling in a corner.

Destiny glanced at the video monitor, raising an eyebrow at the sight of the naked marac sitting in the interrogation room. "Well, I guess we've found the one thing more terrifying than an armed marac: a naked one. Somebody better get him a towel before we all get nightmares." She smirked. "I'm just saying, marac fashion wasn't winning any awards before, but this is a new low."

Busto emitted a low grunt and continued staring at the monitor.

I rolled my eyes, leaning back in my chair. "If this guy doesn't talk, it's not gonna be because he's tough—it's because he's too embarrassed to look us in the eyes. I'd offer him a blanket, but I feel like making him suffer through this might just break him faster."

Destiny grinned. "Maybe we can charge extra for the therapy sessions after this."

I chuckled. "At this rate, we're all going to need therapy. I mean, I've seen some weird stuff out there, but this? This might take the cake. Naked marac in the police station—definitely wasn't on my list of 'things to prepare for as a starship captain.'"

Destiny snorted. "Yeah, 'How to Interrogate a Nude Alien' definitely didn't come up in Gunny's training. Think we should add it to the survival manual?"

Busto made another grunting sound.

I shook my head. "Nah, we'll leave that one for the next poor sap who ends up in this position. They can figure it out like we did—pure improvisation. Maybe they'll have a blanket ready."

Destiny smirked, glancing at the screen again. "Or at least a blindfold for themselves. I mean, this is a team effort, and right now, I'm not sure who's suffering more—him or us."

On the video monitor, Marshal Batts entered, followed by a young woman. Busto reached forward and turned up the sound. "Shut up, you guys, I'm trying to listen."

Destiny slapped him on the shoulder. "Creeps, Gunny, they just barely arrived!"

The door behind us opened, and Sergeant Rowbottom

entered. "Mornin' everyone," he said, finishing it with a yawn.

I pointed to an empty chair. "Grab a seat and some popcorn. The show's about to start."

The Marshal got started by asking for identifying information from the marac. That didn't go very well because they couldn't understand each other.

Batts excused himself for a minute, then returned with the translator box all the maracs wore most of the time. He strapped it to one of the arms of the marac, who barely twitched.

I didn't know marac body language, but this one looked like his mind was about gone.

The Marshal started again, and this time, they got a response.

The alien was named Om'bel, and he was a "mission specialist" for the Nebula Nomads. He explained his duties, which could be best summarized as being a fighter. Om'bel was one of Ban'ach's soldiers.

The interrogation was pretty dull, with Batts and the woman focusing on basic questions for most of it. The alien was not very responsive. I don't know if it was because he was refusing to cooperate or if something was wrong with him. My guess was it was the latter.

But after they'd been going at it for a couple hours, the interrogation suddenly got very interesting.

"So, you don't know where the abducted humans are being kept, right?" Batts asked for what seemed to be like the fiftieth time.

"Where else but with the principal?!" Om'bel suddenly replied in the synthetic voice generated by his translator box.

"The principal?" Batts asked. "Did I hear that right?"

"Yes, where else would they go?" The alien waved an arm, showing a bit more energy compared to earlier. Maybe we'd started the interrogation when he was still in the middle of whatever was equivalent to his sleep cycle.

"Who is this principal?" Batts added.

The alien released a very human-sounding sigh. "The party who hired our outfit."

"And who might that be?"

"I am not at liberty to discuss the confidential business of the principal."

"Okay, I get it. But it's okay for you to abduct sentient beings. Do I have that right?"

"My colleagues—the Nebula Nomads—are working on a sanctioned contract under the strictures of Part 3 of Article 23 of the Commercial Interstellar Ventures Declaration of Imperium Session 4298."

"Good heavens, he sounds like a lawyer!" Destiny said.

On the video, Batts shook his head. "I don't know what any of that means. Please. Tell this dumb human in basic language what you just said."

"It means that our activities are legal. So long as we deliver the product to the principal per the agreed upon terms."

"And what are those terms?"

"I cannot discuss the details. But I'll tell you this much. The humans you are looking for are not even on this planet now. They are somewhere on Luna and have likely been brought into the principal's employment."

"On *Luna*, you say? As in the Moon?"

"Yes, and that is the only thing I'll say on the matter; otherwise, the boss will sever one of my limbs," Om'bel said, shaking a tentacle.

"And you won't tell me who this principal is? Sounds to

me like an organization that has hired you Nomads as a contractor. Is it the Kergan government?"

"I'm not allowed to talk about it, but it is pointless anyway because I don't even know. The boss doesn't tell low-ranking members of her staff those sorts of details."

"But our missing humans are on the Moon. And how are they being employed?"

"That I do not know."

"Please, speculate."

Om'bel wiggled his limbs and closed his eyes. It was body language of some kind that seemed very deliberate, but I didn't know what it meant. "Sure, human, if it will get you to leave me in peace. Most likely the humans have been assigned to rigor pods and their brains mindjacked."

The woman assisting Batts flipped to a new page in her notebook and started scribbling notes again, furiously trying to keep up.

Batts wiped his hand on his face and bowed his head as if telling himself he was too old for this business. "Rigor pods. Mindjacked. Explain these terms."

"We were ordered to take humans that had experience working in the mine."

"In Mineral Park Mine?" Batts asked.

"Yes, where else? The principal wanted humans with experience in mining operations. They were more interested in their minds than in their physical bodies."

"To what end?"

Answering as if he were talking to a small child, Om'bel said, "To operate the principal's systems through a mindjack. That's my guess. It's very common ever since that galactic treaty was passed banning high-end machine intelligence. The humans are being used to operate machinery or computer systems of some kind."

"And this...rigor pod?"

"It's where the humans are confined while they're mindjacked."

"And how often are they mindjacked?"

"How often? Blazing novas, you really don't know anything, do you? Mindjacking isn't something you turn on and off like it was a machine. Once you're mindjacked, you stay that way until somebody decides you've earned your freedom. It's costly to install the hardware, and once it is in there, you're mindjacked until it's surgically removed."

As I listened to Om'bel describe what had happened to Elkin's humans, it was like watching a nightmare play out. If I understood correctly, these humans had somehow been enslaved in the worst way possible: their minds had been hijacked and put to whatever purposes the principal wanted. Even the name suggested that: *mindjacked*.

"So, our missing humans have no freedoms at all?"

"Not really. That would defeat the purpose, wouldn't it? A mindjacked human is a machine that serves the purposes of the principal, whatever those may be. I can only speculate."

Batts waved a hand. "And this principal hired the Nebula Nomads to...acquire assets for mindjacking, correct?"

"Yes, now you get it." And the alien seemed pleased in a condescending manner that Batts had finally understood. "Are we done?"

Batts looked at the woman, and they exchanged an unstated message. Batts turned back to Om'bel. "Yes, for now. I'll return you to your cell, and we'll continue looking for food that fits within your dietary constraints."

Om'bel waved two of his tentacles. "You could always just let me go back to my people."

Batts opened the door and pushed Om'bel out on the rolling chair. He said something I couldn't hear.

I wondered what was going to happen to the marac prisoner. The town was under martial law. There was no judge or jury available to hear the charges. And I doubted the town could afford to maintain a marac in custody indefinitely. I suspected the only release Om'bel would find would be at the end of a gun.

Destiny shook her head, a half-laugh escaping her. "Mindjacked in some pod, working till you drop? Hell, I thought being stuck on the streets was bad, but this? This is next-level messed up. At least when I was scraping by, I could flip off the world and keep moving. But this? No chance. They must've figured that if you can't break someone's spirit, just hijack it. Real nice of them to make slavery sound all fancy."

"I couldn't agree more, Dest," I said. "This is messed up."

Rowbottom leaned toward the monitor. "Yeah, sounds like a dream job—stuck in a pod, working for the 'principal' with no bathroom breaks. Real five-star treatment." He smirked, glancing at me. "What's next? They start handing out mindjacking applications at the local career fair? 'Wanted: hard-working humans with no sense of self-determination.'"

I rolled my eyes, turning to Rowbottom. "I'm sure that'll attract all the best talent. Sign me up."

Destiny grinned. "Hey, it's a real opportunity for growth. You start as a mindjacked drone and work your way up to...well, probably still a mindjacked drone."

Rowbottom chuckled. "Yeah, well, good thing we didn't get 'recruited.' I like my brain right where it is—inside my head, not plugged into some alien server farm."

With this new development, the story here in Elkin just

kept getting weirder and weirder. This Ban'ach was mixed up in some crazy business—the Syderealium. Mindjacking abducted humans. High-tech slavery. On the Moon. How was my crew supposed to deal with this?

The answer was we weren't supposed to. It wasn't our duty. Sure, we'd help eliminate these alien bastards, but there was nothing we could do to help those poor humans who'd already been taken. But at least we could rid the town of any more abductions. I'd have to be satisfied with that.

But what I didn't know is that we still hadn't gotten the complete picture of what Ban'ach was doing. The tale would get even stranger *and* more dangerous, as you'll find out later in this story.

# 16

After the interrogation, Destiny, Busto, Rowbottom, and I headed to the Tumbleweed Tavern for some much-needed food and beer. We ordered steaks, fries, and a round of cold ones. Stafford had even scored a shipment of winter apples from Mexico. How they'd managed to make it across the border without being stolen was beyond me, but biting into one was like tasting a slice of sunshine—sweet and crisp, a rare treat in these bleak times.

I had just finished cleaning my plate and was leaning back, listening to Destiny and Rowbottom swap jokes.

The tavern was packed—every table was filled, and the bar was lined with patrons.

Someone had dropped a quarter in the jukebox, and Strawberry Wine by Deana Carter was playing. I didn't much care for country music, but I had to admit, this one wasn't half bad.

With the buzz of conversation and music, it was hard to hear what Destiny was saying, but whatever it was had Rowbottom laughing so hard he was nearly in tears.

Then, the tavern door swung open. I glanced over and saw a familiar sight—purple tentacles floating in with a head perched on top.

Another marac.

More trouble.

It was like a storm cloud drifting into a sunny day, and right in the middle of the lunch rush, when the place was packed.

My instincts kicked in. I pushed back my chair, shot to my feet, drew my laser pistol, and aimed squarely at the marac's center of mass.

Out of the corner of my eye, I saw Destiny and Busto were already on their feet, weapons drawn, not wasting a second.

After the last few days, none of us were in the mood for marac nonsense. I mean, at this point, if one more tentacled alien wandered into my lunch, I was going to start charging them an entry fee.

The marac froze, its tentacles raised, floating at chest height.

Its wide, black eyes flicked nervously between me and the others. It wasn't armed, at least not visibly—just carrying a satchel slung across its side.

Before anyone could make another move, Stafford rushed over, waving his hands frantically. "Whoa, whoa! Mr. Drake, hold on! She's friendly!"

I shot him a skeptical look. "The marac?"

"Yes, of course! Lower your weapons before you shoot her!" Stafford came up beside me, though I noticed he kept well clear of my line of fire.

I kept my pistol trained on the alien. "Who are you?"

"I am O'hatet, from the Lufen Republic," the marac replied in a calm, synthesized voice from her translator box.

"Please, human, I come in peace."

"You're not Kergan?"

She laughed nervously, her tentacles still raised. She didn't seem like an immediate threat, so I slowly lowered my pistol. "No, definitely not Kergan," she said.

I blinked, taken aback. I'd never met a marac who wasn't part of the Kergan Empire. To me, being a marac and being Kergan were basically the same thing—like assuming anyone in a spacesuit was an astronaut. Turns out, my intergalactic understanding had all the depth of a kiddie pool.

"Come on now," Stafford said, patting me on the shoulder. "She's a friend. You can trust me on this one."

He turned to O'hatet. "Sorry about the welcome, O'hatet. These folks have had a rough time with the Kergan and the Nebula Nomads lately."

"I understand completely," O'hatet said, her voice calm. "I apologize for startling you. May I shake your hand and ask your name?"

I eyed her tentacles, covered in small, sucker-like appendages. Touching her wasn't high on my list of things to do, but she seemed sincere. I reached out cautiously. "Kory Drake."

One of her tentacles wrapped around my palm in a surprisingly firm but gentle grip. Her skin was scaled and dry, like a reptile's, but warm. I had to remind myself that maracs were invertebrates—no bones, just muscle, and cartilage to hold everything together. Honestly, it felt like shaking hands with a warm, friendly snake...if that snake had twelve arms and a translator box.

"It is an honor to meet you, Kory Drake," she said. "I've heard much about you and your crew."

"Is that so?"

She nodded. "This is a small town, and word travels fast. Please, allow me to show my gratitude by buying you and your crew a round of drinks."

I wasn't keen on the idea of being indebted to a marac, friendly or not. "That's not necessary."

"I insist," she said, her tone polite but firm. "It's the least I can do to honor the heroes who rescued Hattie and Graham."

I felt my face heat up. A twelve-armed alien just made me blush. "It was nothing," I mumbled, gesturing to the table. "You're welcome to join us."

"Thank you," she said, floating over to an empty chair and settling herself down, her tentacles forming a neat pillar beneath her to keep her head at eye level with us.

My friends stared wide-eyed. I sat down, gesturing to the others. "Let me introduce everyone." I went around the table, introducing each of my crew, finishing with Rowbottom.

"I know Sergeant Rowbottom," O'hatet said.

Rowbottom grinned. "She's good people, Kory."

Just then, Stafford returned with another round of beers, even setting one in front of O'hatet. I raised an eyebrow. "I didn't know maracs could drink beer."

O'hatet's large black eyes blinked slowly. "Most of us don't, but I've acquired a taste for it during my time on Earth."

"You drink alcohol?"

"No," she said with a slight laugh. "Our bodies don't metabolize ethanol. It has no intoxicating effect on us, though the taste is...interesting. Too much can cause digestive distress, though." She lifted her glass. "But I understand this is an important human social ritual."

Busto smirked, covering his mouth to hide a silent burp.

"Yeah, something like that."

A brief silence hung over the table. My friends were clearly uncomfortable with a marac sitting so casually among us, and honestly, I wasn't sure how to break the ice either. It didn't help that O'hatet didn't seem like she planned on leaving anytime soon.

Destiny broke the silence first. "So, you're not a Kergan," she said, raising an eyebrow. "Are you, like, from another nation or something?"

O'hatet nodded, mimicking human body language with surprising ease. "Correct. I'm from the Lufen Republic."

Destiny blinked. "Wait, how did you get to Earth?"

O'hatet's tentacles shifted slightly as she answered. "I snuck in."

Destiny sat back, looking shocked. "You snuck into a war zone? Why would you do that?"

O'hatet raised a tentacle and pointed it at Destiny. "That's exactly why I'm here. I'm a freelance investigative reporter, and I'm working on a story to expose the Kergan war crimes committed here on Earth."

I glanced around the table—Busto and Destiny both looked as taken aback as I felt. This marac was actually on our side? A marac who cared about humans? It was hard to process.

"What's your goal?" I asked, leaning forward.

"I want what any journalist wants: the truth to be known," O'hatet replied, her voice firm. "The Kergans are destroying your planet and your way of life. The galaxy needs to hear about this. You may be a small star system in an unremarkable part of the Milky Way, but you are aborigines being colonized and exploited. It's an ecological and sociological tragedy. The Kergan Empire doesn't allow a free press, so it's up to people like me to uncover the truth and spread it."

Destiny absentmindedly traced the condensation on her glass. "That sounds dangerous," she said quietly.

"It can be," O'hatet agreed. "But being a marac helps me blend in."

Destiny frowned. "What about the bandits? The Nebula Nomads?"

"They usually leave me alone," O'hatet said with a wave of her tentacle. "I try to steer clear of their business, and they have no reason to mess with me."

I was beginning to realize just how valuable this marac could be as an ally. She could have information on both the Kergan Empire and the Nebula Nomads—maybe even Ban'ach. This was an opportunity I couldn't ignore.

I leaned in. "We recently found out—very recently—that the humans abducted from Elkin are being used as slaves on Luna," I explained. "All of us here have lost someone to the Kergan sweeps. Do you know what's happening to those people?"

O'hatet nodded. "Yes. It's widely known, though perhaps not among your people. Your kind is being enslaved, at the very least. I've also heard darker rumors, but they're unverified. The Kergan Empire's economy has stagnated, and they've turned to slavery to maintain their output."

I shared a quick look with my crew, then told her about Om'bel's interrogation and what we'd learned about the Nomads working for a mysterious principal. "Do you know who this principal might be?" I asked.

O'hatet shook her head. "I'm not sure, but I can find out."

"Could you?" I asked, hopeful.

"Of course," she said. "The information is probably not

public, but as a reporter, I've learned to explore unconventional sources. I'm confident I can dig something up. I'll let you know in a day or two."

"Where can we find you?" I asked.

"I'm staying with the widow Urbana Fontana in the basement of the orphanage," O'hatet replied.

Destiny winced. "Ouch. That sounds noisy."

O'hatet sighed but smiled slightly. "Human children are delightful. Seeing them without parents is a constant reminder of why I do this. I find it...stimulating."

She started to float away, turning back to give us a final wave. "Be safe, my friends. I'll be in touch."

We watched as she glided over to another table, joining an elderly man for what looked like another interview.

Destiny took a long drink of her beer, setting the glass down with a thud. "Okay, so we just had a drink with a marac who's, like, some kind of galactic journalist. Not exactly how I expected today to go."

Busto raised an eyebrow. "Yeah, tell me about it. I've spent the last few days trying to shoot those things, and now I'm supposed to shake hands and chat over beer? Feels a little...weird."

Rowbottom laughed, leaning back in his chair. "Welcome to the new normal. One minute you're blasting maracs out of the sky, the next you're swapping war stories and talking about Kergan slavery over steaks."

I chuckled, shaking my head. "It's surreal. The whole idea that maracs could be against the Kergans? I thought they were all cut from the same cloth. But now we find out they've got their own factions, and some of them hate the Kergans as much as we do."

Destiny grinned, leaning forward. "And did you hear the way she talked about the Kergans enslaving humans?

Like, 'Oh yeah, that's totally a thing they do.' As if it's just another day at the office. What next? They've got a galactic HR department managing their slave labor?"

Rowbottom smirked. "Wouldn't be surprised if they did. Probably with a whole manual on how to mindjack your workers and still make them think they're getting benefits."

Busto shook his head, looking serious for a moment. "We joke, but that's dark stuff. Mindjacking? Humans being used as slaves? That's not something I ever thought we'd be dealing with."

Destiny nodded, her smile fading slightly. "Yeah, you're right. It's messed up. I mean, I knew the Kergans were bad, but this? It's next-level evil."

I leaned back in my chair, staring at the ceiling for a moment. "So, now we've got to figure out what to do about this. If humans are being used on the Moon for who knows what, we can't just sit here and pretend it's not happening. But I guess that's a long-term goal. First things first—survival, and getting back to the base."

Busto held up his glass. "I'll drink to that: getting home." We all drank, even Rowbottom, who wasn't part of my crew but had been sticking around long enough to feel like one of us. I was starting to consider inviting his team to join us when we made it back to California.

Destiny sat quietly, swirling the last of her beer. It didn't take a mind reader to know where her thoughts had drifted. The conversation had hit her hard—her mom and sisters had been missing for months now, likely swept up by the Kergan when they tore through San Jose. Now she knew the horrifying truth: the abductees were being forced into slavery. Was her mom mindjacked into some rigor pod? Were her sisters suffering the same fate?

The worst part was that we might never know. The Kergans had a stranglehold on humanity, and the more we learned, the clearer it became that we were like insects caught in a spider's web—helpless, paralyzed, and entirely at their mercy as they tightened the threads around us.

I wanted nothing more than to get back to Wolf Jaw, have Zeta rebuild *Thunder*, and start hitting the Kergans where it hurt. But first, we had to take care of Elkin's bandit problem. Sure, we didn't have to—Zeta could crank out some gasoline with her nanoforge, and I was sure we could buy an old vehicle from someone in town with one of our Gold Eagles. But I'd given my word to Marshal Batts. And the more I got to know these people, the more I wanted to help them.

And maybe, somehow, I could recover my stolen memories while we were at it.

"Alright, folks," I said, meeting each of their eyes. "It's time we figure out how to take down the Nomads."

Rowbottom nodded. "We took out about half their numbers yesterday. They've probably got no more than a dozen left. If we're gonna hit them, now's the time—before they bring in reinforcements."

"Right," I said, pushing my chair back. "Let's go find the Marshal and get this thing rolling."

We settled our tab, with me handing Stafford a fresh gold chip to cover the cost, and then made our way back to the police station to find Batts and start planning the operation.

# 17

Marshal Batts' office wasn't exactly the kind of place that screamed "battle planning." It was more of a storage closet that had lost a fight with a map factory.

The walls were plastered with faded, peeling maps of Elkin and its surrounding areas, as if Batts was determined to make it look like he knew what he was doing—or at least where we were.

A battered old desk sat at the center, drowning in paperwork and half-empty coffee mugs.

The only thing missing was a dartboard with a picture of Ban'ach's face on it, which, frankly, I would've contributed to in a heartbeat.

Destiny, Busto, Rowbottom, and I squeezed into the room, trying not to trip over a rifle Batts had propped up against his chair. Yeah, that man was ready for action...or maybe just paranoid. Either way, it wasn't comforting.

I leaned forward, clasping my hands like I had any business running a mission this big. "We need to hit the Nomad headquarters at Mineral Park Mine," I said, sounding more confident than I felt. "We'll be the spearhead —my crew and the Army scouts. But we'll need your posse to cover our flanks and provide overwatch. No offense, Marshal, but this is bigger than your usual traffic stop."

Batts grunted, crossing his arms like he wasn't sure if I was insulting him or not. "How many people do you need?"

I glanced at Rowbottom, who gave me a slight nod. I didn't want to admit I was making this up as I went along, so I pushed through. "Fifteen, twenty people should do it. We just need them set up on the ridges around the mine, picking off any Nomads trying to flank us. They don't need to go head-to-head with the Nomads; we've got that covered."

Batts rubbed his chin. "I can get you fifteen. Mostly hunters. They're good with a rifle, but don't expect 'em to charge in guns blazing."

"That's fine," Rowbottom chimed in. "We don't need them in direct combat. Just keep the pressure off our backs. Just like yesterday."

"Exactly," I said, trying to sound like I had this whole thing figured out. The truth was, planning an attack on an alien warlord's stronghold wasn't exactly covered in my starship captain's handbook—mostly because I didn't have one. "We need to hit them fast and hard. We can't give Ban'ach time to regroup or call for reinforcements."

Busto leaned back in his chair, arms crossed like he was thinking hard—which, for Busto, usually meant trouble. "And what about Ban'ach? She'll have that shuttle revved up and ready to fly the second things go sideways. You know how she is—slipperier than Destiny when it's her turn to do the dishes."

Destiny shot him a glare. "Hey, that only happened once. And I was...busy."

I held up a hand, trying to get us back on track. "Busto's right. Ban'ach isn't sticking around for the fireworks. We need to ground that shuttle before we even start the attack."

Rowbottom scratched his chin. "We could send in a small team the night before, sabotage her shuttle. I'm thinking a few well-placed charges, maybe cut the fuel lines."

The Marshal's office felt even smaller as the argument began to heat up. The dusty maps and old paperwork were the least of my concerns now. The air itself seemed to thicken with tension, everyone talking at once as the plan started to unravel before my eyes.

Rowbottom leaned forward, his voice steady but insistent. "We can't just go charging in there without sabotaging her shuttle first. If Ban'ach gets airborne, she's gone—again. We all know she's got an exit plan, and we're not going to catch her with our pants down this time."

"Yeah," Busto added, crossing his arms. "We blow her ship's engines, and she's stuck. Nice and easy."

But Marshal Batts wasn't having it. He rubbed his chin, clearly not liking the idea of sneaking in the night before. "That's too risky. You go in to sabotage her shuttle, and something goes wrong—one wrong move—and the whole Nomad camp's alerted. Then what? They're going to be ready for you when you come in for the real attack. We'll lose the element of surprise."

"And then we're all toast," Destiny chimed in. "Plus, I don't know about you, but I'm not exactly keen on creeping into Ban'ach's backyard at midnight and praying nobody notices. Sounds like a quick way to get dead."

Rowbottom threw his hands up. "It's a small team. We're in and out. No alarms, no drama."

I was starting to feel the headache coming on. The last

thing we needed was an argument before we even had the plan settled. "Look, we all know Ban'ach's going to run the second things go south. If we don't stop her shuttle—"

"And what if we botch the sabotage?" Batts interrupted, his voice rising. "One noise, one set of eyes in the wrong place, and we lose everything. The Nomads'll be waiting for you with guns drawn the second you step foot in there. You really want to roll the dice on that?"

Destiny shook her head, leaning back with a smirk. "Yeah, I'm with Batts. No way am I creeping through their camp like some kind of assassin. I'm not that sneaky, and you're dreaming if you think we'll just waltz in and out of there."

Rowbottom glared at her. "You underestimate my scouts."

"I don't underestimate anyone," she shot back. "But even your scouts can't control dumb luck. What happens when the Nomads decide to do an extra patrol that night, or Ban'ach's shuttle crew is hanging out by the ship? We'll be dead before we even set the charges."

Busto sighed, shaking his head. "So what's the plan then? Let her fly off, and we'll just wave at her shuttle as it heads to the Moon?"

Batts slammed a hand down on the table, silencing the room. "No, we hit them fast. We go in with everything we've got. Hard and quick. No time for Ban'ach to get to her shuttle, no time for the Nomads to regroup. That's how we trap her."

There was a beat of silence as his words sank in. I hated to admit it, but Batts had a point. Sneaking into the Nomad camp to sabotage the shuttle was like poking a hornet's nest with a stick and hoping not to get stung. And if we blew it, we'd lose everything.

I sighed, leaning forward. "Batts is right. We don't have time to risk the sabotage. We hit the Nomads so fast they won't even know what's happening until we're already on them. If we can blitz them and take out their key players, Ban'ach won't have time to escape."

Rowbottom shook his head, clearly unhappy about the idea, but he didn't argue. "We'll need to be precise. No dragging this thing out."

"Yeah, no dragging it out," I agreed. "We hit hard, hit fast, and make sure Ban'ach has nowhere to run."

Busto grunted. "Works for me. Better than tiptoeing around her camp like we're in some spy movie."

Destiny threw up her hands. "Finally, someone's making sense. Let's go in, guns blazing, and show Ban'ach why she shouldn't mess with us."

Batts nodded, the tension starting to ease just a little. "Alright then. We gather the posse, get the scouts ready, and we move in. Hard and fast."

I clenched my jaw, Ban'ach's smug face flashing through my mind. The idea of her slipping away again—after everything she'd taken from me—made my blood boil. She had stolen my memories of my parents, and the thought of getting them back was the only thing keeping me going. Well, that, and the fact that I'm too stubborn to admit I have no idea what I'm doing. Honestly, I wasn't sure what was more terrifying—facing her again or the distinct possibility that I might be in way over my head. Probably both.

I stared at the maps on the wall, my mind drifting back to the memories Ban'ach had ripped away. She wasn't going to get away this time. I was going to stop her, and if I had to destroy her entire operation to do it, so be it.

Batts finally broke the silence. "Alright, I'll gather the posse. We've got one shot at this. You're sure about the timeline? Thirty-six hours?"

I glanced around the table at Destiny, Busto, and Rowbottom. We all exchanged a silent look of agreement.

"Thirty-six hours," I confirmed. "Let's do it."

# 18

That evening, I decided to go and visit the orphanage like I'd been planning. Partly, I was hoping to run into O'hatet again and pick her brain some more. But it was mainly because I remembered my own time in the state-run orphanages of California and how lonely it had been. Maybe it was just morbid curiosity, especially considering how much I was hurting on the inside from the damage Ban'ach had done to me.

Busto and Destiny were tired and didn't want to go, but I convinced Zeta to accompany me. The igna hadn't yet been into town and was interested in meeting some of its inhabitants.

Having no vehicle, we were on foot, but Urbana Fontana's home wasn't too far away. Zeta and I strolled down a gravel road lined with small single-family homes. A few citizens were out and waved to us as we walked by. Zeta got a lot of strange looks.

The Fontana home was a sprawling two-story house in the Santa Fe style. A crudely painted sign on the front lawn said *The Fontana Home for Children.*

I stepped along a flagstone pathway in the front yard to the front door and rang the doorbell.

Sounds of playing children leaked through the walls. It was about 8:30 pm, and I was glad the children had not started going to bed yet.

An older woman opened the door. Her face was creased, and though short, her presence was like a concrete bunker. Even her graying hair, which pulled into a tight bun, gave her a sense of strength.

"Hello, how can I help you?" she said, glancing at Zeta.

I reached out a hand and she took it. "Hi, I'm Kory Drake, captain of the starship *Thunder*," I gestured to my alien friend, "and this is my colleague Zeta. We heard word of your orphanage and wanted to check in on you, if that's okay."

"Oh, please don't call it an orphanage," she said. "It's such a sad word. And I'm not sure the kids are even orphans because I like to think that their parents are still alive somewhere. I like to call it a children's home."

"I understand. Still, I'd like to see the children if it would be okay."

She eyed me up and down. "For what purpose?"

I shrugged. "I'm an orphan myself and spent many years in an orphanage. I suppose I feel a sense of... camaraderie, I suppose you could call it, with the children. I don't think I could do anything to help you, but maybe it would do them some good to see somebody like me."

She opened the door wider and nodded. "Please, come in. I do like to bring visitors to talk with the children. Sorry for the questions. I just had to make sure you weren't some kind of creep. And I'm Urbana Fontana, but everybody calls me Ana."

Zeta and I followed her into a foyer.

In a large living or family room down a short hallway, I could see a group of children gathered around a board game on the floor.

Several girls sat at a table drawing or coloring.

"How many are you caring for, Ana?" I asked.

"Thirty-two children, ranging from ages of nine months to thirteen years."

My jaw dropped open. "Wow! So many?"

She shrugged. "It could be worse, but when they turn fourteen, I send them to board with local families in the community. I'm the only one here full-time, but the home is a community effort."

She led us into the family room, and we stood to the side, watching the children. There were about twenty in the room, all older children over the age of five or six.

"And all of them have missing parents?"

She nodded. "The Nebula Nomads have been abducting the young adults in the area, even the ones who have small children. It's such a tragedy. If we didn't take care of them, they'd just starve."

I noticed a boy of about eight or nine years old off to the side, playing by himself with a notebook and some pieces of loose paper covered with tables and lists.

I pointed to him. "Who's that?"

"That's Leo Finch. His parents went missing last month. Elara and Joshua Finch. Just up and gone one day. Leo came into town, found the Marshal, and said some armed maracs had shown up at their home in the middle of the night and taken his mom and dad away."

"Any siblings?"

"No, just him. An only child. He's had trouble integrating with the other kids."

"What's he doing?"

"You know, I haven't a clue. It's some kind of game he plays by himself. It keeps him occupied. I don't mind. He's quiet and well-behaved."

"Can I talk to him?" I asked.

"Sure. I'll be sending the kids off to get ready for bed in about half an hour, but go ahead until then."

Zeta floated to my side, observing the setting. Some of the kids were looking back at her.

I moved to a seat near Leo and asked, "Is it okay if I sit here?"

Leo looked up at me for a second, then back down at his papers and shrugged. "Sure."

The tables on the sheets of paper were covered with words and numerical values. The notepad had what looked like calculations on it. If it was a game, it was a really strange one.

"What are you playing?" I asked.

Leo sighed. "It's just something I made up."

"What's the goal?"

"You have to fight the Kergans and kill all the bad guys."

"So, it's like a strategy game?"

He nodded but didn't look up at me for a while. I sat there watching him.

Three girls had gathered their courage and approached Zeta. They were now in a conversation with the alien.

After a while, Leo looked up and said, "Who are you?"

"I'm Kory Drake. I'm in town visiting for a few days. Helping with the bandit problem."

"Are you, like, a policeman or something?"

I chuckled. "No, not at all. I'm sort of like a soldier."

"Cool. Have you killed any Kergans?"

I didn't think this was the sort of conversation Ana would want me to have with an eight-year-old, but I felt I should be honest.

"Yes, but I had to. They were trying to hurt me. I had to stop them."

Leo looked at me with a hurt expression. "I wish somebody had stopped the maracs who took Mom and Dad."

I didn't know what to say. Just like him, I wished someone hadn't taken my parents from me when I was just a toddler. They'd died in a car accident, but sometimes it felt like the universe had conspired against them, against me, to rip them away.

And if that wasn't enough, Ban'ach had stolen my last memories of them. Now, no matter how hard I tried, I couldn't recall what it felt like to be with them. I knew, intellectually, that they'd loved me, but knowing that and feeling it are two completely different things.

People forget that it's not enough in relationships to simply say you love someone—you have to make the other feel it. Saying the words without meaning or action behind them is like handing someone an empty gift box. It's the acts of love, even the smallest ones, that truly carry the weight of how much you care. And Ban'ach had robbed me of that. She hadn't just taken my memories—she'd stolen the emotional connection, the feeling of being loved, and left me with nothing but the cold, hollow box that once held those feelings.

I didn't want Leo to grow up without his parents. I didn't want *any* of these children to go through what I had. What the Nomads and the Kergans were doing in abducting people was pure evil that threatened to undermine not just our current generation but the future of humanity that was both symbolized and embodied by our children.

In that moment, I knew that going out and destroying Kergan shipping and killing Kergan soldiers was no longer sufficient. I needed to fix the damage that had been done. And I realized that I *could* fix it, at least a little, if I helped recover the parents of these children. Leo's parents. If my crew and I became the medium through which they were reunited.

It seems like such a small decision—this determination to repair the harm that had been done to myself and the children—but it altered the course of my life. Sitting in the playroom of that orphanage, watching Leo, and feeling my heart hurt, I transformed from a destroyer into a protector. That experience, sitting quietly watching Leo Finch and thinking about my goals in the war, ended up defining who I am today.

Urbana entered the room and announced it was time for the kids to prepare for bed.

There were lots of groaning complaints, but the kids were surprisingly cooperative.

Leo gathered his papers, stuffed them into his notebook, and left with only a glance in my direction.

I didn't mind.

I reminded myself of Leo's parents' names so I wouldn't forget them. Elara and Joshua Finch. I was going to bring them back to Leo. But first, I had to find them. Maybe O'hatet could help me with that.

I approached Urbana as she corralled the kids down a hallway. "Ana, thanks for letting us visit. Zeta and I will let ourselves out."

She patted me on the shoulder. "You're welcome, come and visit anytime."

"One thing. I heard that O'hatet was staying with you."

She nodded. "In the basement apartment. It's tiny, but

she doesn't seem to mind."

"Could I speak with her?"

"She's not in right now, but I'll let her know you stopped by. Is that okay?"

"Sure, absolutely." I walked away with a final wave of the hand and goodbye.

We let ourselves out the front door. As we walked up the road back toward the Marsden home, I couldn't stop thinking about how different I felt compared to when we'd arrived at the house. That need to protect these kids was pushing at me.

"You are thoughtful, Consort," Zeta said. "Zeta senses your emotions are in a tumult."

I remembered that Zeta could sense my feelings through our link, just as I could of hers. "Yes. I saw maybe a little too much of myself in that boy, Leo."

"You are planning something." She said it as a statement, not a question.

"I suppose so, Zeta. I feel like fighting the Kergans isn't enough. I want to repair what has been broken. Those kids represent humanity's future. And their parents have been stolen from them, just like I lost mine. It's wrong. I want to find the adults who've been abducted from Elkin and return them. I want to rescue them. Would the Dominion War Ministry allow us to do that? I know it's a lot to ask, to dedicate an entire warship to freeing some enslaved humans, but I feel like this is the right thing to do."

"Zeta does not know. She must confer with her superiors at the Ministry. But what you desire is not outside the realm of the possible."

"No? Truly?"

"The Dominion's goal is to impair the Kergan war efforts. If recovering these missing humans can somehow be shown to do that, then there is a good chance the Ministry will be supportive of your efforts."

"When can you ask?"

"Zeta will do so immediately, as soon as we return to our lodgings."

I hadn't a clue how Zeta communicated with her superiors. All I knew was that it was silent and appeared to be instantaneous.

"Zeta, how do you talk to them? I'm curious."

"Zeta's capsule contains a syderealdyne transceiver that communicates using waves of sydereal energy propagated through the Syderealium. It is a form of faster-than-light wireless communication."

"Is it fast?"

"Yes, sufficient for Zeta's needs. Both voice and data can be transferred at high rates."

"Does our base have one of these syderealdyne transceivers? In case my crew ever needs to communicate directly with the Ministry? In case something happens to you again?"

"No, you do not have one. It is a protected technology that you must earn. It would cost 900 tribute points to install one in the base."

"900?! You've got to be kidding me! For a stinking radio?"

"Zeta does not set the rules, Consort. The technology is considered sensitive, and therefore, it has a high cost. But you have Zeta in the meantime."

I blew out a forceful breath of air. "Yeah, and it's a good thing, too. I worry that we're too dependent on you. Don't get me wrong: I like you, Zeta. I'm glad we're consorts. But when you died and disappeared out in the desert, it left us nearly helpless."

"That is why Zeta was returned to you. Let this be a sign to you of how much the Dominion values your crew's efforts. They did not want to lose their investment of time and the access to a crew like you who has demonstrated a willingness to do their duty with bravery and imagination."

What she had just said made me feel better. Were we really that valuable to the Ministry? It was kind of sad, in a way. Thousands of humans had to be better qualified than me to captain a Dominion starship. But, as Zeta had admitted, she'd chosen me because I was flairsparked. Maybe that ability was the key, though I had yet to learn the full implications of what it meant to have this strange and mysterious talent.

# 19

Creeping toward the entrance of the Mineral Park Mine, the night air was as still as a sleeping baby. But my heart pounded in my chest, a steady rhythm that matched the silent march of our boots.

I could hear the shuffle of the posse behind me—Elkin's finest citizens, armed and ready, even if their hands trembled more than they should.

Ahead of us, Rowbottom's team had already fanned out, setting up positions along the ridges surrounding the Nomads' base.

We weren't here for a peaceful negotiation. This was a fight to the death, and we had all agreed—no prisoners.

I glanced at Destiny and Busto, both locked in focus.

Destiny had that dangerous glint in her eye, the one that always appeared when she was spoiling for a fight. Her fingers twitched near her holster like she couldn't wait to draw.

On the other hand, Busto was a wall of calm, rifle gripped tight, but his face unreadable. It was the kind of calm that said he'd seen worse than this—a kind of steady resolve that always made me feel like maybe, just maybe, we could actually pull this off.

Destiny caught my glance and smirked. "So, how many of Elkin's finest do you think are going to shoot themselves in the foot tonight? Because I'm betting at least two."

Rowbottom, overhearing, shot her a look, shaking his head. "Don't underestimate 'em, Austin. These folks may not look like much, but half of them are better shots than you'd think. I've seen some of those 'trembling hands' drop a deer from 200 yards easy. Give 'em a chance."

Destiny grinned, raising an eyebrow. "Well, I'll believe it when I see it. But I'm still keeping my toes out of their line of fire."

Rowbottom crouched next to me, his face a mask of grim determination, eyes constantly flicking to the horizon as if expecting something to go wrong any second. And honestly? So was I. Things were too quiet, and that kind of stillness before a fight always made my gut churn.

"Let's move," I whispered, hoping to shake off the creeping anxiety crawling up my spine.

The squad nodded, and we advanced toward the mine entrance, our footsteps barely audible over the suffocating silence.

The hum of a distant generator buzzed through the night air, almost mocking us with how oblivious the Nomads were to their impending doom. They had no idea what was coming. They didn't even deserve the warning.

"Take out the buildings," Rowbottom muttered into his comms, the tension evident in his voice.

In seconds, the first AT-4 rocket shot through the sky, lighting up the darkness like a sudden flash of lightning.

It slammed into the outer structure with a deafening

boom, sending shockwaves rippling through the ground.

Flames erupted, swallowing the building whole as debris scattered like deadly confetti.

Screams cut through the night, the sound of panic setting in as the Nomads scrambled.

And that's when the chaos truly erupted.

"Open fire!" Rowbottom barked, and we obeyed without hesitation.

Busto and Destiny unleashed hell on the soldiers rushing out from the burning structure, cutting them down without mercy.

I squeezed the trigger, watching as another Nomad collapsed under my shot, his body crumpling like a rag doll.

The air was thick with smoke, the crack of gunfire, and the panicked shouts of men who'd realized they were in a losing fight. It felt like being swallowed by a raging wildfire—fury and destruction spreading uncontrollably, consuming everything in its path, leaving no room for escape or mercy. The kind of scene that gets burned into your mind and makes it impossible to sleep for nights after.

"No prisoners," I reminded myself through gritted teeth as I sighted another target—a Nomad darting between two burning buildings, trying desperately to escape.

These people were slavers, monsters, the scum of the universe. They didn't deserve any mercy—none of them.

I fired, and the figure collapsed, lifeless.

We pressed on, moving through the chaos as explosions rocked the mine.

One building after another went up in flames, soldiers falling left and right as we advanced.

We were unstoppable, and the Nomads—unprepared and disorganized—had no way to fight back.

"Shuttle, dead ahead!" Busto's voice broke through the

chaos, and my heart skipped a beat as I spotted it.

A large, sleek shuttle sat nestled against the cliffs at the northeast corner of the mine, its engines powering up, the Nomads' last hope of escape. If Ban'ach got on that shuttle, we'd lose her again.

"Not this time," I muttered, watching as one of Rowbottom's scouts lined up a shot with the AT-4 rocket launcher.

There was a tense moment of silence, the kind that stretches just long enough to make you think everything's about to go wrong.

Then the rocket streaked through the air.

It slammed into the shuttle's engines with a tremendous explosion.

The flames shot up into the sky, and the ship buckled under the impact. The shuttle was done for, its escape plan literally going up in smoke.

I couldn't help the grin that spread across my face. Ban'ach wasn't going anywhere.

Or so I thought.

As we approached the main headquarters, gunfire still crackling around us, the door to the building slammed shut, and a series of clicks echoed through the metal walls. Ban'ach was in there, and she'd barricaded herself inside.

"I demand a parlay!" Her voice yelled from a window, sharp and unyielding. "Come any closer, and I'll blow myself and my guards up. I've rigged the entire building to explode."

I froze, anger flooding my chest.

The last thing I wanted was for Ban'ach to escape again, but I couldn't risk her blowing herself up, either. I needed her alive. I needed my memories back.

"She's bluffing," Destiny muttered, adjusting her grip on

her rifle. "We should just blow the door open and finish her off."

Zeta's voice, calm but firm, echoed in my ear. "Kory, it would be most perilous to permit a Soul Ravager such as Ban'ach to remain alive. She possesses far too much power, and her ilk are seldom, if ever, to be trusted. You must put an end to this now."

I clenched my fists, my mind racing.

Zeta was right. Ban'ach was dangerous—more dangerous than anyone else I'd faced. But she had information. Information about the Kergans, about her employer, and most importantly—about the memories she'd stolen from me.

"I'm not killing her," I said, my voice low but determined. "Not yet. I need her to tell us everything she knows."

"Kory, surely you cannot be in earnest," Zeta said, her voice calm but firm. "You are allowing sentiment to obscure your better judgment."

"Maybe I am," I shot back. "But I need the information she has, Zeta. And she's the only one who can help us."

There was a long pause. Even Destiny and Busto stayed silent, waiting for my decision.

"Very well," Zeta finally said, though I could hear the reluctance in her voice. "But do not say Zeta failed to caution you."

I turned back to the barricaded door. "Ban'ach! We'll let you and your guards live, but only if you tell us everything you know about your operation and employer."

"Agreed. We will exit momentarily," came the voice of the Nomads' boss.

While we waited, Batts' posse surrounded the building, sealing off all possible escape routes just in case Ban'ach tried to slip away.

I grew impatient.

"Ban'ach, come out *now*! Or we will blow the entire building up!"

I was about to signal our fighters to take cover when a *thud* sounded on top of the building and a piece of the roof flew off.

The thudding pulses of a Kergan starship drive started to knead my insides.

A sleek, tiny black shape rose from *inside* the building, pivoted, then accelerated away. It was the smallest Kergan starship I'd ever seen, smaller even than a blackhole.

"No!" I yelled, my hope escaping with the ship. "Storm the building, take them, now!"

I raced forward, my boots pounding against the ground.

The solid steel doors of the Nomads' headquarters loomed in front of us, locked tight.

Appleton moved quickly, planting the breaching charges before pushing us back.

She called out a brief countdown, and then the charge detonated, blowing the doors clean off their hinges in a deafening blast.

Rowbottom's team surged ahead, followed closely by my crew.

We swept through the building room by room, weapons raised, clearing each space.

Of the bandits, we found only three maracs and one human, all of whom surrendered without a fight. Ban'ach, however, was nowhere to be found. One of the maracs claimed she and her lieutenant had fled in the small ship.

I wanted to break something.

Ban'ach had slipped through our grip. Clearly, the large shuttle we'd destroyed had been a decoy. Or, at the least,

Ban'ach had had an escape ship hidden inside the headquarters building for just this type of contingency.

As we continued to clear the building, we stumbled upon two humans locked in filthy, cramped cells. They barely reacted to our presence, their eyes vacant and lifeless, bodies slumped against the walls.

They had no visible implants so that they couldn't have been mindjacked. But something was clearly very wrong. Had they been tortured?

In another part of the room, we found four coffin-sized pods. Each had a display panel, a user interface, and multiple jacks and ports attached.

Peering through the small windows on top, I saw that each pod contained a single human. They appeared asleep, but the technology surrounding them suggested something far more sinister.

"These are rigor pods," Zeta said, floating by my side, her tone measured. "Zeta has never encountered such devices before, though she is well-acquainted with the theory. It seems Ban'ach had intended to deliver these individuals to her principal."

"Can we help them?" I asked.

"Aye, lad, by nightfall, they shall be freed."

I turned my attention to the humans we had found in the cells. Even though we had freed them physically, their spirits seemed shattered. They barely acknowledged our presence, even when members of the posse—people they supposedly knew—tried to engage with them.

"Ah, this is more worrisome," Zeta said, gazing at the prisoners.

"What is it?"

"Can you reach into the Syderealium?"

"Like, right now?"

"Aye."

"I don't think so, not with all the chaos around."

"Very well. With time, you will learn to push away distractions. What Zeta wanted to show you can only be seen in the Syderealium. The two humans have had their glyphshades ravaged. No doubt by Ban'ach herself. Indeed, almost certainly by her, for this is the cruel handiwork of a Soul Ravager."

"What will happen to them?"

"Alas, they will most likely perish," Zeta replied solemnly. "Their physical forms remain intact, but they have been robbed of their will to live. Ban'ach has stolen that from them, as is her vile way."

"But...they haven't been here long. Can't we help them? Keep them alive?" I pressed, unwilling to accept that we had no options left.

"The citizens of Elkin may try to tend to their bodies, but it is doubtful they will succeed. Their consciousnesses have been all but obliterated. Zeta wonders why Ban'ach chose not to mindjack them outright. It seems she is embezzling her principal's resources to prey on human glyphshades for her own twisted gain."

I turned away from the sight of the hollow-eyed prisoners, frustration bubbling inside me like a pot on the verge of boiling over, its heat unchecked and ready to spill out, burning everything in its path.

Was this what we would find when we tracked down the rest of the missing humans? Hollow shells, minds erased, their souls consumed by monsters like Ban'ach?

"Busto, get these people out of here," I ordered, my voice tight. "Let's see if we can save the ones who still have a chance."

One man, barely conscious, muttered weakly as we

lifted him from his cell. He had been taken only the day before, and the ravaging seemed less severe. Perhaps he might recover. Perhaps he would be lucky.

Watching the broken humans shuffle out of the building, I couldn't help but think that this could have been me—if Zeta hadn't intervened if she hadn't pulled me from Ban'ach's clutches. I could have become a hollow husk, mind wiped clean, trapped in the darkness forever.

It should have felt like a victory. The Nebula Nomads were destroyed—dead, fled, or captured. Marshal Batts would arrange for transport back to California, and we could finally go home. But as I watched my crew securing the base and tending to the captives, all I could think about was the one who had escaped.

Ban'ach still had my memories. She still held that piece of me and believed she had won. But this wasn't over. Not by a long shot. Now, I had even more reason to hunt down Ban'ach's mysterious principal, for wherever I found them, I was sure I would find Ban'ach.

# 20

I sat next to Destiny in the cramped auditorium of the Elkin Community Center, which had been hastily converted into a courtroom.

The city council, looking about as qualified for this as I was for ballet, sat at the front like they'd been doing this their whole lives.

Marshal Batts played prosecutor, while the three maracs and one human of the Nebula Nomads we'd captured during the two assaults on their headquarters sat at the defense table.

"Ah, the esteemed judges," Destiny whispered, leaning close with a smirk. "Trained in the sacred art of town hall meetings and bake sale disagreements. I'm sure they'll handle this with all the finesse of a PTA debate."

I stifled a laugh.

She wasn't wrong. Elkin had been operating under martial law for months now, so serious criminal cases were being judged by the five-member city council—none of whom had any legal training, but boy, they did love their dramatic pauses. Let's just say if you wanted a fair trial, you'd better hope you hadn't annoyed them at last week's community potluck.

The defendants were charged with kidnapping, mayhem, and looting—your basic post-apocalyptic trifecta.

We'd been sitting in this stuffy room for three hours, suffering through the presentation of evidence and witness testimonies that seemed more repetitive than a bad country song.

The townspeople, packed in like sardines, weren't exactly a picture of patience. Every so often, the council chairman had to pause the proceedings to toss out some hothead who looked two seconds away from making this a public execution.

Closing arguments had come and gone, and now the judges had returned from their in-chambers conference, which was probably just them bickering over who got the last donut.

The whole room leaned forward, tension so thick it could choke you. The crowd wasn't just waiting for justice—they wanted blood and maybe a side of afternoon entertainment.

"Well, this should be good," Destiny muttered. "I bet Orozco's got a speech all lined up. Probably practiced in the mirror this morning."

I glanced at the city council chairman, Gil Orozco, who smacked his gavel with gusto, calling the room back to order. "The defendants will please rise," he said, his voice brimming with the kind of authority you only get from self-importance.

The maracs and the human at the defense table slowly rose from their chairs.

The maracs were impossible to read—tentacles

dangling, faces blank as ever.

But the human? He was an open book. Pale, sweating, but defiant, chin raised like he was still pretending this wasn't the end of the road. His eyes glared at the judges with all the pride of a man about to walk the plank.

"Leonidas Theodorou, Om'bel, En'ran, and O'arpol," Orozco began, naming the defendants before the council. "We, the Elkin City Council, acting as judges pursuant to the Elkin Marshal Law Ordinance, having heard the evidence, witness testimonies, and the arguments of counsel, have reached a solemn verdict regarding the grave charges brought against you.

"On the counts of kidnapping, mayhem, and looting, this council finds all four of you guilty beyond a reasonable doubt. These crimes are not mere offenses against individuals but violations of the very sanctity of life and liberty. They are affronts to the fundamental principles of our legal and moral order and pose a direct threat to the safety and stability of this town, particularly in these tumultuous times.

"In accordance with the laws governing martial rule, and in light of the limited resources available to render a more humane form of punishment, we, the judges, after careful deliberation, sentence you to death by firing squad—this being the only practical and fitting penalty for crimes of such heinous magnitude. This sentence shall be carried out immediately.

"It is not issued lightly, but with full consideration of the circumstances under which we live and the urgent necessity for deterrence. The law must be upheld without compromise, and those who violate it must face the most severe consequences.

"Let this sentence stand as both a measure of justice for the victims and a stark warning to others who might contemplate similar transgressions: this community will not tolerate lawlessness.

"May justice be served, and may order be restored.

"Marshal Batts, the condemned are remanded into your custody for carrying out their sentences." Orozco smacked his gavel. "This court is adjourned."

The improvised courtroom erupted into a cacophony of cheers, the sound reverberating off the walls like a storm breaking over the room.

Laughter and applause mixed with the quiet sobs of those who had suffered the most. For many victims and their families, it was a bittersweet relief—justice had been served, but their wounds still ran deep.

Tears streamed down faces as some clutched one another, finding a small, fragile sense of closure amidst the chaos.

Yet, for others, the hollow absence of their abducted loved ones loomed large. The verdict did nothing to bring them back, leaving an unspoken grief lingering in the air, an emptiness no court ruling could ever fill.

I felt that new pull, that need to fill the void—to find their loved ones and bring them back.

I hadn't talked to Destiny or Busto about my plans yet, mainly because I had no idea how to approach them. Let's face it: opening up about feelings was not exactly my strong suit—on a good day, I was about as emotionally available as a brick wall. And losing the memories of my parents had been no improvement. But I knew I'd have to bring it up soon.

The condemned were executed at an abandoned rock quarry just outside town.

I won't describe it in detail—there's nothing glorious or satisfying about it. Executing a sentient being, even one who's been lawfully condemned, leaves a weight in the air, a heaviness that clings to you long after the last shot is fired.

There's something about killing an unarmed, bound person that sits wrong, no matter what they've done. It feels unnatural.

As the final echoes of the shots faded, I couldn't help but wonder how the Kergan Military Authority would react when they found out what we'd done to these marac bandits—citizens of the Kergan Empire.

# 21

My crew and I sat at a long table in the dimly lit Tumbleweed Tavern, picking at dinner after the grim events of the day.

The trial and execution had left me without much of an appetite, but I forced myself to eat. Even Zeta was present, her floating form silently observing. Though she didn't eat like us humans—at least not in any way I'd seen—she seemed to enjoy the social atmosphere.

This seemed as good a time as any to bring up what I'd been thinking. I'd already mentioned it to Zeta, but Destiny and Busto needed to hear it, too.

"I've got something to run by you all," I began, stabbing a piece of steak with my fork.

"No, I'm not giving you any more gold chips," Destiny said without missing a beat, her mouth full.

I sighed. "Let me remind you that I've been the one keeping our tab current with Stafford. And, no, this isn't about money."

I took a deep breath. "I've been doing some thinking

about the missions we've been running with *Thunder*. So far, it's all been about hurting the Kergans, destroying their ability to wage war—freighters, the command nexus in Montana, all that."

"We've killed dozens of Kergans, probably more," Destiny said. "And we've cost them a small fortune. I'd say we're doing pretty good."

"Don't forget the frigate we shot down," Busto added with a grin. "Whiskey-One. That felt like a win."

"I haven't forgotten," I said. "We've done good. We've earned the right to rebuild *Thunder* as a corvette, right Zeta?"

"Indeed," Zeta replied in her measured, formal tone. "Your crew was awarded 330 tribute points for destroying that vessel. You possess ample points to upgrade *Thunder*'s hull."

I nodded. "Great. So, here's the thing—I want us to be more than just destroyers. I want us to become protectors."

Destiny frowned at me like I'd grown a second head. "Kory, you do realize the two don't exactly go hand-in-hand, right? Sometimes you've gotta break stuff down before you can build anything worth saving."

"I know," I said, holding up my hands. "But I'm talking about more than just smashing stuff up. We've hurt the Kergans—no doubt about that—but look around you. This town is barely holding itself together. Wolf Jaw's no better. Why not help rebuild?"

"Rebuild? What are we, a construction crew now?" Destiny asked, her confusion clear. "There's not much point when the galaxy's on fire."

"I'm not talking about grabbing shovels and bricks, Dest. I mean, we could make a difference by helping people here. Rescue the ones who were abducted."

She crossed her arms and leaned back in her chair,

clearly bracing for a debate. "Look, I get it. You want to help people. Who wouldn't? But the thing is, we're not exactly the cavalry here. We barely keep ourselves alive on a good day, let alone saving half the planet. You think the Kergans are just gonna roll over and let us play heroes? We're small-time, Kory. We're outgunned, outmanned, and unless Zeta's hiding a magic wand somewhere, we're out of resources."

Her voice softened a little, but the frustration was still there. "We've been surviving by the skin of our teeth. You think turning us into rescue rangers is gonna magically make things better? We can't fix everything. Heck, we can't even find our own families, and now you want us to save a bunch of strangers? That's not how this works."

She looked away, shaking her head. "Survival's already hard enough. If we start spreading ourselves thin, trying to be some kind of intergalactic knights in shining armor, we're just gonna get ourselves killed. And I, for one, don't want to go down because we bit off more than we can chew."

Busto, who'd been quiet up until now, finally spoke up. He leaned forward, resting his elbows on the table and locking eyes with Destiny. "Dest, Kory's got a point. We've been hitting Kergans hard, yeah, but what's it for? Sure, we've taken out a lot of their assets, but what are we building? When this is all said and done, what's left? Just a bunch of debris?"

Destiny scowled, but Busto pressed on. "We've survived, sure, but if we're not aiming for something bigger, then what are we doing out here? Kory's talking about giving people a shot. I know it sounds like a stretch, but we've got a ship, we've got skills, and we've got firepower. We're not a one-trick pony. Hell, we already took down a Kergan frigate and cleared out the Nomads. You think helping out the people of Elkin is any crazier than that?"

Destiny opened her mouth, but Busto wasn't done.

"Look, I get it—survival's tough. But at some point, we've got to stop just surviving and start living. If we can make a difference, why not try? Who knows, maybe taking out these Kergan supply lines and saving people makes us even more dangerous to them. We can hurt 'em in ways they don't see coming."

"Geesh," Destiny said, "my head's hurting, and you haven't even given me the details yet."

"I want us to try and rescue Elkin's abducted humans," I said softly so that other customers wouldn't overhear. "If you want the details, then fill in the blanks."

My friends were quiet for a while.

"That's ambitious," Busto said, leaning back, his brow furrowing. "But we don't even know where they are."

I leaned forward, my voice dropping. "But we do have leads. Om'bel, during that interrogation, mentioned Luna. The abducted people are on the Moon."

Destiny rolled her eyes. "The Moon, sure. And how exactly do you plan on getting them back? Even with *Thunder* upgraded, we're talking about dozens of people, at least, who need to be rescued. How're we transporting them all?"

I ran a hand through my hair. "We'll figure it out."

Busto's face lit up with an idea. "We could capture a Kergan freighter. Board it, take the crew out, and use their ship to haul the humans back."

Destiny crossed her arms. "That sounds reckless."

"Risky, sure," Busto admitted. "But we've pulled off crazier stunts."

"And that's why I want Rowbottom and his team to join us," I said. "We need more people. We can't run *Thunder* with just the four of us anymore. We'll need a bigger crew—two watches, maybe more."

Destiny snorted. "You think Gunny's gonna want to

work side-by-side with Army scouts? You know how Marines are."

Busto waved her off. "Hey, I can tolerate them. They're not completely useless."

Before we could get into more banter, Rowbottom and his team walked in. Vila and Montana spotted us immediately and sauntered over, grinning like they'd just won a bet.

"Well, look who decided to show up," Vila said, clapping me on the shoulder. "What's the plan now, Drake? Another half-cocked mission to get us all killed?"

"At least we don't need a whole platoon to hold our hand," Busto shot back. "How many Army scouts does it take to screw in a lightbulb again?"

Montana smirked. "Says the guy whose last 'strategic' plan was flipping a coin. I'm surprised you all aren't still stuck in a ditch somewhere."

"Careful, Montana," Destiny chimed in, smirking. "Wouldn't want to scuff up those shiny boots of yours. Gotta look good, right?"

Rowbottom raised an eyebrow. "You know, Austin, maybe if you learned some actual tactics instead of shooting first and figuring out where you are later, you'd still be alive when the job's done."

I couldn't help but laugh, shaking my head. "Okay, okay, enough. We're all on the same side here."

"Are we now?" Vila said, arms crossed but a grin tugging at his lips. "You gonna fill us in on this big plan of yours, Drake?"

I leaned forward. "Actually, yes. How would you and your team like to join us in Wolf Jaw? Be part of the crew of *Thunder*?"

Rowbottom blinked, momentarily stunned. "You

mean...with your outfit? On your ship?"

"Yes. As captain, I'm formally inviting you."

Rowbottom looked around at his team. Vila was nodding, Montana was eyeing me like I'd just challenged her, and Appleton seemed eager as ever.

"Well," Rowbottom said, leaning back in his chair. "This just got interesting."

Rowbottom took a long look around the table, his hand still resting on the back of his chair. "You're serious, Drake? You want us to sign up for your crew?"

"Dead serious," I said. "Your team is exactly what we need. I've seen how you operate. *Thunder*'s getting an upgrade, and we need more hands to run her. Plus, with the kind of work we've been doing, we could use more muscle."

Vila smirked, leaning on the back of his chair. "More muscle, huh? Well, I guess you finally realized the real brains of this operation aren't space jockeys after all."

Busto rolled his eyes, half-smiling. "Brains or brawn, you'd still need us to keep you grounded. Or else you'd be tangled up in your own map before breakfast."

Montana chimed in, her voice low but steady. "Look, Drake, we've been in plenty of ops together. But it's one thing to tag along on a mission—it's another to join a full-blown insurgency."

I nodded, meeting her sharp gaze. "True. This is a big step. But you've seen what the Kergan have done to Elkin. You've seen what they're doing to our people. We're not just fighting for survival anymore—we're fighting to take something back."

Rowbottom glanced at his team. "So, this gig, what's the real upside? Are you offering us a permanent place on *Thunder*, or is this a temporary thing until the next crisis blows over?"

"We need a long-term crew," I said. "The ship's getting bigger, and with Zeta's upgrades, we're planning to make a real dent in the Kergans' operations. Plus, we'll need to train for more specialized missions. Rescues, infiltration, maybe even a few boarding operations."

Vila raised an eyebrow. "Boarding operations? As in capturing Kergan ships?"

I grinned. "That's the idea."

"Well, count me in," Vila said, slapping the table. "About time we hit them where it hurts."

Montana wasn't so quick to agree. "And if we do get in too deep? What's the fallback?"

"We won't be alone," I said. "The Collective Dominion backs us up. They've got their own reasons for wanting to see the Kergans weakened. But more importantly, we've got each other. That's our fallback."

Rowbottom exchanged glances with his team and then turned back to me. "Okay, Drake. We're in. But if you get us all killed on some suicide mission, I'll haunt you."

Busto snorted. "Too bad ghosts aren't welcome on *Thunder*."

Destiny grinned. "Unless you come back to fix our broken coffee machine. Then you might have a shot."

Rowbottom laughed, finally relaxing into his chair. "Alright, cosmo-cowboys, let's see if this ship's really worth all the hype."

## 22

"I've got the vehicles, but only about five gallons of gasoline," Marshal Batts said, his tone apologetic as he leaned back in his creaky office chair, arms folded across his chest. The man looked like he'd rather be delivering better news.

I waved it off, trying to reassure him. "Don't worry about the fuel. We've got that covered."

Batts raised an eyebrow, clearly surprised. "Really? How're you pulling that off?"

"Zeta's got a nanoforge. It can produce small quantities of fuel. Should be enough to keep two vehicles supplied for the trip there and back."

Batts sat up straighter, the relief palpable on his face. "Well, I'll be damned. That's a hell of a trick. Alright, in that case, all I need is to round up a couple more folks to act as drivers and guards."

"How big are the vehicles?" I asked, already picturing how we'd fit everyone.

"We've got a Suburban and a Ford Expedition. Can fit

about eight adults in each, plenty of space for your crew," Batts replied. Then his expression shifted, a frown tugging at the corner of his mouth. "Though I heard Rowbottom's team is heading out with you?"

I nodded. "Yeah, they're coming back with us to Wolf Jaw."

He sighed, shaking his head. "Shoot, that's too bad. They've been a big help around here. I hate to lose them, but I get it. You've got a bigger fight to deal with, and they're good soldiers. Elkin'll miss them, though."

"Believe me, I'd keep them here if I could," I said with a small smile. "But yeah, we need all the help we can get for what's coming. Don't worry, though—the vehicles should be big enough for all of us, even if it's a little crowded."

Batts nodded, though I could see the reluctance in his eyes. "Alright. Probably tomorrow, then. I'll let you know as soon as I've got the drivers lined up."

With that settled, I left Batts' office and made my way down two streets over to Urbana's place. Next up on my list was O'hatet.

Since we'd finished off the last of the Nebula Nomads, the town had been buzzing with life again. People were out on the streets, walking with a little more purpose, a little more hope.

Ahead of me, I spotted Martha Marsden with Hattie and Graham in tow. The kids were hauling sacks of groceries while Martha checked something off her list.

I watched them head into the hardware store without even seeing me.

Those kids were lucky. Damn lucky to still have their parents.

Of course, I was glad we rescued them—who wouldn't be?—but I'd be lying if I said I didn't feel that familiar sting in my chest every time I saw a family like that. Not at them, not at all. Just at the universe for not cutting me the same deal. I'd lost my parents before I was old enough to understand what that even meant, and Ban'ach had stolen the last memories I had of them. Now, I was left with nothing but fragments, like trying to recall a dream that slips away the more you try to grab it.

I'd like to think I was going after the abducted humans purely out of the goodness of my heart, but let's be real: I had my own selfish reasons, too. Following Ban'ach's trail wasn't just about justice—it was personal. I wanted my memories back. I wanted to trap her, make her pay, and steal back what was mine.

Until then, every time I saw a kid with their parents, it was like something inside me was pulling apart at the seams.

When I arrived at the Urbana home, I was relieved to find O'hatet in her basement apartment.

"Kory Drake!" she exclaimed, her enthusiasm palpable as she floated toward me, a sheaf of papers waving in one of her tentacles. "Just the person I was about to seek out. I have news!"

I smiled at her excitement. "May I come in?"

"Of course, of course!" She waved her multitude of arms in a sweeping gesture. "Do come in!"

O'hatet moved aside, allowing me to enter.

Her apartment was spartan, with the bare essentials: a small bed, a kitchenette, and a bathroom tucked into the corner.

The room was freezing, the air conditioner blasting at full capacity. I figured maracs must prefer it this way.

I gingerly lowered myself onto an ancient wooden chair that protested under my weight but—thankfully—didn't collapse.

"We'll be leaving town tomorrow, most likely," I said, getting straight to business. "I was hoping you had more information before we go."

"Excellent timing," O'hatet said, her large eyes gleaming. "I've uncovered some crucial details."

"Well, don't keep me in suspense. Let's hear it."

She leaned forward, her voice lowering conspiratorially. "I know who the principal is. And I know where the abducted humans have been taken."

My heart skipped a beat. "It's the Kergan government, right? They're using the Nomads as a front?"

She shook her head. "No, not at all. The principal is actually a large Kergan mining conglomerate—Imperial Mineral Holdings."

I blinked, taken aback. "A corporation? They're behind the kidnappings?"

"Yes," she said, "IMH hired the Nomads to gather humans with experience in mining. They needed them for their operations."

"And where are they being held?" I asked, leaning forward in my seat.

"They've been taken to a Helium-3 mining facility inside Lindblad F, which is a crater on the far side of the Moon."

My eyebrows shot up. "How did you get your hands on this information?"

"I penetrated IMH's internal network," she replied matter-of-factly.

"Was that difficult?" I asked, surprised by how casually she mentioned it.

"For me? Not particularly. I used a bit of social engineering on an unsuspecting IMH engineer and gained access through a backdoor."

I couldn't hide my surprise. O'hatet was sounding more like a seasoned hacker than a journalist. Then again, cracking information systems might be just the tool a good reporter needed in a galaxy like ours.

"This is excellent news," I said, the weight of her discovery sinking in. "We finally have a lead—a starting point."

"I'm glad you think so," she said. "But there's more you need to know...and something I need in return."

I frowned, suspicion creeping in. "What are you asking for?"

Her tentacles shifted, and she fixed me with a serious gaze. "I want to join your crew. To live among you, observe your activities, and report on your insurgency. And perhaps...I could assist you in other ways."

Her request blindsided me. "O'hatet, you do realize how dangerous it is? I can't guarantee your safety."

"I am aware, Kory Drake," she said, her tone calm but resolute. "But I do not expect you to be responsible for my wellbeing."

I hesitated. "I'm not even sure we can support a marac at our base. What would you eat? We're not exactly stocked with marac-friendly supplies."

She waved a tentacle dismissively. "Do not worry yourself over that. This device"—she gestured to a small metal box near her bed—"converts human food into something I can consume. Along with my supplements, I'll be self-sufficient for quite some time. Water and your normal food are all I require. And somewhere to sleep."

I sighed, the thought of having a civilian underfoot—especially one who wasn't human—filling me with doubts. "I'll agree tentatively. But the Collective Dominion has final say. If their War Ministry approves, then you're in." I didn't know how the ignas would feel about a marac living amongst us. Even a friendly one. "Is that good enough for now?"

"It is," she said, nodding.

"Alright then," I said. "Now tell me—what's so important that you needed to make this deal?"

She leaned in. "I intercepted a document on the IMH network that I'm not sure even the engineer was supposed to know about. It references something called 'Project Silver Tangle,' being conducted at the same lunar facility where the abducted humans are enslaved."

"Silver Tangle?" I asked. "What's that?"

She clicked her beak thoughtfully. "It seems to be connected to the discovery of an artifact in an underground vault. The document refers to this artifact as the 'Astral Maul,' and if I'm correct, it's of Primordian origin."

I furrowed my brow. "The Primo-what?"

"Primordians," she clarified. "An ancient alien race that went extinct millions of years ago. They left behind powerful artifacts scattered across this region of the galaxy. Most of these artifacts are dead, but some still function— and they can be extremely dangerous."

"Great," I muttered. "Just what we need—an ancient doomsday device."

Her eyes gleamed with curiosity. "This Astral Maul may be partially functional. IMH scientists are attempting to reactivate it."

"Any idea how dangerous it is?"

"I don't know," she admitted. "But that's why I want to come with you. There's a story here, Kory Drake. A story I need to uncover."

"And you're hoping to play a part," I said, smirking.

"Precisely," she said, tentacles flexing with resolve. "I

want to know what IMH is doing with this artifact and why they're using human slaves."

I rubbed my chin, mulling it over. "If this Astral Maul turns out to be dangerous, we may have to call in the Collective Dominion. But we'll cross that bridge when we get to it."

She smiled—well, as much as a marac could imitate a smile. "Then it's settled. I'll prepare to leave with you tomorrow."

As I stood to leave, a sense of the mission's gravity crept up, but I couldn't help rolling my eyes. The Astral Maul? Really? It sounded like something you'd find in an over-the-top alien movie, but no—here it was, potentially real and tossed right into our lap. Ancient alien artifacts with apocalyptic vibes always show up at the worst possible time. I could practically hear the universe laughing at me as if it had gotten bored and decided to turn our rescue mission into some high-stakes cosmic game show.

And then, of course, the humans. What were they doing tied up in this mess? Just innocent bystanders doing forced labor? Or, knowing our luck, something much darker? My money was on darker. Because apparently, simple isn't a word the universe understands. Instead, it throws ancient death traps and enslaved miners at us like it's trying to spice up our already impossible mission.

# 23

I caught up with my crew back at the Marsdens' hayloft.

Busto was hanging the last of the wash up to dry, his movements calm and methodical, while Destiny lay sprawled on her sleeping bag, snoring lightly.

Zeta hovered in the corner by the open hay chute, not exactly standing guard, but her presence always felt like she was observing something, even if I couldn't guess what.

Busto noticed me first. "Hey, boss. Martha was just over here. The town's throwing a banquet tonight to celebrate the victory over the Nomads. We're the guests of honor."

Destiny's eyes fluttered open, and she sat up, blinking the sleep away. "A banquet, huh? Perfect. Nothing says 'job well done' like awkward small talk over mystery meat and pretending we don't all smell like we've been rolling in hay for days." She stretched and added with a smirk, "Think they'll notice if I nap through the speeches?"

I chuckled. "You'll have to stay awake for at least part of it. They'll expect us to make some kind of speech."

"It's happening at seven at the Community Center."

Busto flipped a wet shirt in the air and clipped it to the clothesline. "How'd it go with Batts?"

"Good enough. We're set to leave tomorrow if he can get drivers and guards together." I hesitated a moment before continuing. "I also stopped by to chat with O'hatet."

Busto gave me a sideways look, his arms folding across his chest. "What happened?"

I filled them in on O'hatet's intel about the Astral Maul and her request to join us on our journey back to Wolf Jaw.

Destiny groaned. "Great, another hitchhiker. Just what we needed."

"She's more than that," I said. "She's got skills. Look at everything she's uncovered about the Nomads' employer. She could be key to figuring out what this Astral Maul really is." I turned to Zeta. "Can you get permission from your superiors to let O'hatet embed with us?"

"Zeta shall submit the request immediately, though she suspects the Ministry of War will leave the decision in your capable hands, Consort," Zeta said in her usual Victorian tone. "But Zeta will attend to it promptly."

Destiny raised an eyebrow. "What's the deal with this Astral Maul anyway? I mean, just what we needed—an ancient, probably super-dangerous Kergan project. Because, you know, life wasn't already insane enough."

"That's why O'hatet's coming with us," I said. "She's our key to unlocking more information about this thing before we dive headfirst into a rescue mission."

Busto went back to the laundry, shaking his head. "Yeah, great, just another mission we're woefully underprepared for. I love those."

We fell into our tasks. Destiny began cleaning her protomatter suit, muttering under her breath about the banquets being another excuse for "polite torture," while I inspected our firearms and Busto made sure we'd have enough supplies for the trip.

A while later, Zeta floated over. "General Pilli has granted O'hatet permission to join our crew, provided that any reports she publishes about our operations be reviewed by his staff beforehand. This is the sole condition."

I nodded. "That's fair. I'll make sure she understands the terms."

Destiny grinned. "Yeah, because after everything we've been through, a little red tape is what's going to stop us."

Zeta drifted closer to me. "Consort, it is time for your training."

I glanced at the gear still scattered around, but I knew Zeta was right. Ban'ach wasn't going to take it easy on me, and I had to be ready when we crossed paths again. "Alright, let's do it."

The next few hours were spent deep in meditation, practicing my ability to enter and exit the Syderealium. Zeta guided me through the intricacies of the Three Laws: Connection, Dominance, and Conduct.

The Law of Connection was clear—every glyphshade, living or dead, was connected by energlyphs. These energlyphs made up a being's willpower, vitality, and experiences. While living beings' glyphshades were tethered to their bodies, those who had died were free to roam the Syderealium.

The Law of Dominance was a warning. Some parts of the Syderealium were ruled by Astral Titans—beings so old and powerful they made Soul Ravagers like Ban'ach seem like nuisances in comparison.

And the Law of Conduct? It dictated balance. The Syderealium wasn't a place for senseless attacks. Beings who preyed on others risked retribution. Soul Ravagers like

Ban'ach violated this law, and it made me wonder how long she could get away with it before someone—or something—bigger came knocking.

A chill ran down my spine as I thought back to the Astral Maul. Its name, its very existence, felt like it was tied to these laws in ways we didn't yet understand.

Destiny would say I was overthinking it, but I couldn't shake the feeling that we were walking into something far more dangerous than a simple rescue mission.

# 24

The Elkin Community Center, which had survived all kinds of events—from awkward middle school dances to local town hall meetings—was packed to the rafters tonight.

The usual dust and dim lighting were drowned out by the warm glow of lanterns, and the tables that once held bake-sale pies were now laden with platters of roasted meats, fresh vegetables, and bread that filled the room with a mouthwatering aroma.

Elkin's citizens had come together, pulling out all the stops to give us a proper send-off, and it showed.

Chairman Gil Orozco stood at the front of the room, his ever-serious face softened by the warmth of the occasion. His salt-and-pepper beard looked freshly trimmed, and his clothes—though simple—were clean and pressed.

He raised his glass, calling for silence. The room quickly fell into a quiet hum as all eyes turned toward him.

"Ladies and gentlemen of Elkin," Orozco began, his voice deep and steady, the weight of leadership clear in every word. "Tonight, we gather to celebrate a victory hard-won by the people in this room—citizens, fighters, and friends who came together when the darkness of the Nebula Nomads threatened our homes, our lives, and our very future."

The crowd murmured in agreement, a few heads nodding.

Orozco paused, scanning the faces of the people in the room—his people, I realized. He carried the town's burdens on his shoulders every day, and tonight, that weight seemed a little lighter.

"I'd like to start by thanking our defenders—both those who live here and those who came from afar to stand with us. The crew of the starship *Thunder* and our own brave Army scouts, who fought alongside us with courage and resolve." He turned toward our table, gesturing with his glass. "Without you, we might not be standing here today."

The townsfolk burst into applause, and I could feel their gratitude swelling in the room. It wasn't the polite clapping you hear at a speech, but genuine, heartfelt appreciation—the kind that made your chest tighten up and your throat a little dry.

Busto leaned over and whispered, "Careful, Captain, they're going to name a pie after you at this rate."

I rolled my eyes. "As long as they don't put me in charge of baking it."

Orozco raised his hand for silence again, and the crowd quieted. "Now, there's still much work to be done. The Kergan invaders are far from defeated. But tonight, we celebrate what we've accomplished—how far we've come—and we give thanks for the bravery of those who fought to protect us. So, to Captain Kory Drake, to his crew, and to Staff Sergeant Rowbottom and his scouts, we say thank you."

He lifted his glass higher, and the crowd followed suit, toasting with an enthusiasm that felt as much like relief as it did celebration.

"And now," Orozco added, his tone lightening, "I believe Captain Drake has a few words for us."

I froze for half a second—of course they were going to make me give a speech. I should've seen it coming. Destiny elbowed me with a grin.

"Better make it good, Kory," she teased. "Try not to mention how we almost got blown up five times. You know, keep it positive."

I stood, pushing my chair back, and gave her a look. "I'll do my best," I said, trying to suppress the smile tugging at the corner of my mouth. As I rose to my feet, the room fell silent again, all eyes on me.

I cleared my throat. "First of all, thank you, Chairman Orozco, and thank you, people of Elkin, for putting on this amazing feast." I waved a hand toward the tables piled high with food. "You've outdone yourselves."

A ripple of laughter spread through the crowd, some folks raising their mugs in appreciation.

"I've been thinking about what to say tonight," I continued, glancing around the room. "And honestly, I keep coming back to one thing: how lucky we are to have found a place like this. Elkin isn't just a town—it's a community. You welcomed us when you didn't have to, you fought with us when it would've been easier to hide, and you've shown us what it means to be brave in the face of impossible odds. I can't say enough about your hospitality, your courage, and your resourcefulness."

I paused, feeling the weight of my next words. "But as Chairman Orozco said, the fight isn't over. The Kergans are still out there, and they aren't going to stop. Not until we stop them. So, my advice to you, Elkin? Keep resisting. Keep standing up for yourselves and for each other. And know this—we won't forget about the people the Kergans have taken. I promise you, we're not done yet."

I gave them a nod and sat back down, grateful the speech was over. The applause that followed was loud and genuine, and I could feel the sense of solidarity in the room. These people weren't just surviving anymore—they were ready to fight for their future.

As I took my seat, Busto grinned and clapped me on the shoulder. "Not bad, Captain. Got a little teary-eyed there for a second. Almost thought you were gonna hug somebody."

"Don't push your luck," I said with a smirk.

Destiny was shaking her head, laughing. "You're all heart, Kory. We should've had Zeta give the speech. She could've bored them into submission with her 'elegant phrasing.'"

Sitting at the end of the table, Zeta looked up from her meticulous arrangement of silverware. "Zeta believes her eloquence is underappreciated, Miss Austin. But Zeta is content to allow Captain Drake the spotlight this evening." She tilted her capsule ever so slightly as if bestowing some ancient wisdom upon us. "Zeta finds that speaking with grace and refinement is often wasted on audiences that prefer...bluntness."

"Yeah, well, bluntness gets the job done," Destiny shot back, eyes twinkling. "And I've seen you in a fight, Zeta—you're not exactly subtle when the lasers start flying."

"Ah," Zeta replied smoothly, "but one must always maintain dignity, even in battle. Zeta believes that there is honor in how one conducts oneself, no matter the circumstances."

Rowbottom, seated across from us, shook his head with

a grin. "Well, that's one way to look at it. But me? I prefer to just win."

Montana, who had been quietly sipping her drink, leaned in with a smirk. "I don't know, Rowbottom. I've seen you trip over your own rifle before. Dignity's a stretch."

Vila chimed in, nudging Rowbottom. "Hey, it's not his fault! Army scouts can't help it—they don't teach coordination at boot camp."

Busto chuckled. "No kidding. I've seen better footwork from drunk chickens."

The table burst into laughter, and for a moment, it was easy to forget that we'd just come out of a battle—or that more fights were waiting for us.

As the night wore on, people started coming by the table to say their goodbyes, shaking hands and offering their thanks. Each time, I felt a tug of guilt—like we were leaving unfinished business behind. There were still people out there who needed saving. There were still battles to fight.

I caught a glimpse of Martha Marsden in the crowd, holding her two kids close. Hattie and Graham. We'd saved them. But how many others were still out there, waiting for someone to show up and rescue them?

By the time the banquet wound down and the people of Elkin had said their final goodbyes, I felt a strange mix of pride and restlessness. We'd done good here—there was no denying that. But Ban'ach was still out there. The abducted humans were still waiting.

As we walked out into the cool night air, Destiny stretched and cracked her neck. "Well, Kory, we survived another one. What's next? We overthrowing an empire before breakfast?"

I smiled, but there was a seriousness beneath it.

"Something like that."

Busto fell in step beside me, his jacket slung casually over his shoulder. "I'm with you, boss. Just say the word."

I looked around at my crew—Destiny, Busto, Zeta, and the scouts who had agreed to come back to Wolf Jaw with us. "We've got a lot of work to do," I said quietly. "But we're not doing it alone."

And as we headed back to our temporary quarters for the night, I couldn't help but feel that this was only the beginning. The Kergans didn't know it yet, but they had a fight coming. And we weren't going to stop until we brought everyone home.

# 25

We left Elkin just as the sun was rising, our two SUVs packed with the newly expanded crew.

There were thirteen of us now—nine from my team, including O'hatet, and four from Elkin, including Marshal Batts and his men as drivers and guards.

Zeta had used her nanoforge to produce an extra twenty gallons of gasoline, which we strapped to the roof, unsure if we'd find fuel along the way. Five hundred miles to Wolf Jaw stretched out ahead of us, most of it through desert and rough terrain, and I wasn't in the mood for any surprises.

Fortunately, the journey was uneventful—if you don't count Bakersfield and Fresno, which both felt like they'd been designed by a drunk maze-builder with a grudge against anyone trying to get anywhere on time.

Roadblocks forced us to take the scenic route, or as I like to call it, "the long way around because the universe thinks I need more patience." At least we didn't run into bandits. Small miracles, right?

The miles blurred together, and by the time we hit the

snow-covered Sierra Nevada, the familiar sight of Wolf Jaw Valley spread out below us.

Two weeks ago, we'd crash-landed *Thunder* in the Arizona desert like a bunch of amateurs. Now, by some miracle, we were finally home—probably smelling worse than the last time we left.

As we approached the southern checkpoint, there was old Archibald Andrews, the same town guard from when we first arrived.

He eyed us with suspicion, his rifle slung over his shoulder as he squinted at our convoy.

Sitting in the front passenger seat, I rolled down my window as Batts pulled up to the gate.

Andrews spotted me, and his scowl melted into a grin. "Well, dog on it! If it isn't Kory Drake!"

I laughed, leaning out the window. "Good to see you too, Andrews."

"Hell, we thought you were gone for good! Last we saw, you were chasing that Kergan warship. What happened to you?"

"Long story," I said, pointing over to Batts. "This here is Marshal Batts from Elkin, Arizona. His people were kind enough to give us a lift back home."

Batts nodded, all humble-like. "They helped us out down in Arizona. It's only right we returned the favor."

Andrews raised an eyebrow as if remembering something. "So, where's your spaceship? Thought you were running some big operation."

The secret of *Thunder* had clearly gotten out—though it wasn't like we'd been subtle, flying a starship over town and firing on a Kergan frigate. "*Thunder*'s down," I admitted. "Crashed in Arizona, but we'll rebuild her."

"Well, I reckon everyone in town knows about it now,"

Andrews said, grinning. "You kind of gave yourselves away with that whole 'shooting Kergan ships out of the sky' thing. Half the town was watching."

I chuckled. "Yeah, subtlety isn't our strong suit."

Andrews' eyes flicked over to the convoy. "I see Austin and Busto there, but who're the rest of these folks?"

"Batts' people, mostly. The others are recruits from Arizona. We'll be staying at the base."

Andrews shook his head. "No problem letting you pass. You boys saved this town from being obliterated. Just make sure you register those new folks with Mayor Best when you get a chance."

"Will do. Thanks, Andrews."

As we drove through the gate, the road narrowed, and soon, the refugee camps lining the outskirts of town came into view. Batts whistled low. "How many people you got in here?"

"Thousands," I replied. "Most of them fleeing from Kergan forces or local bandits. It's been like this for a while."

As we continued, the scars from the Kergan attack became evident.

We passed charred homes, the hydroelectric plant in ruins, and the town's only grocery store, Best One Stop, half-boarded up with burnt-out gas pumps sitting like sad metal skeletons.

Despite the damage, people were moving in and out of the store, and the town itself seemed...alive. Battered, bruised, but still moving.

When we reached the base road, the familiarity of the forest gave me a strange comfort. Wolf Jaw might not be perfect, but it was home.

We found the base—our home—just as we had left it: the front gate smashed, sections of the fence twisted and mangled where I'd driven *Thunder* through at low altitude. A strange sight, though oddly familiar, welcoming even.

We pulled inside and parked alongside our battered 1988 Toyota Van and the Brooks' old pickup truck. It felt surreal being back.

"Home, sweet home," Destiny muttered from the rear bench, her voice tinged with exhaustion, but there was a smile in her words. She wasn't wrong—wrecked or not, it was still ours.

I stepped out of the SUV, boots crunching on the gravel, and headed toward the entrance.

My thoughts wandered, wondering where the Brooks family was.

I didn't have to search long.

The main entrance creaked open, camouflaged in a rock formation that could fool any outsider.

Phoebe Brooks sprinted out, her face flushed, white teeth flashing in the morning light.

"Kory!" she yelled, laughing as she collided with me, wrapping her arms around me. The next second, her fists were swinging. "You assholes!" she half-sobbed, half-laughed, and landed a light punch on my chest. "We were so scared!"

I chuckled, rubbing my shoulder where she'd smacked me. "Sorry, Phoebe, we crash-landed *Thunder* in the Arizona desert. It took us longer than expected to find a ride home."

She stepped back, hands on her hips, still glaring but with a hint of a smile. "Couldn't you have at least radioed? We've got a ham radio, remember?"

That probably would've been smart. "Yeah, uh, didn't even cross our minds. Guess we were a bit busy, you know, surviving."

Before I could say anything else, the rest of the Brooks

family appeared—Ricki, Baxter, and Lynda—all walking briskly from their camouflaged surface home.

Their faces were alight with relief.

We exchanged hugs and handshakes as I introduced the new members of our crew, including O'hatet.

The Brooks weren't exactly thrilled about the marac reporter in their midst, their suspicion clear, but I eased the tension by explaining she wasn't Kergan.

After several minutes of chatter and catching up, I turned to Baxter. "How're we doing on food?"

I braced myself for the worst. Without Zeta and the nanoforge, their ability to produce food and trade goods was likely limited.

"Oh, we put a hold on trading as soon as you all vanished," Baxter said casually.

Destiny raised an eyebrow. "Bet that pissed off the townspeople."

"Yeah, but they've come to rely on us," Baxter shrugged. "It was necessary."

"Well, at least now they'll be happy to see us," Busto added. "I was half expecting them to be mad about the whole 'half their town getting blown up' thing."

Baxter waved it off. "Dora's been here a few times. No sign of anyone blaming you guys. Mostly just worried about what happened to you."

He patted me on the shoulder. "You should go see her soon. I think she'll be more relieved than anyone that you're back." Then he glanced at his daughter, Phoebe. "Well, at least with the exception of Phebes," he said with a chuckle.

I nodded. "We will. But first, we need to eat. You still have supplies?"

Baxter smiled. "Yeah, plenty. Enough to last a few days, even with this big crowd you brought along."

"Good." I clapped my hands together. "Alright, let's get lunch going!" I shouted, leading everyone toward the entrance to the underground base.

The mess wasn't built for this many people, but we'd make do. I knew already I'd have to use our tribute points to expand the living quarters.

Once inside, I took a quick detour and stuck my head into the hangar. Empty, of course. Just as I expected. *Thunder* was a wreck, still somewhere in the desert near Elkin.

The sight of the vacant hangar hit me harder than I thought it would. Rebuilding her would be one hell of a project, but this time, she would rise as a corvette.

As I turned to leave, I spotted Ricki Brooks tailing me. "Hey, Ricki," I said, ruffling his hair.

He grinned up at me, blushing slightly. "Hi, Kory. Glad you're back."

It had only been a couple of weeks since we left, but he'd grown. Another inch, easy. The kid was shooting up like a weed.

"Any more problems with the Pattons while we were gone?" I asked.

"Nope," Ricki shook his head. "They've been keeping to themselves."

I made my way down to the living quarters and mess hall, where it was already bustling with activity. Destiny and Busto were in their usual routine—Destiny rummaging through the pantry with a look of determination while Busto was busy giving her a hard time.

"Careful, Dest," Busto said, glancing over his shoulder as he helped Lynda stir something on the stove. "Last time you were in charge of dinner, we nearly had to declare a state of emergency."

Destiny shot him a look, holding up a can of beans like it

was a prized possession. "I'm expanding your culinary horizons, Gunny. You just don't have the taste buds for innovation."

"Is that what we're calling it?" Busto smirked. "I thought we were just building up a resistance to food poisoning."

Lynda chimed in with a laugh. "I think that's why we keep you around, Destiny—just in case we need to weaponize dinner."

Destiny rolled her eyes. "Well, it's either me or the MREs, and let's be honest, no one's winning that battle."

I squeezed into the mess, elbowing my way between them. "We need Zeta to expand the base and a new mess hall."

Destiny raised an eyebrow. "You saying we're not worth the effort, Captain?"

"I'm saying," I grinned, "if the Dominion has any sort of fire code, we're about to get ourselves in a lot of trouble."

Busto snorted. "They're probably already mad 'cause we lost our first ship. Might as well add over-capacity dining to the list."

The banter bounced around the room as our crowded little crew packed into the space. There was an undeniable sense of warmth, of relief. We were together again. For the first time in days, the ache left by Ban'ach's theft of my memories felt distant, like something I could forget for a while.

# 26

The next three weeks were a whirlwind of activity as we settled back into the base. Zeta, of course, had the hardest job—rebuilding *Thunder* from scratch—but before she could even get started on that, we had to expand the base. It wasn't just my original crew anymore. We had four new members plus O'hatet, our marac guest, so space was suddenly at a premium. And then there was the small matter of needing a larger hangar to accommodate a corvette-sized starship.

Luckily, Zeta had planned ahead when she designed the base, making it modular and easy to expand.

She kicked things off by adding two new pods of sleeping quarters on the second level and expanding the mess hall and kitchen. She even threw in a rec room with an entertainment center and tables for games or crafts—because, you know, nothing says "intergalactic insurgency" like knitting on your off-hours.

I also had her add a new wing to the command center, complete with an office, classroom, and library.

The classroom came equipped with simulators for *Thunder*'s systems, which could be linked together for group training. Nothing like a little hands-on practice to prepare us for inevitable space warfare.

The upgrades went up quickly thanks to the nanoforge, though the process left a mud pit behind that made the base smell like a wet dog for a solid two weeks.

Next up was the hangar, which was no small task. The original hangar was 70 by 70 feet and 20 feet high. The new one would be 100 by 100, but with a 50-foot ceiling. Why so tall? Because corvettes and larger Dominion ships are stack-designed—great for long space missions, but terrible for atmosphere.

The hangar excavation went smoothly once Zeta added a second nanoforge. It was like watching a giant ant colony at work—messy but efficient.

I could have prioritized rebuilding *Thunder* first, but I knew better. Taking care of my people had to come first, especially when we were facing bigger missions ahead. So, while Zeta played mole, digging out the hangar, I focused on training.

Phoebe Brooks, bless her, was already up to speed on navigation and defensive weapons. But Rowbottom, Montana, Vila, and Appleton were complete novices when it came to operating a starship. Their only experience was as the crew of an M3 Bradley, which, as you can imagine, doesn't translate neatly to space combat. Still, they were a well-oiled team and knew how to work together, which was more than I could say for a lot of new recruits.

Destiny took command of the second watch as pilot, with Rowbottom handling engineering, Vila on sensors and offensive weapons, and Appleton managing navigation and defense.

Meanwhile, I kept command of the first watch, with Phoebe on navigation and defenses, Busto on weapons and sensors, and Zeta running engineering.

What about Cindy Montana? I didn't assign her a position on the flight deck. Instead, she became our ship medic and supply officer—basically, the one responsible for patching us up and making sure we didn't run out of essentials. In combat, she'd be holding on tight and trusting the rest of us not to get her killed, but outside of that, she was indispensable. Montana quickly became the crew's unofficial mom, always there to fix our booboos and remind us to eat something other than protein bars before we even thought about dessert.

Training the scouts was...let's say, "challenging." They were smart and motivated, but *Thunder*'s systems were leagues more complex than their Bradley. They soldiered through it, though, and by the end of three weeks, they were getting the hang of things.

Why recruit these particular folks? Simple: they were already a combat-hardened team, and they filled a critical gap. *Thunder* was too small for a dedicated marine detachment, so any boarding or ground operations would have to be done by us. The scouts gave us the firepower and tactical experience we'd need for freeing the humans who were enslaved.

Every morning, Busto led us through tactical drills.

Zeta cranked out additional protomatter suits and weapons to outfit the newbies, and I insisted that everyone —no exceptions—qualify to Busto's exacting standards. That meant small arms, tactical comms, suit maintenance, fieldcraft, and small-unit tactics. The scouts breezed through it, already having that down, but the rest of us had to up our game. It wasn't just about skill anymore; it was about learning to function as a team.

Of course, during all of this, I was still playing the part of a reasonably competent leader—though it felt like I was just one misstep away from turning the whole place into a mud-wrestling match. Leadership: it's mostly pretending you know what you're doing.

What about the townspeople? We reconnected with Mayor Best, who came by the base to meet the new crew members. After a friendly meeting, I took them to Best One Stop to get their visitation permits sorted.

I made it a rule that each crew member should head into town at least once a week, rub shoulders with the locals, and try to unwind a little. It was part goodwill mission, part making sure the townsfolk remembered we were the good guys, and part keeping my people from going stir-crazy. Plus, we had to restart supplying food and fuel to the town under our previous deal with the mayor, even covering the two-week gap while we were busy crash-landing in the desert.

Destiny and I made a point to visit her aunt and cousin, Judith and Earline Fulton. Seeing them was sobering. They'd lost weight and were clearly struggling despite having some of the town's better resources. Judith worked as Mayor Best's secretary, which meant she should've been first in line for whatever supplies were available. Yet, even they were hurting.

The refugees, those without even a house to call their own, were in much worse shape. It made me feel like we weren't doing enough, but we were already stretched thin. The only real solution was to clear the surrounding towns of bandits and Kergans so people could return home. Unfortunately, liberating entire communities wasn't exactly on our to-do list at the moment.

Maybe I should've focused more on Wolf Jaw instead of the missing humans from Elkin, but part of me hoped that the thousands of idle adults in Wolf Jaw would eventually take matters into their own hands. Organize. Fight back. Reclaim their homes. And to be fair, there were some signs of life. Wolf Jaw's police force had grown significantly since the Kergan attack, and Neal Best was making progress procuring small arms for a town armory. Still, it was a fragile kind of progress.

Meanwhile, Zeta had her hands full, completing the hangar expansion and beginning the rebuild of *Thunder*. Watching her work was like witnessing the birth of a giant. Vast, sinewy strands of nanobot threads stretched out from the nanoforges, reaching into the hangar to pull atoms from the Earth's crust, piece by microscopic piece. The new *Thunder* took shape slowly but steadily, layer by layer. It took eighteen days to rebuild the ship from the ground up, but the real magic was in watching her grow.

Then there was Cindy Montana. Turns out, she was more than just a badass with a medkit—she had a degree in molecular biology. I asked her why she hadn't gone the officer route or pursued medical school, but in her straightforward way, she said she loved being a combat medic too much. Officer training school would've stuck her behind a desk, and she preferred being in the thick of things.

I respected that. More than that, I realized her talents were being underutilized, so I convinced her to let Zeta take her under her wing. Montana had the educational background to actually understand how the nanoforge worked, unlike the rest of us, who just hoped it wouldn't explode when we turned it on.

Montana even analyzed the nanobots under a microscope, explaining how they functioned like synthetic microorganisms, using many of the same strategies as living cells and microbes. I had no idea what she was talking about, but Zeta seemed impressed.

Within weeks, Montana could synthesize fuels and basic food ingredients, lifting a massive burden off Zeta. She even wrote a program in Python to automate some of the nanoforge's tasks—an absolute lifesaver for the rest of us who hadn't a clue how to operate what still seemed like magical machinery. Though Montana wouldn't be building starships or fusion plants anytime soon, she made incredible progress in an extremely brief amount of time.

During all this time, O'hatet kept herself busy observing the crew or immersing herself in the library's archives. I had worried that hosting an alien might put a burden on the base—like having a houseguest who never leaves—but she was as unobtrusive as a shadow. She seemed genuinely interested in our activities as insurgents. Though considering our version of excitement involved endless drills and waiting for Zeta's construction, I wondered if her standards were just really low.

Once, after we'd been cooped up in the base for four weeks, I asked her if she was getting bored. She replied, "I am enjoying the lack of excitement." I wasn't sure if that was a compliment or a subtle dig at our monotonous routine. Maybe for her, hanging out with a bunch of idle guerrillas was the alien equivalent of a relaxing vacation.

I knew she was still exploiting her backdoor at IMH to investigate Project Silver Tangle, the Astral Maul, and the plight of the slaves at Lindblad F. Every few days, I'd check in with her, hoping she'd cracked some secret code or uncovered a hidden conspiracy. But she always had little information to share.

"I don't like to reveal the details until I know the entire story," she said, sounding like a cryptic fortune cookie.

I pressed her to let us in on some of the pieces of the puzzle so we could help her brainstorm. "Come on, O'hatet," I coaxed, "even Sherlock needed Watson."

She politely refused. "Your assistance is appreciated but unnecessary at this juncture."

It was like trying to get spoilers from someone who'd already seen the movie—they know everything but won't spill the beans. I half-expected her to pat me on the head and tell me to run along. Still, I couldn't help but admire her dedication to thorough research, even if it meant leaving us in suspense.

# 27

I shifted in the stuffed chair, trying to get comfortable as my friends settled around me.

Destiny and Busto took their usual spots on the couch facing me.

Zeta hovered quietly at my side, her capsule emitting its familiar hum and glow.

O'hatet—well, "rested" might be a better word than "sat," given her lack of legs—was in another chair, her tentacles curling slightly beneath her.

The library door clicked shut, sealing us into the most private room in the base.

"Alright, O'hatet," I began, curiosity gnawing at me, "what's this all about?"

"Thank you for meeting with me, Kory," she said, her tone hushed but deliberate. "I have some new information, things I've known for a while but wasn't ready to share until I had a clearer picture."

Destiny tapped her boot impatiently on the quartz floor. "Please, don't dance around it. Just spit it out."

"I'm getting there," O'hatet said, turning her dark eyes toward me.

"Is this about the rescue on Luna?" I asked, trying to steer the conversation toward what I suspected was her point.

"Indeed," she replied. "I've uncovered more about the situation, though not as much as I'd hoped. Unfortunately, I don't have all the details on the humans at Lindblad F—likely you'll need to perform a reconnaissance to get the full story."

Busto crossed his arms. "That's not what you've been holding back, is it?"

"No," O'hatet said. "The new information I've uncovered concerns Project Silver Tangle and, of course, the Astral Maul."

I leaned forward, both intrigued and a little annoyed that she was dragging this out. "Go on."

"As I suspected, the Astral Maul is indeed a Primordian artifact—ancient and partially existing in the Syderealium. Its original purpose is still debated among the Kergan scientists studying it, but the prevailing theory is that it was designed to monitor life on Earth."

Busto raised an eyebrow. "On Earth? Then why's it sitting up on the Moon?"

"Likely to avoid disturbing the very life it was studying," O'hatet explained. "The Maul appears to be some sort of instrument to record and measure the glyphshades of organisms—probably tracking the consciousness and physical interactions of early hominids. Perhaps *homo erectus* or even *homo habilis*."

"Let me get this straight," I said, trying to piece it together. "They were spying on our ancestors? Studying their minds?"

"Something like that," O'hatet said. "It seems they were particularly interested in the link between consciousness and the physical world."

Busto scoffed. "That doesn't sound like something the Kergans could use against us. What's the big deal?"

"If all it did was record thoughts, sure," Destiny added with a smirk. "But I'd rather not have some ancient alien machine poking around in my brain like it's looking for lost car keys."

O'hatet tilted her head. "I wish that were the full extent of it. But I've learned something else, and this...this is where it gets more concerning."

The room fell silent, all eyes on O'hatet as the tension rose.

O'hatet took a deep breath, her expression growing serious. "The Kergan scientists are attempting to modify the Astral Maul, turning it from a passive observer into an active tool of manipulation. Their goal is to use it to influence the minds of every sentient being on Earth—effectively putting your entire species under Kergan control."

My stomach twisted. "Is that even possible?"

"Zeta fears it is," Zeta said. "The Collective Dominion discovered a similar Primordian artifact centuries ago. Zeta now knows what the Astral Maul is. Zeta will need to inform her superiors immediately."

I rubbed my temples, trying to sort through the details. "So, the Kergans have found a sydereal sensor capable of reading the whole planet, and they're modifying it to manipulate every mind on Earth. Do I have that right?"

"Yes," O'hatet confirmed. "Though I'll need to keep investigating for more precise details."

"Why do they call it the Astral Maul?" Destiny asked.

"That's the Kergan name for it," Zeta explained. "But the real danger isn't just the mind control. Using the Maul could attract the attention of an Astral Titan."

Destiny frowned. "What the hell is an Astral Titan?"

I had learned this from Zeta's lessons. "They're ancient beings who've lived in the Syderealium for millions of years. Each controls a domain, and they don't take kindly to beings like us messing with the fabric of the Syderealium."

Busto leaned forward. "And what happens if we get the attention of one of these Titans?"

Zeta's voice took on a grave tone. "In the worst case, a Titan could consume the glyphshades of every living thing on Earth. It would wipe out all life—down to the microbes. Your planet would be left an empty shell."

Destiny raised an eyebrow. "But it's the Kergans poking the hornet's nest, not us."

"To the Titan, it wouldn't matter. Humans and Kergans would be indistinguishable. The Kergans are essentially trying to usurp the power of a Titan to control you."

I sighed, the weight of it all pressing down like I was trying to carry the world on my back—without a map. The Kergans were like daredevils on a joyride, heading full throttle toward a cliff, convinced they could leap the gap. And we? We were just the poor saps in the sidecar, hoping to survive the landing.

"Seriously, the Kergans are like Evel Knievel," I muttered.

Destiny snorted. "More like Dar Robinson, but without the charm."

"Okay, so they're planning this crazy stunt. How close are they to pulling it off?" I asked.

O'hatet answered, "They plan to activate the Maul in two months."

I slapped my thighs in frustration. "Two months to stop them from turning Earth into a mind-controlled puppet show. Great. Well, this rescue mission we've been planning just became a sabotage mission."

Busto shook his head, muttering a curse. Destiny grinned as if she'd been waiting for the chance. "You know me, boss. I love breaking stuff."

"We need to infiltrate the mine at Lindblad F, rescue the captives, and destroy the Astral Maul."

Busto frowned. "But what do the slaves from Elkin have to do with the Maul?"

"They're being used for the excavation and as cover for the operation," O'hatet explained. "The Helium-3 mining on the surface is a front. This entire project is officially sanctioned by the Kergan Empress, with Ban'ach now running security at the mine."

At the mention of Ban'ach, a cold chill ran through me. Ban'ach, the one who had stolen my memories of my parents. My obsession with recovering those memories still gnawed at me, leaving me hollow—like a vending machine that promised snacks but never delivered. If we got to the mine, maybe—just maybe—I could finally confront her and reclaim what she'd taken from me. I needed those memories back. Without them, I felt like I was just going through the motions, a captain on autopilot. And trust me, nobody wants a captain on autopilot.

Busto cut through my thoughts. "We'll need to scout the crater. Can *Thunder* handle that?"

Zeta nodded. "Aye, Gunny Busto. *Thunder* will have the endurance and range to reach Lindblad F."

I turned to O'hatet. "Will you continue helping us? We could use you on this mission."

She gave a slight nod. "Yes, Captain. I anticipated this

and am prepared to accompany you. I understand the risks and shall continue to render aid."

I smiled, feeling a slight weight lift from my chest. "Then it's settled. Our first task is to propose this mission to the Dominion. Zeta, can you get approval?"

"Aye, Consort. Zeta shall contact her superiors at once."

I leaned back in my chair, trying to digest everything O'hatet had just told us. Destiny's grin had morphed into a full-blown smirk as she glanced between me and Busto.

Destiny leaned back, still smirking. "Kory, you've got a real knack for dragging us into the weirdest situations imaginable. First, we're flying starships; then we're crashing them, and now we're up against mind-bending relics that might just get the attention of interdimensional gods. You know, the usual."

Busto grinned and crossed his arms. "And let's not forget the part where we'll be sneaking into a Kergan base on the Moon. Can't wait to explain that one to the grandkids someday—if we make it out alive."

I chuckled, shaking my head. "You're welcome, by the way. I'm just doing my part to make sure your lives are full of excitement. You think this job comes with a retirement plan?"

Destiny snorted. "Yeah, it's called not dying. Pretty solid plan so far, right?"

Busto raised an eyebrow. "Guess we'll see if it holds up when we're staring down an ancient artifact that could melt our brains."

"Well," I said, leaning forward with a grin, "at least I won't be bored either."

# 28

Five weeks after our return to Wolf Jaw, *Thunder* was finally ready.

This time, I wasn't going to let her come to life without a little ceremony. Our crew was bigger now, and I wanted to make sure they all felt like they were a vital part of the team. Plus, we needed to formalize the chain of command.

So, Zeta and I planned a christening ceremony for the ship and an official crew induction. It wouldn't be fancy, but hey, I figured I could at least give my ragtag group of guerrillas a moment to feel like a real crew, even if I still wasn't sure what I was doing half the time.

I stood at the front of the hangar, the newly rebuilt *Thunder* looming behind me like a monument to defiance.

The starship was a marvel of engineering and a testament to our resilience. Her hull, the same silvery gray doped silicon-carbide as before, gleamed under the bright hangar lights—a squat cylinder sitting on its circular base, 75 ft in diameter and reaching 40 ft tall, including her extended undercarriage.

Sleek lines traced along her sides, interrupted here and there by large lobes containing her tractor pods.

The weaponry had also been upgraded; two turret-mounted rail guns and concealed missile tubes were integrated seamlessly into the design, and a heavy plasma cannon turret gave her a menacing elegance.

Smaller laser point defense blisters sprouted all over the hull.

The flight deck was not visible, hidden in an armored citadel at the ship's core.

Emblazoned on her bow (the top when she was landed) was the ship's emblem, which was added by my request: a stylized thunderbolt piercing through a storm cloud, symbolizing power and knowledge.

The crew was assembled before me, their faces a mix of pride, exhaustion, and determination. Also there standing tall were Baxter, Lynda and Ricky Brooks, all three smiling with quiet pride. Even O'hatet had joined us, floating quietly in the back, her tentacles swaying gently like kelp in a calm sea.

The atmosphere was electric, charged with anticipation and the unspoken promise of what was to come.

I cleared my throat, feeling every eye on me. Public speaking had never been my strong suit, but if there was ever a time to rise to the occasion, it was now.

"Thank you all for being here," I began, trying to project a confidence I didn't quite feel. "When I first took command of *Thunder*, she was just a ship—armed and dangerous, sure, but still just a machine. But in the time since then, she's become more than that. She's become our home, our refuge, and our weapon against those who would oppress us."

I paused, scanning the faces of my crew. Destiny gave me an encouraging nod, her eyes sparkling with unspoken mischief, while Busto crossed his arms with a proud smirk, the corner of his mouth twitching as if suppressing a witty remark. Zeta floated to the side, her octahedral form pulsating with a soft glow—I sensed approval from her through our consort link. Vila and Appleton shared a conspiratorial grin, probably cooking up some modification to our tactical drills that would either save our skins or get us all killed. Montana adjusted her hair, giving me a subtle thumbs-up.

"Today, we christen this new *Thunder* not just as a starship but as a symbol of our resilience. She's been through hell—shot down, torn apart, and rebuilt from the ground up. And in that, she's a lot like us. We've all faced losses, hardships, and moments when giving up seemed like the easiest option. But we didn't. We fought. We survived. And here we are, stronger than ever."

I gestured to the ship behind me. "This ship is a testament to what we can achieve when we work together. She's more than just metal and technology; she's a part of each of us. Every bolt, every circuit, every weld represents the blood, sweat, and tears we've shed to get here. And as long as she flies, she'll carry with her the spirit of our struggle."

I turned to face *Thunder*, lifting a bottle of wine that Zeta had synthesized just for this occasion. The liquid inside shimmered with iridescent hues, and I wasn't entirely sure what it was made of—or if it was technically wine—but it was the thought that counted.

"With this christening, we renew our commitment to the fight," I said, raising my voice. "To protecting those who can't protect themselves. To standing up against tyranny and injustice. To never backing down, no matter how tough things get."

I swung the bottle against the hull. It shattered with a

satisfying crash, the strange liquid cascading down the ship's side like a waterfall of stars, and the crew erupted into cheers.

"From this moment on, let *Thunder* be a beacon of hope," I continued, turning back to my crew. "Let her remind us that as long as we're willing to fight for what's right, we can overcome anything. We are her crew, and she is our sword and shield. Together, we will face whatever challenges come our way. Together, we will find those who have been taken from us, and we will bring them home."

I took a deep breath, letting the moment settle. "Welcome aboard the starship *Thunder*. Let's show the universe what we're made of!"

The crew cheered again, louder this time, and for a brief, shining moment, I felt like maybe—just maybe—I was becoming the leader they deserved. Then Destiny caught my eye, mouthing something about not letting all this go to my head, and I chuckled.

We still had a long road ahead of us, but standing there, surrounded by my crew and the ship that had brought us all together, I knew we were ready for whatever came next.

Just as the applause began to fade, Zeta floated forward, positioning herself between me and the crew. Her metallic capsule glowed brighter, and the ambient sounds of the hangar seemed to hush in anticipation.

"Consort Kory Drake, crew of the *Thunder*," Zeta began, her voice carrying a formal weight that echoed through the cavernous space. "This is a moment of rebirth. By the authority of the Collective Dominion's War Ministry vested in Zeta as your military adviser, Zeta hereby issues the following orders."

Her gaze—or whatever sensory apparatus she used—swept across the assembled crew, her words precise and measured. "You are to take full possession of the starship *Thunder*, now rebuilt and ready for service. From this moment, she is yours to command. She will not simply be a vessel; she will live through your actions, bound to your will, and become the instrument of your mission."

Zeta's tone sharpened as she continued. "This ship, forged with the most advanced Dominion technology, must become more than a machine. It must reflect your resolve, your discipline, and your unity as a crew. Together, you will make her a force to be reckoned with—an extension of your purpose."

Her capsule bobbed subtly, emphasizing the gravity of her words. "Captain Kory Drake, Zeta charges you and your crew with this sacred duty: bring *Thunder* to life. Let her carry the strength of the Collective Dominion and the human spirit against the Kergan Empire. The Dominion places its trust in you."

She paused, her luminescent form hovering silently as if awaiting a response. The crew exchanged glances; even O'hatet tilted her head slightly, a gesture of interest—or perhaps amusement.

I stepped forward, a wry smile tugging at the corner of my mouth. "Thank you, Zeta," I said. "We accept this charge."

My crew erupted in cheers, and I joined them. *Thunder* had been rebuilt, and we were ready to bring the fight to our enemies once again.

Destiny grabbed Phoebe's arm, and the two marched purposefully toward Thunder's hatch, eager to be the first ones aboard.

I stepped in front of them with my arms spread wide, halting them in their tracks. "Whoa, hold on, you two!"

They blinked in surprise.

I grinned. "We're not quite done yet. Back to your spots." Chastised but smiling, they retreated to their places in line.

"There's one more bit of official business before we can call *Thunder* fully commissioned," I continued, making eye contact with Zeta. "Zeta, would you do the honors?"

Zeta floated forward, her expression unreadable but the air of ceremony unmistakable. "Kory Drake, by the authority vested in Zeta as your military advisor and Heliacal Templar, Zeta hereby promotes you to the rank of Lieutenant Commander in the United Humans Confederate Armada and appoints you captain and master of the armed corvette *UHS Thunder*."

I saluted her. "Thank you, Zeta."

The crew looked at me with raised eyebrows and curious glances. I hadn't told any of them what was happening. But after much thought, I realized we weren't just a ragtag group of insurgents anymore. We were a military unit now—a strange one, sure, but a unit nonetheless. It was time to give us structure, ranks, and a proper chain of command.

Zeta had also informed me that a few of Earth's ex-governments had been evacuated by the Collective Dominion and had formed the United Humans Confederacy (UHC), a government-in-exile with its own space force called the UHC Armada. On paper, we were now part of that force, though, in actual fact, we remained under the command of the Collective Dominion Ministry of War. Nonetheless, our crew was about to become official.

I stepped forward again, my voice firm. "Destiny Austin, front and center!"

Destiny's eyes widened. She hesitated for a moment before marching up beside me, coming to attention.

"Destiny Austin, as commander of this unit, I promote

you to the rank of Lieutenant Senior Grade in the UHC Armada and appoint you as First Officer of the armed corvette *UHS Thunder*."

She blinked as I pinned the rank insignia onto her overalls. "Congratulations, Lieutenant Austin," I said with a wink, shaking her hand.

Next up was Busto. He stepped forward with the precision of a Marine who'd seen more than his share of command structures.

"Clemen Busto, as commander of this unit, I promote you to the rank of Lieutenant Senior Grade in the UHC Armada and appoint you Chief Weapons Systems Officer and Commander of the Marine Detachment of the armed corvette *UHS Thunder*."

One by one, I continued the promotions: Phoebe Brooks became an Ensign and Chief Navigation Officer; Ivor Rowbottom was promoted to Ensign and Assistant Engineer; Cindy Montana to Ensign, Medical and Supply Officer; Balbino Vila to Chief Petty Officer and Assistant Weapons Officer; and Moriko Appleton to Chief Petty Officer and Assistant Navigation Officer.

Was I promoting everyone a bit lopsidedly? Probably. But I wanted to acknowledge the huge responsibility they were all about to take on. Besides, ranks are only as important as the people who wear them, right?

As civilians, Baxter, Lynda, and Ricki Brooks didn't receive military ranks, but I appointed Lynda as Base General Manager and Baxter as Head of Base Security. At only fourteen, Ricki had a couple more years to wait before I'd recruit him, though I had a feeling he'd be joining us sooner than later.

I also reminded everyone that, regardless of their fancy new ranks, every single crew member was also part of the

Marine Detachment, meaning we would all be subject to Busto's orders whenever we happened to be part of an away or tactical response team. That earned a few groans, especially from Destiny.

Finally, I called for their attention one last time. "I know this has been a long meeting, and you've all been patient. So, without dragging this out any longer—because I know you're all itching to argue about who gets the best bunk—allow me to give you your first order as captain of the *UHS Thunder*. Crew, man your posts and bring this ship to life!"

Thunderous cheers erupted as the crew rushed forward, lining up to board the ship. I couldn't help but grin as they disappeared inside. We were officially back in business.

# 29

Two days after christening *Thunder*, we had completed filling her stores, charging the chromatic batteries (the corvette carried two), and familiarizing everybody with the internal compartments and systems.

My crew were aboard, waiting for me to take us out on our first flight.

I climbed the gangway and entered through the hatch into the stern airlock. We sat in an atmosphere, so the outer and inner doors were open. This was deck 3, the bottommost deck of the stack.

I walked up a short corridor to the hull's center and climbed a ladder—really more like a steep flight of stairs, but we were supposed to call it a ladder.

The flight deck was located at the center of deck 2. It was an armored capsule containing all the stations used by the flight crew during flight operations.

The compartments surrounding the flight deck contained stores, a captain's day room, and a head.

Deck 3 contained the engineering compartment, missile

magazines, access to the two railgun turrets, and the armory.

Deck 1 was where the crew quarters were located and the mess, lounge, pantry, and medical bay. Access to the plasma cannon turret was also found there.

I entered the flight deck and saw that every seat was taken except for the pilot's. Even the jump seats were occupied by Cindy Montana and O'hatet.

During normal non-combat flight operations, each watch required four persons on the flight deck: pilot, navigation and defenses, weapons and sensors, and engineer. The navigation station was also our communications station.

During combat, each of the normal stations got an assistant, including a co-pilot for the pilot. That meant there were a total of eight stations with consoles on the flight deck, plus two jump seats pushed against a bulkhead. When all the seats were occupied, it made for a crowded and noisy compartment.

I took my place on my acceleration couch. I turned and looked at my crew.

All of us were fitted into protomatter suits, except Zeta, who didn't require one. Even O'hatet wore one fitted to her cephalopod body.

The suits were required for sustained acceleration, acting like both a gee-suit and to augment strength and protect against blunt-force traumatic injuries. For normal flight operations where accelerations were at or below 1 gee, they could be discarded, and we would wear ship coveralls. But for this flight, we would push *Thunder* to her limits, so I insisted on the suits.

I called for a status check from each station. They all gave me the green light.

"Nav, open the hangar," I ordered.

"Roger," Phoebe responded. I saw her tapping at an imaginary object in the middle of the air. But I knew it wasn't imaginary to her. Instead, she was seeing a virtual interface in her HUD and her suit's haptic controls replicated the resistance and texture of buttons and dials.

With a *thunk*, a sliver of daylight appeared above us.

There were no viewports in the flight deck to view outside directly, but the HUDs on our helmets delivered a view of the outside world.

The sliver increased in width as the hangar hatch slid to the side, exposing the rebuilt *Thunder* to the outside world for the first time.

The new *Thunder* wasn't as sexy and sleek as the old one had been, with its shark-like lines and surfaces optimized for atmospheric flight. As a corvette, the new *Thunder* was intended mostly to operate in space. It was as aerodynamic as a brick and would never be able to glide to the ground if it ever lost power. But it made up for these shortcomings by being more powerful, heavily armed, better protected, and having longer endurance. It was a true spaceship in the sense that the word "ship" suggested.

The hangar hatch finished withdrawing. I gripped my flight controls and manipulated them to give us a slight vertical acceleration, and *Thunder* began drifting up through the looming hole in the ceiling.

The 6 ft thick quartz ceiling flew by us, and the corvette cleared the hangar. I punched a button, and the undercarriage retracted into *Thunder*'s belly. I double-checked that the active camouflage was engaged and confirmed that it was so. The citizens of Wolf Jaw now knew of the existence of our starship. Still, there was no reason to go flaunting ourselves and putting on a show, especially considering the risk that nearby Kergans could observe us if we weren't cautious.

"Seal the hangar," I ordered.

"Aye aye, sir," Phoebe replied.

Our flight plan was to conduct a patrol over the western Nevada mountains, searching for Kergan merchant ships we could raid. Combat wasn't the primary goal because we were working up the ship to confirm it was functional. But I wanted to test our weapons and defensive systems and blood my new crew members.

Rowbottom and his team of Army scouts had been rapid studies. They were enthusiastic, and I knew their watch, with Destiny in command, were anxious to have their turn at the primary controls. They wouldn't get that today because this was a relatively short mission. But we would definitely need to sit multiple watches for the visit to Luna we planned to undertake in a few days.

I flew us northeast across the summits of the Sierra Nevada Mountains. We were in the early days of spring, and the mountains were encrusted by thick layers of snowfall that had accumulated for months. I kept our speed at 600 knots, just below the speed of sound, so we remained invisible to Kergan and human sensors.

*Thunder* could accelerate with equal force in any direction because her tractor pods were omnidirectional. Theoretically, I could have flown the ship in any orientation I wanted, including backward and upside-down. But for the sake of crew comfort, I kept us oriented so the maximum acceleration was generally directed through the floor, i.e., vertically, to make it safer to move around. This meant that when accelerating forward, I would tilt *Thunder* forward as we built up speed until we reached a steady velocity, at which point I oriented Thunder with her bow pointing up at zenith so gravity pulled through the floor. I imagined that when in space, outside Earth's gravitational influence, I would orient the bow toward our direction of acceleration.

During a typical mission, we would be in freefall for lengthy periods because *Thunder* had a limited amount of delta-v it could produce on one charge of its batteries. Over 70 km/sec, more than three times what *Thunder* could achieve when it was a Raptor hull. Despite this improvement, it would still take anywhere from 6 to 12 hours for us to reach Luna from Earth orbit, depending on how much charge I wanted to reserve in the batteries.

I parked us on top of an unnamed mountain somewhere in Nevada where our sensors had a clear view of the sky. Phoebe and CPO Appleton monitored for threats, while Busto and CPO Vila controlled our sensor systems. The rest of us relaxed and waited.

The new *Thunder* was a bit of a slug to fly compared to its former iteration. It didn't glide effortlessly through the air as it once did. But it felt more agile, and the amount of power produced by the tractor pods was intimidating. If I had disabled the acceleration governors, I knew I could have easily pushed us so hard it would have killed us. I would have loved to invest some of our tribute point balance toward inertial dampers, but those required a frigate or heavier hull size. Also, an FTL drive would become available when we upgraded to a frigate.

"Contact," Busto called on the intercom, "Kergan civilian vessel, designating Alpha-1, bearing 323 by 21, angles 143, range 2300, closing."

I saw an icon representing the new contact appear on my tactical display. "Any visual yet?" I asked.

"Working on it," Vila said.

"Alpha-1 has friends. Two hostiles. I'm designating them X-ray-1 and X-ray-2," Busto said a minute later.

"Picking up enemy search radars from X-ray-1 and X-ray-2," Phoebe said. "They match the signature of Kergan fighters."

"Escorts," I concluded. "That must be a merchant ship approaching for landing."

"Aye, Captain," Busto said. "We've got a visual."

I looked at my display and saw a grainy image of a block-shaped Kergan ship entering the atmosphere, leading a long trail of glowing plasma. The two escort fighters followed several miles behind and above it, each leaving its own much smaller trail.

"Prepare for battle," I said. "Weaps, get me missile solutions. ASMs for the freighter, IMs for the fighters. Charge the railguns and keep them on standby."

"Aye aye, sir."

"Nav, plot me an intercept course that keeps us quiet."

"Aye aye," Phoebe said. She began tapping at her invisible interface while talking silently to Appleton, who sat beside her.

Soon after, a navigation plot appeared on my tactical display. "Strap in tightly. We're intercepting," I said. I lifted us off and began accelerating along the track Nav had given me.

"ChEng," I called out to the Chief Engineer, Zeta, "how is she holding together."

"Excellent, Captain," Zeta responded. "All systems are in the green."

"Very good, thank you."

I accelerated us eastward, waiting for the ship and its escorts to overtake us. Then we would accelerate to their speed and fire up their asses.

*Thunder*'s new sensors were much more capable than the old hull. We had acquired visuals of our adversaries much earlier, and the images were clearer and had higher contrast.

Our new corvette hull had much larger missile magazines than the old hull. And we hadn't even upgraded them yet. We had twenty tubes for 2,000 lb anti-ship missiles and forty tubes for 200 lb intercept missiles. The missiles were our primary long-range weapons, while the railguns were for medium-range combat and the plasma cannon for short-range fighting.

"I have a missile solution," Busto announced. "We can launch in 90 seconds."

"Roger," I said. "Standby."

The three ships passed us overhead. They were at about 120 thousand feet moving at Mach 5, while we were currently flying at 65 thousand feet and just under Mach 1.

"Weaps, prepare to fire the railguns at those fighters," I ordered. I oriented *Thunder* so that both railgun turrets had a field of fire to the fighters.

"Aye, aye," Vila answered, who had control of the railguns.

"Weaps, fire missiles!" I called out, and at the same time, I pressed the flight controls.

*Thunder* leaped forward, pressing us down into our acceleration couches as I increased our velocity to overtake the freighter.

"Missiles away!" Busto announced.

I didn't even feel the launch of the missiles, though that shouldn't have surprised me. *Thunder* now massed over 500 tons, ten times heavier than it had previously been. There was just too much solid structure for the vibration of the missile launches to reach us.

I watched the missile trajectories as they pursued their prey.

Seconds later, the freighter's velocity shifted southward as it began evasive maneuvers.

Flashes of light appeared as the Kergan fighters' LPDs began firing at our missiles.

Two of our missiles were taken out by the LPDs, but two ASMs impacted the freighter. A single IM hit one of the fighters. The fighter disappeared in a ball of flame.

The freighter broke into two pieces and began tumbling as the hypersonic airstream ripped it to shreds.

The remaining fighter turned toward us.

"Vampire, vampire!" Destiny called out as the enemy fighter released two missiles at us.

"Releasing LPDs!" Appleton said.

Our LPD blisters began firing at the enemy missiles. I couldn't hear the *crack* of them firing from our position buried deep within the hull.

"Engage X-ray-2 with railguns!" I called out.

Moments later, *Thunder* jumped to the side as the two railguns accelerated tungsten darts down their tubes at 10 km/sec. Incandescent traces dashed from our hull across the sky toward the fighter. One of those connected with it, and a cloud of sparks exploded out the rear of X-ray-2, quickly followed by a trail of debris spilling out of the fighter as it began to roll uncontrollably.

"Enemy missiles eliminated!" Appleton announced. Our LPDs had overwhelmed the enemy missiles.

"X-ray-2 is eliminated!" Busto cried out.

The flight crew cheered.

"Mission accomplished," I said with a smile.

The fight had been too easy. I would have never engaged two Kergan fighters like that voluntarily with the old *Thunder*, but our corvette was a much more deadly threat. Our missile magazines were still 90% full, and we were undamaged.

These thoughts occupied my mind as I steered us back to base, satisfied that *Thunder* was in working order and ready for our first full mission.

On the flight back, the crew relaxed and chatted as if they were nothing but passengers. I was proud of them and the skills they had mastered. We had taken the fight to the Kergans and hurt them, though it was clear that *Thunder* had much more potential now as a warship and that using her to hunt freighters was overkill. We needed to fight more worthy prey.

"Secure from general quarters," I said as we flew across the Colorado-Utah border, heading westward.

This released the second watch from their stations, as well as Montana and O'hatet.

They got up from their seats and left the flight deck, probably going up to the crew lounge or maybe the mess on Deck 1.

As Destiny walked past, she leaned down and whispered in my ear, "Don't crash her."

I shot her a smirk. "One time! You crash one spaceship, and suddenly you're 'that guy.'"

# 30

I spent another two weeks training the crew and preparing for our recon mission to Lindblad F.

I'd have gone sooner, but the Dominion War Ministry moved at the speed of bureaucracy—because, apparently, the best way to wage war is to drown in paperwork. Zeta informed me the holdup was due to some bean counter's concern that we might be stepping out of bounds as if we insurgents had time to read a rule book on what types of life-and-death missions we're "allowed" to take on.

It irked me. This was our war, humanity's war. Sure, a few ignas, like Zeta, were fighting alongside us, but the majority of the Dominion? They were basically spectators with better seating and all the popcorn. And if this new United Humans Confederacy government-in-exile was actually functioning, I almost wished the Dominion would just hand over control. Then again, UHC desk jockeys might be just as bad, probably sending us on raids while holding meetings about how many forms we'd have to fill out afterward.

My cell's mission eventually got approval, and I had to admit that we had put the delay to good use, especially for our training as a tactical team. We had even begun including O'hatet in some of our away-team scenarios as a non-combatant who needed to be protected.

We also obtained detailed topographical maps of Lindblad F, and I ordered everybody to memorize them until they knew the terrain like the folds in their finger joints. O'hatet produced some crude maps of the IMH mining installation based on the best information she had, though she had low confidence in them and said we would have to go in assuming we knew nothing.

So, two weeks after shooting down that freighter, we launched on our first long endurance mission, headed to the Moon.

We left in the middle of the night because I wanted our recon to be conducted during the equivalent of local mid-morning when the crew's circadian cycle would be at its peak.

Not that anybody was likely to fall asleep during their first moonwalk.

For the transit from Earth's orbit to Luna, I accelerated us to 7 km/sec, a modest velocity that would see us arrive in lunar orbit in 12 hours. Accelerating at 1 gee, it only took us fifteen minutes to reach that speed, so most of the transit was done in micro-gravity.

We scheduled watch shifts to swap every six hours. So, six hours into the flight, just five hours after leaving orbit, I handed control over to Destiny's second watch. It was their first time flying the ship during a real mission, and I hoped *Thunder* would still be in one piece when I woke up.

I floated out of the flight deck and headed for my bunk on Deck 1 to try and sleep for a few hours. As the pilot-commanders of *Thunder*, Destiny and I shared a private cabin by hot-bunking while everybody else shared bunks in the berthing compartment, which probably smelled like a gym locker by now.

I awoke 30 minutes before the start of my watch. A convenient display in my cabin showed that *Thunder* was about an hour from the point in our transit where we needed to decelerate, and all systems were green.

I floated into the mess and put a bag of coffee and another of oatmeal in the microwave.

Because we were in zero-gee, the food had to be eaten from squeeze bags to keep sticky blobs from floating into the air handling system.

Phoebe and Busto—the Nav and Weaps for my watch—arrived a few minutes later.

"Hey, boss," Busto said with a yawn.

Phoebe reached out and patted my shoulder as she floated by me on her way to the pantry. "Busto snores!" she complained over her shoulder.

"At least I don't whistle," Busto replied. "Now we know what a marac sounds like when they sleep."

I sensed that the sleeping arrangements weren't to everybody's satisfaction. They were accustomed to having their own private quarters back at the base, and it had spoiled them.

I was studying a telescopic real-time image of the Moon on my tablet when Phoebe returned to the table. "Whatcha lookin' at? Can you see Lindblad F?"

I shook my head. "Nope. It's on the far side. We won't see it until we make our orbital insertion."

"Where's it at?"

I pulled up a map of the moon with latitude and longitude lines. "It's here, not too far from the north pole and five degrees from the western boundary between the near and far sides."

She put a hand on my shoulder to hold herself steady while she looked over my shoulder. She smelled nice despite having just woken up. A subtle musky smell mixed with the scent of a flower. "It's not very big, is it?"

"That's just the scale of the map. The crater is 25 miles in diameter and a mile deep. But you should know this. You've been studying the maps just like the rest of us."

She sensed my annoyed tone and squeezed my shoulder. "Yes, but it just looks different when one looks at it from the perspective of the entire Moon. It seems so much smaller."

"Well, the Moon may be smaller than Earth, but it's still a big place. We have a lot of terrain to survey."

Busto sucked a mouthful of coffee and groaned with enjoyment. "I'm still worried they're gonna spot us coming in."

"Zeta assured me that our stealth systems will hold up to scrutiny," I said. "Just as long as we don't go firing weapons or accelerating too aggressively or get too close to one of their radars. We just need to keep our thermal signature down. There's no atmosphere to stir up by going too fast, so that makes things easier, in a way, since we don't have to worry about our speed. Can't go supersonic when there's no air."

I finished my oatmeal and burped. I couldn't breathe through my nose anymore, a consequence of being in zero-gee. Fluid collected in the sinuses, and it felt like I had a head cold. It also made food less satisfying to eat.

Five minutes before the start of our watch, I drifted down to Deck 2 and poked my head into a few of the lockers where we kept our stores. The first one I checked was full of substrate charges for *Thunder*'s nanoforge. That's right, our ship had its own nanoforge, so we could fabricate custom objects if the need ever arose.

The second locker contained an emergency shelter, airlock kits, a rock laser drill, and other excavation supplies.

With a minute left on the clock, I opened the hatch to the flight deck and floated in. The deck was organized with six seats in a half-ring, each with its own console, and two seats in the center facing the backs of the other six. Those two were the pilots' couches. The two jump seats rested against the bulkhead behind the pilots.

Destiny looked up as I entered and gave a quick nod, but her attention remained fixed on her interface, fingers tapping away. "Hey, Captain. I'm just wrapping things up here."

"How's it lookin'?" I asked.

"We had a wastewater leak a couple hours ago, but Rowbottom found the issue."

"Gross. What was it?"

"A stuck valve. It vented into vacuum. We lost about two gallons of water."

"Crap. Did it mess up our signature?" Even a tiny spray of water globules in a vacuum had a distinct radar signature that could give us away while running silent.

"No, I think we're good. Nav didn't detect any scans from enemy radar or lidar. At least, nothing out of the ordinary."

"Okay. I'll ask Zeta about the leak." I suddenly realized Zeta wasn't on the flight deck yet, which was strange. She was never late for anything.

I settled into the pilot's couch. "I have the conn," I said to the flight deck.

"You have the conn," Destiny echoed back, completing the official switch of our watch.

As Destiny, Appleton, Vila, and Rowbottom floated out of the compartment, Busto and Phoebe logged into their consoles. Moments later, Zeta zoomed in and took her seat at the engineering console.

"ChEng! I was worried!" I blurted.

"Sorry, Captain. Zeta was investigating the leak."

"Is everything okay?"

"Aye, it was a frozen valve that wasn't properly seated during construction. Zeta has mitigated the problem for now and will implement a repair once we return to base."

Phoebe glanced up from her station and smirked. "Well, at least we didn't lose anything valuable—like, say, coffee. Two gallons of sewage, though? Tragic, really. I'm sure we'll all survive the heartbreak."

"Hey, that 'sewage' gets recycled," Busto said. "We just lost a couple gallons of the ship's water."

Phoebe shivered. "Yuck, thanks for reminding me of that. I'll just never drink from the water jug again."

The following hour was uneventful. The Moon quickly grew larger in our displays, and the Earth appeared no larger than a quarter held at arm's length. As we entered the Moon's gravitational field and its pull overcame that of distant Earth, we began to accelerate as we fell toward the cratered surface. I made a couple course adjustments with taps of the flight controls to ensure we hit our insertion windows.

Fifteen minutes before our closest approach, I made an announcement on the ship's PA. "Attention all hands. Prepare for acceleration. You have 67 seconds to secure the ship."

The second watch should already be up and preparing for the maneuver. If they were in the mess, they would be checking that food and other items weren't floating around to fall to the floor when I began our orbital insertion maneuver.

Phoebe had my planned course plotted on my tactical display, and I watched the timer tick down to deceleration. I left the controls on autopilot because timing was crucial, and the computer would be much more precise than I could be. My job was to monitor the maneuver and intervene if anything went wrong.

A few seconds before the timer expired, *Thunder* adjusted its orientation to ensure acceleration would be along the vertical axis. The time expired, and the pull of acceleration built up smoothly, ramping from zero gee to just under 1 gee. There was no rumble of engines or detectable vibration in the hull. Just a building force.

Thirteen minutes later, we completed the push, bleeding off 7 km/sec of excess velocity, and entered lunar orbit.

But we weren't done yet. Lindblad F was near the North Pole. Twenty minutes later, we executed another push, completing a plane change in our orbit, putting us into a high-inclination lunar orbit that would see us pass over Lindblad F in eight hours.

We could have come in much faster, but I wanted my watch to be on the flight deck when we descended.

We switched shifts. Instead of returning to bed, I went to the captain's day cabin to study our recon plan again.

I was nervous. None of us had ever performed an EVA, let alone walked on the surface of another planetary body.

Zeta had assured me that we were well-equipped for it and that our protomatter suits were designed for the environment we would encounter.

We carried a small rover stowed in *Thunder*'s small cargo bay. It could carry six passengers inside a pressurized compartment, and we needed it because the distances we needed to traverse were quite large. We had to land the corvette about 20 miles away from the IMH buildings in order to stay below the horizon and avoid detection.

On our first pass on the far side, we got our first good look at Lindblad F. I recorded a high-definition video and spent several hours with Zeta and Busto studying the crater's interior.

It was an almost perfectly circular bowl, 25 miles in diameter at the lip and 10 miles at the bottom of the basin, which was about 7,000 feet below the lip.

The descent from the lip to the basin bottom was 5 to 6 miles long, so quite steep, at least for human senses accustomed to Earth's gravity, but in the Moon's 1/6th gee, it would feel like a gentle slope.

The bottom of the basin was not flat but undulated with hills reaching as high as 1500 feet above the low points.

Roughly 80 square miles of lunar regolith that IMH was mining for its unusually high concentration of the Helium-3 isotope, valuable for its use in compact fusion power plants on many large starships.

Most fusion plants, such as the ones in our base, used the proton-proton reaction because fuel was exceedingly cheap. However, it had a low power density, making the plants impractically large for a vessel like a ship. He-3 was much better suited for that application, particularly for large warships, making it a strategic resource.

Why are there high He-3 concentrations on the Moon? The Sun's solar wind deposited the isotopes into the top layers of the lunar regolith. Collected over billions of years of accumulation, the concentrations were significant, and extraction costs were much lower than isolating He-3 from the atmosphere of a gas giant such as Jupiter.

There's your gratuitous science lesson.

That explains why IMH had supposedly established this mining operation, and it was a good cover. The best fronts are ones based on a slice of the truth. Nobody would have guessed that they were secretly excavating an ancient artifact somewhere under those buildings.

Our images showed three concentrations of buildings in the crater basin. There was a large cluster on the northern edge, situated at the bottom of a valley. The largest buildings were located there, along with what looked to be garages and possibly habitation domes.

Two smaller clusters of buildings were located approximately 3 to 4 miles distant in the southern half of the basin. These consisted of a single dome, garage, and what looked like large mining vehicles.

It was a lot of infrastructure and buildings. The Kergans down there could conceivably have hundreds of humans enslaved.

"I think we should land just north of the northern lip, right here," I said, pointing to a spot north of Lindblad F where the crater lip dipped into a shallow gully or chasm. "The lip will mask our approach from this main cluster. We'd only be about 8 to 10 miles distant."

Busto pinched his lower lip with his thumb and forefinger and nodded. "Yeah, I don't see any signs of ground traffic through there. But, then again, if they use floaters, they won't leave a trail."

Our rover was also a floater. It used traction pods for motive force and only rested on landing pads when stationary. This made for smooth and fast travel that was stealthier, and kept the lunar dust down, though it used quite a bit more power. However, the rover had its own chromatic battery with enough charge to travel for hundreds of miles.

"I want to be on the recon," I said, "and also want to take O'hatet. Who else do you want to bring?"

"Well, we got six seats," Busto mumbled. "I think we should take me, of course, then Rowbottom, Appleton, and Montana. The others we leave here on watch."

"What do you think, Zeta?"

"Zeta concurs," the igna replied.

"Okay, that leaves Destiny in command of the ship with Phoebe on Nav, Vila on Weaps, and Zeta on engineering. It'll be boring, but they'll be ready to extract us on the dime if we get into trouble."

Busto and Zeta left the compartment.

I stretched and considered what we were facing.

This was looking like a much bigger job than I had anticipated. There were dozens of buildings that would have to be cleared, and that wasn't even accounting for this underground vault with the Astral Maul. Furthermore, the buildings were spread out, with those two separate clusters of buildings that were miles distant from the main one. I didn't know how we would manage this rescue with just my crew.

But those were problems for the future. Right now, our task was to gather information so we could make plans. If we needed to modify our goals, we would do that.

# 31

Eight hours later, after completing four orbits of the Moon, I performed one last big push to deorbit us, placing us on a ballistic trajectory ending in a final deceleration and landing just north of Lindblad F.

I ordered general quarters since we were entering into potential danger. Soon, all the crew were suited up and at their stations.

"Captain, I'm picking up a search radar from inside Lindblad F," Appleton reported on the intercom.

"Roger," I replied. "Keep an eye on it and let me know immediately if it switches into acquisition mode."

"Aye aye, sir."

"70,000 feet, minus 2800," Destiny said, giving me our current altitude and decent rate.

It wasn't necessary for her to call it out because the data was on my display, but her regular announcements were like the chorus of a song.

The lunar terrain grew in detail as we continued our descent.

We fell at an acute angle that kept the Lindblad F facilities below the lip of the crater and our horizon.

We were lucky that we were doing this recon during the lunar daytime. If it had been night—lunar nights lasted for two weeks—it would have been much more difficult to make out details. Even using infrared or low-light sensors.

As Destiny called another mark, I gave us a push to decrease our velocity and started looking for a suitable landing spot among the rugged terrain.

The ground below was strewn with large boulders, probably the ejecta of this ancient crater.

I zeroed out our descent velocity and began gliding over the ground at about 500 feet altitude, moving at 90 knots.

Staring down between my legs through the floor, made transparent by my HUD, I spotted what looked like a clearing near the head of the chasm we would drive down. I adjusted my flight controls to direct *Thunder* toward it, performing a small hop to clear the summit of a large hill, then continued descending.

Punching a button on my virtual console, I deployed the undercarriage.

Other than Destiny's callouts, it was utterly silent on the flight deck, other than the whisper of the air handling system and the low background hum of the corvette's dense power systems pushing electrical energy into the tractor pods.

With a final nudge, I brought us to a stop a few feet above the ground and killed the tractors, letting Luna's weak gravity pull us gently the last couple of feet until we contacted the regolith.

*Thunder* bounced slightly on its undercarriage, absorbing the last remaining joules of our kinetic energy.

Slight showers of dust puffed out from the landing pads,

though without an atmosphere, these clouds quickly fell back to the ground.

"Contact!" I called out. "Secure maneuvering systems."

Luna's weak gravity tugged at me. My muscular 250 lb body weighed only 40 lb here.

There was happy chatter in the compartment and my crew buzzed with excitement over the exotic landscape.

Appleton and Destiny compared a nearby boulder to Barney the Dinosaur, and Busto and Rowbottom debated how fast one could safely run on foot.

The six-person away team immediately began preparations for our EVA. We were already in our suits, but we reconfigured those for use as tactical vacuum armor.

After descending to Deck 3, Busto issued small arms from the armory.

Montana exited the ship with Zeta to prepare the rover and remove it from *Thunder*'s cargo bay. Zeta wasn't on the away team but her technical knowledge of the rover was needed in case we encountered problems getting the small craft to operate.

"I have the conn," Destiny said as I rose from my acceleration couch and skipped across the deck.

"You have the conn," I replied. "Remember, don't do anything that I wouldn't."

She chuckled. "You bet, and there's plenty of dumb things you'd do that I also won't do."

"Don't get started." I punched her in the shoulder, feeling her suit harden under my fist, absorbing its energy. It was impossible to give somebody a charley horse when they were wearing protomatter.

30 minutes later, the away team was in the rover, with Rowbottom in the driver's seat. Busto sat at his side, acting as an observer.

The rover was covered by an oblong hemispherical shell with large windows cut into its sides, giving everybody an excellent exterior view. An airlock in the rear gave us access to the outside while maintaining a comfortable atmosphere inside.

Rowbottom lifted us off the landing pads to a height of about a yard above the undulating ground, and we accelerated forward.

I looked behind us as *Thunder* receded in the distance. I had landed us in a valley near some large boulders, and with its active camo enabled, it wasn't long before I could no longer see our ship. The only way we would find our way back would be to follow our recorded navigation points.

We flew down the chasm in the crater's lip like a chute at a water park.

After a mile, we broke through to the other side, and Lindblad F's bowl opened below us.

From this vantage point, we could see many miles. Without an atmosphere to blur distant objects, everything jumped at us in sharp detail.

Rowbottom steered westward, avoiding the large cluster of buildings directly to the south. Though we were flying out in the open, the rover also had active camo and an internal heatsink to dump excess heat, so our thermal signature matched the background.

Descending the crater slope at 30 to 40 mph, in the distance about 5 miles away, I watched colossal mining vehicles lumbering across the lunar surface. They were mounted on massive eight-wheel chasses and had some kind of complicated-looking apparatus attached to the front. There was no sign of a cockpit or other facilities that could support a marac or a human.

"Are those robotic?" I asked.

Busto pointed the rover's optics at one of the trucks and zoomed in. "Hard to say from here, but it looks like it."

O'hatet sat next to me, silently looking out her window. I turned to her and said, "Does this look familiar?"

"I suppose so," she said. "At least, there's no surprises so far."

We circled around the basin for about 20 minutes.

Dozens of the large mining trucks were scattered around. Most were in groups that appeared to be crawling slowly, working at the regolith.

"That one up there," Busto said from the front.

"Okay, I see it," Rowbottom said, and he adjusted our trajectory slightly.

"I spotted one of the mining trucks that's out by itself. We're gonna get a closer look."

I nodded and returned to looking out my window as the landscape swept by in a blur.

"Look, it's barely moving," Busto said. "Approach it from the rear and follow it for a while."

Our rover eased up behind the lone truck and stopped about a hundred feet behind it.

The robotic truck was moving slower than a walking pace, just inching forward.

Dust and gravel sprayed around the forward apparatus which was lowered onto the regolith and doing something to it. Probably extracting the He-3 like a slug foraging on the floor of one of Earth's forests. I almost expected to see a trail of slime behind it.

We followed the truck for 15 minutes without seeing anything change. The truck just kept moving slowly forward.

Busto turned in his seat and looked at me. "What next?" he asked.

"What do you think?" I asked O'hatet.

"I want to tap into it with a network cable," she said.

Busto jerked around to look more closely at her. "You sure about that?"

"The vehicle seems to be unguarded, and I see no signs of sensors looking to the sides or rear. There is a charging and maintenance terminal on the rear." She pointed with a tentacle. "See it?"

She was correct.

On the rear of the truck chassis was a user interface terminal of some kind. The truck was moving so slowly that a person could approach it and easily keep up on foot.

"Busto," I called out, "O'hatet wants to make a field trip to the truck. Can you bring us closer?"

"They might see us," the former Marine said.

"If they haven't already, they're unlikely to if we keep behind them. O'hatet wants to make a hard link to the truck."

He sat there silently for a minute, thinking. "Okay. Rowbottom, bring us up closer, about 40 feet behind it. You stay with the vehicle. The rest of us will exit and support O'hatet."

"Got it, boss," Rowbottom said, accelerating forward to bring us near the truck's rear.

We exited the rover through the airlock.

Busto led the way forward, with O'hatet and me following him.

Vila and Montana kept to our flanks with weapons ready, watching the horizon.

Busto stopped behind the maintenance interface.

The truck loomed above, at least 20 feet tall and probably massing over 100 tons. If it suddenly stopped and reversed, we'd be squished like cockroaches.

The marac came forward with a tablet in her hand, floating on her tractor harness. "This is a standard Kergan computer interface," O'hatet said on our comms. "How convenient."

She dug around in a satchel that hung from her torso until she found a computer cable.

She plugged one end into her tablet and the other into the truck.

Lights on the maintenance panel lit up, and text in an unfamiliar script appeared.

O'hatet tapped at her tablet a few times.

Through her helmet visor, I could see her eyes scanning across the display.

Over the comms, I heard her mumbling to herself as she worked.

She turned from the panel a couple times and looked at her tablet, tapped something into it, then focused again on the panel.

This went on for about twenty minutes.

I started to worry that the driver of the truck would notice us. It couldn't be an AI in there because the Kergans were party to the galactic treaty that forbade the use of machine intelligence. But there had to be an operator somewhere, either hidden in the truck or, more likely, operating it remotely.

As the minutes ticked away with no seeming change in what O'hatet was doing, I grew impatient, then bored, and my thoughts drifted.

I imagined that Ban'ach could be just a couple miles distant, inside one of those buildings we'd seen. She was free, carrying the memories of my dead parents. The strength that Mom and Dad had always been for me had been stolen and now Ban'ach was using it for herself. How could I lose my connection to my parents without forgetting who I was? Without losing myself in this confusing and violent universe?

My ruminations were interrupted by our marac friend. "I have somebody for you to meet, Captain," O'hatet said.

"What?!" The request was so sudden and out of the blue that it left me momentarily speechless.

O'hatet turned to me. "I've made contact with the vehicle driver."

My first thought was that she'd betrayed us. "Why would you do that?"

"Captain, you misunderstand me. Please, trust me, you will want to talk to this person."

"Okay, put them through on the radio so everybody can hear."

A few seconds later, there was a clicking sound on the radio, like a call was being connected. O'hatet's voice said, "Elara, can you hear me?"

"Yes, I'm here," a synthetic-sounding genderless voice responded.

"Good, I have Captain Kory Drake of the starship *Thunder* on the line."

"Hello," I said, "who am I speaking to?"

"My name is Elara Finch."

The name sounded familiar. I'd heard it somewhere before, but it wasn't coming to me at the moment.

"You're...human?" I asked.

"Yes, though I'm not at the vehicle location. I'm at Substation A."

"Why does your voice sound so..."

"Unusual? Yes, you are not hearing my true voice. I am talking to you through a mindjack."

For a heartbeat, I forgot to keep walking forward with

the truck.

This was a mindjacked human I was talking to.

"How?" I asked, confused about what exactly I was talking to.

"I am operating this vehicle remotely." I remembered to keep walking forward at the shoulder of O'hatet, who was tapping something into her tablet. "Please, can you help me? Us?"

"Who is us?"

"There are 161 of us humans here at this mine. We've all been mindjacked." Her voice didn't seem to convey emotional nuances because a computer synthesized it. But I got the sense that if I were hearing her natural voice, tones of desperation would have been leaking through. "Those raiders kidnapped us."

"Raiders?"

"Yes, the Nebula Nomads. They kidnapped us and brought us to the Moon! My husband is somewhere here, but I haven't...encountered him since we arrived. Please, do you know anything about my boy?"

"Are you from Elkin?" I asked. "Elkin, Arizona?"

"Yes! My boy, Leo Finch, is he okay?"

Then I remembered where I'd heard the name Elara Finch before. She was the mother of Leo Finch, the boy I had interacted with at Urbana's home for children.

I'd found one of the abductees! I'd found Leo's mother!

"Elara, I've met your boy, Leo. He misses his parents. He is being taken care of by a woman named Urbana Fontana. Last time I saw him, he was safe."

"Praise God! I've been so worried!"

I looked at the faces of the away team.

Their eyes were locked on mine as they listened to the conversation.

Busto nodded to me.

"Elara, you said that your husband was here also?" I asked, hoping to get more information on the other abductees.

"Yes. I can see his record in the database, but...they won't let me talk to him. However, talking isn't the correct word. They won't let us use our bodies for anything. We're trapped in these rigor pods. It's been months! I'd do anything to hold my husband or my son in my arms. To drink a cold beer. To linger under a warm shower. Can you help us?"

"That's why we're here. But I must urge you to be patient. We're not ready to bring you out yet."

"Why?!" This time, her desperate tone came through clearly.

"Where scouting out this mining facility. At the moment, we need help from *you*."

"Me?!" Elara almost shouted.

"Yes, we need information. This facility is quite large. We need to know about the security, the layout, where the humans are located, and how to bring you out safely."

"Okay, I think I can help you with that."

"There's more. And, Elara, this is important. You must keep this secret what I'm about to tell you. We have evidence of some kind of object being excavated in secret below one of these buildings. Do you know anything of this?"

The radio was silent for several seconds. "Possibly. Some kind of special project is being conducted under Annex C of the Admin Hall. I've been ordered several times to operate an excavator or haul rock. It's unusual work, very different from our normal mining work. I actually kind of enjoy it. It breaks up the monotony."

"What else can you tell me? Have you seen anything else unusual?"

"Not that I recall. It's been several weeks since they had me over there."

"But you know where it is, right?"

"Yes, like I said, it's under Annex C of the Admin Hall."

"Are you able to move around the facility freely?" I asked.

"No, not at all. Our bodies are confined to these rigor pods. The only way to interact with the outside world is through these disgusting mindjacks, and it's all computer stuff. My body is kept medically paralyzed, and all my senses are linked to the mindjack. They work us 18 hours daily, leaving only 6 hours for sleep. And our sleep is manipulated."

"But you have control of this mining truck, correct?"

"Yes, but it's tightly constrained. I have assigned work areas I have to keep within. If I deviate from them, it would raise a flag on the supervisor's board. And they monitor my productivity."

"Who's your supervisor?"

"A Kergan named O'draril. I've never met him in person, but he supervises my mindjack."

"How are you talking to me?"

"Captain," O'hatet interrupted. "We must finish the conversation. We could be detected at any time."

"Your friend is correct," Elara said. "O'draril could notice I'm distracted. He doesn't normally bother me when I'm in the middle of a field working, but it has happened."

"Okay, Elara. This is what I need. My colleague who contacted you is named O'hatet. She is a marac, but not a Kergan marac. She is a friend from the Lufen Republic and is helping us. I want you to give her as much information as possible with our remaining time, anything related to facility security, maps, emergency procedures, locations of these rigor pods, and anything else you can tell us. Can you do that with the remaining time we have?"

"Yes, I think so. I can push the data directly into O'hatet's computer if she has one available."

"Yes, I am ready," O'hatet said.

"Thank you, Elara," I said.

"You won't forget us? Please, promise that you won't!" She cried.

"No, that is why we are here. We've come to rescue the humans who were abducted from Elkin. But it's going to be a few weeks until we're prepared. Don't give up hope!"

Concluding with that remark, O'hatet disconnected our voice channel, and she went back to working with her tablet and the panel as she and Elara transferred the data I had requested.

We had hit the jackpot.

I could hardly believe how easily we had penetrated the facility and made contact with one of the slaves. IMH had practically zero security on its perimeter. But, if they discovered we'd made contact with Elara, all that could change in a heartbeat. We needed to quickly extract the data before somebody noticed our activities.

I paced next to O'hatet, waiting for her to finish.

It took some time, 30 minutes, by the count of my watch.

We'd been following this mining truck for an hour now.

I checked in with Destiny over the LPD comms and confirmed that everything at the ship was quiet. I gave her a status update on our situation and then signed off.

"Done," O'hatet announced and disconnected her cable from the back of the truck.

Busto herded us back to the rover.

We entered through the airlock and took our seats.

We lifted off and returned to *Thunder*, this time taking the long route and circumnavigating the base to get plenty of recorded video of its layout.

# 32

Back in the ship, we cleaned up and stowed the rover.

It was clear to me that IMH's mining facility was too large for us to infiltrate *and* do what needed to be done without extensive preparations. So, I ordered Destiny to set a course for home, and we lifted off to head back to base.

During the transit back, I studied the data that O'hatet had received from Elara Finch. It consisted of a confusing jumble of documents, images, and spreadsheets.

Sitting with O'hatet in my day-cabin, it took us hours to even begin making sense of it. Elara had been scared of being caught by her supervisor and so had rushed through the task, erring on the side of too much information.

There were quite a few files that didn't belong. Like the menu for the cafeteria—for maracs only—and the bathroom cleaning schedule.

Eventually, a coherent picture of the situation began to form.

The IMH mining facility at Lindblad F was divided into three groups of buildings. The main group was called AC-1 and included the Administrative Center, under which we suspected the vault was being excavated. One of the buildings in AC-1 also contained 120 rigor pods in which were imprisoned mindjacked humans.

Two other sets of buildings were called AC-2 and AC-3. These were several miles distant from AC-1 and contained deployed elements of the mining operation. Each contained 30 more rigor pods, though not all were occupied.

Besides the humans, AC-2 and AC-3 also contained habitats for the marac supervisory and technical staff, garages, and parking areas for mining vehicles.

AC-1 contained the same types of buildings as the other two smaller areas, though on a larger scale. In addition to this, there were administrative offices, science labs, the main security building, a small spaceport, and a large He-3 refinery.

Security appeared to be quite small, which initially surprised me. I thought that with this super-secret artifact they were investigating, they'd have many more guards around. But after further thought, I realized they must be trying to avoid attention. On the public face, the only thing they needed to secure were the mindjacked humans, and that was easy because they were stuck in rigor pods.

The weak security is why it had been so easy for us to penetrate the facility's perimeter. What guards were there were located either in the secure buildings where the rigor pods were located, at the refinery, or the Admin Center. In total, there were twenty-six security personnel at the facility. A lot, considering the size of my team, but small compared to the number of buildings and the size of the operation they were securing.

Ban'ach was in charge of the security now. She had escaped us in Elkin and fled to her masters at IMH, and they had assigned her to the Lindblad operation. Probably because she was familiar with the humans she had abducted.

If we planned our rescue operation correctly, I might have an opportunity to face her in the Syderealium and recover my memories. I hoped for this.

I also suspected Ban'ach was involved with the Astral Maul. She was a powerful, flairsparked Soul Ravager who was comfortable with the Syderealium. It seemed like too much of a coincidence that she happened to be working at a place where they were uncovering a Primordian artifact that was known to interface with the Syderealium. Perhaps she wasn't involved with security at all, the job being a cover, and was, in fact, investigating the Maul. Maybe there were other Soul Ravagers at the mining base.

Among the files Elara had given us, we also found emergency procedures. In the case of an attack on the facility by armed intruders, the nearest responder was a Kergan military base 900 miles to the southeast. An emergency request for help would be sent from the Ops Center, and the security guards would have to hold off the attackers until help arrived.

It became clear that any operation we planned would be large and complex. Too big, I feared, for my crew to execute alone. And with the entire Earth threatened by the Astral Maul, the stakes were too large. We needed help.

"Ahhh, gravity," Destiny said with a moan from the couch in the base library. "I never thought I'd miss it so much."

I sat in another chair. Busto was next to Destiny, Zeta floated nearby, and O'hatet rested in a chair.

This was my inner circle of people who I used to arrive at crucial decisions.

"You know you can't trust gravity, right?" Busto said

with a smirk.

"No, Clemen, I didn't," Destiny said with mock respect. "Please correct my ignorance."

"It's because it always brings you down."

"Hyuck, hyuck, hyuck," she said, slapping her knees. "Be careful not to hurt yourself."

I smiled at their byplay.

We'd only just returned from our mission. The rest of the crew were resupplying *Thunder* under Montana's guidance, but I had requested an immediate meeting with my command circle.

"Okay, friends," I said. "We've got some decisions to make. O'hatet, please share with the group here what we found in the data Elara Finch gave us."

The reporter proceeded to summarize what she and I had sifted out of the files and the picture we had pieced together.

"So, they've got twenty-six armed guards," Busto said, "spread across three different areas of the crater basin. That's a lot of area to cover and a lot of dangerous people to neutralize."

"Yes, it's obviously a problem," I said. "But let's not jump too far forward yet. First, I want to list our mission objectives. As I see it, there are two. One, secure the rigor pods with the enslaved humans inside them and transport them to safety. Two, locate the Astral Maul and destroy it."

There was also a third objective, a secret one, for me: Capture Ban'ach and recover my memories.

But I wasn't going to reveal my intentions to my friends. They wouldn't understand, and Zeta might try to stop me. Her ethics didn't permit the stealing of energlyphs, even the recovery of ones that had been stolen. She would not support my plan. I would keep my goal secret and figure out a way to execute it when the time came. After all, I was the commander of this cell, and that had to count for *something*.

Busto and Destiny nodded in response to my two stated goals. "161 humans in rigor pods," Destiny said. "That's a lot, Kory. We're not moving them with *Thunder*. Even if its cargo hold were empty, we might only fit eight pods."

"Ten pods," Zeta said. "Zeta checked the specifications."

"Great. Ten. That's a lot less than 161."

"Obviously, we're going to need some bigger transport," I said. "Any ideas?"

"We could secure the facility, then make a bunch of trips between Earth and Luna," Busto said.

"I doubt that will work," O'hatet said. "That would take days, and the Kergan military would likely learn of the attack within hours if we're lucky. I we're unlucky, then we'd have only perhaps 30 minutes until reinforcements showed up."

"What about constructing a small habitat nearby and moving the pods to there?" Destiny said. "Then we could take our time transporting them to Earth."

"I don't think we have the time to construct it, and it would still take a couple hours to move all the pods," I said. "I think it's too risky."

"We need a bigger ship," Busto said. "There's only one quick way to get one: capture it."

I nodded. "Yeah, the same idea occurred to me. There are dozens of empty Kergan freighters arriving at Earth daily. Surely one of those could fit 161 rigor pods." I looked at our alien friends. "Zeta or O'hatet, do you think either one of you could pilot a Kergan freighter?"

"Nay," Zeta responded. "But you could, Consort."

"Truly?"

"Aye, or one of our colleagues here. The pilot interfaces

are not too different from what you use on *Thunder*."

"What about reading Kergan script? I won't understand the display panels."

"That shouldn't be a problem. Zeta can fabricate an apparatus that translates the text into English on your HUD."

"Okay, well, let's not worry about the details yet. For now, let's assume that we need to capture an empty Kergan freighter. Busto, do you think that's something our tactical team is up to?"

Busto nodded. "I believe so. Those freighters typically have a crew of nine, all civilians. The question I have is whether we can board one without being caught by Kergan naval forces."

"Zeta, what do you think?" I asked.

"We would have to assault a ship that was without escort and immediately after jumping in system," Zeta said.

"Where does that happen?"

"Generally speaking, at any Lagrange point in the system. The Kergan typically use the Earth-Moon L4 and L5 points, or the Earth-Sun L1 and L2 points."

I dug around in my memory, trying to remember what Lagrange points were. It had been part of our training for operating *Thunder* in space. At these Lagrange points, the gravitational force of two massive bodies, combined with the centripetal force of orbit, perfectly cancel out the local gravitational field.

"They typically use the Earth-Moon L4 and L5 because they are closer," Zeta continued. "But the Earth-Sun L1 and L2 are more stable and larger, preferred for long-distance jumps. Being further from the Earth, they are also more isolated, less frequented by military traffic."

I nodded and scratched an itch on my scalp. It had been

two days since I last showered, and I stank from using my protomatter suit. "Okay, so you're suggesting we stake out L1 or L2 and capture a suitable freighter. Correct?"

"Aye, this seems like the most realistic option. Or capture one during its transit from a Lagrange point to Earth."

"Okay, that answers the question about how we get enough transport capacity for the mission. We'll figure out the logistics later, but this sounds like a workable plan to me." I looked at my friends. "Are we agreed?"

There were nods all around. "It'll be a party," Destiny said.

I looked down at the notes I'd scribbled on my tablet. "Next issue: we are too few to pull off this mission. *Thunder* can conceivably be flown by only one person for brief periods. The pilot would have great difficulty controlling the weapons and sensors, but it can be done in an emergency. That means that, in the best case, we have eight people to pull this mission off."

"Less," Zeta said. "Zeta is not allowed to engage in combat directly with Kergan persons. And you will need a pilot for the freighter."

"Great, thanks. We have *six* people to do this thing. And one of them, O'hatet, is a non-combatant, though I need her in the attack team to help us with the computer systems. Five people is nowhere near enough to complete this. We need heavier forces." I looked at Zeta. "Zeta, we need help. Is there anything the Dominion can do?"

The igna rotated on her vertical axis, the glow from the sides of her capsule throbbing. "Aye, Zeta will make a request with her superiors for additional forces."

"You can do that?" I asked.

"Indeed, cells sometimes encounter forces too large to

handle by themselves. There are procedures for requesting a joint attack from multiple cells."

"Like we did at Malmstrom when we hit that command nexus?"

"Correct."

"How long will it take for you to get permission?"

"Zeta does not know. This mission is complex and will require extensive planning and coordination between the cells, which complicates security. How many people do you believe you will need to secure the rigor pods and eliminate the Astral Maul?"

I looked at Busto. "What do you think?"

He took a minute to think about it. His eyes stared into the distance, and I saw the wheels turning behind them. "Four each for AC-2 and AC-3. Twelve to secure AC-1, but make it sixteen instead, so there's a reserve to help with the Maul. I make that twenty armed members of the ground team."

"And five of those will be from our crew. So, Zeta, we need to find at least another fifteen marines and their own transport to and from Luna."

"Aye, Consort, clearly, this will need to be a multi-cell effort. Zeta will begin the request process with her superiors."

That didn't sound like it would be a quick task. But we had other things we could do while we waited for approval. Namely, capturing our freighter.

Though once acquired, I hadn't a clue where we'd hide it. I mean, it's not like you can just park a freighter behind a tree and hope nobody notices. Obviously, it couldn't be one of those monster bulk carriers or even a medium freighter — too big to hide, and let's face it, total overkill for what we needed. We weren't moving an army, just trying to sneak a few things past the bad guys, not start a shipping empire.

As our meeting wrapped up and my friends left the room, I felt the emptiness inside me where the memory of my parents had once dwelt. The feeling of their love was no longer there to strengthen me and give me purpose. The loss was a continuing drag on my emotional health, slowing me down, leaching my enthusiasm like a parasite feeding on my blood.

I had to confront Ban'ach. Somehow, I would do it, recover my memories, and make sure she could never do something like this again to another human.

# 33

*Thunder* came to a stop 100 miles away from the Earth-Sun L1 point.

"Weaps, keep your eyes peeled," I said.

"Aye aye, Captain," Busto answered.

We had decided to choose the L1 point between Earth and the Sun because we hoped that anything looking in this direction from Earth's orbit would be blinded by the Sun's radiation, thus masking our activities. Evidence indicated that this Lagrange point was used infrequently by the Kergan, though there was sufficient traffic to ensure we'd locate a target.

At 903,000 miles distant, the L1 point had taken us two and a half days to reach.

During the transit, we'd seen sporadic traffic. Most of it had been Kergan commercial vehicles, loudly squawking on their transponders to the entire solar system.

We also slipped past Kergan military vessels on two occasions.

Fortunately, running silently without a transponder

and with minimal emissions made us nearly invisible. Space was incredibly vast, and the chances of spotting an object as small as *Thunder* were infinitesimal unless there was some kind of bright signature to call attention to it. When running silent, we appeared to be a small chunk of rock on most sensors.

Since we weren't under thrust, other than station-keeping maneuvers—which were completely automated—I gave permission for each watch to maintain just two people at a time on the flight deck. One to monitor the sensors, the other the flight controls and engineering console.

Just like the old *Thunder*, the corvette's consoles on the flight deck were multifunctional, allowing their users to operate any ship system no matter where they were sitting.

Busto and I left Phoebe with the conn and Zeta on sensors and drifted up the ladder to Deck 1 to grab some food in the mess. It must have been mealtime because nearly all the rest of the crew were present, and it was crowded.

As I floated through the hatch to the mess, a squeeze tube of coffee flew past my head to be caught by Appleton.

"Watch it, Vila," Appleton said with a grin, "you just about decapitated the captain."

I smiled and rapped my knuckles on my head a couple of times. "Yup, there's still something in there."

"That's just the mice," Destiny said with a sparkle in her eyes.

"Hamsters," I responded. "I upgraded months ago."

"And those wheels I hear turning all the time, I thought that was a figure of speech. You really do have hamster wheels in there, doncha?"

That earned some laughs from everybody.

Rowbottom, O'hatet, and Destiny were playing what looked like poker at one of the tables. They were using a deck of magnetic cards so they wouldn't drift away from the table. That also made cheating more difficult.

"I didn't know you knew how to play, O'hatet," I said as I dug through the pantry for a tube of meat-flavored paste.

"My fine companions are teaching me," the marac said. "Poker is a fascinating game. It's as much about watching your human reactions as following the rules."

"How much are you behind?"

"Ha," Destiny guffawed. "She's actually beating us."

Seeing my sister happy warmed my heart. She was the second in command of our unit, but that fact didn't seem to have gone to her head. She had just turned eighteen, but she was still a young girl in many ways. She deserved to enjoy a few more years as a young person.

But war had caught all of us and forced us to do things we never would have thought possible.

I was close to my nineteenth birthday and already the captain of a warship and leader of an insurgent cell. I'd been forced to grow up young because I had nobody else to take care of me. I'd been homeless and without adult supervision since I escaped from the orphanage when I was thirteen. I was fighting for a guerrilla unit against alien invaders, and strangely, it was the most stable home situation Destiny or I had had in over five years.

We drifted at the L1 point for a week.

We saw several ships a day emerge from jump points or depart.

Both Kergan and Dominion jump-capable ships used the same FTL technology. Their drives wrapped the ship into a pocket universe and translated it into the Syderealium. From there, the ship's own tractor pods pushed it across the dimensions to another point in its target universe, then dissolved the pocket. Using the Syderealium as a shortcut drastically reduced travel distances by many orders of magnitude.

It was also relatively cheap, in terms of energy, and reasonably fast, though *how* fast depended on how good one's navigator and computers were since they had to be able to plot an efficient route through the confusing topology of the Syderealium.

Ships could only form sydereal pocket universes in areas with gravitationally flat space, such as points very distant from massive objects or Lagrange points. That's what brought us to the Earth-Sun L1 point.

All that being said, *Thunder* didn't have its own jump drive, so it wasn't a problem we currently had to worry about. When we upgraded to a frigate hull, we would be given an FTL drive.

We saw dozens of freighters during that week, but they were either too big or had escorts accompanying them. Even the small freighters were massive in comparison to *Thunder*. We could have easily fit into the cargo bay of even the smallest ship we encountered.

After five days of this monotonous watch, most of the crew became stir-crazy. *Thunder* was too small to have any significant recreational facilities, and there was barely enough room in the open areas for one person to exercise.

Montana told me her worries about the crew losing bone and muscle mass in the zero-gee environment, so I forced them to use the exercise equipment.

*"Contact Gamma-10 on the scopes,"* Vila announced over the PA. *"Captain to the flight deck."* The announcement cut out.

I quickly finished drying myself off and slipped into my ship coveralls.

I opened the door of the head and flew down the corridor to the ladder, changed direction downward, and arrived at Deck 2 outside the flight deck.

We were on day eight since we arrived at L1.

We only had enough food for another three days out here before we would start eating into our supply reserves. I honestly didn't want to waste five days going home to resupply and returning here. I hoped this new contact would put us in business.

I entered the flight deck and took my seat on the pilot couch. "What you got?" I asked.

"A small freighter just jumped into the system. From what I can see, they appear to meet our requirements. They're alone, and they're small."

I studied the visual of the new ship being recorded with *Thunder*'s optics.

The ship was 90 miles distant and closing, beginning its transit to Earth.

As Vila had said, it was a small ship but clearly a freighter. There was no evidence of external weapons, and the gaping hatches of three decent-sized cargo bays were visible.

It was accelerating at a leisurely quarter gee.

I spoke into the PA and said, "General quarters, this is not a drill."

A couple of minutes later, the rest of my crew began to arrive in their protomatter suits.

Once Destiny arrived, I slipped out to get my own suit on, which only took a minute.

Everybody was in their positions when I returned. Busto and Vila called out parameters to each other as they gathered more information from the sensors.

"Nav, plot me an intercept course," I said.

"Aye aye," Phoebe responded.

"We're doing this?" Destiny said softly from my side.

"Yes, I think so. This looks like the one." I turned to Busto. "Lieutenant Busto, prepare your boarding team."

"Aye aye, Captain." He rose for his couch. "Rowbottom, Vila, and Appleton, you're with me."

The four of them flew out of the flight deck, heading to the armory on Deck 3.

"Ensign Brooks, you're on Weaps," I said.

Phoebe acknowledged my order and reconfigured her console to manage the sensors and weapons systems since my two weapons specialists, Busto and Vila, were on the boarding team.

"Okay, people," I said to the entire deck. "This is going to be a contested boarding action. Remember your training. The enemy appears to be unarmed, but don't take any chances. Nav, prepare to jam their comms. Weaps, watch your fire. We'd like to take them down without damaging the ship. If we destroy their drive, the ship's worthless to us."

I accelerated *Thunder* forward on the plotted intercept course, bringing us up behind the freighter on the same trajectory and a little to the port of the enemy.

I closed aggressively.

"Weaps, hit them with our targeting radar and lidar, full power. Let's wake them up."

"Aye, aye."

"Nav, steer our EW array at their main comms array." I looked at Zeta. "ChEng, prepare to grapple onto the ship. We're making a hard dock on their port airlock."

"Aye aye, Captain," Zeta said. "Are you going to hail them?"

"No, I want them to be caught by surprise."

*Thunder* approached the ship and glided up on their port side with our starboard auxiliary airlock pointed at theirs.

Our ship began to vibrate distressingly as the tractor fields of the two ships began to constructively interfere with each other at this close range, shaking *Thunder*'s hull like a ball of dough being kneaded by a baker.

The enemy freighter suddenly veered off course, trying to climb away from us.

"They've noticed us," I said.

I shifted the flight controls and felt acceleration press me into my chair.

The freighter jinked around, trying to put distance between themselves and us, but our small corvette was far more maneuverable than them. They even tried to ram us from the side, but I only used that to our advantage.

"Deploy grapples!"

Powered protomatter pylons shot out of the side of *Thunder* and slammed into the side of the freighter, sticking in place.

Zeta began to reel us in until, with a deep reverberating *thud*, we slammed up against the side of the freighter.

The pylons reconfigured into a tube connecting our airlock to theirs.

"Boarding team, you are go!" I yelled into the comms.

I configured one of my displays to show me a video of the HUDs from each boarding team member.

Busto and his team were crammed into the auxiliary airlock, each carrying a flechette rifle, sidearm, and combat webbing.

The outer hatch opened.

The tube of protomatter led from it to the other ship's airlock.

Busto shouted something.

Appleton flew forward and planted charges on the hatch. Then she flew back and took cover in the airlock.

The helmet views looked away, and seconds later, there was a flash and roar of escaping atmosphere.

The protomatter tube sealed up the resulting gaps, and soon, the atmosphere stabilized.

I continued to fight with the flight controls, keeping us pressed against the freighter's side.

Our corvette looked like a sea anemone stuck to a huge boulder. Though small and empty, the freighter nonetheless outmassed us by at least twenty times over.

I watched my boarding team rush into the enemy airlock.

The inner door opened without any problems.

Vila and Rowbottom tossed flash-bangs into a corridor, and there was a blast and bright light.

The team pushed forward.

The freighter had a civilian crew. They should have been unarmed and quick to surrender once my armed team was on board. But that's not what happened.

The first sign of trouble was a yell from Appleton, covering the team's rear.

"*I'm taking fire!*" Her HUD showed her crouching behind an open hatch. "*Somebody, cover me!*"

"*On it,*" Vila said.

Moments later, he was leaning out around a corner and firing his gun at where the shots seemed to be coming from.

I watched Rowbottom push down a corridor toward the enemy flight deck.

An object came flying down the corridor toward him.

"*Grenade!*" He ducked into an alcove.

The other team members dropped to the floor.

There was a blast, and their HUDs shook.

Smoke filled the corridor.

Busto asked for a row call.

Everybody checked in, so they were still alive.

Rowbottom pointed forward into the smoke and fired several bursts at something I couldn't see.

Appleton took advantage of the confusion to relocate, turning into an empty compartment and taking cover behind its walls.

*"We're pinned down!"* Busto yelled. *"We must move, or we're dead! Follow me!"*

It shouldn't have been this difficult. There shouldn't have been this much resistance from the crew. It didn't make sense.

Busto flew out of cover and pushed aft toward engineering, in the direction they'd first received fire from.

His gun fired again and again. He was ripping the hell out of the corridor.

He passed the body of a dead marac, leaking globes of purple blood to float in the zero-gee environment.

Rowbottom was still on the forward side, and Appleton had joined him.

They leapfrogged forward, one providing cover fire while the other advanced.

Two more corpses of maracs appeared.

My boarding team had split up, which was not part of the plan. Per our training, they should have stayed together in order to support each other. But in the chaos of the firefight, I don't think Rowbottom and Appleton knew that Busto and Vila had left them to go aft.

Vila passed more marac bodies.

The team had already killed at least five maracs, and yet they continued to receive heavy fire.

I studied the camera view of one of the marac bodies.

"Those don't look like civilians," I said.

Their clothing didn't look right. In fact, the maracs looked like they were wearing armor.

"Lieutenant Busto," I said on the comms. "Those are Kergan soldiers! It's a trap! Pull back!"

Busto cried out, "*It's too late to pull back. We're engaged. I've already killed three of them.*"

Vila seemed confused. He kept flying down one corridor, realized it was a dead end, and then would fly back and try another.

Finally, he followed Busto as they entered the engineering spaces at the ship's stern.

The images I was seeing from the HUDs were too confusing, and I lost track of where my team was.

Anxiety ate into my stomach.

This should *not* have been this hard. Something was wrong. This wasn't just any ordinary freighter.

Suddenly, Appleton's HUD flashed bright yellow, and her physiological telemetry flatlined. Then her HUD blanked out.

"*We're under fire!*" Rowbottom screamed. "*Appleton's hit! I need a medic!*"

"Dammit! Destiny, you have the conn!" I turned to the jump seats. "Montana, you're with me! Grab a weapon!"

"*I'm making my way forward with Vila!*" Busto said. "*The engineering spaces are secured!*"

"*I can't hold them!*" Rowbottom yelled as he tried to apply an emergency compress to Appleton's chest.

There was surprisingly little blood, but she wasn't moving.

He released her, grabbed his gun, and started firing again at movement up the corridor.

I rushed down to the armory and grabbed a gun.

Montana came right behind me, carrying a medic's satchel.

We entered the airlock and flew across it into the other ship.

The corridor was filled with thick smoke, so I switched to IR, which only helped a little.

The sounds of a flechette gun hammering on full automatic sounded forward.

Busto and Vila flew out of the smoke and just about blew me away when I surprised them.

"This way," Busto said, taking the lead. "Watch our rear!"

"I thought you said it was clear," I said.

"I *think* it is, but there's no easy way to know for sure."

He flew forward with Vila and Montana following closely, and I came after, watching our line of retreat.

Something behind us, down the corridor, moved.

I aimed and fired a burst. The buttstock of my flechette gun vibrated against my shoulder.

I fired another burst, then another, until the movement stopped.

A minute later, after more bursts of fire, Busto and the rest of my boarding team came rushing back with Appleton under tow and Montana trying to tend to the wounded soldier.

"Where to, Busto?" I asked.

"The ship! The enemy is pushing toward us!"

Not only had we *not* subdued the enemy crew, they were in the process of executing a counterattack!

If we didn't end this immediately, this would soon turn into a counter-boarding action.

We streamed through the airlock one at a time, up the tube, and back into *Thunder*.

"Captain," Busto yelled, "help me seal the airlock!"

An armored marac appeared at the other end of the tube.

I raised my gun and fired at full auto.

Dozens of hypersonic darts punched into the alien's center of mass and exited the other side, spraying blood and gore.

I raised my muzzle and stepped back just as Busto slammed the outer door shut and cranked on the dogs.

"ChEng and Pilot," I cried on the comms, "get us out of here!"

"*Brace for acceleration!*" Destiny announced on the PA.

Montana was inside the inner airlock hatch on the floor with Appleton, trying to work on her. She curled around the other woman protectively and clamped her hands onto a railing.

*Thunder* jumped like a bucking horse as the tube and grapples disconnected.

A sideways force pushed us, threatening to make us slide down the corridor, but it was only momentary until Destiny reoriented the corvette.

I crawled to Montana. "How is she?"

The medic shook her head. "No heartbeat, Caption! Let me be. I need to focus on her!"

I said a prayer in my heart for Appleton.

She was my age, barely an adult. I had sent her into combat, and now she was dying.

Rage filled me.

"Lieutenant Austin, blow that ship away!" I ordered.

"*Aye aye, sir!*" Destiny responded moments later.

I shook Busto's shoulder to get his attention. "I need to get back to the flight deck."

"Go!" he said and gave me a gentle shove.

I half ran and half flew toward the ladder to Deck 2, as *Thunder*'s acceleration fluctuated while Destiny maneuvered.

When I was halfway up the ladder, the hull rang several times as both railgun turrets began to fire.

When I entered the flight deck, the turrets were still firing at a rate of about once every three seconds.

I flew to my chair, strapped in, and looked at the displays.

Destiny had flown *Thunder* forward of the freighter and was sitting there firing railgun slugs down its long axis, gutting the ship.

Atmosphere vented from dozens of gaping holes in the freighter's hull.

Occasionally, there would be a bright flash as a slug hit something substantial and converted its kinetic energy into vaporized metal.

The cargo ship was no longer accelerating. All electronic emissions had stopped, and running lights extinguished.

I saw several marac bodies floating in vacuum along with thousands of other pieces of debris.

"You can stop now, Dest," I said softly.

She allowed another four slugs to be fired, then said, "Weaps, cease fire." She sighed and folded her arms. "You have the conn."

"I have the conn. Destiny, take weapons. Phoebe, return to navigation and defense."

They acknowledged my orders and reconfigured their displays.

"Captain," Phoebe said, "I'm detecting a Kergan acquisition lidar scanning this area. Range is 915,000 miles. Doppler indicates they are accelerating at 20 gees in our direction."

"That's got to be a Kergan warship," I said. "They could

be here in half a day. Let's get out of here."

I took one more look at the freighter's shattered hull, feeling disappointed in myself and my crew.

We had practiced and trained for this boarding action. What had gone wrong?

I accelerated *Thunder* away from L1 and the warship's trajectory.

Their lidar wasn't in tracking mode, which meant they probably still hadn't seen us, at least not among the thousands of objects floating around us.

We should be able to slip away before they got there.

"Busto, what's the status of CPO Appleton?" I said on private comms.

*"She's gone, Captain. She took a round to the heart,"* Busto said.

"Roger."

I'd lost one of my crew.

I felt dead inside.

# 34

Chief Petty Officer Moriko Appleton died instantly from a flechette round to the heart. It happened as a consequence of orders I had given her.

I took her death hard.

She was the first person who ever died while serving under my command.

She would be far from the last, but one always remembers that first one. Just like I remember the first person I killed, that Kergan MP I blew up while rescuing Destiny from detention in San Jose.

One thing I've learned over my long career is that it's impossible to prepare for all possible contingencies when it comes to combat. You can be the best trained and equipped warrior in the universe, with fleets of ships and armies behind you and a bullet-proof battle plan, yet still, somebody will die.

Risk is a part of war. If it were risk-free, it wouldn't be warfare. It would only be bullying. When it comes to combat, your enemy has just as much right to use deadly force as you do. All it takes is one bullet to end you. Or terminate the man or woman standing next to you. Or a soldier deployed on the next hill over.

We didn't have a morgue on our small ship, and it would be at least two days until we reached home. Zeta used our small nanoforge to construct a coffin for Appleton. After Montana cleaned her up, we placed her body in it, her hair braided and dressed in a clean ship suit.

Our entire crew gathered together to say farewell. Then we shot her coffin into solar orbit.

Zeta said that eventually, her coffin and body would intersect with Earth and burn up on reentry.

I was angry.

At Busto, for letting his boarding team get split up.

At Phoebe, for not properly jamming the freighter's comms.

At Destiny, for not stopping me from deciding to board that ship.

But mostly, I was angry at myself because I was sure it was my fault we had failed. We had practiced and planned, so it must have been me who was lacking somehow. It was my responsibility.

It was foolish of me to believe these things, but at that time I still hadn't learned the cost of war. I was being irrational, and I took it out on my crew.

"Busto, why did you let your team get separated?" I asked Busto in a private meeting in my day cabin.

He shook his head, his dark eyes hiding emotion. "Fog of war, Captain. It wasn't something I chose for us to do. It's the kind of thing that happens in combat."

We reviewed the recorded HUDs from our armor during the boarding action, trying to find the moment when things went wrong. There were plenty of small things we could have done better, and we made note of them, but I couldn't find any one thing that would let me place the blame on my friend for Appleton's death.

I met with Phoebe, Zeta, and Destiny, those on the flight deck when we started the boarding action. "Phoebe, why didn't your jamming work on the freighter? How did that warship find out about our attack?"

She looked down at her lap and clenched her fists. "I don't know, Captain. I jammed them like you asked. I swear I did."

"Captain," Zeta said, "Ensign Brooks made no errors. The problem is that the jamming only stopped the freighter from being able to receive communications. But they could still transmit. They must have sent a distress message to Kergan forces on Earth. This far away, *Thunder*'s jamming would have had no effect on receivers all the way at the planet."

I felt my face flush in embarrassment for singling out Phoebe. "So, Phoebe didn't do anything wrong."

"Correct, Consort."

So, it was my fault then. She'd only been following my orders.

"Okay, I apologize, Ensign," I said.

She nodded. "Maybe next time we should shoot their comms array with the plasma cannon."

I nodded. "That's a good suggestion. We'll remember that."

Half a day after we left L1, we passed the Kergan warship, which was coming in the opposite direction.

I had directed *Thunder* in a long curve back to Earth, so we were still 100,000 miles distant from the large and dangerous ship at the closest approach. Too far to get a visual, but based on its performance profile, Zeta concluded it was a Kergan light cruiser.

We managed to avoid detection.

By the time we returned to base, thirteen days had gone by. Nearly two weeks were spent on the endeavor, and we had nothing to show for it except for a dead comrade and a frustrated crew.

Morale hit rock bottom. Busto blamed himself for the death, probably because *I* was questioning his actions during the operation. Not vocally, but I thought it, and it rubbed off on him.

I couldn't afford *not* to trust the former Marine, and honestly, I didn't have a good reason not to put my faith in him. But we had passed through a bad experience together, which degraded our relationship. I found myself arguing with him over stupid things on more than one occasion.

But time heals all wounds. Even emotional ones if we allow it. Busto and I were friends, and that held us together until we could smile and laugh again. And we learned some things that helped us find that.

We continued to investigate our failure. We finally figured out what had gone wrong thanks to Zeta's access to Dominion intelligence sources.

"Consort, Dominion intelligence has studied the data your crew gathered from the enemy freighter," Zeta said. The entire crew was gathered for her briefing. "This was not your fault."

"Please explain," I said.

"Intelligence indicates that the freighter was not a civilian ship."

Busto snorted. "That's obvious. Tell us something we didn't already know."

"It was carrying a platoon of Kergan Imperial Marines on some kind of counterinsurgency mission," Zeta said.

"Holy *shit*," Busto said.

"Was it a Q-ship?" Rowbottom asked.

"I don't think so," Busto said, "because it wasn't armed. But it was some kind of secret troop transport."

"Indeed, Lieutenant," Zeta said. "You are fortunate to be still alive. You managed to eliminate a very dangerous target." She looked at me. "Captain, your crew caught the ship completely by surprise. If that had not been the case, none of you would have likely survived. The Dominion Ministry of War extends their compliments for a job well done."

"Damn, it was pure luck, then," Vila said.

This news helped to recover some of our low morale. It had just been bad luck that we'd picked that particular ship and a testament to our training that we survived the encounter and destroyed the transport.

We replaced Appleton. Busto did some recruiting in Wolf Jaw and ended up hiring a woman named Darya Novikova. She was a former Army infantry sergeant with the 10th Mountain Division. She was twenty-nine, physically fit, intelligent, and good with weapons. A natural leader. We started her training for the Nav position on *Thunder* and as part of Busto's tactical team.

On the trip back home, we also received some good news. The Collective Dominion Ministry of War approved our request for reinforcements.

"In light of this Astral Maul and the threat it represents," Zeta explained, "the Ministry has increased the priority of your mission and designated it of strategic importance. This qualifies it for a higher allocation of military assets."

I clapped my hands. "Excellent. What are we getting?"

"Three additional insurgent cells will be made

available. You, Consort, will be in command of the operation. The other cell commanders will report to you."

"I assume we'll get to meet them beforehand, right? I mean, I understand the need to keep the cells isolated from each other, but we can't do this without close coordination."

"Indeed, a rendezvous will be planned, and you will meet there. Zeta will receive further details within the next week."

"Yeah, because we've already wasted two weeks. We've only got six weeks until this Astral Maul becomes operational. And we still need to capture a freighter."

I wanted to take at least one of our new allies to make the capture. I wasn't taking chances again on encountering more Imperial Marines without having at least twice the number of people on the boarding team. By the time we met with them and traveled out to L1, we'd only have five weeks left until the operation. Three, if it took us another two weeks to find a suitable ship to capture.

The clock was ticking, and we were all feeling it.

# 35

Destroying the freighter carrying the platoon of Imperial Marines had earned us a nice chunk of tribute points. I used those to purchase tech upgrades that would make us a more potent boarding force.

At the top of the list were weapons drones that the crew could remotely pilot from the flight deck. This was a way for us to augment our boarding team while still leaving people in command of the ship. The drones were eight-legged spider-like robots that massed about 90 lbs. They carried a flechette gun, laser carbine, or single light plasma cannon. They were also excellent at melee combat and were protected by protomatter armor.

I also purchased maneuver packs for our protomatter suits for zero-gee combat. These contained miniature tractor pods that allowed us to fly like Zeta and O'hatet, even in Earth's gravity.

During the week before we met with the other cells, we practiced with the new equipment and trained Darya Novikova for her roles. It was a time spent strengthening ourselves and preparing for the upcoming mission.

The rendezvous with the additional cells took place at the Badlands National Park in South Dakota. A week after returning to our base, I loaded the entire crew into *Thunder* and flew us to there. We left O'hatet behind at the base because the Ministry of War didn't want her meeting with the other cells for security reasons.

The Badlands were flat, arid, and devoid of humans. It was centrally located on the North American continent, making it easier for our cells to meet up. That implied that our new comrades were based in areas far from our own, though the Ministry forbade us from telling each other where our respective bases were located.

We were the first to arrive. We landed *Thunder* adjacent to the bank of a stream that wove through the landscape like a snake.

The air was cold and windy, so we waited inside *Thunder* for the other ships.

The first sign of another ship was when it materialized out of thin air, it seemed, just as it was landing not too far away from us. We hadn't even picked them up on our sensors until the last moment. It was a corvette identical to ours.

I ordered my crew to remain on the ship until all the cells had arrived. The last two ships arrived a few minutes later. They were also corvettes.

This delighted me. The four ships combined would be a significant force!

Dressed in our ship coveralls and winter coats, the nine of us exited *Thunder* and walked toward a flat area roughly in the middle of the ships.

Soon after we emerged, the hatch in another of the ships

opened, and its crew climbed out and walked over to meet us.

A middle-aged man led. He was almost as tall as me but thinner, with pale blue eyes and cropped hair starting to gray at the temples. Beside him floated an igna in a cube capsule instead of an octahedron like Zeta's.

I walked up to them with Zeta at my side. I held out my hand. "I'm Kory Drake, captain of the *Thunder*." The man took it. I gestured to Zeta. "This is my consort, Zeta, of the Collective Dominion."

The man nodded. "Marvin Ivers, captain of the *Fullback*. This is my consort, Elpha." He stood there and eyed my crew.

He didn't look particularly pleased. I noticed that his crew were significantly older than mine. There were eight of them in total; most appeared to be in their thirties or forties, and some were overweight.

Captain Ivers seemed to be judging me and finding me wanting. It was probably my age. "So, you're the one in charge of this here, shindig, is that right?" His accent sounded Canadian or perhaps Northcentral US.

"Yes, that's correct," I responded. "Let's wait for the other crews to join us before I go into details." I looked at Montana. "Ensign Montana, maybe there's some kind of shelter we can assemble to get us out of the wind?"

"Sure, boss." She waved to Vila. "Vila, give me a hand." They marched back to our ship.

The next crew joined us, and we exchanged greetings. The captain was named Victor Cobb, and his igna consort was Xyra, in another cube capsule.

Cobb was the captain of the corvette *Invictus*. He was about Busto's age, and ten people were on his crew, including Xyra and himself. They were a mix of middle-aged and young adults, somewhat older than us but younger compared to the crew of the *Fullback*.

The last crew to arrive were from the corvette *Defiant*. The captain was a young woman in her early twenties. "I'm Annica Stenberg, captain of the *Defiant*." She pointed to the igna in a spherical capsule next to her. "This is Omri, my consort."

Stenberg had a plain-looking round face and was short. Her features beamed with friendliness, and I immediately felt comfortable with her. Stenberg's voice sounded familiar, though I was sure I'd never met her.

"Where have I heard you before?" I asked as we shook hands.

She had a crew of nine, like us, and they were also young, with about half of them in their late teens or early twenties.

Her eyes gleamed. "Yeah, you sound familiar, too. Warlock-two?" She raised an eyebrow.

I snapped a finger and pointed at her with my eyes wide open. "Hah! You're Warlock-one! At Malstrom!"

She laughed, and suddenly, she grabbed me in a hug and patted me on the back. "You saved our asses!" she roared. Turning to her crew, she said, "You guys remember that?"

Several of them nodded and smiled.

"We still owe you those drinks," one of her crew said.

I waved my hand at her crew. "Looks like you're all doing well. Nice to finally meet you and put a name to the voice."

She released my hand and stepped back.

We went around the crowd that had gathered, shaking hands and exchanging names. It had become chaotic and noisy, with almost forty strangers meeting for the first time.

Montana and Vila were assembling an canopy, though it wouldn't be big enough for everybody.

I joined Ivers, Cobb, and Stenberg under it with our consorts. We ordered the rest of our crews back to our ships to keep their eyes on the sky and their bodies out of the elements. The eight of us were enough to make whatever decisions were needed.

"Okay, so you all should have received a preliminary briefing from the Dominion Ministry of War," I said.

Cobb and Stenberg nodded.

Ivers clapped his hands, then held them wide. "We were in the middle of a big campaign. What's this show all about? My crew didn't appreciate being yanked away."

I held up my hand. "First of all, remember to avoid telling each other any information that could give away the location of your respective bases. It's crucial that we maintain operational security of our facilities because they're difficult and expensive to relocate."

I turned to Ivers. "I'm sorry this mission has interrupted your other activities. But I think once you hear about this new mission, you'll understand why the Ministry re-tasked you."

I put my hands in my pockets and paced several times, thinking about how to proceed. "We discovered that a Kergan corporation, under contract with the Kergan Empire, is excavating a dangerous alien artifact on the far side of the Moon. If they succeed in activating it, it will threaten the safety and well-being of every living being on Earth. Furthermore, the facility at which this excavation is taking place employs 161 enslaved humans. Our mission is to rescue those humans and destroy the artifact."

I then spent the next hour describing what we'd found so far and our planned operation. Zeta interjected several times to give further explanations, for which I was grateful.

The three captains made me feel inadequate, and Ivers was definitely not happy to be here. I wondered what his problem was. Maybe he just didn't like not being in charge.

"So, you just want some glorified stormtroopers, it sounds like," Ivers said after I had finished the briefing. "That's what we are to you."

"Ivers," Stenberg said, "that's not what I heard. It sounds to me—"

"He needs warm bodies to soak up some of the fire from these Kergan guards," Ivers said, pointing a finger in my direction. "Look," he said, gazing into my eyes like I wasn't worth his time, "I know you've been fighting just like the rest of us, but you're just a kid. Me and my crew are gonna do things our way. I don't care what the Ministry says about it."

"Consort," Xyra, Ivers's igna consort, said, "you remain under orders of the Dominion. Captain Drake is in command of this mission, and you must follow his instructions."

I stepped up to him closely and summoned a face of stone. "Or I could just request another cell. If you're not going to cooperate, I'm sure the Ministry will find me somebody else," I said.

Why did there always have to be that one person who pissed in the pool? I was sure the rest of his crew must be good people, but Ivers was a real piece of work, one I didn't want to deal with.

He waved his hands. "Okay, okay, okay! I get it. That won't be necessary. Let's just get this over with so we can move on with our lives."

"As I was trying to say," Stenberg said, "it sounds to me like this facility is too large for one cell to handle on its own. Multiple mission objectives exist, and each cell is too small to split up."

"That's exactly right," I said. "Each of our crews is a team of people. You all know how to work with your people. The outlying groups of buildings at Lindblad F need to be assaulted, and once that's begun, it will be too difficult for the other cells to help if it's needed.

"Since we have four cells, I plan to have two cells attack the AC-2 and AC-3 clusters, one cell at each. You secure the rigor pods and wait for the freighter to arrive and load them.

"The other two cells will attack AC-1 together—the central group of buildings where the artifact is located—since resistance will likely be greater."

"You also said you still needed to capture a freighter," Captain Cobb said.

"Yes, we already made one attempt and failed." I told them the story of fighting the Imperial Marines. Iver shook his head with a disgusted look but didn't say anything.

"We can't afford to waste any more time capturing this ship," I said. "It's crucial to the plan. That's why I'd like one of your ships to accompany us and provide backup."

I was worried nobody would volunteer because it would be a tedious mission. But Stenberg raised her hand immediately and said, "We'll do it. *Defiant* will come with you."

I nodded in thanks. I now also knew I wanted her crew to join mine in the fight for AC-1.

"Okay," I said, "we'll plan on *Fullback* assaulting AC-2 and *Invictus* AC-3. My crew will pilot the freighter and lead the attack on AC-1 and the artifact, with *Defiant* joining us. I'll ask O'hatet, a friendly marac who's working with us, to forward you all the data we've collected from Lindblad F and IMH."

We agreed to use the Ministry of War as our medium of exchanging messages since we had no means of communicating directly except in person. The operation was planned for four weeks in the future, pending the successful acquisition of the freighter. I had the assignment to pick the date for our mission to capture the freighter and coordinate with Stenberg and *Defiant*.

The meeting concluded. We packed up the canopy, said farewell, returned to our ships, and flew away.

# 36

Two days later, we set out for our second attempt at capturing a freighter. After rendezvousing with *Defiant* in Earth orbit, we headed for L1, flying in a line-astern formation with *Defiant* trailing us by about ten miles.

We got lucky — and in more ways than one.

First off, we only had to wait a day before a suitable ship showed up. Another small freighter, eerily similar to the one we'd botched before, emerged from its jump the very next day.

In consultation with Captain Stenberg, we decided to station her four-person boarding team on *Thunder*, which saved us the headache of coordinating two ships grappling simultaneously.

Our plan was simple: *Thunder* would latch onto the freighter while *Defiant* stood off, destroyed the freighter's comms array, and added an extra layer of intimidation.

*Thunder* got a bit crowded with thirteen people aboard — O'hatet stayed back at base, but even so, our life-support systems were pushed to their limit. Luckily, we only needed to manage it for a few days.

We intercepted the freighter just as planned. Stenberg and her crew were a pleasure to work with—professional, competent, and committed to the cause.

*Thunder* grappled onto the ship, and our eight-person boarding team stormed aboard, with three combat drones leading the way, remotely controlled by Destiny, Phoebe, and Montana.

Meanwhile, *Defiant* knocked out the ship's comm array, ensuring no distress call would go out.

The nine maracs aboard the freighter surrendered without a fight. There was no cargo onboard, just empty holds—one of which was perfect for transporting the rigor pods we'd need.

After the chaos of our first attempt, this one almost felt...anticlimactic. A little part of me felt silly for being so tense, but Captain Stenberg assured me that her crew was just as relieved everything went smoothly for their first boarding operation.

Once the freighter was secured, we transferred Stenberg's team back to *Defiant*.

I assigned Destiny, Phoebe, and Rowbottom to stay aboard the freighter as a prize crew, with three of Stenberg's crew remaining to guard the marac prisoners.

And speaking of prisoners...that was a problem. If the freighter's crew had been dead, things would've been simpler—morally messy, sure, but logistically tidy. But they'd surrendered, expecting we'd protect them. And I intended to keep that promise. The only snag? We didn't exactly have provisions at the base or in Wolf Jaw to house marac prisoners. Something had to be done with them, and soon.

\* \* \*

The captured freighter was named *Enthart'a ir Mo'shy'uim*. Destiny decided the name was too long and unilaterally rechristened it the *Moshy*.

*Moshy* was a small freighter but nonetheless huge in comparison to *Thunder*. At 350 ft long, with a square cross-section of 50 ft on a side and massing 3,800 tons, she was bigger than our entire base combined. But we needed to find a way to hide her from the Kergan Military Authority until the mission to Luna.

I decided the easiest thing to do with her would be to hide her in the same place where we would need her: on the Moon. To that end, on the return trip from L1, we took *Thunder* and *Moshy* on a detour to Luna and parked the freighter inside a deep crater on the north pole where it would be perpetually in the shade. We put the ship's systems on standby and hoped nobody would notice her.

*Defiant* picked up the guards from *Moshy*, and *Thunder* picked up the prize crew and the prisoners.

We returned home to our bases to finish preparing for the rescue mission.

*Thunder* was stuffed to the gills because of our prisoners, and we had nowhere for them at the base. We sealed them in an empty storage closet for the time being.

"I know you're going to say no," Destiny said to me in the base mess as we ate, "but I think we should execute them. Their empire is the one that destroyed our countries. Because of them, at least a billion humans have already died!"

Busto shook his head. "Two wrongs don't make a right. What you propose is not the sort of people we are. I believe in the Golden Rule: Do unto others as you would want done unto you."

Destiny dropped her fork on her plate and folded her

hands on the table. "Look, they may be civilians, but they're just as guilty as the soldiers. If it weren't for their support, there would be no Kergan empress and no Empire going around and enslaving people. I see execution as a justified punishment and a tidy solution."

I held up a hand. "Destiny, I understand how you feel, but we're not going to execute them. If we did that, I wouldn't be able to sleep at night."

She shrugged. "I knew that's what you'd say. I'm just telling you what *I* think."

"And you know that I respect your viewpoint." I shifted my attention to Busto. "But I *do* think there should be consequences. This freighter crew *doesn't* get a get-out-of-jail-free card." He lifted an eyebrow. "I want to deter this crew from getting involved again with trafficking the stolen wealth of humanity."

"And how do you plan to do that?" Busto said.

"I had a conversation with O'hatet about marac morals. Have you ever seen a marac with a tattoo?"

Destiny and Busto sat there thinking for a moment. They shook their heads, and Destiny said, "I don't think so, but it wouldn't make them look any freakier than they already are."

"Maracs as a species abhor body art. They see it as intervening in what nature gifted them. It involves some kind of eco-ethical mumbo jumbo that O'hatet tried to explain to me, but I didn't get. The important point is that tattoos are looked down upon to such a degree that maracs who have them become essentially social outcasts."

I saw a light illuminate in Destiny's eyes. She nodded. "I know where this is going."

"We're *going* to release those maracs," I said. "We can't keep them in detention; they're too dangerous to have around here, and I'm unwilling to kill them."

"But you're going to tattoo them…" Destiny said with a smile.

"Yes, with a punitive tattoo on their foreheads right between their four eyes."

"What's it gonna say?"

"I haven't decided, but it doesn't matter. What's important is that they're permanently marked and won't ever be able to be hired again as ship crew."

"They could just get it removed," Busto said.

I shook my head. "It's not so easy for them. Their skin doesn't renew as fast as ours does and is much more sensitive to damage from the lasers one would normally use to burn the tattoos away. That's probably one reason maracs detest them so much."

And that's the story behind why we tattooed the nine captured crew members of *Moshy* with *Thunder*'s hull emblem on their foreheads.

When the prisoners realized what we were going to do, you would have thought we'd brought out a torture rack. They lay there and cried in the marac fashion and screamed and resisted so much it took five people to hold each individual down while the tattoo was applied.

I almost felt bad about it. Almost.

The day after giving them our mark, we covertly flew the prisoners to a remote area south of Portland, Oregon, far from our base, and released them to fend for themselves.

I was confident they would soon encounter a Kergan patrol and find safety. But they would never crew a space freighter again, of that O'hatet had assured me.

# 37

Nearly all of our time over the ensuing weeks was dedicated to training.

There was tactical training with Busto that every crew member was obliged to participate in.

There was flight training in the simulators and occasional flight tests. Zeta's requirement that all crew be cross-trained in the other crew positions significantly increased the effort it took to keep us qualified.

I also spent one or two hours training with Zeta in the Syderealium daily. She taught me how to defend myself from other glyphshades and took me exploring.

There was much hidden knowledge in the Syderealium, though it was challenging to learn because my mind was too accustomed to modeling a 3D physical universe. Many objects in the Syderealium were fleeting and depended on the attention of a glyphshade to maintain coherence.

Zeta taught me how to construct weird topologies, like miniature worlds. She said that such techniques were behind how starship FTL drives functioned. Indeed, Zeta hinted that there would come a day when I might be capable of physically transporting myself through the Syderealium.

She also helped me prepare for how the Astral Maul would present itself in the Syderealium. We planned to handle the Maul purely on the physical side since we didn't understand how it worked on the sydereal side, but Zeta wanted us to be prepared.

The Astral Maul generated an attractive force that influenced other glyphshades. The force could be modulated such that it evoked specific feelings and motivations. More importantly, it could be focused on a particular region of the physical universe near where it rested. This was why it was a threat to Earth.

It also made the Maul a threat to our assault force and our mission.

I sat with O'hatet in *Thunder*'s mess at the main table with the captains of *Fullback*, *Invictus*, and *Defiant*. Busto and Destiny stood behind me against a bulkhead, and Zeta floated at my shoulder.

The executive officers and consorts of the other captains were also here. It was crowded in the mess, but it was necessary to have these planning meetings because we were just 60 hours away from initiating the Lindblad F operation. This was our last opportunity to meet in person.

"Captain Ivers, *Fullback*, and your crew will conduct the assault on AC-2." I pointed to my tablet, which lay on the table displaying a map of Lindblad F. "Captain Cobb, *Invictus*, and your crew will assault AC-3. The two groups of buildings are nearly identical. Each has six guards, only two of whom are on duty at any given time."

"Yes, Captain Drake," Ivers said, looking annoyed.

"We've already studied the plans in depth. You need not repeat all this again."

"Please let me finish, Ivers," I glared at him. "There's a reason I'm repeating it. As I was saying, your two crews are responsible for AC-2 and AC-3. I expect you to finish first before we're done at AC-1. One of my people, Ensign Phoebe Brooks, will command the freighter *Moshy* and land adjacent to the rigor pod chamber to load your recovered rigor pods. You will help her with the loading."

I pointed to the central cluster of buildings on the map. "The crews of *Thunder* and *Defiant* will assault AC-1, minus the pilots who are needed at the controls of those ships and *Moshy*. I've already assigned two of my people to piloting and can't afford to reduce the size of my ground team any further, but we need a cargomaster on *Moshy*." I looked at them questioningly.

Stenberg raised her hand. "I've got the largest crew. I can offer CPO Thomas Martinez for that task."

I nodded in appreciation, though wishing one of the other crews had offered. "Thanks. That's settled, then. Brooks and Martinez will be on *Moshy*." I leaned back and folded my arms. "That leaves sixteen people for the AC-1 assault team, one of whom is a non-combatant," I pointed to O'hatet.

"Why is she going?" Ivers asked.

"We need her to penetrate the facility computer network and disable their communications.

"So, the reason I'm reviewing all of this is because I'm concerned we don't have enough people to complete the tasks we need to do at AC-1. Remember, not only do we have to rescue the majority of the mindjacked humans—there are 120 of them there—but we also have to locate and neutralize the Astral Maul. I need assurances that the crews of *Fullback* and *Invictus* will advance to AC-1 to assist once your objectives are completed. Do I have that?"

"Yes," Cobb said.

Ivers waived a hand. "Sure, if we have time. But we're gonna be on our own out there, and I can't guarantee anything."

"Ivers, just get your rigor pods loaded as fast as possible and then relocate your people to AC-1 to provide us reinforcements," I said, my face flushing and my heartbeat picking up. "If that's not plain enough, then I'll make them orders."

"Yes, I understood the first time. We'll be there," he said, screwing his face up like he'd bitten into a lemon.

The more I was around Ivers, the less I trusted him. The man had a chip on his shoulders and obviously thought he was destined for bigger things. I'd learned he was a former officer of the US Navy Reserve and had experience as a ship's officer. For some reason, he thought that put him into an elite category in which none of us were members.

At least I wasn't the only one he had a problem with. He treated Cobb with complete contempt, and Stenberg he talked to like she should have been married and staying home with children.

Deep down inside me, I remembered that I had no right to judge Ivers because I wasn't the most trustworthy person, either. I was going into this mission with a secret objective that I'd not shared with anybody. One of my secret tasks inside AC-1 was locating Ban'ach and somehow induce her into a sydereal duel that would enable me to recover my stolen memories.

I knew my intentions would possibly jeopardize the entire mission, but if I didn't corner Ban'ach, who knew when I would again have the opportunity?

"And just how many tribute points are we going to be awarded from this mission?" Ivers asked. That was another thing about him I didn't like. The guy was obsessed with accumulating tribute points.

"I don't know," I said.

"Does it really matter?" Destiny said from behind me, disdain evident in her voice. "Or are you just shopping for the juiciest tasks?"

Ivers stiffened and turned his head to her. "Listen, you little—"

"We're talking about enslaved humans and a doomsday artifact," she continued, talking over him. "That's what the stakes are, *Captain*."

I held up a hand to signal calm. "Captain Ivers, the Ministry hasn't given us that information. But they've always been generous with their rewards. I'm sure you'll agree that that will be the case here. Nobody is going to shortchange you. This is a critical mission."

"You've got a far easier task than we or the *Defiant* have, so stop your bitchin'!" Destiny said, almost yelling.

I gestured at Busto with my chin, and he grabbed her arm and pulled her out of the mess. She rolled her eyes at me and followed him out.

Ivers looked like he was about to blow a gasket. "Captain Drake! Your crew are insubordinate and insolent! I don't know what kind of ship you run, but if she were on *my* crew, I'd have her in the brig over an outburst like that!"

I sighed and ignored his outburst. This wasn't the US Navy, and my crew happened also to be my friends.

And Ivers was an ass.

Secretly, I smiled on the inside, seeing Destiny get under his skin. But letting that show would only get him worked up even more, and I needed him on our side if we were going to succeed at this mission.

# 38

I strolled along the path outside our base with Phoebe at my side. She had her arm looped through mine and was pressing her body against me as we gazed up at the Moon, which was nearly full.

"Just think, in less than 24 hours, we're gonna be up there," Phoebe said. "I have a hard time believing that we already walked on it. Like Neal Armstrong. It just seems... unreal." She leaned her head on my shoulder.

It was apparent to me that Phoebe had feelings for me. Perhaps a bit of a crush. And I hadn't tried to dissuade her.

I didn't have any romantic feelings for her, yet a genuine affection had grown and started filling in some of the gap left by the missing memories of my parents. Was she a friend? Definitely, without question. She was also beautiful in her own way and had a lithe body that always made me blush whenever I saw her naked while switching in and out of her protomatter suit. But I'd never felt a desire to take our relationship any further than what it was.

"Well," I said, looking at Earth's largest satellite, "it's not going to be as pretty this time. You know, it will be lunar night during the mission."

"Yeah, Zeta already told me about it. Did you plan that on purpose?"

"No, it's just how the schedule played out. I'm happy, though, it'll make it just that much harder for the Kergans to spot us." I turned us down a path leading to the glen's brook. "Are you scared?"

She shrugged. "I don't know. I suppose so, a little. It's nerves, mostly. I don't want to let you down."

"You won't."

She shook her head. "I've got that huge freighter to pilot all by myself. And you guys are going to be inside that base getting shot at while I'm safe on the flight deck. I feel bad. Yeah, you know, that's why I'm anxious. I'm worried about you!"

"Well, I need you, Phoebe. Besides Destiny and me, you're our best pilot on the crew. I've got Destiny stuck flying *Thunder*."

She giggled. "I bet she's happy about that!"

"You know how she is. She's a little bloodthirsty, but I need her at the controls of *Thunder* just in case bad things happen, and we need to bug out."

She leaned in and looked into my face with a grin. "I know what's goin' on. You're just protecting the two girls you care most about!"

The thought hadn't occurred to me. But I could see how it might appear to other people. Is that why Ivers was treating me like garbage? No, he was just an asshole. No, I was confident I had picked Phoebe and Destiny as the pilots because they were my best choices.

I patted her hand and chuckled. "Sure, because I just can't live without you ladies."

She smiled and looked down at the path as we strolled along the bank of the brook. I could tell what *she* thought the truth was, and it seemed to please her, so I didn't say anything to persuade her otherwise.

"I just keep thinking about all those orphans in Elkin you told me about," Phoebe said. "How many of these people we're going to rescue have children down in Elkin waiting for them?"

"I counted fifty-eight. Some are single parents, but most are mother and father, both taken by the Nebula Nomads."

She was quiet for a while. I steered us up a path back toward the base. We'd been gone on our walk for a good twenty minutes now.

"You've never told me about your parents," Phoebe said.

I felt a chill run through my bones. That gap in my memory was suddenly looming like a sinkhole, ready to swallow me.

My reaction must have shown on my face because she said, "I'm sorry, if you don't want to talk about it, it's okay." She shook her head and looked away from me.

I patted her hand. "You don't know?"

She halted and turned to me. "What?"

"Destiny hasn't said anything to you? Or Zeta?"

Her face twisted into a scowl. "What are you talking about?"

I sighed and looked at my feet. "You know about that encounter I had with the Soul Ravager in Elkin, right?"

"Yeah, this Ban'ach."

"She stole something from me."

"Yeah, I heard she hurt you somehow, but everybody's been so hush-hush about it. I didn't ask because you seemed okay. Maybe a little sadder than I remember you, but you've been under a lot of stress." She grabbed both of my hands and squeezed them. "What is it?"

"Ban'ach stole my memories of my parents."

"What?!" she gasped. "You mean you can't remember them?"

I shook my head. "It's strange. I can remember *remembering* them, if that makes sense." She nodded. "But it's like a gaping hole in my past. I no longer have memories of what it felt like to be with them. Or of their faces. Nothing. It's all gone."

She released me and held her hands to her face. "That's awful!" She gaped at me. "I can't imagine what that must feel like!"

I tried to shrug it away. "I lost them when I was only three years old. I didn't have a lot of memories."

"But, still. Some of my sweetest memories are of my early childhood. Of Mom holding me on her lap in church while singing songs about Jesus. And Dad tickling me while dressing me for bed. And going to the park with them. You know, I heard this child psychologist once talking about the myth among the population that humans don't have memories from being babies. He said that wasn't true, but that when we're small children, everything is feeling. Our brains don't remember in a linear fashion, but our bodies remember. He said that's why people who suffer emotional trauma tend to cuddle up in a fetal position. That's because they remember being secure in their mother's womb. Their bodies do."

She reached up and cupped my cheek. "Oh, Kory, I'm so sorry!"

I felt something clenching in my heart, and my eyes teared up. There was so much sympathy in her voice. Tears started to flow down my cheeks.

She hugged and held me, and for the first time since my loss, I wept. For what Ban'ach had taken from me. I would never be the same person again. That evil alien had altered my personality permanently.

# 39

"Range 100, bearing zero-zero-niner," Novikova announced as *Thunder* skimmed over the lunar landscape at scarcely 200 ft altitude, following the undulating terrain. Lindblad F lay just over the horizon.

I checked my tactical display and saw that *Defiant*, *Invictus*, and *Fullback* trailed us by five minutes, with *Moshy* another minute behind them. We had departed from the north pole above an hour ago and were making our slow, careful way southward to our destination.

*Thunder* was in the front, tasked with taking out the IMH comms array with precision fire in a surprise strike before they could send out a distress signal. Hopefully, that would buy us a couple of hours of breathing room while we conducted the raid on the facility.

Destiny was piloting and would remain in that seat until the operation was completed. After dropping us off, her job was to hover over Lindblad F and interdict any vehicles that tried to flee, using lethal force if necessary. Being the only one on the ship, her hands would be full, but I trusted in her completely.

Mountains passed beneath us, then a broad valley that was pockmarked by thousands—perhaps even millions—of craters of all sizes, from miniature bowls barely big enough to hold my clenched fist to monsters that spanned from horizon to horizon.

I saw it all in low-light imaging—the so-called starlight optics—because it was lunar night at this longitude and would remain so for another ten days.

The terrain was uniformly cold, so the infrared imaging was useless. Fortunately, there was enough illumination from the stars to see details in the monochrome tapestry the starlight optics delivered.

We dared not activate the terrain following radar or lidar lest our opponents detect the emissions. Even using LPD waveforms was too risky. The enemy were just too close.

Our ground speed was 1100 knots. I calculated in my head—20 miles per minute. We'd arrive in 5 minutes.

Another minute ticked by, and Busto shuffled his feet to lean forward and check his combat webbing.

The ground team was fully suited and geared up. I had my flechette gun, plus four extra magazines—nearly five hundred rounds of flechettes.

My laser pistol was strapped to my hip, my tractor pack on my back, and my combat webbing carrying a knife, first-aid supplies, suit repair kit, grenades, my share of our demolition charges, a couple energy bars, water bladder, and other useful gear. I was so loaded down that I barely fit into my acceleration couch.

The only one not like me was Destiny, who would remain on the ship. Phoebe was already on *Moshy* with Martinez.

I looked at O'hatet. Her gaze was penetrating and unreadable. With her four eyes, each completely black, she always reminded me of trying to stare down a giant spider. Noticing my attention, she waved a friendly tentacle at me.

*Two minutes left*, I noted on the display.

The rim of Lindblad F was visible on the horizon, with the cleft in it where we'd driven down it on the rover.

"Weaps, you are free to acquire and engage," Destiny said.

"Roger, weapons free," Vila said.

His job was to locate the comms array and blast it with the plasma cannon turret. He tapped one of his booted feet nervously on the deck, shaking his head and stretching his shoulders.

The crater rim passed underneath us, and the crater basin opened below us.

Destiny kept us high rather than descend into it to give Vila a wider field of fire.

The deck tilted downward as she reoriented *Thunder* so the turret—which was on the bow of the corvette pointing at zenith—could fire downward.

"Acquiring..." Vila said. He tapped his fingers on his interface. "Acquired. Commencing fire."

I felt nothing, but brilliant white flashes burst across the display, traveling downward at a portion of the complex, too fast to track their motion, and exploded against something.

The firing paused, and then Vila fired another burst that lasted about two seconds.

"Okay, I think I got it!" he said.

"Roger. MARDET prepare for insertion!" Destiny called out.

That was the call for our Marine Detachment to get

down to Deck 3 and wait to exit the ship.

There was an organized scramble as the eight of us lined up and streamed off the flight deck. As I left Destiny, I reached out, patted her on the shoulder, and nodded at her.

She winked at me in return.

Busto and Rowbottom were in the lead, with O'hatet, Montana, Zeta, and myself in the middle, and Novikova and Vila watching our flanks.

We had to exit the ship in two groups because the airlock was only big enough for four of us at a time.

It took 30 seconds to cycle it, so it was over a minute before we were all on the pitch-black floor of the crater.

A habitation dome loomed above us to one side.

A blocky building next to that held the Admin Center and the facility's security office—our first objective.

The MARDET from *Defiant* would hit the opposite side and meet us inside. They should have been landing about right now.

It was quiet.

That's the weird thing about walking around on the moon. From photographs, it looks like a barren wilderness, but it's much spookier than that. Sound doesn't carry in a vacuum, so the only thing I could hear was my own breathing, the *thud* of my footsteps, and the squeaking of my gear that transferred through the atmosphere of my suit.

Busto made a hand signal that meant we should space ourselves out. That was important so an enemy couldn't drop a grenade on us and take us all out simultaneously.

Though the blast from a grenade wouldn't be very effective in a vacuum, the shrapnel was still potentially deadly. Our suits would probably stop it, but it would still wreck equipment and slow us down.

Rowbottom carried a large box.

He and Busto moved forward to what looked like a random place on a wall of the Admin Center, though it was anything but random. We'd used the architectural drawings Elara Finch provided to identify ingress points.

Rowbottom opened the box and pulled out a device made of thick, flexible plastic. It was a temporary airlock made of ballistic plastic designed to contain the explosion from a breaching charge.

Within 30 seconds, they had the airlock assembled and ready.

Rowbottom placed several breaching charges in a circular pattern and closed the inner and outer flaps.

He pressed some buttons on a control panel, and the edges of the airlock adjacent to the building molded themselves. The seal was made of protomatter, and by the time it was finished, it had made an impermeable and permanent bond with the structure.

The former scout stepped to the side, and seconds later, there was a flash and the airlock filled with smoke and its sides bulged out.

Rowbottom pressed some more buttons, and the airlock vented the interior, leaving it in vacuum.

He opened the outer hatch.

We crammed ourselves into the tent-like device.

The person in the rear sealed the outer hatch.

The inner hatch opened slowly, letting the atmosphere vent into our space without a sudden explosion.

Anybody in the building right now would probably have felt their ears pop if the breaching charge hadn't already blasted their eardrums.

My team rushed through the breach into a lobby of some kind.

It was filled with smoke, and I could hear alarms

blaring either because of the pressure change or the smoke.

My team spread out, and moments later, I heard calls of "clear!".

Busto signaled us to proceed.

Rowbottom took point, heading deeper into the building, looking for the security office.

He arrived at a corner, turned it with his gun raised and aiming, and immediately fired a burst, then dropped back into cover.

He waited a few seconds, lowered himself to the floor, then popped out again, firing another burst.

Signaling us forward, he rose to his feet.

When I got to that corridor where he'd fired, I saw two armed and very dead maracs lying on the floor.

Rowbottom and Busto were inside a room—the security office—ransacking it.

O'hatet flew forward into the room and sat at a control console of some kind.

"Disabling alarms," she said. Seconds later, all the alarms silenced themselves. "Unlocking secure areas."

Her tentacles flew across a screen, tapping one after another on icons, which changed from purple to yellow. It was marac symbology, and purple was an important color to indicate danger. Probably because their blood and skin were purple.

"*This is Firehouse actual,*" Ivers suddenly announced over the comms. "*We have breached AC-2 and are proceeding to our objective, over.*" The MARDET of *Fullback* had been assigned the callsign "Firehouse."

A minute later, I received similar announcements from Cobb and Stenberg.

I heard a loud *bang* in the distance and knew the MARDET from *Defiant* was breaching the building. Their objective was to secure the habitation dome and detain civilians.

Our next job was securing the rigor pod berth, eliminating any guards we found, and transporting the rigor pods outside.

A flechette gun fired behind me in the corridor.

"Contact!" Novikova yelled.

Another long burst of flechettes and the blast of a grenade.

I rushed to Novikova and Vila's position just as Vila rushed forward into the corridor, firing from the hip and screaming at the top of his lungs.

Novikova shook her head and chased after him.

Three marac security guards armed with what looked like taser stun weapons were firing at the soldiers without any effect.

Vila smashed into them and started beating the daylight out of them with his rifle buttstock.

Soon, Novikova joined him.

I appreciated Vila's decision. His quick thinking had made him realize the guards couldn't hope to hurt us, so rather than kill them, he'd taken them prisoner.

A minute later, the three guards were bound and secured to a railing in a corridor with cuffs.

"Firehouse and Firefly, this is Fireball, report!" I called on the comms. "Fireball" was the callsign for *Thunder*'s MARDET, and "Firefly" was for *Invictus*'s.

"*Fireball, Firefly, IC-3 is secure, and all resistance has been eliminated,*" Cobb said on the radio. "*Proceeding to move pods.*"

I looked at my watch. Only five minutes had elapsed since we'd breached the building. It felt like an hour.

"Firehouse, report!" I said again.

Nothing. Ivers was probably too busy to hear my

request.

There wasn't anything I could do about it now. We had to head to our next objective.

"*Firefly, this is Moshy, moving to your location,*" Phoebe announced on the comms.

Right now, the freighter would be passing overhead, moving toward IC-3 to pick up their share of the mindjacked humans.

We were making progress! Our plan was in motion!

"*Fireball, this is Fireplace actual; we have breached the AC-1 hab and are securing it!*" said Stenberg on comms.

"Roger Fireplace," I replied, glad to hear that she and her team had reached the central group of buildings and were now just one building over from our location. We could now provide mutual support for each other.

We left O'hatet to monitor the security system, with Novikova and Montana to guard her and set up an aid station.

Busto, Rowbottom, Vila, Zeta, and I proceeded deeper into the complex, searching for the rigor pod berth. It was to the east through an underground tunnel.

"*Fireball, this is* Thunder, *small shuttle departing IC-1 in direction of Anaxagoras Base.*" Anaxagoras Base was the nearest Kergan military base. "*Engaging.*"

"Roger, *Thunder,*" I replied.

Busto took us down empty corridors with equally empty labs and offices branching off them.

It surprised me how few people were about. Maybe we'd gotten lucky and hit the Admin Center during off hours. Of course, that would mean Fireplace—*Defiant*'s MARDET—would have significantly more civilians to deal with.

"I've got movement!" Busto hissed.

He made a hand signal, and we all took cover behind a wall that opened into the tunnel we needed to take.

"Five or six armed maracs are closing," he said. "Check your suit seals."

I looked at my suit control panel on the inside of my left arm and verified suit integrity.

Busto set the fuse on a plasma grenade and tossed it far down the tunnel.

Muffled screeches and whistles of maracs sounded.

A few seconds later, the grenade detonated with a flash of blazing white light and a pulse of overpressure that squeezed my lungs.

Busto and Rowbottom leaned out into the tunnel and began firing while I watched our rear.

Pressure alarms started whooping as the atmosphere vented out of a breach, though it felt like a small one. About ten seconds later, the alarms cut out. The automated systems must have sealed it.

Flechettes flashed past us, and my men returned fire.

We exchanged fire with the maracs for several minutes. It sounded like there were only two guards who were firing back, but the berth was right at the end of the tunnel behind them.

I saw a marac enter the corridor behind us, dressed in armor and carrying what could only be a plasma cannon.

A second marac trailed him.

I raised my gun and fired several bursts. "Contact, rear!" I yelled.

Moments later, Vila was firing at my side.

The maracs had stumbled right into us, and we shot them before they could respond. But where had they come from? That side of the building was supposed to have already been cleared.

Busto and Rowbottom advanced down the tunnel, firing their guns at full auto.

A minute later, Rowbottom yelled, "Clear!"

The rest of us picked ourselves off the floor and moved into the berth.

We found ourselves in an underground chamber with thick concrete walls and ceiling.

Over a hundred coffin-sized white pods rested on the tile floor and a mezzanine.

Five marac corpses lay near the entrance, leaking purple blood onto the floor. Two of them were unarmed and looked like civilians. Perhaps technicians.

"*Fireball, Fireplace,*" Stenberg called on the radio, "*civilians are secure. Be advised we are advancing to rigor pod berth.*"

"Roger," I said on the comms, then to my team, "Okay, guys, Stenberg's on her way with her team. Let's get moving with these pods."

The rigor pods were completely self-contained systems with their own power and life support, making them easy to transport. I had feared that we'd need to wake up the mindjacked humans before we could move them, leaving over a hundred confused and scared recently freed slaves, none with space suits, to somehow get onto the freighter. The pods made that job much easier, and they protected our charges. Though they did require a connection to external power, they could run on internal batteries and supplies for several days when needed.

The downside was that the pods were heavy, massing nearly 350 lbs, including the human inside. But in the Moon's weak gravity, it worked out to just 58 lbs. Two people could easily move individual pods. On the other hand, we had 120 of them to get out of here, and we were one level underground.

"Let's start getting them to the surface!" Busto yelled.

Zeta flew down the rows of pods, guiding Vila, who started disconnecting power and plumbing.

I looked in the small window on the nearest pod and saw a man who appeared to be sleeping. His face was gaunt and heavily bearded, and his hair was past his shoulders. Apparently, nobody had bothered to groom the captives.

Stenberg's team of five arrived at that moment. They'd left two on their ship and three back at the habitation dome guarding the civilians.

Soon, everybody was busy with their tasks.

Now was the perfect time for me to go look for Ban'ach. Would she be with the civilians in the dome? Hiding somewhere in the offices? In the excavation? Or somewhere else? With my people busy, I could just slip away and search.

But I couldn't go through with my plan. These people, my friends, had all risked their lives to follow me on this mission. I found myself unable to betray their loyalty by going off and pursuing my own agenda when we were in the middle of the job. I just imagined what Destiny would say if she found out. How Phoebe would look at me. The way Busto would treat me afterward.

I forced my thoughts of Ban'ach to the side, jogged through the berth until I found Busto, and said, "Where do you need me?"

"Good! Help me with this pod, Captain."

I picked up the foot of it and he the head. We carried it together to a service elevator, stacked it on another pod, and then returned for more.

*"Fireball, this is Firefly, our pods are loaded and we're proceeding to your position,"* I heard Cobb say on the radio.

I still had heard nothing from Ivers' status. "Negative,

Firefly. Firehouse has been silent. Please proceed with caution to AC-2 and render whatever assistance Firehouse and *Fullback* might need."

"*Roger, proceeding to AC-2. Firefly out.*"

"*Moshy,* Fireball, once you are loaded, proceed to the east side of the berth at AC-1."

"*Roger, we'll be finished loading in five mikes,*" Phoebe responded.

What was going on at AC2? Why was Ivers not responding to any of my calls?

I could have really used *Invictus*'s crew here at AC-1, but more importantly, I had to ensure things went smoothly at the two smaller groups of buildings.

Abruptly, a terror began to grow within me. A sense of pending doom that set my heart racing and my breath coming to me in gasps. I crouched on the floor and looked for the threat.

Nothing.

All my colleagues had frozen in place. Some were looking around, like me, while others had curled up into balls and were protecting their heads.

All work had halted. My smoothly running crew of people were suddenly frozen in fear. And there didn't seem to be any logical reason for it.

# 40

I felt exquisitely terrifying anxiety, more than I'd ever experienced. It felt like I had just turned around and found a wild thousand pound tiger stalking me. Or a loaded semi-truck rushing straight at me at 60 mph. Or Destiny losing her balance and about to tip over the edge of a precipice.

Sweat streamed down my cheeks.

My chest hurt.

*We are so screwed!* I kept thinking.

*Why did I get us into this?*

*I'm so stupid.*

*I just want to go home!*

*I'm too small, too weak!*

Zeta flew into my field of vision and bumped against my helmet. "Consort! Ignore it!"

"What's happening?!" I cried.

"Adjust your suit's air mixture. You're hyperventilating!"

I hesitated, trying to decide the most important thing to do right now. I was exposed! I needed to hide!

A figure screamed and ran out of the berth. One of Stenberg's people, I thought.

"Consort! Do it!" Zeta bellowed in a voice I'd never heard her use before.

It snapped my attention back to what she was saying.

My suit air.

Okay, that was easy.

I raised my inner arm, tapped it, and soon entered my air control panel.

"Increase your oxygen mixture to 100%."

I did that. Immediately, I felt my head clear up.

"Go to your medical panel."

I did that, just going on autopilot, following her instructions. I could do this.

"Inject 10 mg of lorazepam into your blood."

I scrolled through the menu, made my selection, set the dose, and executed.

I let out a long breath and lay on the tile floor.

Within seconds, a weight seemed to lift off my shoulders, and my thoughts returned under control.

"What just happened?" I asked.

"It's the Astral Maul. Somebody is trying to operate it," Zeta said.

*Damn, that was terrifying.*

In just a heartbeat, the Kergans had completely neutralized my team.

I had to get them back under control.

The sense of pending doom still loomed over me, but whatever medication my suit had given me had helped, and knowing the Maul was causing the feeling helped me push the sensation away.

I set my comms to the open channel. "Okay, people, you're probably feeling scared shitless right now and don't know why. Listen to me, and I'll get you out of this, but you must promise to follow my instructions exactly." I then walked them through the steps for changing their suit air and injecting the anti-anxiety meds.

I began to hear some chatter on the radio, which was a good sign.

"Listen up," I said. "That was the Astral Maul that did that. Somebody's trying to use it against us. We *must* get these pods loaded and neutralize the Maul. I need you to be brave, push the mental discomfort into a closet in your mind, and focus on your immediate tasks. You are all brave people, the best of humanity. I know this because otherwise, you wouldn't be here trying to rescue these people. Stand firm. Let's show these Kergans we're no pushovers."

Soon, my people were back on their feet, and though there was less energy and purpose behind their movements compared to before, they were quickly back to moving rigor pods.

The low lunar gravity made it much easier to move the rigor pods than it could have been otherwise. Even so, with just ten people to do the job, of whom two were needed to provide security, it took a while to move the 120 pods.

*Moshy* relocated and landed just outside the berth's service airlock. One of its huge cargo hatches opened, and I saw the 30 pods Cobb's people had already rescued.

Martinez came down the ramp and started giving us instructions on how to load the pods onto the ship.

In the lunar darkness, there were very few lights, and those we had created sharp shadows, even from the pebbles strewn around our feet.

I was struggling with a pod alone when I got a call from Cobb. *"Fireball, Firefly, I...uh...got a bit of a problem out here at AC-2."*

I stopped pulling on the pod and set it on the lunar regolith. "Say again, Firefly?"

*"I can't find Firehouse or Fullback. The berth at AC-2 has been breached, and there are dead maracs. I also see human blood on the floor. Some of our people must have been wounded."*

"I think it was the Astral Maul. What about the pods?" If Ivers had damaged any of them, I would hunt him down and punish him.

*"They look intact."*

"You don't have time to play detective. Get those pods out to the airlock and prepare for pickup from *Moshy*. We'll worry about Firehouse later."

Maybe Ivers' people got into a firefight, some of his people got wounded, and he bugged out without telling me. But my best guess was that the Astral Maul had hit them hard, and Ivers had fled the battlefield.

I was mad, but I could do nothing about it now. We'd just have to complete the mission with the people I still had.

*"Roger,"* Cobbs said with a tone of frustration in his voice.

I pulled on the pod, sliding it up the loading ramp to *Moshy*'s cargo hold, then down a row to where Martinez was waiting with a set of clamps.

"Right here, Captain," he said to me, showing me where he wanted the legs of the pod resting.

I followed his instructions and watched as he tied the pod down securely, patted it, and said, "All set."

I marched out of the cargo bay, doing a quick count while I did so. 102 were lashed down, including the thirty from AC-2. We had another forty-eight to load here. Then *Moshy* would need to relocate to AC-2 to collect their pods.

I cycled through the berth airlock and looked for Stenberg.

The looming doom still hung over me like a shadow, but I ignored it.

Finding Stenberg, I approached and tapped her on the shoulder. "How are we doing?"

"As good as can be expected, we've got just these eighteen left to move up the lift."

"Excellent. The rest of our teams can take care of that. I need to conference with you, Zeta, and Omri."

I called Zeta and Omri over, and soon, the four of us huddled in a circle.

"Okay," I said, resting a hand on Stenberg's armored shoulder. "As soon as these pods are loaded, our next phase is to locate that vault, secure it, and destroy the Astral Maul. Captain Stenberg, you weren't originally part of that plan, but without either of the other two teams here to help, I'm gonna need you."

"You've got it. Just tell me what to do."

"I need you to put Omri, along with a couple of people to guard her in the security center because I need O'hatet. Can you do that?"

"Yes. What about my last two? You want them to go with your team?"

"No, do whatever you need with them to secure our retreat out of this facility. My team will proceed to the excavation. But you're my reserve, just in case we get into problems, so please standby to come pull us out if we need it."

"Okay, you got it."

"And when Cobb gets here, send him into the excavation."

"What about Ivers?" she said with a shake of her head.

I shrugged. "He, his crew, and his ship are gone."

"What?!"

"Cobb found evidence of a fight at AC-2, and the guards were dead, but the pods hadn't been secured. No sign of *Fullback*. I think that Astral Maul's mind attack broke them."

"Did they *leave*?"

I nodded. "I think so. Somebody got scared and fled, it seems."

She cursed and hefted her flechette gun in a manner suggesting she wanted to use it on Ivers.

I patted her on the shoulder. "Okay, we got a plan. Let's do it!"

The last of the pods were going up the elevator.

I walked around the empty berth and gathered my people. "Where's Rowbottom?"

"He just went up the elevator," Vila said. "He'll be back in a minute."

I pointed at Vila. "Go to the security command center and collect Novikova, Montana, and O'hatat. Bring them back here."

"Aye aye, sir."

I picked up my tablet, flipped to the screen with the facility map, and studied it.

The excavation was supposed to be somewhere underneath the Admin Center. But was the entrance there or somewhere outside? We hadn't yet descended into the Admin Center's basement level, so I guessed that was where we'd find it.

And maybe Ban'ach, if I was lucky. I hadn't given up on finding her, only delayed my intent.

Five minutes later, I had all my people gathered together, all of us except for Destiny and Phoebe. "O'hatet, you know better than any of us where to go. Guide us, please."

"Yes, Captain. Follow me," and she took off flying for the

berth entrance to the tunnel.

I tapped on Novikova's shoulder. "Keep next to her and make sure she doesn't get shot."

O'hatet took us back through the tunnel, past the battle-damaged corpses of the marac guards we'd killed.

We descended a stairwell through two levels, looking for hostiles but finding none.

We entered a large room, like a warehouse, but it was empty except for a large hole in the floor surrounded by excavating equipment.

Two marac guards floated there.

My team shot them down before they could raise their guns.

We ran forward up to the edge of the hole. It was about 10 ft square and dropped perhaps 30 ft into the lunar rock before bottoming out in a corridor that I couldn't see from this vantage point.

A rickety scaffolding and ladder rested against the excavation wall.

Busto grabbed the carbon fiber trellis and looked like he was about to descend.

"Hold on," I said.

Busto stopped and looked at me.

"Okay, my friends," I said. "We don't really know what we're going to find down there. If the last fifteen minutes of terror is any evidence, it means this is going to be painful. Those bastards are trying to bring the Astral Maul online, and we're paying the price for it."

"They're probably trying to stop us," Montana said. Everybody looked at her. She shrugged. "It's what I'd do if I were in their place. We blew through their security and defenses here like it was nothing but tissue paper."

I nodded. "Montana is probably right. We're not just

facing Kergans here but also a mysterious alien artifact. This could be deadly. If you feel you can't do this, then please stay up here and guard our rear. Anybody who goes in there, I need to know we have each other's backs."

I turned and looked each one of them in the eye. They nodded and held their weapons ready.

At that moment, I realized I had in my team the best people in the world. Leaders often brag that way about their people, but I truly believed it. We had trained together for this mission. I had just watched them suffer an attack by the Astral Maul and survive it. There was nobody else in the universe I would have rather had at my back.

"Very well, Lieutenant Busto, please lead us down into the vault."

# 41

Busto saluted, then turned and began climbing down the trellis.

Suddenly, he stopped, looked up at me, and smiled. He tapped something on his control panel and floated down the shaft instead of climbing. He'd remembered his tractor pack.

That did it for the rest of us. We all enabled our tractor packs and followed in a line into the vault.

At the bottom, I found myself in a long corridor cut out of ancient stone.

Dim lighting hung on the ceiling.

The corridor unfolded 100 yards distant, ending at an immense steel door that stood slightly ajar as if to tempt the unwary into entering.

I flew up to join Busto at the door. It wasn't open all the way. Only a crack of light showed through a gap about three inches wide.

Busto nudged it further open with the muzzle of his rifle.

The door was made of six-inch-thick steel and must

have weighed thousands of pounds, but it was so well balanced that my friend effortlessly swung it on its hinges.

It revealed another chamber. But it seemed this one was not made of stone or even metal.

The walls and ceiling were paneled with a material that shimmered like calm water.

The floor was covered with a rubber-like substance that absorbed the sound of our footsteps and provided excellent traction.

There were no individual lights, but illumination instead seemed to emit from every surface in an ambient glow, leaving no shadows.

The proportions of the room were not human. The ceilings were too low, such that my nearly two-meter frame had to hunch my shoulders uncomfortably. However, the corridors were much broader than one would typically see in a small building. Everything was low and wide, probably designed for the Primordian body.

We were inside the Astral Maul.

"Captain," O'hatet said. "Please join me."

She floated at the start of a corridor, pointing down its length. "This way, I think."

"Okay," I said. "Let's do this." I turned to Busto. "Leave a few people here to secure our exit," I said.

He nodded. "Novikova, Montana, and Rowbottom. You watch this entrance. Nobody comes in or out without my say-so. Got it?"

"Aye aye, sir," Rowbottom said.

Busto, Vila, O'hatet, Zeta, and I began to advance down the corridor.

Our surroundings were strange. I couldn't quite make out the end of the corridor. It just seemed to stretch on into the infinite distance.

After we had walked about 20 feet, I turned around, expecting to see the entrance chamber. Instead, I saw the opposite end of the corridor stretching forever.

"Um, where did..." I said.

"Captain, there are illusions down here," O'hatet said. "It's part of the Maul's defense mechanisms."

I sighed. "You never said anything about defenses."

"I thought it was obvious."

"How are we supposed to find our way back?"

"Zeta senses a hyperdimensional topology here," Zeta said. "We must use the Syderealium to find our way."

I shuddered to think what would happen if one of my friends wandered off. Would we lose them forever? "Everybody, stay close."

"Consort," Zeta said, "pause for a moment and enter the Syderealium."

I nodded and dropped to a sitting position on the floor. I shut out distractions and focused on the transcendental sequence, embracing it.

What had been so difficult when I was a novice now seemed easy. Within a few seconds, I entered the Syderealium, the blank shroud over my glyphshade lifted, and I saw my energlyph-covered body flying through a structure. Nearby were several other clusters of energlyphs. They didn't look like human bodies, but I somehow knew who each one was just by glancing at them. They were my companions.

We were no longer in the corridor but rather in something like a large building lobby with many hallways leading off it. "Which one leads to the Maul?" I asked.

"We are already inside the Maul," Zeta said from within the Syderealium. "What you see here is the true structure of what's in the physical realm."

"Okay," I picked a doorway at random. "Let's try that one."

I ended the sydereal projection and took a minute to reorient my senses.

I couldn't see the doorway I had selected, but its direction and distance were ingrained in my memory. "Follow me, people. Stay close."

I moved in the direction of the doorway and started walking.

Busto trailed me with his hand resting on my shoulder.

We walked for a long time, many minutes. The edge of the corridor didn't seem to be getting any closer.

"Boss, are you sure about this?" Busto said, worry evident in his voice.

Even though the illusion was as confusing to our senses as a hit of LSD, I was confident in what I'd seen in the Syderealium and knew we still hadn't reached the doorway.

"Don't worry, I know where we are," I replied. And I *did*, in a peculiar way. For one thing, I knew that we had actually reached a surface and were now walking up it, though there had been no sensation that gravity had changed. We were spiraling around the outside surfaces of the corridor.

You are probably asking, how did that work? Well, the Syderealium is a place with infinite dimensions. A straight line there generally doesn't translate into a straight line in our physical universe. That's why I had to view it in the Syderealium for it to make logical sense.

This corridor was a manifold inside the high-dimensional space, with no walls or ceilings. Every surface was a potential floor, and winding paths that weaved without any sense to them actually, when viewed from the Syderealium, were perfectly straight edges.

When I knew we had arrived, I reached out my hand and felt a panel under it, though I couldn't see it with my physical eyes. But it was there. I pressed on it until it gave way.

A door opened in front of us, seemingly out of thin air.

"I think I'm gonna throw up," Vila said.

"Yeah, I'm not feeling so hot, myself," Busto said. "This is very disorienting. What's in the next room?"

"I don't know. We're searching," I said.

"How long have we been here? It feels like at least an hour."

"Lieutenant, do not trust your sense of time in this place," Zeta said. "Time flows differently."

Then Busto opened his faceplate and vomited onto the rubbery floor.

Luckily, there was a breathable atmosphere down there, so he didn't immediately asphyxiate.

"Damn. This is like being airsick, only worse," he said.

"We'll call it syderealsick," I said with a grin.

I wasn't feeling any of the disorientation they were. Probably because I'd seen this place in the Syderealium, and that knowledge had been ingrained into my memory. "Let's go."

I walked into a new chamber. It was an empty room with walls the color of sandstone and a floor and ceiling of crystal. I knew the place.

I turned around and saw that my team had followed.

"This looks almost normal," O'hatet said.

I smiled, then walked to the nearest wall, put my foot up on it, pivoted, and started walking up the wall.

I didn't stop until I reached the ceiling.

I pivoted again, stepped onto the ceiling, and walked across it to the middle.

I was now hanging upside down. Or, rather, all of *them* were upside down, and I was right side up.

Vila slumped down—or pardon me—up to his feet and cradled his head.

"Come now, people," I said, "the next doorway is up here. You must follow me."

"So much for looking like a normal room," Busto said.

It took a few minutes, but eventually, I got my team oriented correctly and up next to me.

I reached down, found an invisible panel right where I knew it would be, pressed on it, and a new door opened in the floor—or was it the ceiling? The orientations were all relative now.

I stepped through the door, falling. Not accelerating, though, because there was no rush of air.

A platform appeared ahead of me, and I moved closer to it. Or maybe it was moving, and I was stationary. I had no frame of reference to tell which it was. But we soon came into contact with each other, and I touched it with my feet.

The floor of the platform was white marble with black grains. My team floated down near me.

Busto and Vila's faces looked green, and O'hatet was hanging back, her body trembling.

The platform stretched into the distance. I could not see any end to it.

Short columns of stone about 3 ft tall were arranged on it in rows. Objects rested on top of each one. Each column held something different.

On the closest column rested the complete skeleton of some sort of large rodent.

On another was an unusual looking large backpack that seemed strangely familiar.

"That's a parachute," Busto said.

One column held a slab of asphalt pavement. It looked like it had just been cut from a road somewhere on Earth. The remnant of a yellow-painted double-line ran across it.

Another column held a glass vial on a pedestal. A liquid in the vial fumed and emitted a noxious scent.

"Careful," Zeta said, "that is concentrated sulfuric acid."

Yet another column held what had to be a completed homework assignment of some kid in elementary school. A single sheet of paper. The name "Quandale Dingle" was written in messy pencil at the top, and below it twelve arithmetic problems in addition and subtraction had been completed.

It was such an everyday item, and it was just sitting there alone on a stone column.

There was a small bronze statue of an angel on another column.

A Phillips screwdriver—well used, rusted, and smelling of damp and mold—on the one next to it.

There were hundreds of columns, maybe even thousands, and all the objects were unique and seemed randomly selected from human civilization.

"What is this place?" Vila said, looking a little less green.

"I believe it's a museum," I said.

He chuckled. "Who would be interested in this stuff?"

I looked at him and held his eye. "Not us."

That shut him up, and he was quiet for several minutes.

It felt like three or four hours had passed since we'd entered the vault, but I knew Zeta was correct. We had no way to know. We just had to keep pushing forward. But my stomach was complaining.

We stopped for fifteen minutes and ate some rations while discussing where to go next.

"I need to peek again at the Syderealium," I said.

After finishing my food, I rested in my meditative posture and entered the Syderealium.

I found us on a large patio with the glowing lavender sky of the Syderealium looming over us. My team was huddled together.

Then, I noticed a cluster of glyphshades in the distance, approaching us. I didn't know who they were but sensed their hostile intentions.

I jumped back into my body. Opening my eyes, I said, "We're about to have company. Take cover."

That got everybody's attention, and we grabbed our weapons and hid between the columns.

The stone I leaned against held a rather large dead spider, though perfectly preserved.

A couple minutes later, Busto hissed at me and pointed at something in the distance.

I hurried up close to him, looked around his column, and saw a group of eight or nine armed maracs approaching us. They were still about 100 ft away.

# 42

Busto and Vila whispered for a few seconds, and then Vila moved off and disappeared behind a group of columns.

When the maracs floated within 50 feet, we sprung from behind our columns and opened fire.

A burst of flechettes flew right by my head and smashed a grandfather clock on a column to pieces.

I ducked behind my cover.

A grenade detonated, flinging dust and debris in all directions.

I switched to a different column, glanced over it, and saw a marac hiding with his back to me, and I shot him with a burst of three flechettes.

I dropped back behind my cover just as it was sprayed with a burst of gunfire.

Busto and Vila pressed forward, assaulting the maracs, who had all taken cover.

I stayed on our flanks, guarding against the maracs trying to get around us.

I shot another marac when it tried to circle behind us.

Zeta and O'hatet were following me but staying in cover.

Over the next ten minutes, the gunfire became more sporadic, with occasional bursts of automatic fire, until one final long one split the air with a mighty crescendo.

Busto jumped out of cover. "We're clear!" he yelled.

Our team gathered back together. Thankfully, nobody was wounded on our side. We'd killed nine maracs.

"How are we on ammo?" I asked.

"I'm down to my last two magazines," Vila said.

I gave him two of mine and another to Busto, leaving me with just one spare magazine. They were our firepower, and I would rather they had the extra ammo than me.

"We must be getting close," I said.

"Yeah, those guards weren't just wandering randomly," Busto said. "Which way, boss?"

I pointed over his shoulder. "We're almost to the end of this patio."

"Patio?"

"Sorry, that's what it looks like in the Syderealium. We're headed to a small building I saw in the Syderealium."

He shook his head and laughed. "Okay, dude, I'm completely lost. I guess you're like the Cheshire Cat."

I sucked water from my bladder. "Well, if this is Alice's Wonderland, then I suppose that might be true."

He nodded. "It might just be that. I keep thinking armored playing cards are about to break through the walls and come at us with pikes. It certainly wouldn't be any stranger than what we've seen so far."

My understanding of the maps O'hatet had shown me was that the Maul was not physically very big. At least in our physical universe. But it was now clear to me that the inside of the Maul was not fully contained within our universe. It had a weird multidimensional topology that spanned far more space than would be possible in our universe.

"We are traveling on a manifold through a much higher dimensional domain," Zeta said. "It is all bounded by the physical dimensions of the external Maul walls found under the IMH mining facility but contains a volume of space much larger than its size would suggest."

"How big?" I asked.

"Zeta does not know, but it could potentially be larger than the Earth's surface area."

"Zeta, how is that even possible?"

She twisted on her axis and emitted a sharp whine. "This Maul is a pocket domain of high dimensions that's been sequestered from the Syderealium by the Primordians control the artifact."

"We could get lost," I said, fear looming in my chest again. "We might already *be* lost."

"Do not fear, Consort. You are following the path you found in the Syderealium. It is leading us correctly. Do not lose sight of it."

I knew she was right. We wouldn't have stumbled on that patrol of maracs if we hadn't already been close.

I wanted to send a message back to the other teams not to enter the Maul, but our radios had stopped working as soon as we entered this place. At least there was air, though we'd seen no water, food, or animals of any kind.

We rose to our feet, and I took the lead again, walking in the direction I knew would take us to the core.

After about half a mile, the columns ended, and a vertical concrete wall stopped us. It stretched to the sides seemingly forever, and the top lay in shadows.

I thought I could hear the trickle of flowing water at the

edge of my hearing but saw no evidence of it.

"We have to go up this," I said.

Vila slapped his hand on the perfectly smooth concrete face. "How the hell are we supposed to do that?"

I smiled at him, then pressed my foot against the wall, pushed up and off the floor, and found myself standing on the wall and looking at my friends hanging from what now looked like the wall. The concrete wall had become the floor.

Vila's face twisted. "Not this again." He turned away and shook his head.

I started walking across what was now the floor, not waiting for my friends. I knew they'd follow.

I headed for the shadows ahead, knowing that hidden within them was an entrance to a chamber where I'd find the core of the Astral Maul.

I glanced behind me and confirmed that my friends were following.

Physical laws were obviously different in this place. It all felt like magic, and yet I knew it wasn't. This was a technological artifact whose workings defied human understanding and perhaps always would. That's why it was so dangerous for the marac to be playing with it.

I followed the path in my mind, left from my glimpse of it in the Syderealium.

Would I find Ban'ach at the end of it?

I figured there was a good chance of that. The Kergans needed somebody like Zeta or me who could navigate this place, and what better person than her?

The shadows deepened, and I waited for my friends to catch up.

We latched onto each other with hands and tentacles on shoulders. Zeta let me hold her in the cradle of my arm, where the heat emitting from her body made me sweat.

The shadows soon became impenetrable, and I lost track of all my senses.

I kept walking forward, though I felt no pressure of a surface under my feet. Yet, I knew I was still treading the path.

These borderlands were yet another defense mechanism of the Astral Maul, depriving potential foes of their senses. But I had the Syderealium to guide me.

At last, a dim light appeared ahead, and as I approached it, the shape of a doorway appeared as if out of mist.

"This is it," I said. I glanced back and was grateful to see all my friends still were with me.

"Once more unto the breach, dear friends, once more," Busto said from behind me.

The doorway was shut by a shining door made of glass or polished metal. It had no handle I could see, but when I approached, it slid to the side of its own volition, revealing a short hallway and a foyer.

I entered, and my team gathered behind me.

We found ourselves standing on a balcony several levels high overlooking a cavern that held something that looked like an industrial machine about the size of a two-story house.

Pipes, cables, and conduits projected and ran in a thousand directions, weaving around each other and plugging into a numberless ensemble of ports and plugs. Plumes of vapor billowed from pipe joints. The hum of powerful alternating electrical currents came from the mighty mechanism, and the air smelled of ozone and hot metal.

A control console shaped like a crescent moon rested on the floor to one side with display panels situated like whiteboards. Glowing icons and alien script covered them.

Several chairs were positioned behind the consoles, and a group of maracs rested in them or floated nearby.

They were a good 200 feet distant, but I immediately knew who Ban'ach was, even though I'd not yet met her in person. In this place, it seemed so obvious.

I'd found her.

"Let's plant the charges and get out of this place," Busto said.

"No, we can't blow it from here," I said. "It'll have to be the outside."

"That wasn't the plan!" he hissed.

"You know that the plan was always subject to change when it came to the Maul. We didn't know what we'd find. I fear that the dimensional weirdness we're seeing will affect the charges. Or the time distortion."

I pointed at the group of people. Undoubtedly, Kergan scientists were trying to bring the Maul into operation. And the strange assemblage of industrial machinery must have been the Astral Maul's core. "Capture them."

"Captain, I—"

"Just do it, Busto. We don't have time to argue."

He cursed, turned to Vila, and began whispering instructions.

"We're going to try and capture them," I told Zeta.

"Is that necessary?" Zeta responded.

To complete our primary goals, no, it wasn't, but I wasn't going to kill Ban'ach when she still held my memories. Otherwise, it would be like killing a part of myself.

"Zeta, I don't have time to explain. This is what we're doing."

Without waiting for her response, I moved to the side where I'd seen what looked like a stairwell.

Something in the shadows whipped out a limb and grabbed me, looping around my torso until my weapon and arms were trapped at my sides.

Crying out, I fell into a black pit.

# 43

One second, I was standing on the balcony; the next, I was plummeting downward.

I landed on a hard surface with a sudden jolt that left me gasping for air.

Whatever had me tied up kept me from losing my footing, but the impact shot through my knees, hip, and back. The only thing holding me up was the trap that had a hold of me.

I reached my fingers out and felt chords of something wrapped tightly around me, like a snake. But my arms were trapped against my torso.

I surveyed my surroundings. I stood in a small room. The walls, floor, and ceiling were utterly featureless.

Whatever opening I had fallen through was gone.

"Busto! Zeta! Vila!" I yelled but heard no response.

I could sense Zeta through our link. She was somewhere above me, but my instincts said she was *miles* distant!

How could I have fallen that far? I should be dead. Then again, who knew how this strange world would play with my link?

An opening in one wall appeared. Suddenly, without warning or any noise, it was there, whereas it had been a solid wall one moment before.

Ban'ach floated into the room.

She was larger than any other marac I'd ever seen. Her tentacles were thick and muscular, her eyes deep tunnels of intelligence. She wore flamboyant clothing of turquoise leather trimmed with red. Her upper skin wasn't the typical purple I'd seen in most marac, but instead was colored a soft green. I had heard there were other races of marac, but this was the first one I'd seen. Compared to the small purple maracs who comprised the Kergan masses, Ban'ach was green and large.

Behind her came two purple maracs, carrying flechette rifles, which were immediately pointed at me.

"Ah, yes, my flairsparked!" Ban'ach called out with a bird-like voice. "How delightful!" Her beak clacked together several times, just barely visible at the center of her twelve arms.

"I'm not yours!" I replied.

"You don't say." She flipped a tentacle, then floated closer, drifting along my side, around my back. One tentacle reached out and touched my protomatter suit.

"No, no, this won't do. I'm going to release you. Don't move." She said something to the guards in their whistling and screeching tongue. Probably instructions to kill me if I disobeyed.

The arms that had me trapped suddenly loosened and retracted.

The guards came forward and grabbed my weapons and stripped my combat webbing off of me.

I shrugged my shoulders and folded my arms over my

torso to loosen stiff muscles.

Ban'ach returned to float in front of me, just out of arms reach.

She touched my suit, and suddenly, it started to retract from my body.

I pulled on the protomatter, trying to cancel the order, but it didn't obey and kept rolling down my body, exposing my limbs, torso, and head.

Soon, I was standing completely nude on top of a blob of unformed protomatter.

Ban'ach drew in a sharp breath, and her entire body shook. "Your species is disgusting."

Her eyes studied every square inch of my body, running up and down my limbs as she circled me. If she was disgusted, she had a strange way of showing it.

She reached out occasionally with tentacles and touched me in various places, sometimes in an almost caressing fashion. She spent quite a few seconds playing with my hair. And not just the hair on my head, if you know what I mean. I was soon blushing.

"Where are your companions?" Ban'ach asked.

Maybe she hadn't found them yet. Or maybe she was just playing games.

*Please, Zeta, please, Busto, keep safe! Keep together!* I prayed.

"I don't know what you're talking about," I replied.

She whipped a tentacle in a slashing motion, which I understood to be marac body language for "no". "You could not have killed off that squad of soldiers all by yourself. I know you are not alone."

I tried to change the subject. "What do you want with me?"

I had to find a way to force her to project into the Syderealium. I knew how to project myself but not how to force it on somebody else. Zeta had refused to teach me those skills, and I got the sense that she didn't know how to do it. It was considered forbidden knowledge.

Ban'ach reached out and caressed my chest. "Oh, my sweet, human energlyphs are incomparable. When we flairsparked maracs discovered this, it caused quite an uproar in the Empire. The Empress herself is said not to be found without a human around for her to...feed upon."

"I don't know what you're talking about."

"Come, now, you may be human, but somebody has been training you. Something has changed since we last met. Is it that igna who follows you around?"

I kept my mouth closed. Giving her any information about my friends would only endanger them.

"Silent? Not even a question about Mom and Dad?"

Rage exploded inside me, and I leaped at Ban'ach.

Piercing pain thundered through my spine, and I dropped to the floor.

I screamed until my voice stung.

The pain slowly dissipated, leaving me panting and sweating.

I rose unsteadily to my feet.

Ban'ach held up a small cylindrical device in her tentacle. "This is a nervebreaker, specially tuned for human nervous systems. I would suggest not trying that again unless you like the feel of it." The tip of her tentacle played with the trigger on the end of the cylinder.

A bead of sweat ran down my chest. "You stole my memories of my mother and father from me. I'm warning you now; one day, I will kill you for it."

She laughed. "Is that so? And how will you do that once you are an Emptied?"

Emptied? I failed to hide the fear this name suggested.

"What else did you expect?" she said. "Taking Mom and Dad was just the start of what I had planned for you. The flairsparked are so much more enjoyable to consume. It's like the difference between water and nectar. One needs water for survival, but nectar makes life worth living. Those humans who aren't flairsparked are like the water. I give them to the Empress and my other sister Soul Ravagers. But now, nectar like you is something special I save *all* for myself. Why would I share?" She traced my stomach muscles with the tip of an arm, playing with my belly button and letting the tip go lower into my nether regions.

She seemed to be trying to get some kind of physical response from me. She played with me like a doll. Because that's all I was to her. An object to be used and then discarded.

I glanced at her guards and wondered if this sort of activity was something that disgusted them, but they were standing silent without expressions on their alien faces.

"I had planned to keep you to myself," she said, "and sip from your glyphshade. Just a little each day to keep me happy. There isn't much life worth living for anymore. I bet you couldn't guess how old I am. Hmm?"

I shook my head. "I don't even know how long maracs live."

She waived a tentacle. "Generally, not more than 150 of your solar years, and the vast majority less than 120. But Soul Ravagers, we benefit from our skills with the Syderealium. For example, I am 283 years old and look like I'm 40. The Empress, may Vad'or bless her reign forever, is over a thousand years old."

So, the Empress of the Kergan Empire was a Soul Ravager, just like Ban'ach. Something was alarming about this news. Somehow, the feeding of Soul Ravagers on glyphshades was tied to the longevity of the Soul Ravagers.

"But I'm not so greedy as to recognize other potential uses for you," Ban'ach said. "You are the most powerful flairsparked I have ever encountered. That comparison includes hundreds of other alien species, not just humans. Some of them don't even have flairsparked. You humans possess a rich population of flairsparked, one reason you are so satisfying, but you, Kory Drake, shine like a supernova compared to them. I had planned to feed on you myself. But you could be an even more valuable political asset."

"What do you want?"

"I plan to gift you to the Empress and let her do with you as she chooses."

"She'll just feed on me."

"Possibly. Even probably. But perhaps not."

"I won't do anything for you. You stole my parents from me!"

She circled me, sniffing.

As she did this, I split my mind and started meditating on the transcendental number while the other half followed her.

I'd never tried to enter the Syderealium without meditating before and didn't even know if it would be possible. What would I do when I got there? But somehow, I sensed the key to forcing her into a projection was first getting myself there. The sequence of numbers started to flow, $0.1...2...3...4...$

"What if I returned them to you?" Ban'ach said.

I lost my concentration and had to start over again. "What?"

"It's a simple matter. It would hurt me. I have enjoyed those two energlyphs ever so much. It is clear you drew tremendous strength from them, and they have likewise fortified me both physically and mentally. But the Empress, may Vad'or bless her reign forever, must have you whole and unblemished. I would not leave my marks on her."

"And what do you get out of this?" I said with one part of my mind as the other struggled to start my meditation again. *0.1...2...3...4...5...*

She jerked to a stop, turned to face me, and weaved two tentacles together in an intricate pattern. "I earn the debt of the Empress, may Vad'or keep her."

"Political power, you mean." Almost, I could feel the veil of the Syderealium beginning to lift.

"Yes, perhaps. What else do I have to live for now? Purpose, that is what I seek. Countering this pointless insurgency you humans are conducting is beneath my abilities."

"But, the Astral Maul? That must be quite the achievement, you finding it." I was in the Syderealium. But only half my consciousness was there, and it felt sluggish as I tried to keep the other half focused on Ban'ach, keeping her distracted.

She rocked her body back and forth. "I didn't find it. I'm only here because I am a trained flairsparked. These fools can't navigate the Maul without one of us. But who will benefit from the Astral Maul? Not I, at least not in my current role."

"You need the attention of your Empress."

I studied the glyphshades of the two guards. They were within easy reach. In the physical universe, I was helpless, but here in the Syderealium the guards were like mice and I the cat.

Zeta had never taught me how to attack and steal energlyphs, but I had a basic idea of how to do it. It was a question of focused willpower, which could be shaped into a blade that would cut an energlyph from the glyphshade's vine and attach it to my own. It was the reverse operation of defending. But could I properly focus my willpower when my consciousness was split like this? It was like trying to drive and text at the same time. Neither task could be done properly.

"Yes, I need that in order to find purpose," Ban'ach continued. "*You*, Kory Drake, are my key to that. So, this is my deal. Cooperate, and I will return your energlyphs to you and make you whole and turn you over to the custody of the Empress, may Vad'or bless her reign. The alternative is that I keep you for myself, will feed on you slowly, until you are an Emptied."

I focused on the closest guard. My glyphshade brushed up against his. His physical body seemed to shiver, and his weight shifted, but then he froze in place again.

From the guard's perspective, I must have just done the equivalent of walking on his grave.

Back in the Maul, I said, "I'll have to think about it."

Ban'ach bobbed up and down, and her skin flushed. "Do not play with me, Drake! I sense that you are not taking me seriously!" She lashed out a tentacle, and the tip slapped me painfully.

I nearly lost my hold on the Syderealium. The pain was enough for the veil to almost fall on me.

I drew on my willpower and slowly my sydereal presence solidified.

And then I realized that what I'd just done to keep myself in the veil—focusing my willpower like a razor blade —was precisely what I needed as a weapon.

Keeping my willpower focused, I lashed out at the guard's glyphshade.

Energlyphs exploded away like a dandelion being blown on with a mighty breath. I felt that my attack was clumsy, but it was the best I could do.

I drew the free energlyphs toward me, calling them and offering sanctuary on my glyphshade.

They came closer because they didn't want to disassociate, which is what would happen to a free-floating energlyph. I felt them attach to me, and suddenly, new emotions, feelings, and experiences flooded my mind. They were strange, alien, yet fulfilling.

I realized I'd drawn myself too strongly into the Syderealium and lost track of Ban'ach. But I needed more time!

I opened my physical eyes again, found myself on the floor, and saw Ban'ach staring down at me. A dot of blood was trailing down my chest from where her tentacle, like a whip, had opened up the skin on my chest.

"You humans are so delicate!" she said with rage.

I had become unresponsive for a few seconds, and she seemed to have concluded I had fainted after she struck me. She didn't yet know I was fully awake, but in the Syderealium. But I couldn't keep up the pretense too much longer.

I looked at the nearest guard. He was still staring forward, but his eyes seemed frozen. He most certainly wasn't okay.

His arms holding the gun slumped, and the weapon fell until it was hanging by only the sling.

Ban'ach heard the noise and turned to him.

I rushed back into the Syderealium, focused my willpower like a blade, and attacked the second guard.

My blade cut into him, and thousands of energlyphs flew loose, which I called to myself, sucking them into my glyphshade.

They attached to me, and new sensations and emotions

filled me.

Then I slashed at him again, and a smaller cloud of energlyphs burst forth, which I drew to me.

I fed.

The new energlyphs felt like water on the tongue of a man dying of thirst.

The glyphshades of the two guards were now sparse husks. The Syderealium seemed to tremble around me. I thought I could hear Zeta yelling something from a long distance.

"What has happened here?" I heard Ban'ach say.

She was still in the physical world. I knew I should return my attention to it, but I felt so...full. I just wanted to rest here for a little while.

"Wake up!" Ban'ach yelled. I heard the sounds of a beating taking place. "Get up!"

I could sense my physical body still lying on the floor of that cell. Unconscious because all of my mind was in the Syderealium at that moment trying to consolidate around the new energlyphs.

I turned my attention to Ban'ach's glyphshade.

It was a massive monstrosity of energlyphs. Millions, and millions of nodes of energy, organized into a complex hierarchy of branches. A fractal pattern, each branch drilling down into yet smaller branches. She seemed to fill the entire domain. I knew that I was looking at an old and powerful being. She was a Soul Ravager, and she'd stolen from me.

I focused my willpower and slashed her. But instead of breaking and scattering, her energlyphs bounced.

I tried again, and in response I heard a surprised gasp from Ban'ach in the physical world.

"By Vad'or's sack, you're projecting!"

A tentacle slapped against my physical body. Then again.

"You've emptied them!"

Then she surprised me by laughing uproariously as if she'd just understood the punchline of a highly clever joke.

"Oh, the Empress is going to *love* you!" She laughed more. "Like a goreclaw, you are! Already a Soul Ravager, and untrained at that."

She whipped me again and again, laughing the entire time while blood streamed from my stinging wounds.

"You see? You overate, you idiot. You gorged yourself!" She sighed. "Well, I suppose there's not much to be done about this. I can't have you out there trying to take a bite out of *me*, now, can I?"

In the Syderealium, I continued lashing out at Ban'ach, but her energlyphs were too resilient. It was like trying to cut a steel thread with a razor blade.

Then, Ban'ach was there, in the Syderealium—just me and her.

# 44

Her glyphshade didn't change in structure, yet I could feel her staring at me with malevolent focus. "You naughty little puppy. Look at the mess you've made!"

She effortlessly pushed me away.

She studied the husks I had left of her guards. "You eat like a wild animal. But what more could I expect? You have no control, no training. I'm surprised you got this far." She laughed again. "Oh, no, no, no, we can't leave you out in the wild, little human!"

"Give me what's mine!" I yelled and focused my willpower again, plunging it into her like a lance.

She jumped to the side. "That is quite enough!" she roared, fear showing behind her voice for the first time. "Get control of yourself!"

"Give them back!" I jabbed at her.

I really didn't have a clue what I was doing. To Ban'ach, I must have looked like a caveman holding a laser pistol. I rushed at her, stabbing all around.

She tried to dodge, but something got through, and I

saw several tiny energlyphs break free from her.

I pulled on them, and they attached to me. They were so small I barely felt anything change.

But Ban'ach's reaction was far from subtle. "You are a monster!"

"Who's the real monster here, Ban'ach?! At least I don't feed on the helpless!"

"You're an uncivilized bruit, and I'll rein you in or destroy you if you won't submit. You're too dangerous to be left free!"

Then she attacked. All her willpower focused on one giant blow that manifested as an exotic-looking war mace.

But Zeta had trained me well. I saw her attack coming and deflected it easily, leaving her spinning as she tried to recover from her wild swing.

"Untrained, am I?" I taunted.

She attacked again, this time feinting with a blade on the right while trying to sneak in with a blow from her mace on the other side. But I ducked, and both attacks passed over me.

I stabbed at her again and hit something. A few more tiny energlyphs broke away, and I sucked them in.

I knew there was something wrong with my attacks. I wasn't able to summon the bruit force that Ban'ach could. I was fighting with a needle while she held weapons of war. But I could still make her bleed, and she knew it.

But how much longer could this go on for? I was tiring.

A roar and trembling sounded from a distance, slowly increasing in violence.

I looked in that direction and saw a structure that looked like a crystal palace. It had towers and ramparts and windows like slits. The noise was coming from it.

Ban'ach attacked me again.

This time, I moved inside her attack and grappled her, pressing my glyphshade up against hers. She was much larger than me, but I wrapped a stranglehold around a portion of her that I instinctively knew to be a debilitating hold. Don't ask me how I knew.

She screamed. "You vile monster!" I heard panic in her voice.

"You created me!" I roared. "I would have never come after you if you'd just left me alone, you greedy alien bitch!"

"We're *all* in danger, you nitwit! Look!" She seemed to point in the direction of the crystal structure.

"What is it?" I responded without releasing my grip on her. I knew if I let go, she would be all over me again.

"That's the Astral Maul on this side! It's unstable! You've contaminated this domain!"

"I've contaminated it?"

"Yes, with your clumsy attacks. You've left energlyphs to drift free and evaporate. The Astral Maul is feeding on the energy. We're in danger, you idiot!"

"Not any more danger than we already were. If the Astral Maul blows, and I die, it will be a price worth paying!"

She squirmed powerfully under my grip. We were in such close proximity, I could read many of her energlyphs. They gave me random glimpses into her psyche.

I sensed a complex female, bored with life and lacking fulfillment.

Then I saw them. *My* energlyphs. My mother and father. They drifted by me, and I grasped for them. My glyphshade brushed up against them, and for a fleeting moment, I felt the warm skin and smell of shampoo I associated with my mother's hugs. I heard my father's deep, happy laugh as he tumbled with me on the grass in our backyard. I felt whole again, like myself.

Then they were gone, drifting away. I focused my willpower, drawing upon all my mental capacity not just to focus it but to shape it into a blunt instrument, like what I'd seen Ban'ach using. A sydereal mace. I swung it at the branch holding my energlyphs.

My blow struck.

Ban'ach screamed.

Dozens of glyphshades blew away from the branch, some of them quite large, and while she was stunned, I sucked them in, feeling strength flow into me. But I didn't find my parents among them. They were still attached to her branch. My blow had been powerful but had barely scratched her.

But I had her in my power, and she knew it.

She squirmed under me, and I could sense her terror. Nothing like this had ever happened to her before. She didn't need to tell me because I could feel it myself. I could see myself through *her* perspective.

She had not lied. I was the most potent flairsparked encountered in thousands of years. I had the potential to use my talents to rule worlds, dominate civilizations, and even force the galaxy to bow down to me.

But I didn't want any of that.

I just wanted my parents back.

So, I fought, striking Ban'ach again and again.

She was so robust and skillful. It was only a matter of time before I overcame her, but how much longer could I hold on to her?

I had completely forgotten about my friends and the reason we had come here. I was thirsty for blood! For Ban'ach's sydereal blood! I would not be sated until I drank deeply from her. Until what had been taken was returned.

In the physical world, I sensed movement. I devoted a trickle of my attention to it.

I sensed people in the cell with me and Bana'ch.

It was Busto and Zeta, and my other companions. They stood in the open doorway.

"What's wrong with him?" Busto asked.

"He is in the Syderealium!" Zeta yelled, her voice tense and her words clipped. "He is battling with Ban'ach!"

"Let me just kill her."

"Nay, if they are locked in battle, you could kill both of them by accident! Wait for Zeta! She goes!"

Suddenly, Zeta's glyphshade was next to me. She took a few seconds to study the battleground. "No!" I heard her cry out in sorrow.

Something tugged at me. "Kory Drake, release her!"

"No!!! I almost have them!"

"Nay! Zeta forbids it!" A blow of sydereal energy struck both Ban'ach and me, and I lost my grip on her.

I flew backward.

Ban'ach's glyphshade went limp, and I knew she'd returned to the physical world.

"Zeta, what have you done?" I called out. Her glyphshade was beautiful and elegantly constructed.

"No, Consort, what have *you* done! You have done what is forbidden! You have become a Soul Ravager!"

"Never!" I cried out in anguish. "I would never!"

"Kory Drake, it is not our origins that define us, but our actions. You chose wrong."

I felt filthy like I had just bathed in a cesspool and rinsed off with urine. "What do I do?"

"Right now, we must leave this projection."

"No, Zeta! What's going to happen?!"

"Zeta does not know. This event is unprecedented. Zeta

must confer with the Supreme Council." She shoved me. Zeta *shoved* me hard, and it hurt, not just physically but in my heart.

I yielded and performed the mental exercise that returned my mind wholly to my physical body.

I opened my eyes. I lay on my back on the floor with drool running out of my mouth.

Busto twisted on the floor, twitching and screaming.

Ban'ach was gone.

I ran to my friend. Moments later, he calmed down and opened his eyes.

"What happened?" I asked.

"I don't know," he said. "Ban'ach woke up, looked at me, and suddenly I was on the floor screaming."

I stood and glanced out the door. Vila and O'hatet were picking themselves up off the floor. "Ban'ach?" I asked.

"Gone," Vila said.

I went back to the room and approached Zeta. She wouldn't let me come close.

"Zeta! Please!"

"Keep your distance, Consort!" she said. "It's all that Zeta can handle, and we have this link between us."

"I'm sorry! Tell me how to fix this!" I found myself weeping for the hurt I'd caused my friend, even though I couldn't understand what exactly I'd done wrong.

"Zeta does not know if it can be fixed. Zeta needs time. Keep your distance until then." She studied my body. "You are naked. Gather your suit and belongings."

I nodded, wiped the tears away, and stepped into my suit.

"It's more than time to blow this place," Busto said. "We've been hearing strange rumblings."

"What happened to the other maracs in that chamber?"

"They ran away. We're not chasing them. If they get out in time, they live; if not, they die when we blow this place."

A couple minutes later, we organized ourselves, then headed on the return path at a run, exercising none of the caution we'd moved at before.

Somewhere ahead of us was Ban'ach. Would we catch her? Did I *want* to catch her? How Zeta reacted to my actions made me lack confidence in my judgment.

Were the memories of my parents so vital to me that they were worth destroying my friendship with Zeta?

Were they worth endangering my crew?

I didn't have an answer. So, I secretly wished I wouldn't reencounter Ban'ach, at least not soon, so I wouldn't have to face the dilemma.

In trying to destroy the monster, it seemed I had begun turning into one myself, at least in the eyes of Zeta.

# 45

The strange and confusing world that was the Astral Maul trembled around us as if the ground were about to split asunder and swallow us.

We fled from the cell where I had been interrogated, stopping briefly in the central chamber where the control console for the Maul was located.

A huge wall-sized display contained dense text and figures, but in no language I could understand. It flashed in bright colors, primarily purples and yellows.

"It's kerganese script," O'hatet said. "This console isn't part of the original artifact. The Kergan installed it as a way to control the Maul."

"Can you read it?" I asked.

"The words, yes, but most of it makes no sense. Mostly technical jargon. But there are a lot of error messages."

"The artifact is destabilizing this domain of the Syderealium," Zeta said. "An Astral Titan will be attracted and destroy it. The foolish Kergans attempted to manipulate forces they did not understand! We must flee before we are destroyed along with the Maul!" She started moving toward the staircase that led up and out of the chamber. "Come, all!"

I rested a hand on O'hatet's broad head. "Let's go, there is no time."

Busto and Vila were so nervous they practically danced. O'hatet waved her arms and said, "It is a shame they destroyed this artifact. We could have learned so much from it." She turned and followed.

We climbed the staircase to the balcony, then jogged to the strange opening that led us down the wall that was really a floor.

As we crossed the bare concrete, the air began to fill with smoke that smelled of ozone and a sweet and sharp scent I recognized as nitrogen oxide. Somewhere nearby, there was a highly energetic source burning the air. My suit HUD displayed warnings about toxins and to keep my helmet sealed.

We reached the museum of columns, running through it and even flying on our tractor packs for short distances when it permitted us to cut corners, though the gravity in this place was strange and caused the tractors to behave erratically.

As we ran down the endless hallway through which we had entered, I felt a swirl of emotions that had no logical origin. Elation, fear, jealousy, courage, sadness, excitement, my feelings cycled through them rapidly, jerking my mind around until it became difficult to concentrate on the path ahead. I knew the feelings weren't my own but were being forced on me by the Maul.

"Persevere, my friends!" Zeta yelled. "The Astral Maul is unstable!"

If the strange Primordian machine could do this to us,

what would it be like if it was unleashed upon Earth with the Kergan Empire at the controls?

After running for what seemed like hours, I realized I could no longer remember where we were.

"Stop!" I yelled. "I need to enter the Syderealium again."

"It's too dangerous!" Zeta cried.

"I can't see where we're going anymore. I've lost track of our path."

"Then do not remain long, Consort."

I sat on the ground, forced my tumultuous feelings into the background, and began the meditations that would transport my consciousness into the Syderealium. One minute, I felt joy; the next, anxiety. Then, a raging hate that had no target. But I shoved these emotions away and forced myself to project into that other world.

Once inside the Syderealium, I again beheld the path and saw our exit not too far away.

Satisfied, I was about to leave, when I sensed a presence behind me. I turned around.

Blazing light and heat engulfed me.

A body as bright and significant as the Sun loomed over me. Its presence so intense that I felt my glyphshade beginning to disassociate, my energlyphs tugging at their bindings, being pulled into this *thing*.

**"Mortal, how dare you walk in my presence!"** a deep bass, roaring voice said so powerfully it made my soul vibrate.

I looked away, unable to withstand the glory of this being. "Who are you!"

**"I am Pyrakos the Boundless. What abomination have you brought into my domain?!"**

The firmament of the Syderealium trembled from the voice of Pyrakos. I had encountered one of the Astral Titans!

Its attention was upon me. I knew I was doomed.

"Oh, Great Pyrakos, it was not I who built this Astral Maul. My companions and I came to stop it before it would disturb your realm. My enemies are trying to use it against my people. Have mercy on us!"

Yeah, I know, it was a pathetic speech. But I'd never spoken to a god before, so it was the best that could have been expected on such short notice.

**"I care not for your petty squabbles, mortal!"**

My energlyphs pulled at me, Pyrakos's essence drawing them in, threatening to unmake me. Nevertheless, I remembered Zeta's training and applied my will to keeping myself intact, somehow resisting the god, though I don't know how I managed it.

**"You are a strong one. Few can withstand my presence. Have you a name?"**

Dared I give him a reason to remember me? Honestly, did I want this immortal and omnipotent being to know of me?

One thing I'd learned on the streets was to be polite. If you find it strange that a homeless youth would have learned that, just remember that being rude to another street person was a good way to earn yourself a knife in the gut.

"I am called Kory Drake by my people," I said after a moment of hesitation.

**"Kory Drake, will you swear an oath to destroy the Astral Maul once you return to your material plane?"**

"Yes!"

**"Swear it!"**

"I, Kory Drake, do swear by my energlyphs that I will destroy the Astral Maul!"

**"So be it, Kory Drake. This oath hereby binds you.**

**Now, be gone with you!"**

With that final word, he cast me out of my projection.

I opened my eyes to the physical world.

A piercing pain behind my eyes greeted me. My mouth was as dry as a desert.

Busto knelt next to me, grasping my shoulder. "What happened?" he asked.

I shook my head and pushed him away. "It doesn't matter. There's no time. We need to get out of here and plant those charges."

I rose to my feet.

The path ahead was now clear in my memory. We were almost to the exit.

I started forward but noticed my companions standing there staring at me like I had sprouted an extra arm. "Run!" I roared and turned my back on them.

I had met a god of the Syderealium!

I saw one and survived!

What did it mean?

Why had Pyrakos not consumed me?

Perhaps only because through me, he could destroy the Maul. I had become the willing instrument of a god.

"Thank God!" Cobb yelled as I emerged from the Maul into the vault.

He, Stenberg, and a portion of their crews stood guard around the entrance. Some of them were lying on the stone ground, looking confused. Two of them appeared to be unconscious.

"What happened?" I asked.

"A marac emerged a few minutes ago. We tried to capture them, but they fired some kind of area weapon that stunned us."

"That would be Ban'ach. She escaped us inside the Maul. Where did she go?"

Cobb and Stenberg looked at each other and shook their heads. "I don't know," Stenberg said. "We were all left squirming on the floor."

"*Thunder*, this is Fireball, be advised that Ban'ach is loose and may attempt to flee on a shuttle or other ship," I said over comms while Cobb and Stenberg finished helping their fallen team members get back to their feet.

"*Roger*," Destiny replied.

Busto and Vila started planting the charges around the Maul entrance and throughout the excavated vault.

These would collapse the vault, though not likely destroy the Astral Maul itself. For that, we had loaded eight GAMs—or ground attack missiles—into *Thunder*'s missile magazines, which we would launch after departing the facility.

"Captain Stenberg," I said, "have your Kergan captives been evacuated yet?"

"Yes, they've been moved to AC-3," she said.

I checked the people's progress planting the charges and saw they still had a few more minutes.

"Captain Cobb, what happened at AC-2?" I asked the captain of *Invictus*.

He shook his head. "We weren't able to figure it out. The best we could determine is that the crew of *Fullback* left in their ship sometime between when they made initial entry and when we finished up at AC-3. My guess is that those emanations we were getting from the Astral Maul spooked them."

"Did you get all the rigor pods evacuated?"

"Yup, they're all loaded. All 161 of them. We're only waiting on you people."

Suddenly, Destiny spoke up on comms. *"Fireball, Thunder, enemy shuttle in sight fleeing from a pad north of the Admin Center. I'm in pursuit."*

"Roger," I said.

That must be Ban'ach. I still hoped to recover my memories, so I didn't want Destiny to kill her, but at the same time, I didn't want her to escape because that could create complications for us.

*"I'm getting hit with significant jamming,"* Destiny said. *"They're really bookin', holy smokes!"*

The comms went silent for a bit, and I felt my shoulders tense up, waiting for the outcome of the pursuit.

*"Fireball, I've lost them!"* Destiny reported.

"Roger, *Thunder*, return for team extraction." I clapped my hands. "Okay, everyone, it's time to take our leave!"

There was nothing we could do about Ban'ach at the moment, and she was probably headed to the nearest Kergan military base. We needed to get out of here before she called in a counterstrike team.

"Clear the vault!" Busto yelled.

The three crews filed up the trellis work at the vault entrance.

Vila came last, pulling the detonator cable behind him. The blast would likely cause this entire section of the building to subside into the lunar surface.

We marched to the outside.

All three remaining corvettes, along with *Moshy*, were parked there.

I received a message from Phoebe that the freighter's cargo was loaded and secured, and they were ready to depart.

I gave the signal to Busto.

He pressed something in his hand, and the ground

shook. Sparks and debris flew into the dark sky from the other side of the Admin Center. The roof collapsed.

We loaded into our starships.

I ascended to the flight deck and took my customary seat next to Destiny.

"I almost had her!" Destiny said, a visible blush on her face.

"Don't worry about it," I said. "She must have had an escape already planned."

"She had some crazy countermeasures on that shuttle! I couldn't get any of *Thunder*'s weapons to lock and she disappeared from sensors almost immediately after lifting off."

I patted her knee. "There'll be a next time. I still need what she took," I said softly so Zeta wouldn't hear me.

Once everybody was strapped in, I lifted us out of Lindblad F, with the other three ships following.

"Weaps, you are cleared to fire on AC-1," I said.

"Aye aye, Captain," Busto replied.

About 30 seconds later, I watched on my tactical display as the GAMs departed our magazines, streaking for the facility.

They struck with giant balls of sparks and glowing rock, spilling tons of lunar rock into the sky.

The Moon now had eight new craters where the Astral Maul used to be.

"Search lidars coming over the horizon," Phoebe announced. "The signatures match two Kergan frigates."

"Okay, let's get low and fast," I said. "Nav, keep an eye on *Moshy*."

My tactical display indicated the direction from which the Kergan warships were approaching but not their distance because their lidar emissions gave us no ranging information, and we hadn't yet picked up their hulls on our sensors.

I steered *Thunder* down, reducing altitude, until we were weaving through valleys in the lunar landscape.

Phoebe piloted *Moshy* from behind us, the lumbering bulk of the freighter struggling to keep up.

*Invictus* and *Defiant* scattered in different directions, hoping to split the pursuit. "*Godspeed*, Thunder!" Stenberg called out on the radio.

"*Moshy*, move ahead of us," I called on the radio.

"*Roger*," Phoebe replied.

The strength of the enemy lidar emissions grew stronger. Their directions split, and two sources indicated they were crossing our stern from starboard to port. But one of the sources stubbornly stayed on the same bearing, indicating they were pursuing us.

*Moshy* passed us on the port side. Her navigation lights were extinguished, so all I could see on the visible spectrum was an occlusion of the stars.

Phoebe piloted the ship expertly, moving in front of us so I could guard her rear and draw enemy fire targeting the defenseless cargo ship.

"Radar signal bearing one-nine-seven," Novikova said. "The signature matches that of a Kergan frigate. Based on the signal energy, I calculate a high probability they've seen us."

"I've got a firm reading on thermal," Busto said. "Designating Zulu-3."

"Dang it!" I said. "Okay, prepare for battle!"

# 46

"Weaps, range to Zulu-3?" I asked.

"I'm working on it," Busto said. "Approximately 50 to 60 nautical miles."

We had *Moshy* with us carrying 161 helpless humans. Even worse, that frigate outmassed us by three times over, was more heavily armored, carried stronger armament, and could accelerate harder. If *Invictus* and *Defiant* had stayed with us, we might have been able to fight Zulu-3 together, but their location was unknown, and they were out of contact.

"Source is crossing slowly from port to starboard," Novikova said a minute later.

"They're closing on us at 650 feet-per-second," Busto said.

I racked my brain for a strategy, some trick I could use. I had to rely on *Thunder* and the wits of my crew to protect *Moshy* and get us home alive.

"Zulu-3 emissions signature has changed to acquisition mode," Novikova. "They're trying to lock onto us, Captain!"

"Comms, any contact with *Invictus* or *Defiant*?" I asked.

"No, last contact was about 10 minutes ago," Destiny responded, who was acting as the communications officer while Phoebe was out of the ship.

"Montana, how many combat drones do we have available?"

"Four in the armory and another three in crates," the medic said from her jump seat.

The combat drones had powerful tractors and could theoretically accelerate quite fast.

"ChEng, our combat drones: Could they be programmed to produce emissions that looked like our ship?"

"Aye, Captain," Zeta said. "That could be done with no modifications. All we need to do is have them transmit a random signal over their comms at high power. Furthermore, their protomatter armor could be reconfigured to make them look like our hull on sensors."

"Truly?"

"Aye."

"Do it. Montana and Weaps, help her. Shove any available drones out the airlock and program them for random trajectories leading away from us." I waived at them. "Quickly!"

The three crew members unstrapped themselves and flew quickly toward the hatch.

I needed to buy us some time while they completed the task. I pressed the transmit button for the comms. "*Moshy*, follow me; we're going to use the terrain to mask ourselves."

"*Roger*," Phoebe said.

Ahead of us, *Moshy* banked and turned to pull in behind *Thunder*.

Below, I saw a narrow chasm between two soaring mountains. I guided *Thunder* down into it, the gap between the nearly vertical walls barely wide enough to let the freighter through.

I dropped *Thunder*'s speed until the passing rocks were no longer a dangerous blur.

Suddenly, the chasm opened up into a valley covered with a field of boulders.

I entered a low circling turn over it, looking for somewhere to land.

Phoebe extended the larger ship's undercarriage, and her speed dropped until she came to a hover over a gap between two rocks the size of office buildings.

I surveyed the cluttered landscape and spotted a gap in the rock debris perfectly suited to *Thunder*.

I decelerated, extended our undercarriage, and brought our ship to rest on the ground with a gentle *thud*.

"Go to total EMCON," I said.

Multiple replies of "aye aye" sounded on the flight deck. My crew went through systems, shutting them down to minimize and control our emissions.

Phoebe would be doing the same from her side.

All external lights were extinguished, and we were still in the lunar night, so it was pitch black outside the ship. I believed I had picked a good landing spot.

We were resting inside a deep bowl inside a mountain range. Thousands of boulders surrounded us, some so giant they dwarfed *Thunder*. I tried to imagine what cataclysmic event could have broken them off Luna's crust and thrown them down here. It was beyond my comprehension.

Where were those drones?

"Zulu-3 emissions have gone back to search mode," Novikova said in almost a whisper. There was no need to talk so softly, but I think it was just her natural reaction to us hiding.

The indicator light for the ventral airlock flashed.

Moments later, I watched on the display as four figures flew away from *Thunder*.

Seconds later, each of them ballooned in size until they were approximately the size of *Thunder*, and they began transmitting random chatter on the radio that appeared to be encrypted comms. They were composed almost entirely of vacuum, each massing no more than 300 pounds, but they looked convincingly like our ship.

Zeta, Busto, and Montana floated back onto the flight deck.

"Drones are away, Captain," Zeta said as she strapped back into her console station.

"Excellent," I replied. "Weaps, as soon as we have Zulu-3 back on sensors, I want you to compute ASM and railgun firing solutions. Charge the railguns for maximum armor penetration. We're going to shoot these guys in the ass."

*Thunder*'s current railguns were heavier versions of what we'd had mounted on the Raider hull, so we wouldn't have to overcharge them and potentially damage them.

"Aye aye, sir."

I watched my display and saw the blocky outline of the Kergan warship passing about 20 or 30 miles to the southeast, flying high and fast. Fortunately, they hadn't passed directly overhead, or they would have immediately seen us. Regardless, they were obviously distracted by the fleeing drones.

"Zulu-3 has acquired Drone-4," Novikova said. "They have weapons lock."

"I've got that solution, Captain," Busto said, "but some of our missile tubes are masked by these rocks."

"Okay. Prepare to fire what you can on my command."

Zulu-3 was flying away from us, but I knew they would return as soon as they fired on the decoy and realized what it was. I needed us to act before they saw through our deception.

Zulu-3 flashed with bright light as it fired its railguns.

I lifted *Thunder* out of the bowl, retracting our undercarriage. As soon as we cleared the nearby boulders, I yelled, "Fire!"

*Thunder* shuddered twice as both railguns fired 10 lb tungsten darts at velocities of 186 miles per second.

Nearly at the same time, ten heavy ASM missiles launched from her magazines and accelerated at 30 gees toward Zulu-3.

The railgun darts crossed the distance to the enemy frigate in a third of a second. One missed, but the other impacted in an explosion of sparks like a detonating fireworks shell.

On my thermal display, I saw *Moshy* lift off and begin flying in the opposite direction of the frigate, hugging the terrain.

I accelerated toward the frigate, closing the distance before they could fire on us, hoping the railguns would recharge quickly.

The frigate's LPDs fired. There was no atmosphere to scatter and reveal the beams of coherent light, but our fired ASMs began to explode one after another.

"Prepare another flight of ASMs!" I ordered.

The railguns finished charging. "Fire railguns and weapons free!"

Vila had control of the railgun turrets. He aimed them and fired.

*Thunder* shuddered.

More of our missiles exploded before they could impact

the frigate.

Another.

Another.

Then, a massive explosion bloomed against the frigate. One of our missiles had made it through. Incandescent debris flew out from the frigate.

Moments later, our saturated sensors cleared, and I saw Zulu-3 still flying. Damaged, with a yawning crater in its flank, though still flying.

"Vampire, vampire!" Novikova yelled.

Four icons representing enemy ASMs appeared on my tactical display, rapidly closing with us.

"Enable all defensive systems!" I said.

One of the enemy missiles disappeared in a ball of light.

Four IMs fired from *Thunder*'s light missile magazines and accelerated toward the threats.

Another enemy missile blew up.

I pulled *Thunder* into a tight turn, trying to confuse the missile tracking logic.

Our ship shuddered, and warning lights flared.

"We took a railgun slug to the stern," Zeta said. "Atmospheric venting in compartments 17 and 22."

Our railguns fired again.

We released ten more ASMs.

One of the enemy missiles passed by our IMs and LPD firing, closing with our stern.

*Thunder* quaked abruptly, throwing me forward so hard it wrenched my right shoulder against my restraining straps.

Alarms whooped.

Smoke pumped out of an overhead air vent.

*Thunder* tumbled.

I studied my attitude sensors and quickly applied

compensating force to the flight controls, bringing the ship back under control.

"Heavy damage amidships!" Zeta yelled. "Railgun turret 2 is damaged, and ASM magazines are disabled. We're venting atmosphere from Decks 1 and 2."

My display showing *Thunder*'s status was a wall of red warnings and error messages. The enemy missile had exploded on our side and opened a huge hole.

On my sensor, *Moshy* was fleeing, now 40 miles away. There was no evidence that Zulu-3 had even detected them. Maybe they would manage to get away.

"Keep firing!" I ordered.

"Railgun is rebooting!" Vila responded.

"ASMs are offline!" Busto said.

We were a sitting duck and as good as dead.

I was happy to see Zulu-3 take another hit from one of our most recently fired missiles, hitting almost the exact same spot on its hull and seeming to do minimal damage.

The frigate closed with us, coming in for a kill shot.

I flew *Thunder* down into a valley, hugging the ground, aiming for a mountain pass, trying to get the terrain between us and Zulu-3. One of the mountains zoomed past our starboard side, masking us temporarily from the enemy ship.

I flew us around the shoulders of the mountain, attempting to play for time.

The enemy captain was too clever. He raised the altitude of Zulu-3 until it could look directly down upon the mountain, revealing everything at its base, including us.

I looked for more cover, but there was nothing nearby.

Our weapons were damaged and rebooting. If we took one more missile hit like the last, we'd disintegrate.

I knew we were dead.

Suddenly, multiple missile icons appeared on my threat display. At first, I thought they were coming from an unseen enemy, but they weren't flying toward us but toward Zulu-3.

Zulu-3 turned away and accelerated, though more sluggishly than it should have. We'd obviously damaged them.

Additional missile icons appeared, again accelerating toward Zulu-3. There were now at least fifteen missiles pursuing the frigate.

"Dominion corvette on thermal!" Busto said.

"It's *Defiant*!" Destiny cried out.

"Thunder, Defiant, *standby for an ass saving!*" Stenberg called out on the comms.

My crew cheered.

Friendly missiles exploded one after another as Zulu-3's defenses engaged them. But there was no way they were going to get them all.

Two missiles penetrated their point defenses and exploded against the frigate's hull. Glowing debris flew in all directions.

Zulu-3's hull split in half.

"*Defiant*, about time you returned the favor!" I said on comms with a huge grin on my face. "*Moshy*, enemy eliminated, return to formation."

I watched on the display as the freighter executed a tight turn and accelerated back to us.

*Defiant* approached and took up a position above and behind us.

"Thunder, *you've got heavy damage amidships,*" Stenberg said.

"Yes, we're aware. Repair work is underway."

"I've got the signatures of a Kergan flotilla on threat

sensors," Novikova announced.

"Then, let's get the hell out of here."

I accelerated us away from our battlefield with *Moshy* and *Defiant* following, staying low and pushing for the horizon.

An hour passed of low-level frantic flying until we could no longer detect any warships or their emissions.

*Thunder* had taken heavy damage amidships. We had lost about half our stores, one railgun, twenty ASM missile tubes, the medical bay, the rec room, one of the primary tractor pods, two attitude tractors, and three LPD blisters. Given our hull damage, I was worried we wouldn't be able to enter Earth's atmosphere.

"We are flight-worthy," Zeta assured me a couple of hours later after we were well into the middle of our transit back to Earth. *Moshy* and *Defiant* were still in formation with us. "Just keep our atmospheric indicated airspeed below 215 knots."

"Roger," I replied. That would be pretty slow, but we only needed to enter the atmosphere when we were directly above our destination.

We were headed for Elkin, Arizona. We needed to get these mindjacked humans out of their rigor pods and remove their mindjack implants, and there was no better place to do that than in their own hometown.

Our medical bay was destroyed, and *Moshy*'s was not configured for humans. But we convinced Captain Stenberg and the crew of *Defiant* to agree to accompany us to Elkin so we could use their medical bay for the mindjack removal procedures.

I owed Captain Stenberg in a big way. We all did. But, considering the fact that we'd rescued them first back during that mission at Malmstrom, perhaps now we were even.

I realized how important it was to have allies. Both of our ships would have been dead at one time or another if it hadn't been for the other. My crew owed our lives to them just as they did to us.

Bonds like these are what tie warriors together into an exclusive fraternity. As a former Marine, I knew this was likely something Clemen Busto learned many years ago.

But it was new information for me. Next time I saw Stenberg, she was getting a hug, whether she wanted it or not. I was so glad to be alive.

Maybe I could convince the Collective Dominion Ministry of War to keep our two ships together from now on.

# 47

I stood between Busto and Destiny at the side of Elkin's high school gymnasium. A glass of apple cider in one hand, a small paper plate stacked with cookies in the other.

At least half the town of Elkin was present for this celebration, including nearly all the people we'd rescued from Lindblad F.

It had taken us two days to decant all 161 of them from their rigor pods and remove their mindjacks, but we'd done it.

Also present were the entire crews of *Thunder* and *Defiant*.

When our ships had landed on the outskirts of Elkin, we'd at first caused people great fear, thinking a Kergan force was invading them. Then their emotions changed to friendliness when they realized their old friends Busto, Destiny, and me were among us.

And then, they'd seen what our cargo was in *Moshy*. Nearly all the humans who had been abducted from their town, alive, if still trapped in their rigor pods. But our arrival caused a sensation as families were reunited.

Overnight, we managed to empty Urbana's Home for Children and did it in the best way possible: by bringing their parents home.

A tall, attractive woman with blond hair and a man built like a tank with brown hair approached us arm-in-arm. Clinging to the woman's blue dress was Leo Finch. Of course, I recognized the couple: Elara and Joshua Finch, two of the slaves we had rescued.

"We heard you were leaving!" Elara said as she came to a stop in front of us.

I shrugged. "Our work's done here."

"We could use people like you around here," Joshua said. "There's plenty of empty homes. I'm sure we could find someplace for you."

Destiny smirked. "Oh, don't encourage him, folks." She patted my shoulder. "This boy has a hard time turning down free housing."

I smiled. There was a time when that had been true, and I was so happy it was behind us. "We already have a home back in California. But we'll be sure to stop by and visit from time to time."

Elara let go of her husband's arm and embraced Destiny. Then she reached out her arm and pulled Busto and me into the hug.

She stepped back. Tears streamed down her cheeks. "Thank you so much! I wish there were some way we could pay you back for what you've done."

I looked at the small family standing before me. Leo, smiling shyly, but obviously comfortable with his mom and dad. He was a different boy than the one I remembered from the orphanage. Smiling and more willing to talk.

"I'm just glad to see you three back together." I spread

my arms wide. "For all of you that are back together. It made it all worth it."

"I heard there was quite the excitement on our way out of that mine," Joshua said.

"Just be glad you got to sleep through it," Busto said.

The town had already heard our story multiple times of the escape from Lindblad F. It was well on its way to becoming a legend.

Loud laughter suddenly rang out across the gym. I looked and saw Vila in the middle of sharing a joke with three members of *Defiant*'s crew.

We'd had a couple days of downtime to relax, and I'd gotten to know Stenberg's crew better, especially Stenberg. I'd spent several hours with the young woman, and we'd become good friends.

While sitting under a tree in the town park, I'd told her about my desire to see a unified effort.

"We can't fight this war with the Kergans as individual cells," I said.

"But the Dominion wants us kept separate for security," Stenberg said as she carved a stick with her belt knife.

"And look at what that almost got us? Both our crews dead and our ships destroyed." I tossed a pebble. "No, there is strength in numbers. I would like us to join our efforts."

She shook her head. "The War Ministry won't like that. It'll be like having all their eggs in one basket."

"But do you agree with me or not?"

"Yes, you make a good point."

"Then we don't ask them. We tell them how things are gonna be."

She chuckled. "Kory, you are one of the most stubborn people I've ever met. You don't let anything get in your way, do you?"

I thought about Ban'ach and my memories she had fled with. "I wish that were the case," I said sadly. Zeta was still avoiding me, treating me like I was coated with sewage.

"Look," she said, "let's have Zeta and Omri discuss it." Omri was Annica Stenberg's igna consort. "We both depend on our consorts, so we can't do anything without their permission."

"Unfortunately," I replied. "I wish we humans could conduct this insurgency the way we wanted."

"But we need the Dominion's technology and their consorts. You know that. Without them, we're screwed." She shifted her stick and started gouging out a figure in it. "Still, you've made a good point. I'll talk to Omri. You talk to Zeta."

"Okay."

And that's what I'd done. I'd gone to Zeta and explained my proposal to unify *Thunder*, *Defiant*, and their two crews into a single cell that would be able to tackle more difficult operations against the Kergans.

The response I got shocked me. But maybe I shouldn't have been. She hadn't said more than a half-dozen words to me since she stopped my attack on Ban'ach.

"Consort," Zeta said, "what you propose is feasible. Zeta will speak with Omri and the Ministry. But whatever happens, you will not be a part of it, at least not in the near future."

My jaw dropped open. "What do you mean?"

"Do not think that Zeta has forgotten what happened inside the Astral Maul? You committed a grave offense when you attacked Ban'ach in the Syderealium."

"I was defending myself!"

"You stole energlyphs from her. You are a Soul Ravager!"

"I am not! How could I be? I never signed up for that.

Nobody trained me. I just acted according to instinct."

"Zeta understands, yet you acted contrary to our laws of the Syderealium, you destabilized the balance of sydereal forces, and you attracted the attention of Pyrakos."

"That wasn't me! That was the Astral Maul!"

She spun on her vertical axis. "Perhaps, and yet, perhaps not. It is extraordinary you escaped that god."

"He needed me."

"Gods do not *need* us mortals," she replied with disdain. "You cannot trust anything they promise."

"Fine, but why does any of this matter?" I asked. "What I did is done, and I can't take it back."

Zeta was quiet for almost a minute. I could hear the soft hum coming from her capsule. "You have been summoned to the Collective Dominion," she finally said.

I took a step backward. "What does that mean?"

"You are to be formally charged with sydereal battery by the Office of Sydereal Enforcement."

I threw my hands in the air. "I'm not even a citizen of your country!"

"You are under military discipline and subject to Dominion jurisdiction."

"But I live on Earth! What are they gonna do about it?"

"Kory, Zeta is disgusted by your behavior. You must understand that you will be declared outlaw if you refuse to comply and respond to these charges."

"What does that mean?"

"You will be cast out of the crew of *Thunder*, and any citizen of the Collective Dominion may legally kill you without it being a crime."

"That's barbaric!"

"It is our way. Respond to the charges or be declared outlaw."

I shook my head. "Why are you doing this to me?"

"It is not Zeta. You chose to ignore her council when she warned you not to try to recover your lost memories from Ban'ach. These are the consequences."

"If I agree to respond," I said, "what will happen to me?"

"Zeta does not know. Your situation is unprecedented. Typically, it takes years of training for a flairsparked to learn how to execute the sort of attack which you did. Some, including Zeta herself, will argue that it was a crime committed without premeditation and in self-defense. Perhaps such a legal defense will work. But others will claim that doing what you did is too dangerous to go without punishment."

I couldn't believe it. In the eyes of the Dominion, I was now a criminal suspect. I felt betrayed by Zeta because her people would have never known anything if she hadn't told them. Then again, maybe she didn't have a choice in the matter. Still, I felt like she should have been doing more to protect me.

I couldn't imagine losing *Thunder* and my crew. They were like family to me. It had given me purpose. I would definitely lose all of that if I became outlawed.

"If I agree, what is going to happen? What about our consortship?"

"Regardless of what you choose to do, Zeta must terminate her consortship with you."

I couldn't find words to respond. *It's over.*

"Zeta is the crown princess of the Collective Dominion," she continued. "She cannot be seen to be associated with a Soul Ravager. It is her duty to ensure that the evil you've done is corrected.

"Zeta has been recalled to the Dominion. A ship is coming for her. If you choose to respond to these charges, you will be given a place on the ship for the journey."

My friend was abandoning me! "So, it's going to be a trial of some kind?"

"Zeta does not know. Your case will be heard by three judges of Zeta's people who are knowledgeable in sydereal matters."

"What about my friends? My crew? *Thunder*?"

"They will remain on Earth and continue with their missions. Another igna Heliacal Knight will be sent to form a consortship with Destiny Austin."

"Does she know any of this? Destiny?"

"No."

I sighed with relief. At least there was one person who hadn't betrayed me. It would have shattered my heart if I'd learned that Destiny was discussing this business behind my back with Zeta.

There was no good choice, but I refused to become an outlaw. Stenberg had been correct. Humanity couldn't conduct this fight against the Kergan Empire without the help of the Collective Dominion, so I needed to repair my relationship with Zeta's people. And perhaps one day, Zeta would forgive me.

"I'll do it," I said.

"Very well, Consort. Zeta's people are just and fair. But she cannot be associated with you."

I realized how much pain I must have caused her by my actions. I was pulling her away from this fight.

My emotions twisted inside me. I'd only tried to bring justice to Ban'ach, to punish her and correct the evil she did to me.

Oh, how the consequences had been twisted so foully!

I had lost my friends, my ship, and my purpose. Ban'ach, when she learned of this, would rejoice.

And still, I refused to give up my goal of recovering my memories from Ban'ach. Mom and Dad were my foundation stone. My psyche depended on them. I could not sustain this fight without them on my side. I needed my two stolen energlyphs returned.

And maybe the Dominion needed somebody like me, a flairsparked human. If I could prove that to them, perhaps they would show me mercy for my actions. Because who was the true enemy here? It wasn't me. It was Ban'ach, the Empress, and the Kergan Empire. They were a selfish and malign force that needed to be removed from the galaxy. They, and all the other Soul Ravagers who would enslave and feed upon humans and other sentient beings.

Ban'ach and the Soul Ravagers had to be stopped, and I would not rest until they were.

## *THE END*

Kory Drake will continue his story in the next *Starship Thunder* book: ***Memory's Shadow***.

**Please rate or review my book online!** As an indie author, I *depend* on your reviews to legitimize my books in the eyes of those who have not read them.

# About Joseph McRae Palmer

Joseph McRae Palmer writes speculative fiction. He is also an engineer in the telecommunications industry and holds a Ph.D. in Electrical Engineering from Brigham Young University. Joseph was born in Provo, Utah, but raised in Sitka, Alaska, and graduated from high school in 1993. Later, he served as a missionary for two years in central Mexico. He and his wife of more than two decades, Beatriz Palmer, are parents of one son and three daughters, and as of 2023 they reside in northern Utah, USA.

Joseph's fiction site: www.josephmcraepalmer.com